D0353745

Water Bound

A SEA HAVEN NOVEL

CHRISTINE FEEHAN

piatkus

PIATKUS

First published in the US in 2010 by The Berkley Publishing Group,
A division of Penguin Group (USA) Inc., New York
First published in Great Britain as a paperback original in 2010 by Piatkus

A CIP catalogue record for this book
is available from the British Library.

ISBN 978-0-349-40008-2

Printed and bound in Great Britain by CPI Mackays, Chatham ME5 8TD

Papers used by Piatkus are natural, renewable and recyclable
products sourced from well-managed forests and certified
in accordance with the rules of the Forest Stewardship Council.

Mixed Sources
Product group from well-managed
forests and other controlled sources
www.fsc.org   Cert no. SGS-COC-004081
© 1996 Forest Stewardship Council

Piatkus
An imprint of
Little, Brown Book Group
100 Victoria Embankment
London EC4Y 0DY

An Hachette UK Company
www.hachette.co.uk

www.piatkus.co.uk

For Mike Carpenter
and our beloved Lillyana

ACKNOWLEDGMENTS

I could never have written this book without the help of two wonderful men. Mike Carpenter spent hours and hours teaching me about sea urchin diving. He graciously took us on several boats, and got us a ride down the river into the Albion Harbor and out to face the wild ocean swells. He provided amazing research and answered every question no matter how ridiculous. Any mistakes are mine alone, as he went over the material numerous times with me. Mike, I hope I did right by you.

Cody Tucker helped me understand a world that most of us can only see from the outside. He spent a good deal of time helping me understand what it was like going from a world where one didn't quite fit, into another where everything was vivid and beautiful.

And of course, our beautiful Lillyana, who shows us every day what true courage is.

Thanks to Mark King, Skip Williams and Clint Wyant for answering questions regarding firefighting and sheriff procedure along the Mendocino coast. I, of course, am writing a work of fiction and therefore took a few liberties!

1

FLAMES raced up the walls to spread across the ceiling.
Orange. Red. *Alive.* The fire was looking right at her. She
could hear it breathing. It rose up, hissing and spitting, following her as she crawled across the floor. Smoke swirled
through the room, choking her. She stayed low and held
her breath as much as possible. All the while the greedy
flames reached for her with a voracious appetite, licking
at her skin, scorching and searing, singeing the tips of her
hair.

Chunks of flaming debris fell from the ceiling onto the
floor, and glass shattered. A series of small explosions
detonated throughout the room as lamps burst from the
intense heat. She dragged herself toward the only exit, the
small doggy door in the kitchen. Behind her the fire roared
as if enraged by her attempt to escape.

The fire shimmered like a dancing wall. Her vision tun-
neled until the flames became a giant monster, reaching
with long arms and a ghastly, distorted head. It crawled

after her on the floor, its hideous tongue licking at her bare feet. She screamed, but the only sound that emerged was a terrible choking cough. She turned to face her enemy, felt its malevolence as the flames poured over her, trying to consume her, trying to devour her from the inside out. Her scream finally broke past the terrible ball blocking her throat, and she shrieked her terror in a high-pitched wail. She tried to call out, to beg for water to come to her, to save her, to drench her in cool, soothing liquid. In the distance the shriek of the sirens grew louder and louder. She threw herself sideways to avoid the flames . . .

Rikki Sitmore landed hard on the floor beside her bed. She lay there, her heart racing, terror pounding through her veins, her mind struggling to assimilate the fact that it was just a nightmare. The same old familiar nightmare. She was safe and unharmed—even though she could still feel the heat of the fire on her skin.

"Damn it." Her hand fumbled for the clock radio, her fingers slapping blindly in search of the button that would stop the alarm that sounded so like the fire engine from her dreams. In the ensuing silence, she could hear the sound of water flowing, answering her cry for help, and she knew from experience that every faucet in her house was running.

She forced herself to sit up, groaning softly as her body protested. Her joints and muscles ached, as if she'd been rigid for hours.

Rikki wiped her sweat-drenched face with her hand, dragged herself to her feet and forced her aching body to walk from room to room, turning off faucets as she went. At last only the sink and shower in her bathroom were left. As she went back through the bedroom, she turned on the radio and the coastal radio station flooded the room with music. She needed the sea today. Her beloved sea. Nothing worked better to calm her mind when she was too close to the past.

The moment she crossed the threshold of her bathroom, cool sea colors surrounded her with instant calm. The green slate beneath her feet matched the slate sea turtles swimming through an ocean of glossy blue around the walls.

She always showered at night to wash the sea off of her, but after a particularly bad nightmare, the spray of the water on her skin felt like a healing wash for her soul. The water in the shower was already running, calling to her, and she stepped into the stall. Instantly the water soothed her, soaked into her pores, refreshed her. Her personal talisman. The drops on her skin felt sensual, nearly mesmerizing her with the perfection of their shape. She was lost in the clarity and immediately zoned out, taken to another realm where all chaos was gone from her mind.

Things that might ordinarily hurt—sounds, textures, the everyday things others took for granted—were washed away like the sweat from her nightmares or the salt from the sea. When she stood in the water, she was as close to normal as she would ever get, and she reveled in the feeling. As always she was lost in the shower, disappearing into the clean, refreshing pleasure it brought her, until abruptly the hot water was gone and her shower turned ice-cold, startling her out of her trance.

Once she could breathe without a hitch, she toweled off and dragged on her sweats without looking at the scars on her calves and feet. She didn't need to relive those moments again—yet night after night the fire was back, looking at her, marking her for death.

She shivered, turned up her radio so she could hear it

throughout the house and pulled out her laptop, taking it through the hallway to her kitchen. Blessed coffee was the only answer to idiocy. She started the coffee while she listened to the radio spitting out local news. She dropped into a chair, stilling to concentrate when it came to the weather. She wanted to know what her mistress was feeling this morning. Calm? Angry? A little stormy? She stretched as she listened. Calm seas. Little wind. *A freaking tsunami drill?*

Not again. "What a crock," she muttered aloud, slumping dejectedly. "We don't need another one."

They'd just had a silly drill. Everyone had complied. How had she missed the report in the local news that they had scheduled another one? When they conducted drills of this magnitude, it was always advertised heavily. Then again . . . Rikki sat up straight, a smile blossoming on her face. Maybe the tsunami drill was just the opportunity she'd been looking for. Today was a darned-perfect day to go to work. With a tsunami warning in effect, no one else would be out on the ocean, and she would have the sea to herself. This was the perfect chance to visit her secret diving hole and harvest the small fortune in sea urchins she'd discovered there. She had found the spot weeks ago but didn't want to dive when others might be around to see her treasure trove.

Rikki poured a cup of coffee and wandered out to the front porch to enjoy that first aromatic sip. She was going to make the big bucks today. Maybe even enough money to pay back the women who'd taken her in as part of their family for the expenses they'd incurred on her behalf. She wouldn't have her beloved boat finished if it weren't for them. She could probably fill the boat with just a couple of hours' work. Hopefully the processor would think the urchins were as good as she did and pay top dollar.

Rikki looked around at the trees shimmering in the early morning light. Birds flitted from branch to branch, and wild turkeys walked along the far creek where she'd scattered seed for them. A young buck grazed in the meadow just a short distance from her house. Sitting there, sipping her coffee and watching the wildlife around her, everything began to settle in both her body and mind.

She'd never imagined she would ever have a chance at such a place, such a life. And she never would have, if not for the five strangers who'd entered her life and taken her into theirs. They'd changed her world forever.

She owed them everything. Her "sisters." They weren't her biological sisters, but no blood sister could be closer. They called themselves sisters of the heart, and to Rikki that's exactly what they were. Her sisters. Her family. She had no one else and knew she never would. They had her fierce, unswerving loyalty.

The five women had believed in her when she'd lost all faith, when she was at her most broken. They had invited her to be one of them, and although she'd been terrified that she would bring something evil with her, she'd accepted, because it was that or die. That one decision was the single best thing she'd ever done.

The family—all six of them—lived on the farm together. Three hundred plus acres, which nestled six beautiful houses. Hers was the smallest structure. Rikki knew she'd never marry or have children, so she didn't need a large house. Besides, she loved the simplicity of her small home with its open spaces and high beams and soothing colors of the sea that made her feel so at peace.

A slight warning shivered down her body. She was not alone. Rikki turned her head, and her tension abated slightly at the sight of the approaching woman. Tall and slender with a wealth of elegant blonde hair untouched by gray in spite of her forty-two years, Blythe Daniels was the oldest of Rikki's five sisters and the acknowledged leader of their family.

"Hey, you," Rikki greeted. "Couldn't sleep?"

Blythe flashed her smile, the one Rikki thought was so endearing and beautiful—a little crooked but providing a glimpse of straight white teeth that nature, not braces, had provided.

"You're not going out today, are you?" Blythe asked, and nonchalantly went over to the spigot at the side of the house and turned it off.

"Sure I am." She should have checked all four hoses, darn it. Rikki avoided Blythe's too-knowing gaze.

Blythe looked uneasily toward the sea. "I just have this bad feeling . . ."

"Really?" Rikki frowned and stood up, glancing up at the sky. "Seems like a perfect day to me."

"Are you taking a tender with you?"

"*Hell* no."

Blythe sighed. "We talked about this. You said you'd consider the idea. It's safer, Rikki. You shouldn't be diving alone."

"I don't like anyone touching my equipment. They roll my hoses wrong. They don't put the tools back. No. No way." She tried not to sound belligerent, but she was *not* having anyone on her boat messing with her things.

"It's safer."

Rikki rolled her eyes. How was having some idiot sitting on the boat while she was under the water not diving alone? But she didn't voice her thoughts, instead she tried a smile. It was difficult. She didn't smile much, especially when the nightmares were too close. And she was barefoot. She didn't like being caught barefoot, and in spite of Blythe's determination not to look, her gaze couldn't help but be drawn to the scars covering Rikki's feet and calves.

Rikki turned toward the house. "Would you like a cup of coffee?"

Blythe nodded. "I can get it, Rikki. Enjoy your morning." Dressed in her running shoes and light sweats, she managed to still look elegant. Rikki had no idea how she did it. Blythe was refined and educated and all the things Rikki wasn't, but that never seemed to matter to Blythe.

Rikki took a breath and forced herself to sink back into the chair and tuck her feet under her, trying not to look disturbed at the idea of anyone going into her house.

"You're drinking your coffee black again," Blythe said, and dropped a cube of sugar into Rikki's mug.

Rikki frowned at her. "That was mean." She looked around for her sunglasses to cover her direct stare. She knew it bothered most people. Blythe never seemed upset by it, but Rikki didn't take chances. She found them on the railing and shoved them on her nose.

"If you're diving today, you need it," Blythe pointed out. "You're way too thin, and I noticed you haven't gone shopping again."

"I did too. There's tons of food in the cupboards," Rikki pointed out.

"Peanut butter is not food. You have nothing but peanut butter in your cupboard. I'm talking real food, Rikki."

"I have Reese's Pieces and peanut butter cups. And

bananas." If anyone else had snooped in her cupboards, Rikki would have been furious, but she just couldn't get upset with Blythe.

"You have to try to eat better."

"I do try. I added the bananas like you asked me. And every night I eat broccoli." Rikki made a face. She dipped the raw vegetable in peanut butter to make it more edible, but she'd promised Blythe so she faithfully ate it. "I'm actually beginning to like the stuff, even if it's green and feels like pebbles in my mouth."

Blythe laughed. "Well, thank you for at least eating broccoli. Where are you diving?"

Of course, Blythe would have to ask. Rikki squirmed a little. Blythe was one of those people you just didn't lie to—or ignore—as Rikki often did to others. "I've got this blackout I found, and I want to harvest it while I can."

Blythe made a face. "Don't speak diving. English, hon, I don't have a clue what you mean."

"Urchins, spine to spine. So many, I think I can pull in four thousand pounds in a couple of hours. We could use the money."

Blythe regarded Rikki over the top of her coffee mug, her gaze steady. "Where, Rikki?"

She was like a damn bulldog when she got going. "North of Fort Bragg."

"You told me that area was dangerous," Blythe reminded.

Rikki cursed herself silently for having a big mouth. She should *never* have talked about her weird feelings with the others. "No, I said it was spooky. The ocean is dangerous anywhere, Blythe, but you know I'm a safety girl. I follow all dive precautions and all my personal safety rules to the letter. I'm careful and I don't panic."

She didn't normally dive along the fault line running just above the Fort Bragg coast because the abyss was deep and great whites used the area as a hunting ground. Usually she worked on the bottom, along the floor. Sharks hunted from below so she was relatively safe, but harvesting urchins along the shelf was risky. She'd be making noise, and a shark could come from below the shelf. But the money . . . She really wanted to pay her sisters back for all the expenses they'd covered for her in helping with her boat.

Blythe shook her head. "I'm not talking about your safety rules. We all know you're a great diver, Rikki, but you shouldn't be alone out there. Anything could go wrong."

"If I'm alone, I'm only responsible for my own life. I don't rely on anyone else. Every second counts and I know exactly what to do. I've run into trouble countless times and I handle it. It's just easier by myself." And she didn't have to talk to anyone or make nice. She could just be herself.

"Why go north of Fort Bragg? You told me the undersea floor was very different and the sharks were more prevalent there and it kind of freaked you out."

Rikki found herself wanting to smile inside when just seconds earlier she'd been squirming. Blythe saying *freaked out* meant she'd been spending time with Lexi Thompson. Lexi was the youngest of their "family."

"I found a shelf at about thirty feet covered with sea urchins. They look fantastic. The fault runs through the area, so there's an abyss about forty feet wide and another shelf, a little smaller but still packed as well. No one's found the spot. It's a blackout, Blythe, uni spine to spine. I can harvest a good four thousand pounds and get out of there. I'll only go back when no one's around."

Blythe couldn't fail to hear the excitement in Rikki's voice. She shook her head. "I don't like it, but I understand." And that was the trouble—she did. Rikki was both brilliant and reclusive. She seemed to take her talents for granted. Blythe could ask her to program something on the computer, and she'd write a program quickly that worked better than anything else Blythe had ever tried.

Everything about Rikki was a tragedy and Blythe often felt like holding her tight, but she knew better. Rikki was very closed off to human touch, to relationships—basically to anything that had to do with others. She had allowed each of the other five women into her world, but they could only come so far before Rikki shut down. She was haunted by her past—by the fires that had killed her parents and burned down her foster homes. By the fire that had taken her fiancé, the only person Rikki had ever let herself love.

"You had another nightmare, didn't you?" Blythe asked. "In case you're wondering, I turned off the three other hoses around your house."

Blythe didn't ask how the water had gotten turned on. The entire family knew that water and Rikki went hand in hand and that strange things happened when Rikki had nightmares.

Rikki bit her lip. She tried a causal shrug to indicate nightmares were no big deal, but they both knew better. "Maybe. Yes. I still get them."

"But you're getting them a lot lately," Blythe prodded gently. "Isn't that four or five in the last few weeks?"

They both knew it was a lot more than that. Rikki blew out her breath. "That's another reason I'm going out diving today. Blowing bubbles always helps."

"You won't take any chances," Blythe ventured. "I could go with you, take a book or something and read on the boat."

Rikki knew Blythe was asking if there was a possibility she would get careless on purpose, if maybe she was still grieving or blaming herself. She didn't know the answer so she changed tactics. "I thought you were going to the wedding. Isn't Elle Drake getting married today? You were looking forward to that." Another reason why the ocean would be hers and hers alone. Everyone was invited to the Drake wedding.

"If you won't go to the wedding and you need to go to the sea, then I'll be happy reading a book out there," Blythe insisted.

Rikki blew her a kiss. "Only you would give up a wedding to go with me. You'd throw up the entire time we were out there. You get seasick, Blythe."

"I'm trying gingerroot," Blythe said. "Lexi says there's nothing like it."

"She'd know."

Lexi knew everything there was to know about plants and their uses. If Lexi said gingerroot would help, then Rikki was certain it would, but Blythe was *not* going to sacrifice a fun day just because she feared for Rikki's safety. Rikki's life was the sea. She couldn't be far from it. She had to be able to hear it at night, the soothing roll of the waves, the stormy pounding of the surf, the sounds of the seals barking at one another, the foghorns. It was all necessary in her life to keep her steady.

Most of all, it was the water itself. The moment she touched it, pushed her hands into it, she felt different. There was no explanation for it. She didn't understand it, so how could she explain to someone else that when she was in water, she was at peace, completely free?

"Blythe, I'll be fine. I'm looking forward to going down."

"You're spending too much time alone again," Blythe said bluntly. "Come to the wedding. All of the others are going. Judith can find you something to wear if you'd like."

Rikki had a tendency to go to Judith for advice on what to wear or how to look if she was going to an event where there would be a large group of people. Blythe obviously mentioned her on purpose in the hopes that Rikki would change her mind.

Rikki shook her head, trying not to show a physical reaction, when her entire body shuddered at the horror of the thought of the crowd. "I can't do that. You know I can't. I always say the wrong thing and get people upset."

She had met Blythe in a group grief-counseling session, and somehow, Rikki still didn't know how or why, she'd blurted out her fears of being a sociopath to the others. She never talked to anyone about herself or her past, but Blythe had a way of making people feel comfortable. She was the most tolerant woman Rikki had ever known. Rikki wasn't taking any chances when it came to doing anything that might alienate Blythe or any of her other sisters. And that meant staying away from the residents of Sea Haven.

"Rikki," Blythe said, with her uncanny ability that made Rikki think she read minds. "There is nothing wrong with you. You're a wonderful person and you don't embarrass us."

Rikki tried desperately not to squirm, wishing she were already at sea and as far from this conversation as possible.

She adjusted her glasses to make certain she wasn't staring inappropriately. Sheesh. There were so many freakin' social rules. How did people remember them? Give her the ocean any day.

"And you don't need to wear your glasses around me," Blythe added gently. "The way you look at me doesn't bother me at all."

"You're the exception, then, Blythe," Rikki snapped, and then bit down on her lip hard. It wasn't Blythe's fault that she was completely happy or completely sad, utterly angry or absolutely mellow. There was no in between on the emotional scale for her, which made it a little difficult—whether Blythe wanted to admit it or not—for her to spend time with other people. Besides, everyone annoyed the hell out of her.

"I'm different, Blythe. I'm comfortable being different, but others aren't comfortable around me." That was a fact Blythe couldn't dispute. Rikki often refused to answer someone when they asked her a direct question if she didn't feel it was their business. And anything personal wasn't *anyone's* business but hers. She felt her lack of response was completely appropriate, but the individual asking the question usually didn't.

"You hide yourself away from the world, and it isn't good for you."

"It's how I cope," Rikki said with a small shrug. "I love being here with you and the others. I feel safe. And I feel safe when I'm in the water. Otherwise . . ." She shrugged again. "Don't worry about me. I'm staying out of trouble."

Blythe took a swallow of coffee and regarded Rikki with brooding eyes. "You could be a genius, Rikki. You know that, don't you? I've never met anyone like you, capable of doing the things you do. You can memorize a textbook in minutes."

Rikki shook her head. "I don't memorize. I just retain everything I read. I think that's why I seriously lack social skills. I don't have room for the niceties. And I'm not a genius. That's Lexi. I'm just able to do a few weird things."

"I think you should talk about the nightmares with someone, Rikki."

The conversation was excruciating for her, and had it been anyone but Blythe, Rikki wouldn't have bothered making an effort. This conversation skirted just a little too close to the past—and that was a place she would never go. That door in her mind was firmly shut. She couldn't afford to believe she was capable of the kind of thing others had accused her of—setting fires, killing her own parents, trying to hurt others. And Daniel . . .

She turned away from Blythe feeling almost as if she couldn't breathe. "I've got to get moving."

"Promise me you'll be careful."

Rikki nodded. It was easier than arguing. "You have fun at the wedding and say hello for me." It was so much easier being social through the others. They were all well liked and had shops or offices in Sea Haven—all were a big part of the community. Rikki was always on the outside fringe and was accepted more because she was part of the farm than for herself. The residents of Sea Haven had accepted the women of Rikki's makeshift family when they'd moved here just a few short years earlier, all trying to recover from various losses.

She forced a smile because Blythe had been the one to give her a place to call home. "I really am fine."

Blythe nodded and handed her the empty coffee cup. "You'd better be, Rikki. I would be lost if something happened to you. You're important to me—to all of us."

Rikki didn't know how to respond. She was embarrassed and uncomfortable with real emotion, and Blythe always managed to evoke real emotion, the heart-wrenching kind better left alone. Rikki felt too much when she let herself feel, and not enough when she didn't. She pushed out of her chair and watched Blythe walk away. Rikki was angry with herself for not asking Blythe why she was out running so early in the morning—why she couldn't sleep.

Blythe, of all the women, was an enigma. Rikki was an observer, and she noticed how Blythe brought peace to all of them, as if she took a little bit of their burdens onto herself.

Rikki sighed and threw the rest of her coffee out onto the ground. Sugar in coffee. What was up with that? She glanced up at the clear sky and tried to concentrate on that, to think of her sea, the great expanse of water, all blues and grays and greens. Soothing colors. Even when she was at her stormiest and most unpredictable, the ocean brought her calm.

She went back into her house, leaving the screen door closed but the back door wide open so she wouldn't feel closed in. She quickly polished the cupboards where Blythe had touched them, leaving undetectable prints, washed the coffee mugs and carefully rinsed off the sink around the coffeepot.

Rikki hummed slightly as she packed a lunch. She needed a high-calorie meal, lots of protein and sugar. Peanut butter sandwiches, two with bananas, even though there was an old saying that bananas were bad luck, and a handful of peanut butter cups and two bags of Reese's

Pieces would keep her going. Her job was aggressive and hard work, but she loved it and reveled in it, especially the solitary aspects of being underneath the water in an entirely different environment—one where she thrived.

Extra water was essential, and she readied a cold gallon while she prepared and ate a large breakfast—peanut butter over toast. She might not like sugar in her coffee, but she wasn't stupid enough to dive without taking in sufficient calories to sustain her body functions in the cold waters.

She ate, toast in hand—she didn't actually use her dishes. Her sisters had given her the most beautiful set with seashells and starfish surrounding each plate. She carefully washed the entire set on Thursdays and her wonderful set of pots and pans on Fridays—and she always had them displayed so she could look at them while she ate her sandwich.

She'd washed and bleached her wet suit the night before, and made certain that her gear was in repair. Rikki repaired all her own equipment religiously, waiting for that one moment when all her senses would tell her there'd be a calm and she could go diving. Her gear was always ready and stowed at all times, so the moment she knew she could make a dive, she was ready.

Her boat and truck were always kept in pristine condition. She allowed no one except the women in her family to step onto her boat—and that was rare. No one but Rikki touched the engine. Ever. Or her baby, the Honda-driven Atlas Copco air compressor. She knew her life depended on good air. She used three filters to remove carbon monoxide, which had killed two well-known locals a few years earlier.

She knew the tides by heart thanks to the *Northern California Tidelog*, her bible. Although she'd committed the book to memory, she read it for fun daily, a compulsion she couldn't stop. Today she had minimal tide ebb and flow with hopefully no current, optimum working conditions where she wanted to dive.

Despite Blythe's concerns, Rikki really did consider safety paramount. Rikki stowed her wet suit and gear in the truck along with her spare gear—divers, especially Rikki, generally kept a spare of every piece of equipment on hand just to be safe. Rikki kept hers in an airtight locked container, which she checked periodically to make sure everything was in working order. Moments later she was driving toward Port Albion Harbor, humming along to a Joley Drake CD. The rather famous Drake family lived in the small town of Sea Haven. The Drakes were friends with her sisters, particularly Lexi and Blythe, who was actually a cousin, but Rikki had never talked to any of them—especially not Joley. She loved Joley's voice and didn't want to chance making social mistakes around her.

Strangely, she'd never been bothered by others' opinions of her. Friendships were too difficult to manage. She had to work too hard to fit in, to find the right things to say, so it was easier just to be herself and not care what people thought of her. But with someone she admired— like Joley—she was taking no chances. Better to just keep her distance entirely.

Rikki sang along as she drove down the highway, occasionally glancing at the ocean. The water shimmered like jewels and beckoned to her—offering the peace she so badly needed. She'd had a few months reprieve from her nightmares, but now they were back with a vengeance, coming nearly every night. The pattern was familiar, an affliction she'd suffered many times over the years. The only thing she could do was weather the storm.

Fire had destroyed her family when she was thirteen. Definitely arson, the firefighters had said. A year and six months later, a fire had destroyed the foster home she was staying in. No one had died, but the fire had been set.

The third fire had taken her second foster home on her sixteenth birthday. She had awakened, her heart pounding, unable to breathe, already choking on smoke and fear. She'd crawled on her hands and knees to the other rooms, waking the occupants, alerting them. Everyone had escaped, but the house and everything inside had been lost.

The authorities wouldn't believe she hadn't started any of the fires. They couldn't prove it, but no one wanted to care for her after that. No one trusted her and in truth she didn't trust herself. How had the fires started? One of the many psychologists suggested she couldn't remember doing it, and maybe that was the truth. She'd lived in a state-run facility, apart from the others. Fire starter, they'd called her, and the death dealer. She'd endured the taunts, and then she'd become violent, protecting herself with ruthless, brutal force when her tormenters escalated to physical abuse. She was labeled a troublemaker and she no longer cared.

The moment she turned eighteen she was gone. Running. And she hadn't stopped until she'd met Daniel. He'd been a diver too.

Rikki turned her truck down the sloping drive leading to the harbor, inhaling the fragrance of the eucalyptus trees lining the road. Tall and thick, the trees stood like a forest of sentinels, guarding the way. The road wound around and the Albion Fishing Village came into view. She drove on through to the large, empty dirt parking lot and then backed up to the wooden guard in front of the gangway connecting to the dock.

As she unpacked her gear, the last remnant of her nightmare faded. Now, in the daylight beside the calming influence of the ocean, she could almost be grateful for the nightmares. They always heightened her awareness of safety measures on the farm, and the recent spate reminded her it was time to check all the fire alarms, sprinklers and extinguishers. She could never risk growing complacent again.

Even if she was not the one who had somehow started the fires, someone else had. It seemed clear to her that someone wanted her and everyone near her dead. She'd almost run from Blythe and the others in order to protect them, but Rikki had been so beaten down, so close to the end of her rope, she couldn't have survived without them. And despite everything, Rikki wasn't ready to die. Thankfully her newfound sisters had realized how important fire safety was to her, and they had spent the extra money on everything she'd asked for.

Rikki walked along the dock until she came to her baby—the *Sea Gypsy*. She didn't buy clothes or furniture, her home was stark, but this—this boat was her pride and joy. She loved the Radon, all twenty-four feet of her. Everything on her boat was in impeccable condition. No one touched her equipment but her. She even did her own welding, converting the design of the davit to make it easier to haul her nets on board.

The river was calm and the boat rocked gently against

the bumpers. There was a soothing mixture of sounds, water lapping and birds calling back and forth. There was one lone camper trailer in the park and no one in sight. The harbor was nearly deserted. She went through all her checks and started the engine. Rikki untied the lines and cast off. A familiar eagerness raced through her veins as she pushed the *Sea Gypsy* from her dock.

For Rikki, no feeling on earth matched the thrill of standing on the deck of her boat with the powerful engine, a 454 MerCruiser with a Bravo Three sterndrive and two stainless steel propellers, rumbling under her feet and the river stretching out in front of her like a wide blue path. The wooden bridge spanning the river, with a sandbar and rocks on either side, was her gateway to the ocean. The channel was narrow and impassable in low tide or heavy swells. With the wind on her face, she maneuvered the boat out of its slip and kept a low throttle as she moved along the channel. The sandbar to her right could present problems, and she kept to the center as the *Sea Gypsy* swept around the curve to enter the actual sea.

Double-crested cormorants vied for space on the closest sea stack, a small island made of rock where the birds nested or rested. She sent them a smile as she judged her mistress. She never fully trusted the weather reports or tide books—she had to see for herself exactly what mood the ocean was in. Sometimes, in the protection of the harbor, the sea felt and looked calm, but the waters beyond the land mass could betray her angry mood. Today, the ocean was calm, the water smooth and glistening.

The *Sea Gypsy* swept out into open water and Rikki relaxed completely. This was her world, the one place she was truly comfortable. Here, she knew the rules, the dangers, and understood them in a way she could never understand social situations and human interactions. As the boat rushed over the water, the sky overhead was blue and clear, the surface below as smooth as the California coast ever managed to be. She had a great engine, built for speed—a gift from her sisters and one she could never begin to thank them for.

She rushed passed caves, sea stacks and cliffs—from here the coast appeared a different world altogether. Pelicans, cormorants and osprey shared the skies with seagulls, sometimes diving deep, their bodies sleek and streamlined as they plummeted into the depths after fish. Little heads popped up here and there as seals surfaced close to shore, hunting for a meal. Two seals played together somersaulting over and over in the water.

Spray burst up the cliffs in a display of power as the sea met land. She lifted her face to the salt air, smiling at the touch of water on her face. She began to sing, one hand weaving a dancing pattern in the air as she maneuvered the boat with the other. Singing was almost a compulsion, each time she found herself alone where no one could see or hear her. An invitation. A language of love. The notes skipped over the surface to the sides of her boat as it rushed over the water.

Tiny columns began to form, sparkling tubes that danced over the surface like mini cyclones. The sun gleamed through them, lending them colors as they twisted and turned gracefully. Some rose high, leaping above the boat in thin rainbows to form an archway. Laughing, Rikki shot through it, the wind and water on her face and ruffling her hair like fingers.

She played with the water, out there in the safest place

she knew, with the shore in the distance and the water leaping all around her boat. Water was drawn to her in some mysterious way she didn't understand, coming when she beckoned, saving her life numerous times, making her feel at peace when everything and everyone she loved had been taken from her. Under her direction the water plasticized, forming shapes. The joy bursting through her there on the water where she was so alive could never be duplicated on shore where, for her, there was only vulnerability and emptiness.

She anchored the *Sea Gypsy* just off the shelf but gave herself plenty of scope just in case a large wave did come at her out of nowhere. She checked her equipment a final time. Eagerness rose inside her, unmarred by any hint of fear. She loved to be in the water. Being alone was an added bonus. She didn't have to try to adhere to conventional social customs. She didn't have to worry about hurting someone's feelings, embarrassing her chosen family or having people make fun of her.

Out here in the water she could be herself and that was enough. Out here she couldn't hear the screams of the dead, feel the scorching heat of a blazing fire or see suspicion on the faces around her.

After rubbing herself down with baby shampoo, she warmed her suit by pouring hot water from the engine in it before putting it on. Once again, she checked her air compressor—her lifeline. She'd spent a great deal of money on the Honda 5.5-horsepower engine and her Atlas Copco two stage air compressor with the three extremely expensive filters, two particulate filters with a carbon filter on top. Divers had died of carbon monoxide poisoning and she wasn't about to go that way. She had a non-locking Hanson quick release on her end of the main hose so she could detach quickly if necessary. She carried a thirty-cubic-feet small bailout—her backup scuba tank—on her back. Some of the divers dove without one, but since she usually dove alone, she wanted the extra protection. Rikki didn't care to be bent by an emergency ascent. She wanted to be able to come up at the proper speed should anything happen, such as a hose getting cut by a boater who did not see her dive flag.

Donning her weight belt and then her bailout, she put on the most important instrument, her computer, which kept track of her time so there was no chance of her staying down too long. She had a compass to know where she was and where she wanted to go. Grabbing her urchin equipment, she slipped into the water, taking four five-hundred-pound-capacity nets with her.

The massive plunge into the water felt like leaving earth and going into space, a monumental experience that always awed her. The cool liquid closed around her like a welcome embrace, bringing with it a sense of peace. Everything inside of her stilled, made sense. Righted. There was no way to explain the strange sensations she experienced that others obviously didn't feel when being touched. Sometimes fabrics were painful and noises made her crazy, but here, in this silent world of beauty, she felt right, her chaotic mind calm.

As she descended, fish circled her curiously and a lone seal zipped past her. Seals moved fast in the water, like small rockets. Normally they would linger, but today, apart from a few scattered fish, the sea seemed empty. For the first time, a shiver slid down her back and she looked around her at the deserted spot. Where had all the fish gone?

The San Andreas Fault was treacherous. A good nine

hundred feet deep or more, it was a long black abyss
stretching along the ocean floor. At around thirty feet
deep, a high shelf jutted outward, and the extensive jagged line of rock was covered in sea urchins. The drop-off
was another good thirty feet across where a shorter shelf
held an abundance of sea life as well.

Rikki touched down at the thirty-foot shelf and immediately began to work. Her rake scraped over the urchin-
crusted rocks along the shelf wall, the noise reverberating
through the water for the sea creatures to hear. She worked
fast, knowing that sharks could hunt her from below,
whereas normally when she worked on the ocean floor
she wasn't in as much danger.

Her feeling of dread increased with each stroke of her
rake. She found herself stopping every few minutes to
look around her. She studied the abyss. Could a shark be
prowling down there in the shadows? Her heart rate increased, but she forced herself to stay calm while she
went back to work, determined to get it over with. The sea
urchins were plentiful and large, the harvest amazing.

She filled her first net in a matter of twenty minutes,
and as the weight increased, she filled the float with air to
compensate. In another twenty minutes she had a second
bag filled. Both nets floated just to one side of her while
she began working to fill the third net. Because she was
working at thirty feet, she knew she had plenty of bottom
time to fill all four five-hundred-pound nets, but she was
getting tired.

After finishing the last bag, she hooked all four bags to
her hose and stayed on the bottom while she let the bags
go to the surface, holding the hose to slow the urchins'
ascent and to keep the air from leaving the float once it
reached the surface. She climbed her hose a foot a second

until she hit ten feet where she stayed for five minutes to be good and safe before completing her ascent.

Working in the water was exhausting because of the continual flow of the waves. The wash could push forward and back against a diver, and exposed as she was and having to be careful not to fall into the abyss, harvesting the urchins had made her arms feel like lead. At the surface she hooked the bag lines to the floating ball and climbed on board. Using the davet, she hauled two full nets aboard and stored them in the hold. Exhausted, she sat down to rest and eat two more peanut butter sandwiches and a handful of peanut butter cups, needing the calories before bringing in the last two nets.

The strange dread that had been building in her seemed to have settled in the pit of her stomach. She sat on the lid of the urchin hold and ate her sandwiches, but they tasted like cardboard. She glanced at the sky. It was clear. Little wind. And the sea itself was calm, yet she felt threatened in some vague way she couldn't quite comprehend. As she sat on her boat, she twisted around, looking for danger. It was silly, really, the feeling of impending doom. The day was beautiful, the sea was calm and the sky held no real clouds.

She hesitated before she donned her equipment again. She could pull up another four nets filled with sea urchins, bringing her total to four thousand pounds, enabling her to pay a good amount of money toward the farm. She was being silly. This part of the ocean had always given her a bad feeling. Resolutely Rikki put on her weight belt and hooked her hose to her belt before reaching for her tank.

The air around her suddenly changed. It was charged, and pressure pushed on her chest. She was still reaching for her tank when she felt the tremendous swell building

beneath her. Rikki turned her head and her breath caught
in her throat. Her heart slammed against her chest as she
stared at the solid wall of water rising up out of the sea
like a monstrous tsunami, a wave beyond anything she'd
ever witnessed.

2

THE wave rose over Rikki like a solid wall, lifting the boat as the swell reached her. She threw her hands into the air as if warding it off, singing her song to the sea as she was launched forward into the swollen water. She went under, rolling with the turbulence, falling, her weights taking her down. She caught at the hose attached to her suit and shoved the regulator into her mouth, grateful she'd been prepared for a dive and that she'd taken enough precautions to give the boat plenty of scope.

She sent up a silent prayer that she wouldn't go into the abyss, or go down too fast or too deep, or any of the other hundreds of disasters that could happen. She tumbled, somersaulting through the murky depths. Her heart was racing, but she knew she had to stay calm. Every instinct in her body was screaming at her to get the hell out of there, to fight to get back to the surface as fast as possible, but at the very best that would mean a helicopter ride and being stuck in a chamber, something someone like Rikki could never do.

In spite of the wild ride, her breathing remained the same, as she tried, in the inky darkness, to figure out where she was. She didn't want to end up in the abyss. Her body screamed at her to fight, that if she didn't she would be dead, but her experience kept her calm, accepting of the ocean's power. Don't panic. Calm. That was life under the water. Death was fighting. She simply rode out the wild ride, relying on her diver training and instincts.

Something large crashed into her, knocking her backward. She glimpsed a body smashed hard against the smooth rocks of the shelf. He wasn't in dive gear, she saw that much before he disappeared. Swearing, she swam after him, kicking strongly, knowing the water was too cold to be without a wet suit. He had no scuba gear, no way to breathe, and he was being thrown repeatedly against the rocks, which luckily were smooth from years of hard swells shaping them into polished artwork that few people would ever see. That art would most likely save this man's life.

Kelp wrapped around her arms and held her prisoner for a moment, but she stayed still. Panicking got one killed faster than anything else. Eventually the long bulbous tubes released her and she swam toward the shelf. It took her a few bad moments to find him. His body lay against the rocky shelf, the sweep of the kelp holding him prisoner and then releasing him. He was continually pushed against the shelf, and she noted in a calm part of her brain that she'd have to check him for spines if she managed to get him to the surface.

He wasn't fighting the kelp or trying to stabilize his body against the sweep of the ocean. She snagged his arm and he whipped around, his wide eyes staring directly into hers. She indicated the regulator and pushed it into his mouth. There was no panic in his eyes, which was good and probably indicated he was an avid diver, but there was no real fear either, and that scared her. He couldn't just accept death—not if he wanted to live through this. The water was freezing and she had to get him topside as soon and as safely as possible. She didn't know how badly he was injured. Minutes—seconds counted now.

She kept her arms around him, kicking strongly for the surface, willing him to hang on. She kept her gaze fixed on his, using her eyes, telling him she'd get him to safety. He was a big man. He didn't fight her, which surprised her. Most people would have panicked. The cold was getting to him, making his movements lethargic and heavy, but each time she pushed the regulator into his mouth, he didn't protest and he knew enough to blow out when she was using the regulator.

They stared at one another, and she swore that she felt as if she were falling into his eyes. He didn't take his gaze from hers, not once, not like everyone else always did. It was as if they were so connected that if they looked away from one another, neither would make it to the surface. She felt as if the water flowed through her to him and back again, binding them together in a strange ritual she didn't understand. It was hard to breathe, even with the regulator. Her entire being was absorbed into his as if their heartbeat were the same, their pulse one single beat, their lungs in unison. She'd never felt so close to another human being, not even Daniel, her fiancé. She felt *part* of this man, as if they shared the same skin, the same lungs. Their eyes were staring into each other's souls.

At ten feet, she indicated her gauge and held him to her, her hand clinging to his shirt collar, anchoring him. For the first time he moved, pressing his hand to his heart and then up to the side of his head. She spotted a blood trail and realized he was injured. He wasn't just cold: he'd been slammed against the rocks and hit his head. That changed everything. She needed to get him to the surface much faster than she'd thought. She kicked, but he shook his head, indicating he was fine and to wait at least the required minute.

Rikki watched him closely, now a little nervous that a shark might be attracted and come up beneath them. Her stomach was in knots, an ominous sign. She took the regulator, taking in air, and then pointed up. He made no response but didn't protest as they once again began their ascent. He was heavy and getting heavier by the moment. She felt the exact moment when he stopped breathing, saw his eyes go lifeless, but he was still calm, no fighting, no panicked moment where he grabbed and fought her. He simply was gone and she was left alone, staring into glassy eyes.

She kicked hard, taking them to the surface, rolling him onto his back, trying to keep the regulator in his mouth while she looked around for the boat. It had survived the huge swell thanks to the extra scope she'd used. It was difficult fighting her way across the distance with her burden, and she was already exhausted from the wave battering her. It took a few moments to dump the nets from the float ball and attach the hooks to his belt. There was no way to pull his weight into the boat. She would have to use the davit to haul him to the deck.

She'd left the nets full of urchins in the water. She always left the davit line in the water to hook one float to and to save her the trouble of hooking it up from topside.

Scrambling on board, she tore off her gloves and tossed them aside as she ran to the davit and pressed the button to raise him from the water. She caught his arm and guided him over the gunwale. His body flopped limply onto the deck. Nearly sobbing with her effort, she rolled him over and tore open his shirt to lay her ear over his heart. Nothing. Frantically she put her fingers to the pulse in his neck.

"Damn you, don't you die on me. You were breathing a minute ago." She rolled him onto his side and lifted his middle, trying to clear his lungs, and then she began CPR in earnest, using her regulator to push air into his lungs, just as she had in the water. Twice she thumped his chest hard, trying to kick-start his heart.

"Come on, come back," she hissed, and kept working his heart. She was determined. He'd been sharing her air, *looking* at her. "You are *not* doing this."

She put her ear to his chest again. There! Faint. Fluttering. "That's it. You're fighting," she encouraged. "You want to live."

She really looked at him then. He was all muscle. Total muscle. His chest and ribs were covered in scars. Bullet wounds. Knife punctures and slices. Burns. She sank back on her heels gasping. *Torture.* This man had been tortured methodically over time. He'd been wounded repeatedly. Who was he? Where had he come from? She looked around. There was nothing in sight, no boats, no ships, nothing at all, and she hadn't seen anything before she'd gone down the first time.

"Hold on," she said aloud, "I'll put out a Mayday and we'll get you out of here fast."

She turned her back on him and hurried over to the VHF radio. As she reached for it, a hand shot past hers and yanked the cable out of its socket, before whipping around her neck and jerking her backward against a hard chest. His forearm was nearly choking her.

She dug her fingers into his pressure points and turned into his arm, applying enough weight to spin out, although he caught her by her hair and jerked her back into him. She clamped both hands over his, dropping straight down and spinning, coming back up, nearly breaking his wrist before he let her go. He closed in on her fast, too fast to avoid.

Outraged, Rikki erupted into a fury of fists, feet and head butting. She was slight, but she had honed her skills on the street, in foster homes, in state-run homes, even in gyms. She knew how to hit in order to do the most damage, and when she was attacked, she fought back with everything in her. The man was obviously badly injured, but he was enormously strong. He seemed to know which pressure point would do the maximum amount of damage, and he was a big man, very muscular.

Not one of her blows rocked him, but twice she kicked his thigh dangerously close to his groin. He closed in on her quickly, wrapping his arms around her and taking her down hard. She hit the deck, facedown, his knee digging into the small of her back, his sheer size pinning her so it was impossible to move. He spat something at her in a language that sounded like Russian. She couldn't understand the words, but the razor-sharp edge of the knife against her neck said it all for him. She froze, her breath hissing out in a long exhale of sheer anger.

He must have known she was more angry than scared. In spite of his injuries, the knife never wavered. He spoke in a foreign language, obviously asking her something. His voice was intimidating, commanding, *authoritative*.

That only added fuel to her rage. She forgot the knife for a moment and kicked back at him. "Speak English or kill me, but do something soon or I'm going to shove that knife down your throat." Because in spite of everything, she was getting a little claustrophobic with him on top of her and her face pressed into the deck of her boat. She had a bad habit of losing control when she was pushed this far and she didn't trust herself, not with a knife against her throat.

There was a short silence. "Who are you? What did you do to me?"

Her heart jumped. He spoke English with an accent. Certain tones appealed to her, and his voice had something rich that settled inside of her—that sent her temperature up another notch. "I'm the person who saved your sorry ass, and believe me, I'm sorry I bothered. I dropped two full nets of spines to save your sorry dead ass. I'm the captain, so you can just get the hell off my boat. And while you're at it, get the hell off of me."

She didn't dare move again because the knife didn't, but sooner or later, he was bound to pass out again. She couldn't imagine that he wouldn't, and then she'd throw his ungrateful ass back to the sharks.

Lev Prakenskii kept his weight solidly on the little hellcat spitting and snarling beneath him. He was sick, disoriented and his head hurt like a son of a bitch. He had no idea where he was or what was happening, but he had to assess and make sense of the situation fast. He was on a fishing boat. Only one person appeared to be aboard—a woman with a major attitude problem.

She wasn't cool and calm like an operative. She wasn't afraid like a target would be. She was furious. He couldn't see that she had any weapons, only the tools of her

craft. He'd never seen an immaculate fishing boat, but if
there was such a thing, this was it. Everything looked to
be in pristine condition, although worn with age and
weather. He could kill her instantly, either with the knife
or simply by snapping her neck, and throw her body overboard, seize her vessel and escape, or . . .

She made a sound of sheer anger, rage running through
her like the tide. He could actually feel her resistance coming at him in waves, when she should have been scared
out of her mind. There was something valiant about her.
And she really had pulled him from the sea and revived
him, that much was true, so maybe he owed her more
than a quick death. She spoke English with an American
accent.

"Who are you?" he hissed in a menacing voice. He
"pushed" fear at her, wanting to subdue her quickly because his strength was running out.

"I'm your worst nightmare," she hissed back, in no way
intimidated. Her black eyes never left his face, never
blinked. She had a fierce stare that intrigued him when
little did anymore. She didn't appear intimidated. In fact,
she was so furious, it occurred to him she might be thinking of trying to attack him.

Laughter rippled through his mind. He hadn't laughed
in years. He couldn't remember feeling amused, yet there
it was. He was exhausted, his head seemed to be splitting
open, he had no idea where he was or who was trying
to kill him and he wanted to laugh. This little slip of a
woman thought she was his worst nightmare. She had no
idea what she'd just pulled out of the sea. She used an interesting choice of words to describe herself. He was fairly
certain she was exactly what she looked like—a diver,
one who had risked her life to save his. He was exactly

what she'd said *she* was—everyone's worst nightmare, the real deal.

She stiffened, hearing the sound that had escaped his throat—something between a groan and laughter. His amusement only dumped more fuel onto her rage.

"You'll pay for that," she hissed.

"I'm sorry." It was just that she was . . . extraordinary. And for the first time in his life, he wasn't certain what to do with someone.

"While you're laughing, you'd better not put one cut in my wet suit. You already broke my radio. Get. Off. Me." She enunciated each word. "You weigh a ton."

He'd been careful with the knife. His body was shaking from cold, but he'd kept his hands steady. It was an insult for her to think that he might accidentally nick her wet suit. And she should have been worried about him cutting her throat. He let his breath out and knew his strength was waning. He had to make a decision. Life or death. He had no doubt he could manipulate a woman—he had more weapons in his arsenal than guns—but he was weak and that made him vulnerable.

A little reluctantly, he removed the knife from her throat and eased his weight from her. The moment she was free, the woman flung herself onto her back and sat, pushing backward with her heels to put distance between them. Overheated, she tore off her wet suit top, uncaring that she was exposing soft skin to his startled gaze. She dragged a sweatshirt from behind her and yanked it over her head.

They stared at one another across the deck. The moment their eyes met again, his heart contracted. She had the blackest eyes he'd ever seen, turbulent—stormy—a dark, fierce velvet that appeared almost as liquid as the

sea itself. She looked like a wild thing, moody and beautiful and out of reach.

"Who are you?" she demanded.

That was a good question. Who exactly was he? He
had many names. Many faces. People who saw him rarely
survived. Damn, he was tired. He brushed at his face and
his hand came away smeared with blood. What should he
tell her? He needed her now. Needed an ally, a place to
hide, to recuperate. What would appeal most to a woman
like her? And that was the problem: it was difficult to get
a handle on her.

He read people easily. It was a gift of birth, of training,
of years of experience. But she was difficult. She fought
with the fury of the devil, was obviously a free soul out
here on the sea and had the most direct stare he'd ever
seen on anyone. He hunched his shoulders to make himself look smaller and less intimidating and wiped at his
face again, deliberately smearing more blood.

"You look like hell," she observed. "I can't call the
coast guard because you ripped out my VHF. I'm going to
have to get you to shore as fast as possible."

He held up his hand. "No. I can't be seen." He forced a
trembling note into his voice. "I think someone's trying to
kill me."

"That's a shocker," she said, sarcasm dripping from her
voice.

It wasn't exactly the reaction he was going for. And
people thought *he* was a social nightmare. Where was all
the womanly concern and sympathy? She was looking at
him with dark, stormy eyes that still said she wanted to
kick the crap out of him. She wasn't the most forgiving
woman he'd ever run across. He tried a tentative smile.

"I can't blame you for being upset. I was disoriented.

I think I was just in survival mode." That much was the truth. "I didn't really understand what was going on. I thought you had attacked me."

She took a breath and nodded, accepting his explanation. He had the feeling he would have to stick close to the truth with her. And what the hell was the truth? He didn't know anymore. He found himself rubbing his temple and wincing when he touched the raw, jagged edges of a wound.

"I can't remember what happened. Do you know?" That sounded pathetic enough to touch even a skeptic. And he was beginning to really like her face, that pixie face with the incredible bone structure. She hadn't taken her enormous eyes off of him, almost hadn't blinked. She looked at him like he was a tiger crouched on the deck of her boat, ready to attack at any moment. She hadn't exactly relaxed.

Her eyes were too big for her face and were heavily fringed with black lashes. Her hair was thick and a little wild, with ragged edges making her look even more like a pixie. Her chin was stubborn, her mouth generous. She regarded him with suspicion, but he could see she might just have an Achilles' heel—a soft spot for someone in trouble.

"A rogue wave knocked me off the boat. I found you in the water, but I have no idea where you came from. There's a shelf down about thirty feet and you were being slammed into that. The fault line runs along there and I managed to snag you before you dropped off it." She poured cold water onto a clean rag and handed it to him, keeping her hands in sight and her movements slow. Then she handed him a glass. "Drink this."

He took the tumbler from her, his fingers brushing hers.

His heart jumped. Raced. His breath hitched. He frowned as he took his time drinking the contents. He didn't have reactions to women—not real reactions. Not like that. Not unexpected and for no reason. His body was freezing. It felt as if he'd been beaten with several two-by-fours over and over. It wasn't as if he needed sexual relief. So why the hell would he react to her touch? He didn't like puzzles. And he sure as hell didn't like things he couldn't explain.

"Your name." It wasn't a question this time.

He ran his fingers through his wet hair and kept his expression as blank as possible. He frowned as if trying to remember. What to use? He needed something as close to the truth as possible. There was just something about her that raised a red flag. Like maybe she was one of those rare people who sensed lies. And he was damned good at lying—he didn't know any other way of life. "Lev. I think it's Lev. I can't remember much."

"Are you a criminal? A smuggler?"

He frowned and rubbed at the blood with the wet cloth. "I don't know."

Her expression didn't change much. Her lips compressed and some of the storm in her eyes dissipated. He'd been right not to deny the accusation. She was more comfortable with his lack of knowledge than if he'd denied being a criminal. He obviously wasn't a fisherman. He was armed and he looked dangerous, even as battered as he was. She wasn't going to buy an innocent act.

"Do you know how you got out here? I didn't see any other boats before or after the wave hit."

He looked her straight in the eye and allowed a touch of fear in his gaze. "I don't know. My mind is a blank. I can't remember what happened to me or who I am. But every time I think about going to the authorities, I get this very bad feeling." That was a calculated risk. She was alone on a fishing boat out in the ocean. A maverick. A loner. One who didn't frighten easily. She probably had an aversion to authority and police and questions. It was a connection between them, small, but at last he'd found one. He could find more.

"You need a doctor. What the hell am I going to do with you?"

Triumph swept through him. His teeth were chattering now, and he could feel the edges of his brain fuzzing over. He held on to consciousness grimly. "Thanks for pulling me out of the water." He touched his chest as if it hurt. "You did CPR."

She scowled at him. "I used the regulator."

It seemed important to her to let him know she had not touched her lips to his, no matter how tempting the thought might be. And—strangely—he found it tempting. She had a very attractive mouth and he mentally kicked himself for noticing. *Never* allow emotions to come into play. His life was at stake. She was . . . expendable. A stranger. She meant nothing.

He attempted a small smile, although his face seemed frozen. "From the feel of my chest, the CPR was vigorous."

"I'm not good at anything medical."

He allowed his gaze to slide over her. She was too thin. He doubted if anyone would call her beautiful—but she had a certain wild appeal, smelling of sea and salt and wet suit. "However you managed it, thank you." She seemed too fragile to have pulled him on board by sheer strength, so she was resourceful and tenacious. Admiration for her snaked inside of him and settled somewhere he didn't want to think about.

She held up her hand. "Don't try to stab me. I'm just getting you a blanket."

Lev noticed she'd used the word *try*. She still thought she was the one in control. He watched her every movement carefully through half-closed eyes. It didn't matter that he was in bad shape. He was alert and coiled, ready to spring should she make one wrong move. She was trapped on deck with a dangerous predator—and she moved as if she knew it, keeping her hands in sight as she pulled a blanket out of the locker for him—yet he knew she didn't accept the knowledge. She obviously didn't want to get too close so she tossed the blanket to him.

Lev didn't disabuse her of the notion that she was safe—out of his reach. He could be on her in a second and he knew just about every way there was to kill someone. He sighed as he wrapped the blanket around himself, still shivering uncontrollably. "Thanks," he murmured again. He was injured more severely than he'd first guessed because she was definitely getting under his skin. He had the feeling he was just as uncomfortable with her as she was with him.

"Look. You have a concussion, and if you've lost memory, it's severe. You were really battered against the reef before I could get to you. I have to get you help. We can't just stay out here."

"I'm not going to die," he reassured her. "Can you recover your bags?"

She blinked. Shocked. He'd definitely shocked her. "My bags?"

"With your catch. You said you dumped your catch in order to rescue me."

She waved that aside. "You need help. That comes first. I'll come back out and see if I can recover them later."

She looked down at the water and for the first time he could read her expression. There was longing. Need. Not for her lost catch, but for something else. His mind, as clunky as it was, as shadowy and hazy, began to form an idea that left him a little shocked. An element? Could this woman be element bound? Where there was one bound to an element, there were at least three others. He'd read about such a thing but had never run across it. It was a miracle of nature. But there was that look on her face, almost loving, certainly in need.

"Have you always lived your life by the sea?"

She shrugged. "I don't like being far from the water. And it's how I make my living."

It seemed impossible to just stumble accidently over something that had the potential for tremendous power. A key to one of the elements. Water. He shook his head and instantly his vision blurred, reminding him he was probably hallucinating anyway. He looked her straight in the eye again. "I'm not going to a hospital. I can't afford too many questions, not when I have no answers. Just get me back to shore and I'll find my way."

Rikki scowled, turning away from him, trying to think when those intense eyes had her more than a little rattled. His eyes were a piercing blue, like the sea itself. He was gorgeous. She didn't get close to men who were gorgeous. She judged his height to be over six feet. Wide shoulders, a thick, muscular chest, narrow hips; he was all muscle. The man was a walking mythology statue—a poster child for women's fantasies. His face was all hard angles and planes. He looked tough and she had no doubt that he was. He was shivering continually.

Cursing under her breath, she knew she couldn't just leave him. "You know you could have a blood clot. You hit pretty hard."

"I'll be fine." He settled deeper into the blanket, and long lashes veiled his blue eyes, giving her some relief. "Go get your catch. I'm not going to a hospital, so it doesn't matter where we are or how long it takes us to get back to the harbor."

Rikki studied his face. He could take the boat while she was down searching for the nets, but it seemed silly not to just kill her and throw her overboard. She was very tempted to try to recover her catch. She couldn't afford the loss of the urchins or her gear. Selfish or not, it was how she made a living and the farm needed cash coming in.

"Take the keys with you if you're worried," he said, without opening his eyes.

"I can rig a motor," she said, "so I'm guessing you can as well."

He opened his eyes and looked straight into hers with that penetrating stare that shook her. Ocean blue, his eyes held no real emotion. None. Flat and as cold as the deepest sea. Yet they were brilliant, like two sapphires mesmerizing her. She shook herself. Or like a cobra. He was her catch, fair and square, no matter how difficult he was to handle. She'd been the one to pull him out of the sea—and that made him hers.

"Do whatever you feel comfortable doing, but truthfully, I'll need you to get me out of here. I don't have a clue where I am or which direction I would go to get back to the harbor."

She studied his face. He wasn't exactly lying, but he wasn't telling the truth. He had no doubt that he would find his way to shore—and neither did she. He was a resourceful man.

"Drink some more water. This won't take long," she said, making up her mind. She was going to take him at his word. If the boat started up, she might be able to "dance" the water right over the top of him and spill him right back into the sea.

Lev watched as she poured hot engine water inside her wet suit top and then stripped off her sweatshirt and pulled on her vest with a diver's immodesty. He couldn't help but think she didn't notice him as a man, more like a catch she'd pulled from the sea. A part of him was a little disgruntled over that, while another part wanted to smile. She was very focused once she decided on a course of action. She reached for her gear, hurriedly shrugging into her bailout tank.

He watched her get ready to dive through narrow, brooding eyes. He wanted to move, to put his hand in the water and feel the response to her when she went in, but he couldn't summon the energy. Instead, he watched her go in. Watched the water reach for her. Welcome her, as if it enveloped her and held her.

He held his breath as she disappeared beneath the shimmering surface. She looked peaceful, like part of the sea itself, not awkward like some divers he'd observed over the years. And the water poured over and around her, caressing her body . . .

He pulled himself up short. What the hell was he thinking? He was losing it. The continual rocking of the boat made him feel slightly nauseated, which he would have found mildly alarming if his brain wasn't quite so fuzzy. As it was, his queasiness was just another discomfort among so many. Mostly the cold bothered him. Even his insides were cold. Pain he could manage. He'd lived with pain as a child every damn day. He could walk on glass and keep going. But the cold . . .

He couldn't stop shivering. With her off the boat, he could relax, just for a few minutes—try to get oriented. Try to remember what the hell had happened to him and who wanted him dead this time. Survival mattered. He had a strong sense of self-preservation, and this unique woman with her solitary lifestyle could be his best chance. He needed to have a plan.

The sound of the water lapping at the boat was soothing. The Honda ran lightly in the background as it fed her air. Occasionally there was the cry of a gull overhead. He didn't look up. It was too much effort. This woman went from rage to calm in seconds. She was controlled. Had good instincts. She could see lies better than most. She had incredible eyes. His body jerked. Where the hell had *that* come from? Women were tools. That was what this one was. A tool. To be used. Like anything else handy.

He leaned his head back until he could rest a little more comfortably. Just this once, he wanted to disappear. Be someone else. Anyone. He wanted to be like all those people running around living their lives. What the hell was normal? He didn't even know. He solved problems. He killed people. He moved in and out of the shadows and never emerged into sunlight. That was his life and he'd always lived it without question. And why could he remember that when he didn't know which of the names or faces in his mind were really his? What the hell difference did it make that she had incredible eyes? And a very generous mouth.

He wiped his face and looked down at the amount of blood on his hand. Head wounds tended to bleed pretty badly. He should stitch it up, but he was too tired. His arms felt like lead. It was easier resting beneath the light high-tech silver survival blanket and thinking about—*her*. What was it about her that appealed to him? He'd slept with many beautiful women. Seduced them. Used them. Took the information essential to what he was working on, and then in some cases disposed of them if it was needed.

He wasn't capable of emotion. Emotion got in the way, and by the time he was twelve, he'd learned not to let himself feel anything for anyone. There were moments of weakness and this was one of those moments. It would pass. He was tired, hungry, cold, and had no idea what the hell had happened to him. His mind simply blanked when he tried to remember what he'd been working on. Who he'd been after. Who was after him.

His life was a game of cat and mouse. Survival was always the prize. If he didn't know what the hell was going on, he was already down. He *needed* the woman. She was a tool for survival. His wanting to stay with her had nothing to do with her eyes or mouth. Or her fiery temper. Her absolute passion. What would it be like to feel passion? To have someone with those eyes look at him and no one else? Look at him for no other reason than because she thought he was *hers*?

He pressed his fingertips to his temples and applied pressure. He must be really weak and sick to be thinking like this. There was no belonging. No home. No *hers*. There couldn't be for someone like him. He was a machine. He wasn't human. He'd lost his humanity nearly forty years earlier in a school where children were taught to kill. To serve. To be robots—no more than puppets. He frowned. What in the hell was going through his mind? One didn't question service, or who or what they were—*but*, he'd been programmed from his childhood. There was no deprogrammer for someone like him. Only a bullet in the head at the end of the day. Odd that he could remember details of his past yet not the why of it or what the hell had happened to him.

He'd tracked a preacher once, one who liked boys and often visited Thailand. His appetites were insatiable. Right before Lev had shot him, the man had told Lev that he had no soul. At the time he hadn't even thought about it. Why now? Why was he suddenly contemplating the truth of that? The woman had looked at him with her large, heavily lashed eyes, dark as midnight. Suspicious. But she'd *looked* at him. Into him. She *saw* him. And for one moment, while she'd looked at him—he had seen himself.

His heart thudded, and for the first time since he'd been a child, fear gripped him hard. She'd seen *inside* of him. No one could see him. He'd built a fortress, strong and powerful, surrounding that one small broken piece inside of him that he'd never been able to harden. She'd seen it—he was certain she had. His fist hit the side of the boat, hard. He had to kill her. He had no choice. She couldn't live, not if she knew he was vulnerable.

He forced air through his lungs. It would be easy. Cut her air line. Leave her down there. Take the boat and sink it somewhere. She'd vanish in the ocean like so many fishermen did. It was the smart thing to do—the logical thing. He didn't move. Not one muscle. He just crouched there, waiting for her to come back. Waiting to see her eyes again. And that was just about the stupidest thing he'd ever done in his life.

He thought he might have been unconscious for a short

while. The boat creaked and rocked, and the motion would have been soothing if it hadn't been for the nausea and the ever-present headache. His skull felt like it was about to explode. He was thirsty, but it was too much effort to lift the water to his mouth.

He sat there and tried to piece together his life. It came to him in images, jagged pictures, all violent. Scraps of boyhood memories haunted him with blood and pain. Bullets slammed into his body, piercing flesh and bone, shattering his insides. He felt the blade of a knife, stabbing at him over and over, cutting deep. Something pounded the soles of his feet. Pain engulfed his body. He accepted it. He could stand while in pain. Fight while in pain. Perform while in pain. He could withhold information, lock it away in a part of his mind even he couldn't access.

Discipline. The word repeated itself over and over in his head. He murmured it like a talisman to hold on to. *Discipline*.

"Yes," a voice agreed softly. "Discipline is important."

The voice was soft. Feminine. Too young. He shook his head to clear it. So many of them died and he couldn't stop it. Like a flood.

"Shh," he cautioned. "Don't make a sound, no matter how much it hurts. You can live with the pain. They'll just hurt you more if you make a sound."

"I won't. Don't worry. I won't make any noise."

A cool hand touched his forehead and he caught the wrist, pinning it down. His eyes flying open. He didn't like anyone touching him. The face in front of him wavered— he couldn't center on it. He tightened his grip, not understanding what was happening to him. It was difficult to see, but eventually, through all the haze, he made out a pair of heavily fringed eyes looking back at him. His world

narrowed to that intense gaze. Black as night, so black the
eyes were nearly purple. Liquid, like the sea on a stormy
night. A man could drown there if he let himself. His
breath hissed out. "Sex is a tool. Nothing more."

"It's all right. It's going to be all right."

He shook his head. "I can't save you if you won't listen
to me."

"It's all right. I'll get you out of this."

Her choice of words puzzled him. *He* was the one to
get *her* out. But he'd failed. He'd failed them all. How
could she know what needed to be done when he didn't
know? She didn't try to fight his hold on her, rather she
stayed very still, almost as if she knew any movement
might set off his instincts—and none of his instincts were
good.

Discipline mattered. Pushing the shattering pain away,
he forced his brain to function. His thumb stroked back
and forth over the inside of her palm. She'd removed her
mittens and he was touching bare skin. The center of
her palm drew his attention until he pressed the pads
of his fingers there, tracing two small circles over and
over, as if he could etch them into her skin.

"They're missing," he muttered, his eyebrows drawing
together in a frown. "The symbols. They should be right
here."

"You've got a concussion," she explained. "You need to
be in a hospital."

He closed his fingers around her hand, holding tightly.
"They'll kill me. If you take me there, they'll find me and
they'll kill me."

"Don't worry. I'm not going to let anyone kill you."

He had no way of telling her he was her enemy. He
couldn't form the words. And that told him he really wasn't

thinking clearly at all. *Everyone* was either his enemy or a tool. There were no friends in his business. He just needed a safe place to rest, to figure out what was going on.

"I'll take you somewhere safe."

Her voice was soft. Melodious. A fantasy. He knew a hallucination when he was in one. There were no beautiful eyes promising him a sanctuary, looking at him as if they saw inside of him and past every shield, stripping him down until he was vulnerable. If someone really saw him, they'd kill him and throw his body overboard, not fight to save him—and if they didn't manage his death, he'd have to kill them to protect that vulnerable part of himself.

"You're in danger." He tried to warn her. If she was real and she was looking at him like that, then for once in his life, he had to take the job personally. Just this once. For those eyes.

What the hell? Was she stripping off her clothes? Her wet suit? No one actually hung up their wet suit, did they? She used a bucket of fresh water to rinse off the salt water and wiped herself down without embarrassment, as if he wasn't really there watching the towel glide over her body before she pulled up her jeans and half buttoned a shirt. There were scars on her legs and feet; he was certain of it. He'd mapped out her body in his head. He was mesmerized by the shape of her, the look of her soft skin. So thin but still complete.

All the while she'd dressed, her movements were quick and efficient—there were no flirty moves or hints of seduction, almost as if she thought herself alone, although those black, black eyes bored right through him. She had no adornments, no piercings, not even in her ears, but she did have a tattoo flowing down one hip. Tears? Water droplets? She'd kept it away from him and that only intrigued him more. He had a mad desire to lick those shimmering drops from her skin. The deck beneath him vibrated. The boat rocked more.

"Stay away from the nets. Those spines aren't poisonous, but they can puncture you and break off in your skin. I had surgery after one went through my hand. They'll go through a car tire and cause flats. When I close my eyes at night, sometimes I see them everywhere and I can't get away from them, like they're hunting me. They can be bad news. I've got them away from you, but don't move around."

He wanted to laugh at the warning. He should be afraid of *sea urchins*? That really was laughable. He was so far into the hallucination, it was insane. Sea urchins? Spines? Where the hell was he? A theme park? He felt along his thigh and found the reassuring presence of his knife. A pro would have searched him and found multiple weapons. She hadn't touched him, other than to pound on his chest and get his heart working again.

What was real? What was in his mind? His skull squeezed down on his brain and little explosions went off so that he grabbed his head and just held it. The boat threw him around a little, as if they were speeding through the water, but she left him alone. He needed that space to gather his defenses and come up with a plan of action. Every movement of the boat was agony, but he was used to pain and it steadied him. He used it to concentrate, to bring his splintered mind back under his control.

First thing, assess his situation. Basically he was fucked. He had multiple identities, but he had no idea which ones were safe to use or which was real. He couldn't remember how to get access to money or weapons. He wasn't certain what he had with him. He knew he was in danger, but from whom or what, he had no idea. He was in enemy territory, but there was no clue as to how he'd gotten there or what his mission was. He had no idea who he was supposed to report to. If his head wasn't hurting so damned bad, he'd smash it against the wall out of sheer frustration.

He could only glimpse pieces of his past. Fragments of violence, of running, of danger. He didn't have a family. Nothing soft in his life. Nothing vulnerable. He had no friends. No one he trusted. What the hell kind of life did he live anyway?

"Nothing makes sense," he murmured aloud. "*She* doesn't make sense."

3

―――――

"I have to get you to my truck and then come back and take the catch to the processing dock. Someone will have seen me coming in, so we have to hurry."

The woman bent over him, trying to slip an arm around his back. Lev slapped her arm away and looked her steadily in the eye, wanting her to know he meant business. "If this is a trap, I'll kill you."

"I know, tough guy," she responded.

There was something wrong with her answer—with her voice—with that steady gaze. She didn't fear him. *Everyone* feared him. They looked at him and saw the killer. She reached for him again and he blocked her arm. Exasperation crossed her face. Not anger or fear, but the exasperation one might feel toward an unruly child. She rubbed her forearm.

"Listen to me, *Lev*." She pronounced his name wrong, but he liked the way it rolled off her tongue. "We're about to have company. I'm trying to get your sorry ass into

the truck and out of sight before that happens. Cooperate with me, or stay here and let whoever is hunting you
shoot you."

He stared into those black, black eyes. Soft and liquid
and stunningly beautiful. Where the hell had she come
from? She was like a sea nymph, rising out of the ocean to
drag him from a watery grave. He shook his head at the
pure nonsense. He didn't read fairy tales and he sure as
hell didn't believe in them. She sure as hell didn't talk like
the princesses in the books either.

He nodded his head but waved her to his left side, leaving his right hand free. He was ambidextrous—he could
kill with equal precision from either side—but he was
weak and he wasn't taking chances. She wrapped her arm
around him and surprisingly, considering how thin she
was, the woman was strong.

His legs were pure rubber, but he forced them to move.
One foot in front of the other. He could hear her breathing
with the effort of taking his considerable weight. She
barely came up to his shoulder. It made him feel like less
than a man, leaning on her that way. He hated it, hated the
idea of being so helpless that he had no choice. He muttered under his breath.

"Are you swearing at me in Russian?" She looked up at
him as she helped position him near the dock. "Put your
hands on the gunwale and for God's sake, don't fall in. I'll
get off and help you onto the dock."

He thought he'd been swearing silently, not out loud.
That only served to remind him he was very far gone. He
wasn't grounded enough in reality to trust himself. He
gripped the gunwale, allowing his gaze to sweep the harbor. It was surprisingly empty. He knew immediately that
he hadn't been here before. He remembered places, like

maps laid out in his head. He could actually "see" grid marks, and once he'd been somewhere, the map was indelibly printed in his mind. Of course, he couldn't trust his mind right now. He wasn't even absolutely certain who he was—which of those numerous identities was really his—or what he was supposed to be doing.

The woman stepped easily onto the dock and reached for him. There was determination on her face, and God help him . . . compassion. What the hell was he? A lost puppy? He kept his head down, although he didn't see anyone close or paying attention. She walked him to an older model truck kept, like her boat, in great condition. He'd bet if he raised the hood, the engine would be gleaming and polished.

"I have to get my gear and take care of the uni. If I drive you to the house and come back, I'm doing something out of the ordinary and someone will notice. You can lie on the seat while I take care of business. Stay under the blanket and out of sight. The thing is, this is going to take a little time."

He tried not to look alarmed. He was already swimming in and out of reality. He wanted to be hidden away, to be out of the open, where he had a better chance of regrouping and surviving. "Why so long?"

"They'll hoist the nets off my boat, weigh them and put them in totes for the forklift to take them to the truck. It takes time, but most of the boats didn't go out so it doesn't look like there's a wait at all. I'll have to clean my boat as well. I can't take the chance of spines from the sea urchins on deck. I can bleach my gear at home."

It made sense, but all he wanted to do was close his eyes and sleep. He needed somewhere safe. He forced a nod.

"Are you absolutely certain you'll be fine? I can take you to a hospital . . ."

"No." He said it firmly. "I'd be dead inside an hour."

"So you're certain someone's looking for you?"

They'd tried to kill him, hadn't they? Otherwise, she wouldn't have had to drag him half-dead out of the sea. He shrugged and concentrated on getting into the truck without his head falling off or falling in a heap at her feet.

She helped him inside and handed him the blanket. He caught her hand, his thumb tracing circular patterns in the middle of her palm. "Tell me your name."

"Rikki. Rikki Sitmore." She flashed a small grin. "I have a last name."

He had the impulse to smile. There was something irresistible about her. He wanted to tell her he had multiple last names, but he refrained.

"I'll try to hurry, but it will take time."

"You said that."

Rikki made a face at him, rolled her eyes and slammed the door closed. There were reasons why she didn't go near people—they were all crazy. She'd pulled him out of the sea, and if she'd been thinking *at all*, she would have left him there. Now he was her responsibility. Shoving her sunglasses firmly onto her face to cover her usually direct stare, she climbed back aboard her boat. For some reason she could look straight at Lev, and strangely, the way she looked at him hadn't bothered him as it would most people.

Shrugging, she pushed off with her boat and swung around the other boats tied up to the dock to bring hers under the platform. The hoist was already in position and Ralph lowered the hooks for her to attach her nets to the scale.

"You came in early," he called to her. "I just got here."

She shrugged.

"No one else went out today," Ralph said, scribbling on paper and attaching the name of her boat to the white totes he filled with her urchins.

Rikki was relieved at that. She liked the other divers, and the thought of that monstrous wave running them over was frightening.

"Saw you had company. Something wrong?"

She stiffened but forced a casual shrug. "No," she muttered after a long awkward silence. The men were used to her sullen answers and rarely tried engaging with her.

She turned quickly away, leaving him to deal with the bins himself. Normally she helped, but she didn't want to chance him asking her any more questions. She drove her boat back to her berth and scrubbed it down meticulously as she always did, losing herself in the task while the water lapped at the *Sea Gypsy*, rocking her gently. She focused completely, not allowing anything into her mind but the sheer feeling of her boat, the sky and gulls surrounded by water. She loved the way the droplets of water glistened on the deck like diamonds, prisms of glittering colors, each unique and beautiful. Sometimes she got caught up in looking at them for long periods of time. She had to force her mind to stay focused on finishing as quickly as possible, and it took discipline not to disappear into the routine and flow as she usually did.

Each net was put away carefully, her hoses rolled in the way she *had* to roll them, a loose, precise circle that appealed to her. No one ever touched her equipment. They didn't put it away exactly as it was supposed to go, which was another reason she didn't have a tender on her boat.

But how could she explain how uncomfortable it was to Blythe—people touching her things and meaning to do well, but only making her crazy by not putting things *exactly* where they should be. There was a right way, and no one seemed able to comprehend that.

She sighed and pushed her glasses on her nose. She'd stalled as long as she could. Her boat and equipment were as clean as she could get them. She had inspected her air compressor and the hoses, and now, if there wasn't a dead body on the seat of her truck—yuck—she would have to face the music and do something with him. Better the dead body. If none of her family was home, she'd be stuck with him, and she had absolutely no idea what to do with him because no one—*no one*—came into her house while she was in it.

Blythe was the only person she let in and she couldn't be inside while Blythe was. She pushed her thumbnail into her mouth and chewed on it, frowning as she made her way back to the truck. She stood outside for a moment, drawing in air, steeling herself to be in such close confines. He was in her truck. That was almost as bad as him being in her home. She was beginning to wish she'd never pulled him out of the water.

Biting her lip hard, she yanked open the door. Lev exploded out of the blanket, wrapping both hands around her neck and pinning her head to the seat. She couldn't move, couldn't breathe. Fury shook her before panic set in. His fingers were like steel pins, cutting off her airway. Her world began to go black and small stars burst in her brain. Just as suddenly, he let her go. She slipped to the ground, coughing, holding her throat, gasping desperately for air.

Her glasses had come off. When she could finally breathe, she glared up at him, her eyes meeting his. He looked more confused than ever—not remorseful, confused. And damn it all, she was the one with no social graces, and at least she knew enough to know that he should be feeling *tons* of remorse.

"Get the hell out of my truck," she snarled, reaching to snatch her dark glasses and shove them back on her face. She avoided rubbing at the marks she knew would be on her throat. It felt swollen and tight. He could have easily killed her. She recognized that he could have in seconds. The knowledge didn't make her any less angry.

"I'm sorry."

"Get. Out."

Instead of obeying, he moved back across the seat to give her room. She sat there in the dirt a moment, swearing under her breath.

"Everything okay?" Ralph called. He stood on the platform, frowning, hands on his hips.

Color swept over her face—she could feel it as she scrambled to her feet. Ralph squinted, trying to see into her truck. She glanced at Lev. He was hunched over, his face hidden, the blanket around him.

"Just slipped in the gravel," she called, and climbed into her truck. She started the engine without looking at Lev and lifted a hand toward Ralph before driving out of the parking lot. She counted to a hundred before she glanced at her silent passenger. "Are you insane? Because if you are, just say so. I'll drop you wherever you want to go and we're done."

"I said I was sorry. It was a reflex." He shivered continually beneath the blanket.

"A reflex. I see. Killing people is a reflex."

He looked at her then, his blue eyes piercing through her sunglasses. "I didn't kill you."

She snorted. "You tried."

"If I'd tried, you'd be dead."

"That's twice."

"I said I was sorry and I am. My head is pounding, and I can't seem to tell the difference between what is real and what I'm hallucinating."

"Then you're going to the hospital."

"No. You might as well kill me yourself."

Rikki sighed. "Don't tempt me." She stopped at the stop sign at the top of the hill and tapped out a rhythm on her steering wheel while she considered what to do. He was unstable, no question about it, and she was no nurse but . . . She sighed again and turned right toward Sea Haven.

The farm was located just off of Highway 1. The drive to the property was lined with trees of every kind, great towering giants. Even redwoods. She loved the redwoods, which were so majestic and regal. She thought of them as sentries guarding the way to the farm. The double gate was ornate. Lissa had made it, welding and twisting the iron into a work of art. All of them loved it. Once the gate was open, she drove in slowly, making certain it closed behind her. She focused completely on her surroundings, blocking out Lev while she entered the farm.

She knew every tree and shrub. She knew where everything was and if anything had been disturbed, and she always paid close attention to detail. Blythe warned her that she was paranoid, but before entering her home, Rikki always walked around it, circling to look for signs of someone nearby. Footprints. Crushed leaves. Gas cans. Kerosene. Anything flammable.

She drove to Blythe's home first. She was the first choice to rid Rikki of Lev. He needed someone strong, and Blythe was no-nonsense and would see right through him if he lied—she hoped. Mostly she just wanted to get rid of the man. She knew the minute she pulled up to the large house that Blythe hadn't returned.

"Damn it," she hissed aloud. "How long does it take to get married? Five minutes?"

"Do you want to get married?" he asked, confused.

"No. Let me think. I was going to find somebody who could take care of you. Blythe or Lexi are the best ones I would think, but . . ." She didn't want Lexi with this stranger. She was too young.

"I want to stay with you."

She flicked him a quick, angry look. "Well, you can't. No one comes in my house. I don't like it."

His teeth chattered. "Just for a little while, until I can figure out what's going on. I don't even know my own name for certain."

What choice did she have? She hadn't done a single thing right yet. But how was she going to manage having someone in her home? Her sanctuary? She didn't even know if it was dangerous, but she guessed it probably was. If she was starting fires, she was starting them in her sleep when she was under stress. Having this stranger in her home would definitely be stressful.

"I don't know what to do." For the first time, she was really beginning to be afraid. "Maybe I could just get you warm. You can wait for Blythe in my house."

"Who's Blythe?"

"My sister. Sort of. It's complicated."

She drove to her house, watching the drive, looking for tire tracks. "Stay here," she ordered as she parked her truck and jumped out. She hesitated with the door open. "If you lay one hand on me when I come back, you'd better make certain you kill me, because you won't live through it if you don't."

Lev watched her mouth compress into a line of warning. He thought she looked more like temptation than danger. She fascinated him. She hadn't screamed, not once. She hadn't reacted in any of the ways a woman alone with a killer should have acted. "Take off your glasses."

She stepped back. "Why?"

"I want to see your eyes."

"You really are crazy." She started to turn away from him.

"Rikki."

It was the first time he'd called her by name and her shoulders stiffened. She turned her head and looked at him over her shoulder.

"I need to see your eyes. Your eyes . . . ground me."

Her tongue moistened her bottom lip. She frowned, but her hand went up to the frames, her fingers curling there for a heart-stopping moment while she decided whether or not to indulge him. He found his breath remained trapped in his lungs. She whipped off the glasses and he could breathe again. He found himself there, in the bottomless depths of her eyes. The very deepest sea had come alive and looked back at him. Found him. Saved him. Something broken in his head righted itself. He took a deep breath and nodded.

She pushed her glasses back on her nose and walked away from him. He didn't take his eyes from her as she searched the ground surrounding her house. She was

looking for something, and she was meticulous about
her inspection. She had a small porch on the front of
her house, and like her boat and truck, it was immaculate.
She crouched down and peered at the dirt near a hose.
The hose was wound around a cylinder very neatly and
there was obviously a lot of hose, but he couldn't detect a
single kink it in it.

She disappeared around the corner of the house and he
shoved the door open immediately, his heart contracting
until it hurt. For a moment he was afraid of it stopping. It
had hurt like that right before it had stopped. He remembered the moment vividly. He'd been drowning in her
eyes, controlling the pain, so connected he was part of
her, living and breathing, and then she'd looked down toward the murky depths, breaking the contact. At once the
pain had struck, violent and brutal—his chest tightened
until he thought he might explode, and then he was sinking into blackness. Emptiness. A void, cold and dark and
merciless.

He didn't like losing sight of her, not when she was his
salvation—and that made no sense to him. Nothing made
sense. He tried a few cautious steps and had to grip the
door. The ground tilted and his stomach lurched.

"What are you doing? Didn't I tell you to wait?"

Again he had that strange reaction to her waspish tone,
and he wanted to smile. He couldn't shake his head because it might explode, and if he answered, he might
vomit. He kept his teeth tight and reached blindly for her.
She stepped up to him and took his weight. They both
nearly toppled to the ground before he managed to steady
himself, using her like a crutch. Her breath hissed out of
her, and he hoped he hadn't hurt her. She wrapped her

arm tight around his waist, muttering to herself as she walked him toward her door.

Again he had the impulse to laugh, which was insane when every step made him sicker. The ground rolled and little rockets exploded behind his eyes. She began to tremble and slow, as if she was reluctant, as they gained the porch.

"Maybe you should sit outside in the chair there and rest," she suggested.

"I have to lie down." He really did. And it was going to have to be soon.

He heard her grind her teeth. She propped him against her and unlocked her door, shoved it open and took him inside. He felt her shudder and attempted to ease his weight from her, but his legs turned to rubber. She kept him upright with surprising strength.

"A few more steps and you'll be in the bedroom. I'm going to lay you down and try to get your wet clothes off."

She sounded dispassionate, as if he wasn't a man at all. She didn't seem embarrassed by the thought of removing his clothes, but then she was a diver and he knew they often had to strip with other divers around them. He didn't mind that she wasn't embarrassed, but it vaguely bothered him that she didn't see him as a man. With his head pounding so hard and his chest so tight, he wasn't certain of anything, so he dismissed the notion as idiotic.

The moment he stretched out on the bed, he closed his eyes and let her work. She found his knife in one boot and his holdout gun in the other. There was another knife strapped to his leg. Another gun in his belt. A third one in a harness. Another knife and three small daggers in loops at his belt. She didn't say a word but her breathing changed.

She inhaled several times quite sharply. That made him want to smile too. She found his throwing stars and the two throwing knives, but she missed the garrotes sewn into his clothing.

"What are you? Some kind of assassin?"

He didn't answer. She was tugging his clothing off of him, and he knew the instant she saw him as a man. Her hands stilled and she made a single sound, a low note he couldn't quite interpret. He opened his eyes and caught her looking, her eyes enormous and beautiful, the lashes fanning the sweep of her high cheekbone. She looked up at him and he felt a physical jolt.

She cleared her throat and tugged on his jeans. "Lift up."

It was more difficult than he thought it would be. His energy was gone and his body felt like lead. He couldn't control the continual shaking. She tossed aside his clothes and wrapped blankets around him, enclosing him in a warm cocoon. He found it interesting that she didn't say a word about the numerous scars on his body.

When she turned away, he caught her hand. He waited until she looked back at him. "I need my weapons. Just in case."

"You won't shoot me. Or stab me. Or throw one of those thingies at me."

"No."

She snorted. "How would you know? You don't know what you're doing half the time."

"Still."

She sighed and began stacking weapons on the bed beside the pillow. "Fine. But I'll be royally pissed if you try to kill me again. It's getting old."

He frowned as he watched her pick up his clothes and the wet blanket she'd taken off her boat. She didn't have an ounce of self-preservation. He was a stranger. She had marks from his fingers on her neck. He'd put a knife to her throat. Still, she'd given him back his weapons and turned her back on him as if it were all of little consequence to her. She wasn't afraid of *him*, although he had a nagging feeling she was afraid of something—maybe not fear exactly, but she was worried or anxious.

He watched her through narrowed, half-closed eyes, keeping his breathing regulated so that she dismissed him to take his clothes to the laundry room. He heard her but couldn't see her as she started up the washing machine. Then she was back, meticulously wiping up her hardwood floor until it gleamed. She must have warmed some blankets because she stripped off his blanket and tucked two more around him, still muttering to herself under her breath.

He really was far gone and confused, because he was beginning to find that habit rather adorable. As long as he remained focused on her, he didn't think about pain or what the hell had happened to him. Or who wanted him dead. Or who he was supposed to kill. He didn't want her out of his sight. She moved with a quiet efficiency that reminded him of the way water flowed. She paid attention to detail, and he noticed that she inspected the windows in the room. Once she ran her finger along the ledge and muttered a little to herself.

She left the room and returned with a cup of water. He could see stream rising as she bent over him. "If you drink this, it will help warm you up. I've got to clean up the wound on your head. You're still bleeding and it's a mess." She slid her arm under him and helped to half lift him, enabling him to take a few small sips of the warm water before she laid him back down.

"Thank you."

She regarded him with her enormous black eyes. "You're a mess. You really should be in the hospital."

He had the feeling she wanted him in the hospital, not because she thought he might die but because she wanted him out of her house—of her bed.

"I can't."

She frowned at him and rubbed the bridge of her nose. "You're pretty damned stubborn, aren't you?"

He thought that was evident and not worth answering, so he just let himself disappear into her eyes. She had beautiful eyes. He loved how liquid and soft they were. She started to move away and he caught her arm. "Don't go."

"I don't like people touching me."

He should have let go of her, but instead he rubbed the pads of his fingers up and down her bare arm. Her shirt was still half buttoned, and he was tempted to stroke her flat belly just to know the texture of her.

"I don't like it either," he said. And it was true. Funny. He'd never admitted that to anyone. It didn't particularly matter, he did what had to be done, but he didn't like it—maybe not in the same way she meant. His was a matter of personal space, a natural avoidance of closeness with others. But Rikki . . . He studied her face. "I don't think my touch bothers you that much."

She blinked. She rarely blinked, but he'd struck home. She compressed her lips and then narrowed her eyes at him. "You're pretty arrogant for a man who can't move with a pile of weapons sitting next to him."

"You have such a penchant for violence."

She looked outraged. "*I* do? You're the one being hostile. I'm Mother Teresa here. And I don't like sick people."

"Do you like anyone?" Amusement was creeping in again. He was beginning to like the feeling. "Anything?"

"Not particularly." She snatched her arm away from him as if just remembering he was touching her and she was supposed to be protesting. "And you especially."

She rubbed at her arm as she stalked away from the bed toward the bathroom. The rubbing turned gentler, almost a caress, or maybe that was just in his mind. Figuring her out was fast becoming an obsession, but perhaps it was because as long as he was concentrating on her, he didn't have to look at himself—and he didn't bear close scrutiny. Not now, not when he felt exposed and vulnerable.

She returned, this time with a warm washcloth and a small, very tidy emergency kit. "This might hurt. Lexi might do a better job. Do you want me to wait for her? She's good with people, especially people in pain. It's sort of her thing, helping them."

"You do it. We've come this far and I'm used to you now. I wouldn't want to accidently attack Lexi."

Her expression changed, her dark eyes going stormy. "You keep your hands off of her. I would have no problem sticking your own knife right through your heart if you touched her."

So she had a protective streak. Another Achilles' heel. He'd been beginning to think she was cut off from everyone. But there it was. The storm. The promise. And she was dead serious. He liked that. He didn't want a saint. He was no saint and one would never be able to live with . . . What the *hell* was he thinking? He really had taken a blow to the head.

The warm cloth moved over his head. She wasn't rough, but he wouldn't call her gentle either. Evidently she wasn't the soothing type, but she took care of the wound with the same efficiency she did everything. She was meticulously detailed, taking her time to close the gaping laceration with butterfly strips. She removed every trace of blood from his face and neck before she was through. He heard her washing her hands and all the equipment she used before she returned to him.

"I'll let you sleep." There was uneasiness in her voice.

"Don't go yet." Because he didn't dare go to sleep. He might really kill her if he woke up disoriented. He needed to be able to figure out what the hell was going on. He wanted to breathe her in, feel her inside and out, until he could identify her anywhere, anytime. He was almost there, a few more minutes and she'd be inside of him. He just needed . . . *something*. It was there in his mind, that elusive something. A few more minutes . . .

She gave him that little frown he was becoming familiar with. The moment she made that face, his heart contracted. God, she had some kind of hold on him, as if she had stolen a part of him there under the sea.

"Look." She spread her hands out in front of her. "In case you haven't figured it out, I'm not exactly normal. I can't have anyone here. As soon as Blythe gets back, you're going."

He kept his gaze locked with hers. "In case you haven't figured it out yet, I'm not exactly normal either. You're safe with me. I know the feel of you. Your scent. I won't make the same mistakes again."

"I'm taking a shower."

Oh, God. She was killing him. Making him want to

laugh out loud. Where had his sense of self-preservation gone? He didn't feel emotion—that was far too dangerous. He shivered beneath the blankets, suddenly afraid for her. For himself.

"You're still cold. I should have thought to rub you down with some warm oil. Lexi makes it and I use it sometimes when I come in from a dive. It warms you up fast. Can you roll over, because I'm not rubbing your front."

"Why not?"

"If you want a massage, turn over."

He managed it, although he had to grit his teeth and he didn't bother lifting his head from the pillow. He kept his face turned toward her and his hand inches from his gun. The safety was off, and he could aim and fire in a heartbeat if she made a wrong move. Yeah. That was more like him. He recognized that man. Breathing a sigh of relief, he watched her face while she drew down the blanket and then poured oil into her hands.

The first touch of her hands alarmed him on a gut-wrenching level he didn't understand. He hadn't lied when he said he didn't like anyone touching him. He had control of his body at all times. Complete, absolute and utter control. He could manipulate others through his practiced touch, because of his extensive training in every possible way of sexual pleasure, but he was the one who commanded his body's response, not his partner. He decided who and when, and he was always—*always*—in control. Until this moment.

His breathing changed. Heat rushed through his veins. He told himself it was the oil, spreading warmth over his skin, but he felt the sizzling, scorching heat spreading lower, centering, until, of its own volition, without his consent or command, his groin stirred, grew heavy and thick, and pulsed with need. He had a head injury, pain crashed through him if he dared to move his head, yet he was hard as a rock. What the hell was going on?

He took a breath and let himself absorb the feel of her hands on him. She massaged the oil into his shoulders, her fingers lingering in the long slash along his shoulder blade. Then her palm glided to his arm to trace the bullet wound there, and his body trembled. She massaged deep with her strong fingers, rubbing the oil into his biceps and then down his forearms to his fingers. His breath stilled in his body.

Her fingers were magic, sliding over his, in between, the oil absorbing into his skin while he melted into her. The warmth of the oil added to the illusion of becoming part of her. His heart beat a strange rhythm, pounding for her. He wanted to taste her in his mouth, breathe her into his lungs, be part of her body, seek refuge deep inside her. A long-ago instinct stirred in his broken mind, something he'd once heard, a long-ago childhood memory about a woman who would complete him. An element he needed.

"You haven't asked me." He needed distraction.

With his head and heart pounding and his groin full to bursting, with her hands moving along his back, easing every ache while the warmth poured into his body, he was desperate to divert himself from the unfamiliar needs of his body. And she was a need now. Like a drug infused through his skin. Through all his senses. His body absorbed the oil, but it was really her pouring inside him.

"Your scars? Would you tell me if I asked?"

"What I know. The bullet that nearly severed my spine." He waited until she found it, until the pads of her fingers stroked over the spot like a caress. "Amsterdam. I know that but not why or who. The knife along my hip was Paris and one up by my shoulder blade, Egypt. I know where I was with each of them, but not why."

"I should have taken you to the hospital."

She was frowning again, he could tell by her voice. He wished he could see her face, but she was working on his buttocks and he lost his own voice as well as his ability to think straight. Little explosions were going off in his head—and his groin. His cock was hot and heavy and so full he was leaking. Her hands went to the backs of his thighs.

Impersonal. He repeated the word silently over and over to himself. She would have done the same for anyone needing help. He'd have to kill any man she touched like this. His body should have been relaxed, not ready to take possession of hers. He was acutely aware of her every movement. Her breath. The swing of her hair. The beat of her heart. Her hands moving over his muscles, pressing deep, stroking and gliding. He knew she was wholly focused on what she was doing—not on *him*—and God help them both, he wanted her to notice him.

He needed her to see him as a man, not some damned pet project. Or worse. Maybe she was caught up in the way the drops of oil landed on his skin in the same way she seemed to be wholly focused on water.

He gathered his strength, pushed pain to the back of his mind and shifted his weight, easing off the monstrous hard-on she couldn't fail to notice. It took her a moment to look up from kneading his calves. Her hands stopped abruptly and he heard her shocked inhale. He rolled over, needing to see her face—her eyes.

She shoved back away from him, her eyes widening, the long lashes veiling her expression. As she went to pull away, she held up her hands, palms out, defensively, as if warding him off. Long-buried, maybe even unknown instincts took over. His hand whipped up, pushing air toward her left palm. Sparks danced between them, silver and gold, like tiny fireflies. She cried out and cradled her hand to her, that little frown drawing his attention to her soft mouth.

"Let me see."

"What did you do?"

"I don't know. Let me see."

Her gaze dropped to his heavy erection and her eyes grew stormy. "Just put that away."

There it was again—that urge to smile. "It's not a weapon. And you put it there. You take it away."

"Well, we found out one thing out about you, didn't we?" She snatched the blanket and flung it over him, tenting his monstrosity of a hard-on. "You haven't had sex in a long time."

She was close so he caught her wrist and turned her injured palm over, drawing her hand closer for his inspection. Two faint marks, circles intertwined one through the other. He pressed the pad of his thumb over the marks and rubbed in a circular motion.

"If you think I brought you home so you could have sex, you picked the wrong person. I don't do that sort of thing with just anyone."

His fingers tightened around her hand. "I'm glad to hear that." He moved his thumb and the circles had faded, leaving only a faint redness. Instead of remorse over marking her, he felt a strange satisfaction. He let go of her and allowed his eyes to close. The massage had driven the last vestiges of cold from his bones and left him exhausted.

"Talk to me from the door when you need to wake me up. Make certain I'm alert before you come in."

"What happened to 'you're safe'?" she asked aloud and, sending him another frown, she stalked out, leaving him to sleep.

4

HER sisters had to come home soon. Rikki paced back and forth on her front porch. How long did a reception last anyway? Were they going to be dancing all night? She rubbed her itching palm down her thigh and then pressed her hand hard against her tummy. What on earth had ever possessed her to *bring someone home and put him in her house*? She must have been out of her mind. No one stayed in her house. She couldn't stay in there with him. Now she had to sit outside and wish she had a cup of coffee. She wasn't going inside to make one either.

She stuck her thumbnail in her mouth and chewed on it. What if he needed something? What if he croaked? In her bed. Sheesh. The repercussions of her idiotic decision were mind-numbing. He was a complete stranger and most likely a homicidal maniac, judging by his weapons and his reflexes. She paced back and forth, huffing out her breath and mumbling curses and threats toward him under her breath.

It wasn't even safe to have him in her house. If Blythe
and the others were right and she wasn't a sociopath, then
someone was trying to kill her and anyone who might live
with her. *Or*, she hated people near her so much that she
tried to kill them by burning them alive, and then didn't
remember it. Either way, it wasn't a good scenario.

She whirled around and glared at the door. She couldn't
go into her own house. A man. A man with a very large . . .
She buried her face in her hands. Why did she have to
think about *that* part of his anatomy? She should be thinking about how insane he was, all of his scars and how he
got them, or his weapons and what it all meant.

She'd thought about him naked while she'd showered
and washed her hair. Her body had actually reacted to
the sight of him. She'd felt a blush start somewhere in her
tummy and move up to her neck. Fingers of awareness
crept down her spine and tingled over her thighs. Her
womb pulsed with need. Her beloved water, instead of
wrapping her up like a blanket and comforting her, had
felt sensual on her skin.

She'd meticulously bleached her wet suit and hung it
up, scrubbing her bathroom and shower after use, and then
put his clothes in the dryer. She'd paced back and forth in
her living room while the walls drew closer and closer together and her lungs couldn't get enough air. To escape the
knowledge of him naked in her bed, she'd fled her own
house in desperation.

She pressed the heel of her hand against her forehead. What the hell had she been thinking, bringing him
into her house? No one went into her house, it just wasn't
done. Well, Blythe did, to get her coffee, but they always—
always—drank it out on the porch. She never took
chances. Not with the women who had believed in her,

who offered her a family—who loved her in spite of all her failings.

She bit at her thumbnail. Where were they? Why weren't they home? Blythe had to come home and save her from her own stupidity. She needed him out of her house now. The pacing lasted hours. Eventually she realized she had to go check on him. There was nothing else for it. If she was lucky, he'd be dead already and then she wouldn't have to figure out how to get him out. Maybe she'd just dump him back in the sea.

Feeling a little elated over the thought, she squared her shoulders, took a long look around and steeled herself to go back inside. The moment she entered the house, she felt his presence. He seemed to fill up every room. The house smelled of Lexi's oil, the faint scent of almond and lemon. Rikki rubbed the bridge of her nose, and after a moment of indecision discarded her sunglasses. The house was dark and he was probably asleep. She knew she wore the glasses as much for armor as she did to keep others from being uncomfortable with her direct stare. The way he looked into her eyes . . .

She huffed out her breath and moved as silently as possible to the doorway of her bedroom. He took up the entire bed. His breathing was even, but somehow, she knew he was instantly aware of her presence. Like a predator. The uneasiness building inside of her flared into a massive ball of churning bile. She was going to have to keep him. Here. In her home. That was the consequence for her stupidity.

She didn't dare turn him over to one of her sisters—not even to Blythe. He was too dangerous. She pressed her fingertips to her temples. What was wrong with her? She really didn't have survival instincts the way other people did. Although her "sisters" teased her that she was paranoid, she acted without thinking things through. This man could never go to Blythe's house with his weapons and his reflexes. Rikki was responsible for him, not the others. She had to protect the others.

"Fear has a scent to it."

Her heart jumped. "If you think I'm afraid of you, you're mistaken," she answered. "I don't have people in my home, and I thought I could ask one of the others to deal with you but I realized I can't do that to them."

"So you're stuck with me."

"Something like that." She knew she sounded moody and less than gracious, but he'd disrupted her entire world. Her home was her sanctuary and he'd invaded it.

"When you say you don't have people in your home, you mean that literally, don't you?"

"Yes." Now she sounded sullen. "I don't even like talking to people." He might as well know she wasn't going to be any kind of soothing nurse for him.

"How are you at finding some kind of aspirin?"

She shrugged and went through the bedroom to her master bath. All medicines were kept in her personal bathroom. She had a guest bathroom, always kept meticulously clean, but no one had ever used it. Still, she wouldn't keep her personal medicines in the guest bathroom. She found the bottle and shook out two pills. She never drank water in the bathroom either, so she had to go into her kitchen to get the water. She passed him without saying a word, or giving him any explanation of what or why she was doing anything. His opinion of her didn't matter. She had her ways of doing things and they suited her just fine.

As always when she turned on the tap, the water pouring out appeared to be a silvery stream of shimmering beauty. She could see perfection in each individual crystal drop. She couldn't resist touching, allowing the water to cascade over her hands, her skin, and to meld with her in that comforting way, like living gloves. She turned her hands palm up and allowed the water to hit the exact center of her left palm, where the faint, disturbing marks had faded, yet sensation seemed to remain, as if she'd been branded in some way beneath her skin.

The water was not only soothing on her palm, but sensual, flowing over her skin like silk. She felt a stirring between her legs, a throb of heat, a rush of fire through her veins. Her breasts ached. Small teasing sensations, feather light, like fingers drifting down her thighs.

What the hell are you doing?

She heard the voice clearly in her head. *His* voice, thick with desire, with the same need that coursed through her entire body.

Gasping, she jerked her hands out from under the running water. She caught the echo of her gasp from the other room. For a moment her body pulsed with desire so acute she couldn't think straight. Feeling was everything. Sensations of need, of lust, of desperate desire flooded her mind. She even caught an image of him licking his way up her thigh to her hip, his tongue tasting the droplets of water running down her leg. His desire? Hers? She couldn't be certain. She only knew that she'd never experienced such need and it was all wrapped up with a complete stranger.

She could still feel his muscles within his body, hard and defined—he'd felt like velvet over steel. Somehow the pads of her fingers had absorbed him into her, so that he lived and breathed in her. She looked wildly around her kitchen, and for the first time since she'd moved in, her home was no longer her refuge. She pressed her thumb hard into her palm and abruptly ran out onto the porch where she could breathe. She actually put her head between her knees, feeling a little faint.

"Rikki?"

She turned her head without lifting it, still bent over, and their eyes locked together. At once she felt as if she was falling into him—becoming part of him. He was wrapped in a blanket and stood swaying in the doorway. Beads of sweat dotted his forehead and his skin looked gray.

He cleared his throat. "Are you all right?"

He looked like hell, but he was asking her if she was all right. She straightened slowly, never breaking eye contact. She doubted she could have even had she tried. She was a prisoner now, connected to him, a part of him, and she didn't have a clue what to do about it.

"I don't know. You?"

He smiled unexpectedly, a brief flash of white teeth, although his blue eyes didn't change expression at all. "My head hurts." His eyes warmed then. "And so does my body. Whatever you were doing, it felt like you were touching me—intimately."

She pressed her thumb harder into the center of her palm. "You need to go back inside before you fall down."

"Come with me."

She sighed. "It's difficult."

"Because you don't let anyone in your home."

His blanket slipped and she caught a glimpse of the

long sturdy column of his thigh before he righted it. He'd said home, not house. His description appealed to her.

"Come on." She stepped close to him and slipped her arm around his back, allowing him to lean on her. "Get back in bed. I'll give you some aspirin. Can you eat anything?"

"No. I still feel sick. I think I took a pretty ugly hit on the head." He swung the door closed behind them and locked it.

"Good thing you're hardheaded." She glanced at the door and then up at him. "Are you worried about visitors? It's not like I get many."

"Your family."

She nodded. "Yes, my sisters come by, but as a rule, they don't come into the house. Blythe gets coffee sometimes in the morning and sits out on the porch with me. They just open the door and call to me."

"I wouldn't want to accidently shoot anyone."

She scowled at him as she lowered him to the bed. "Keep up the threats and I'll throw your weapons in the well."

"Did you think that was a threat?" His voice was mild. "I was giving you a warning. I don't have a clue what the hell happened to me. Only a sense of danger and one very large instinct for self-preservation. I really wouldn't want to hurt anyone you cared about."

She could see sincerity in his eyes, but she didn't altogether trust his motives. More likely he was issuing a warning, so she would keep everyone away from him and he could hide without worrying. *In her house.* Her scowl deepened as she helped to prop him into a sitting position. She tucked blankets around him with the same meticulous attention to detail she did everything else.

She waited until he took the aspirin and drank the water before she spoke again. "I put your extra ammo under the bed. You've got enough to start a small war."

Lev studied her face. She had a stubborn little chin. He decided to push her a little more. She hadn't thrown him out yet. "Don't let them know I'm here."

"My sisters?" She gave him that little frown he had already begun looking for. "I don't lie to my sisters."

"I'm not asking you to lie. Are they going to ask if you have a man in your house?"

She toed at an imaginary speck on the hardwood floor. "No."

"Then we don't have a problem, do we? I should be out of here soon."

"You can't even walk by yourself." She held up her hand to stop him from talking. "I'll think about it." She continued to look at him through the thick veil of her lashes. "Are you going to explain?"

"Explain what? I can't remember my own name."

"Why I heard your voice in my head. And don't tell me it didn't happen. I may be strange, but I don't hear voices."

Her eyes went as black and shiny as obsidian. He was fascinated by that. The storm warnings.

"It was your voice. You said, 'What the hell are you doing?' You didn't say it out loud. It was in my head."

He couldn't look away from her gaze. He wanted to wake up to those eyes every morning. See them the last thing before he slept. Take them with him into his dreams. No one should have eyes like that. "I might be telepathic." He shrugged. "I don't have an explanation."

She should have accused him of being crazy but she didn't. "I know some people have extraordinary gifts. There's a family in the village . . ."

She broke off as if she were giving him classified information. Something stirred in his memory, but he couldn't pin it down. The glimpse eluded him before he could catch and hold it to him. Frustrated, he studied her face. He liked looking at her. She had angles.

"I don't know about extraordinary gifts—I was trying to come up with a plausible explanation. Are you telepathic?"

"No! Absolutely not." She rubbed her palm as if it were hurting her.

He held out his hand. "Let me see."

She cradled her hand protectively against her. "I don't think so." She pushed back her hair. "Look, it's really late. Why don't you go back to sleep. You shouldn't be sitting up anyway. We can sort all this out later."

He kept his hand out. "Let me look."

"Has anyone ever told you that you're pushy?"

He felt amusement welling up again. His head hurt like a son of a bitch, but he was ready to smile. "I can't remember much, so I'm going to say no."

"Given your personality, that's most likely a lie," she pointed out and stepped closer to the bed, her reluctance showing in the slow offer of her hand.

His fingers closed around her wrist and he drew her toward him with a steady, firm pressure. Each time the pads of his fingers touched her skin, he felt absorbed—connected to her—as if he was sinking deeper into her. He was almost desperate to join their bodies together. The feeling she gave him from just touching, skin to skin, was exquisite. She delighted him. Intrigued him. Made his body ache in wonderful ways. It was a new experience and one, at first, he didn't want, but now that he was beginning to reason again, he could enjoy every moment, every breathtaking sensation.

He rubbed the pad of his thumb over the center of her palm, tracing the two joined circles, although he couldn't see them. His brain mapped positions and recorded them for him. Every instinct, every memory of her was exact. He knew precisely where those circles had sunk beneath the skin of her palm. He pushed healing warmth at her. He'd learned to heal his own body from minor injuries when he was a child, using the energy around him. He surrounded her hand with the energy he drew on and pushed it into her palm.

"Does that feel better?"

There was silence. He looked up and met her gaze. She wasn't looking at her palm; instead, her eyes were glued to his face. He felt the now-familiar jolt in the vicinity of his heart when he locked gazes with her.

"You can do things other people can't," she whispered, sounding slightly awed. "My hand was aching and it doesn't now."

"I'm glad. After all you've done for me, I haven't shown much in the way of appreciation." He retained possession of her hand, stroking his thumb back and forth, blatantly trying to mesmerize her. He didn't want her leaving him, not with his heart pounding and his head so damned confused. Sometimes, like now, he thought she belonged to him.

"Lexi can heal things, but with the things she grows. She can mix together various plants and make you well in hours. She's amazing. And she can grow anything at all. She does almost all the gardening, although we all help. But she can't just touch someone."

He sent her a small smile, tugging a bit until she sank down onto the bed beside him. She automatically smoothed out the blanket as she sank lower, but she didn't remove her other hand from his as he brought it up for his inspection. "I don't think it's fair to say I healed anything. You didn't have a cut." He brought her hand up to his throbbing head, brushing her fingers across the Steri-Strips.

Rikki tugged until he reluctantly released her. "Get some sleep. It's very late, and I get up early. I won't go out on the boat tomorrow, but I'll see if I can pick up any news about what may have happened to you in the village."

As she stood and half turned from him, he felt the first hint of unease that immediately put him on alert. He struck hard and fast, catching her wrist and dragging her down beside him. "Someone's coming up your road."

"We'd see the headlights."

"They just turned onto it, but they're definitely on the road leading to your house, not one of the others." Even in his weakened state, he'd caught glimpses of the layout of the farm. He'd already mapped out several escape routes in his head. She wiggled, trying to get free, but she obviously was more worried about injuring him further. "Stop it, and listen," he hissed. "I'll cover you from the living room. If they come up to the house, open the door and leave it open, but step to one side. I have to be able to see you, so stay within sight of the left side of the room."

"It's my sister. She knew I went out for a dive, and she's just checking that I'm home safe. She'll come to the kitchen door, not the front door. And you need to mellow out. Sheesh, you'd think you *want* to shoot someone."

"You think I can't tell that you're worried someone's hunting you? You have thread on the windows, and you

checked all of them to make certain they weren't touched.
You circled the house looking for footprints and any dis-
turbances in your plants. Even the layout of the plants is
more to catch an intruder than for looks."

Headlights suddenly spilled light across the wall in the
living room, proving him right.

"Every door is locked, not with standard locks but security locks, and when I bolted the door, you didn't protest. You were more worried about what's out there than
what's inside this house with you. Don't argue with me.
Help me into the kitchen and I'll cover you from there,
just to be on the safe side."

She regarded him with suspicion, and he couldn't
blame her. He still hadn't made up his mind what to do if
she told anyone about his presence. He was confused and
knew that made him doubly dangerous, a wild animal
trapped and fighting for survival. The bits and pieces
coming into his brain weren't good. Not any of them. The
only thing good was this woman staring back at him with
enormous witch eyes, dark with distrust.

Again, he noted, there was no fear. None. He wondered
what it would be like to see trust in her eyes. She gave a
small nod.

"It's Blythe," she assured, "but if you feel safer 'covering' me, then I'm fine with that."

She didn't add her usual warning, but her mouth was
set in a stubborn line. He had the sudden urge to lean forward and kiss her. His head nearly exploded before he realized he had actually made a move toward her. She hadn't
moved and their lips were inches apart. They stared at
each other. She made a little moue with her lips and
slipped off the bed.

Lev released her immediately and, trying for a modicum

of modesty, wrapped the blanket closer around him, even as he grabbed his favorite gun.

Rikki was silent as she wrapped her arm around his waist and helped him to stand. She didn't know why she was indulging him. She should have just picked up the gun and hit him over the head with the silly thing. It was just a little disturbing that he had caught her security measures, as injured as he was. Not once had any of her family noticed—and she liked it that way.

She set him in a chair and went out onto the porch off the kitchen, leaving the door open as instructed. She watched Blythe exit the car.

"Did you have a good time?" She called out loud enough that Lev couldn't fail to realize it was, in fact, her sister and he could just put away his gun.

"I was worried about you. I tried to call you on your cell several times. And I left four messages on your machine." Blythe closed her door and came up the stairs. She reached for Rikki and hugged her.

Rikki tried to hug her back. She didn't mind Blythe touching her, but she always felt awkward, unsure what to do in return, so she usually stood and waited for it to be over, feeling foolish. She recognized Blythe was distressed.

"I'm sorry. I never think to check my messages and I don't have a clue where that cell phone is." She looked around as if she might find it in the flower bed.

Blythe came all the way onto the porch and dropped into her favorite chair. "There was a huge wave, Rikki, it came out of nowhere. The Drakes stopped it, but I was afraid you were caught out at sea when it came."

"I was. It knocked me off my boat," Rikki admitted.

She kept her body between Blythe and the door at all times, standing upright and making certain Lev didn't have a shot if he felt so inclined. She wasn't about to place Blythe in danger.

Blythe paled, her soft brown eyes going wide as she searched Rikki for damage. Rikki couldn't stop her hand from drifting up to her neck to cover the smudges there. "I was just about to go down for another load when it struck, so I had my gear on. No big deal."

"Of course it was a big deal. Tell me what happened."

Rikki shrugged. "I was thrown from the boat and went down about thirty feet. I just shoved my regulator in my mouth and I was fine."

Blythe shook her head. "Honey, you can't keep diving alone. You need a tender."

"If I'd had a tender in the boat, they wouldn't have had on a suit or a tank, and they would have been in the water right along with me. Instead of my own survival, I would have had to think of someone else. I don't have to worry about anyone else when I'm out there. If something happens, I depend on myself. Tell me about the wedding," she added to change the subject.

Blythe smiled immediately. "It was so beautiful. *All* of them ended up getting married. Jonas and Hannah had to stand up for all of them. Elle and Jackson were taking off for their honeymoon. I think they're traveling through Europe. I think everyone left for a honeymoon with the exception of Jonas and Hannah because they'd already had theirs."

Rikki frowned a little at the mention of Jonas and Hannah. Jonas Harrington was the local sheriff and he always made her uneasy. She'd caught him eyeing her a few times, and she had the feeling he'd delved into her past and was watching her in case there was a local fire. Maybe she was just paranoid, but she stayed as far from him and his deputies as possible.

"Any other news?" she prompted.

"I think Joley might be pregnant," Blythe said, "but that's just a guess."

That wasn't exactly the news Rikki was looking for. "Did you all have fun?"

Blythe nodded. "Everyone asked where you were. Lexi danced up a storm. That girl is amazing on the dance floor. I wish I could learn her moves." She laughed softly, her eyes bright with pride. "She and Lissa were very popular tonight. Everyone wanted to dance with them."

Rikki smiled. Lissa and Lexi tended to be the center of attention wherever they were. No one could help but look at them. She was as proud of them as Blythe was.

"You look tired, Rikki," Blythe said. "You should be in bed."

Rikki shrugged. "I always worry until everyone is safe at home." It was a grudging concession to admit it, but then with Blythe she was often more forthcoming than with anyone else. There was something motherly about Blythe—and Rikki had forgotten what that was like. Blythe could wrench emotion out of her when no one else could.

Blythe gave her a smile that started a faint glow inside of Rikki. "I know you do. The others carpooled. They're already in their homes and are safe. Get some sleep."

Rikki had no idea how she was going to do that, but she managed a nonchalant shrug and waved as Blythe headed back to her car. Rikki waited until the car was safely away before going back inside. The lights were out, but when she glanced at the chair where she'd placed Lev, she could see it was empty. Startled, she looked around the room, her heart pounding.

He was lying facedown on the floor, at an angle where he would have been able to get past her with a shot at Blythe while she was sitting in her chair. Gritting her teeth together she slammed the door closed and locked it before stalking across the room to toe him in the ribs.

"You are really annoying. I mean *really*."

"I told you exactly what to do and you didn't listen," he snapped back, his tone impatient. "I hurt like hell thanks to your inability to pay attention."

Her breath hissed out as anger mixed with adrenaline poured through her. "I paid attention, you cretin. I don't take orders from you or anyone else. It didn't occur to me that you'd be so determined to shoot someone that you'd take the chance of hurting yourself further. I swear, if you do one more thing to piss me off tonight, I'm going to put your sorry ass back in my truck, drive you to the cliffs and toss you over. Now get up."

He stared up at her for a long time. Her eyes were hot, his ice-cold. They looked at one another for an eternity, Rikki trying to sustain her anger, which was usually easy enough to do. She was either happy or sad or angry—there was never an in between for her. Right now she was confused. He was just such a strong man, tough as nails. Obviously hurting, sprawled out on the blanket, naked, with his gun in his hand. He hadn't turned the weapon toward her, even though she was threatening him. And he'd thrown the blanket on the floor instead of wrapping himself in it to stay warm.

Her heart jumped. Even in his weakened state, he'd seen *her*. He'd seen her need to have everything in her house a certain way. Lying naked on the floor was *not* okay. Well . . . maybe she could make an exception in his case. She studied his body. Perfectly symmetrical. Every muscle was defined. Chiseled. Like a sculpture. His skin flowed over the framework of his bones and muscles. Large bones, dense and strong. He looked a little like the pictures she'd seen of the early Olympians, warriors every one of them, fighters in a time when it was necessary. She watched the way his muscles moved beneath his skin as he shifted position, the art of the motion and the fluid grace fascinating her.

"Rikki."

His voice startled her. She'd been so caught up in the flow of muscle beneath skin, she'd forgotten what she was doing. What had she been doing? She blinked at him, bringing him back in focus.

"While I appreciate the fact that you like my body, I could use a little help getting up."

"What?" Even to her own ears she sounded confused.

His voice gentled. Turned soft, almost seductive. "Come here."

She felt her body's instant response to his tone, almost as if he hypnotized her. She'd actually stepped forward without thought—without consent—a wholly natural response to his summons. She frowned at him. "Who are you?"

"I wish I could tell you. Whatever I am, Rikki, *who-ever* I am, it isn't a good thing."

She slipped her arm around his back and used her leg muscles, honed by fighting the currents beneath the ocean as they shoved her back and forth, to help him to his feet. "Maybe. And maybe you would have shot me just now if you're all that bad. Give yourself a break and just get in bed and go to sleep. We can sort all this out in the morning."

He seemed heavier this time, and a small bit of blood trickled down the side of his head. She bit her lip. She shouldn't have listened to him. She should have overcome her own aversion to the hospital and just taken him.

"The bathroom. All that water you keep shoving down me is beginning to be felt."

She hesitated, nearly panicking. *Her* bathroom was only a few steps away, while the guest bathroom was at the other end of the house. Her things. For a moment she couldn't breathe. He was invading—*everywhere.*

"Rikki, it's okay if you want me to use the other bathroom. I can make it."

Again his voice stroked over her with gentleness. It made her feel small and silly to have to have everything her way. It wasn't like she had an obsession with germs—it was that everything had to be a certain way.

"That's ridiculous, we're right here." She forced herself to help him through the door.

Once outside of the bathroom, she leaned against the wall with her heart pounding and every muscle tight and protesting. For a moment there was chaos in her brain. What if he touched her things? Messed up her towels? Moved her soap dispenser? She could feel her pulse pounding. Little things could make her explode with anger. She'd worked on it, did breathing exercises, but still, when people messed with her things . . .

And what if that was the kind of thing that triggered her mind to set fires in her sleep? She was distressed, overtired and *someone was in her house.* She put her head between her knees, feeling sick. She knew better than to trust herself. And if a maniac was out there, destroying homes because she was in them, she'd just placed Lev's life in danger.

What's wrong? I can feel your distress. It's pouring off you in waves.

She stiffened, slowly straightening, looking around her. It was his voice again, distinctly his voice. And he knew she was upset.

Don't talk to me in my head. Deliberately she thought the words rather than saying them aloud, uncertain of what to expect. Could they really talk to one another telepathically? It was long suspected in Sea Haven that the Drakes could talk to one another, but she'd never had a single telepathic experience—until she'd encountered Lev.

The door opened and he hung on to it, his blue eyes drifting over her, searching her expression, her eyes. "Are you okay? I know this is difficult for you."

He was the one who was injured. She frowned again and wrapped her arm around him. "You washed your hands, didn't you?"

His smile fascinated her. "Yes, ma'am. I'm all about cleanliness."

He was teasing her. She'd never been good at the concept, although living around the other women the past four years had helped her. Lexi was a terrible tease, and as young as she'd been, with the horrific background she'd had, they all had protected her as much as possible. If teasing was how she needed to cope with stress, then even Rikki was willing to learn to deal with it for her. Rikki didn't dare look up at his face as she took him on through to the bedroom. She was getting used to that face, the angles and planes, the shadows and scars. His face appealed to her in the same way his body did. She was afraid once she focused on it, she'd be captured and would reveal the strangeness of her mind to him.

She tucked the blankets around him. "You need to go to sleep, Lev. It's very late."

"I can't."

She met his eyes, and her stomach took a plunge, as if she'd dropped into a deep blue sea. He was looking up at her. He was a tough, scarred man, a warrior with a million weapons. His eyes were flat and cold, yet she could see his confusion, his vulnerability. She realized exactly why she'd brought him home—why she'd taken such a chance—what she saw in him. *Herself.* She was looking at a man who was utterly, absolutely alone. He was confused and had no idea what or who he was. Something shifted inside of her. Softened.

Blythe had found Rikki when she was exactly the same way. She'd been completely alone and so confused about herself. She still didn't know if she caused fires, or if she'd been responsible for the deaths of her parents and the loss of three homes. She had no idea if she'd killed the only man she'd ever loved. For all she knew she was a murderess. She was terrified to trust herself, let alone anyone else. Just as this man was.

She actually felt connected to him in some way she couldn't break. She couldn't abandon him. Maybe it was payment for what Blythe and the others had done for her. All she knew was—there was no way to walk away from him. She acknowledged the danger. He very likely could be just what he appeared, a killer of some kind, but somehow that didn't seem right to her.

He'd done two things that stuck out in her mind that were a bit contrary to his being completely evil. He hadn't killed her when he obviously had the opportunity, and he'd dragged himself from a kitchen chair to the floor, causing himself a great deal of pain, in order to protect her from an unknown threat. He'd observed that she was worried about intruders, and he'd risked further injury and certainly a great deal more pain in order to protect her. He could have protected himself from the bed. No one, *no one*, had ever done that for her before.

"You don't have to worry," she reassured him, looking him straight in the eye. "I'll watch over you. If anything suspicious happens, I'll wake you up. Just go to sleep now."

"You're asking me to trust you."

She couldn't help herself. There was one unruly strand of hair that spilled into the middle of his forehead. She brushed it back with gentle fingers. "I trusted you, bringing you home, going down for the uni and leaving you alone in my boat. I left the keys in my truck. I know you noticed them. I gave you back your weapons."

"You didn't trust me when the woman came tonight."

"Blythe. Her name is Blythe and I owe her everything. I can take a chance with my life, but not with hers. All I'm saying is, you came home with me. Let me watch over you tonight, and then tomorrow you can go back to being whoever you want to be."

His blue eyes moved over her face as if memorizing every detail and looking deeper, under her skin, behind her eyes, deeper still, as if he might judge the truth of what she was saying.

"How will you sleep?"

Her fingers reluctantly left his face. "You're in my house.

In my bed. It's safer that I be out of the house and stay awake, and I can't explain to you why."

It was his turn to frown. "But you'll talk about this with me tomorrow."

She shrugged, not committing to anything and unwilling to lie. What would she say? I might be a psycho? But then, he thought he was one as well. "Good night, Lev. If you need me, I'll have the kitchen door open."

Rikki snapped off the bedroom light and left him. Either he'd drift off or he wouldn't, but at least he could rest. She dragged a spare blanket from the linen closet and made a fresh pot of coffee for herself before going out onto the porch and settling into the hammock swing. It was her most comfortable chair and she planned to spend the night there.

It was always cold in the evening and already the fog blanketed the trees and gardens, snaking its way into the yard so she could barely make out her sleepy flowers and shrubbery. She loved the feel of the fog on her skin, those drops of mist that shrouded the night in a wet veil of silver. She snuggled beneath the blanket, pulling in her feet, a little uneasy.

She put her apprehension down to having a stranger in her house, but still, she couldn't settle. Twice she walked around the house, wishing she could make up her mind whether or not to get a dog. Airiana loved animals and was always bugging Rikki, and all the others, about getting dogs for protection. A dog was one more thing for her to worry about if a fire started in the night.

She sipped at her coffee and looked at all the places she'd studied a thousand times. Vantage points where someone might be able to hide in concealment and spy on her home and family. How paranoid did it make her that she scouted all the areas and visited them regularly to check for signs someone had been watching her? She sighed and kicked at the railing with her bare foot. Very paranoid, but she wasn't ever going to stop. It was the only way she ever managed to sleep at night.

5

FLAMES raced up the walls and poured across the ceiling, liquid fire, running like rivers through the house, consuming everything in sight. The roar was loud, angry, and the flames reared back, looking—seeking. The orange and red inferno rolled into giant fiery balls, while wind rushed from wall to wall, fanning the conflagration. Heat filled the rooms, and great black gaping holes appeared in the walls. Chunks fell from the ceiling while the inferno blazed hotter.

Water! Come to me! Help me. Water!

Lev woke, gun in his fist, heart pounding, head throbbing, but most of all, his left palm was so painful, it felt like someone had shoved a knife through it. He could hear the sound of water all around him, in the bathroom, the kitchen, outside, even on the roof. He forced himself into a sitting position, wiping at the beads of sweat dotting his forehead with his arm. What the hell was going on? The echo of that frightened female voice still reverberated through his mind.

His brain didn't feel as fuzzy. He had a whale of a headache, but he could think. His dream . . . No, *her* dream. Rikki. She was dreaming or, more precisely, having a nightmare, and somehow she was projecting her nightmare to him. He pressed his palm to his leg while he breathed away the last remnants of heat and fire surrounding him.

Struggling to his feet, he managed to stagger into the bathroom and turn off both the shower and the sink. The basin had filled up, and water had run onto the floor, so he dropped a towel on the mess and went on through toward the kitchen. The sound of water pulled at him again as he went down the hall, and he pushed open a door to find the laundry room. Water ran in the washing machine. He turned that off, spotted his neatly folded clothes sitting on the dryer and pulled on his jeans, hastily buttoning a couple of the buttons as he made his way into the kitchen.

The floor was flooded and water cascaded from the sink—the faucet was on full blast. He turned it off and went outside. Overhead, the skies had opened and poured water down, the main concentration on the house and yard. He looked out over the surrounding trees and saw it was raining, but not with the same force as around the house— around Rikki.

Sound asleep, she was curled up in a hammock swing, a blanket around her, expressions of fear crossing her face as she cried imploringly, palms upward toward the water. His little sea urchin diver was definitely bound to an element— and a strong one at that.

"Come here, *lyubimaya moya*." He reached for her. She was so slight that even in his weakened state, he doubted if he'd have trouble carrying her. He gathered her against his bare chest, whispering to her when she began to struggle. "I'm bringing you in. You can bring the rain with you if you like, but it isn't doing your house much good."

Her lashes lifted and there she was. He felt the jolt through his entire body, the sensation of drowning in a sensual sea. He smiled at her. "I'm taking you inside. If you keep wiggling around, we're both going to end up on the ground."

"I don't like anyone touching me."

"I know." He made no move to put her down. Already the rain was lessening in intensity. He carried her into the house and kicked the door closed behind him, noting that her bare feet were covered in burn scars that obviously went up under the hem of her jeans. "Are you worried that someone might set your house on fire?"

She studied his face for so long, he didn't think she'd answer him. "Yes."

The word came out reluctantly, and for the first time, her gaze shifted from his. He carried her carefully through the kitchen. The floor was wet and needed to be mopped. She didn't notice. She was too busy trying not to touch his bare chest or struggle so hard he fell. He pretended not to notice her dilemma, choosing instead to figure out what she wasn't telling him. Whatever it was, it was important.

He put her on the bed and sank down beside her, deliberately leaning his weight against her. He didn't have to fake weakness. His legs were rubbery and his palm—damn—it hurt like a son of a bitch. He pressed his thumb deep into the center, but before he could use healing energy, she reached out and took his wrist, drawing his hand to her. She had that little frown he found so endearing on her face.

"Is your hand hurting?" She rubbed the pad of her thumb over his palm, tracing imaginary circles there. "I dreamt that your hand was hurting."

The pain was gone the instant her thumb stroked over his skin. He was used to strange occurrences—he was gifted psychically in many different ways—but he'd never had a connection to another human being, at least he didn't think so. He'd hit his head pretty hard, and he wasn't remembering a whole hell of a lot about his life. Only images of violence, a gut instinct telling him someone wanted him dead, and yet he was fairly certain he would have remembered something like this.

His strange reactions to her felt completely foreign— but right. He knew it didn't make sense, but at the moment, nothing did. He needed to be with her. He needed to take the fear from her eyes. He . . . *needed*.

"You dreamt the house was on fire. *This* house." He'd get into the water aspect later. Right now he could give her peace. He closed his eyes and centered himself, allowing his mind to expand, to stretch, to seek the energy of others. He couldn't find anyone close to her home. If someone had been close, they'd left no trace of themselves behind, which was difficult to do. "We're alone, Rikki. I can't tell you how I know, but I do. Just like the way you manipulate water, I know if someone is close."

His revelation should have made her feel more secure, but instead she looked haunted. Just for a moment. He caught a flash of terror in her eyes, and then her expression went blank, distant, as if she'd wiped her mind clean like a slate. He heard her breathing change, just for a moment, a quick inhale and then she exhaled, a long slow breath of air that gave away her agitation.

"What time is it?" she asked. "I have to clean things up."

"Nearly four. What you need to do is to lie down and rest."

She mumbled something incoherent under her breath and went out of the room. He could hear her mopping the floor in the kitchen. It occurred to him that this wasn't the first—or last—time she'd done this. So fires were a recurring nightmare. And she feared someone would start one. She was barefoot and he'd seen the burn scars on her feet when he carried her—his mind was already cataloging each whorl and ridge.

He sighed and brushed his hand over his face, and then just sat on the edge of the bed, rubbing his palm with his thumb thoughtfully while the rain beat on the roof and she scrubbed her floor in the kitchen. Those burns were no accident, then. It was no wonder she worked under the water. It was where she felt safe. Her legs and feet probably hurt when she walked on land, but in the water she was more fluid. He knew the scars would make her skin feel tight and stretched, so walking could be painful.

Mapping the scars in his mind, he traced the pattern in the air and pushed warm healing energy toward the air sketches. As a rule, healing had to be done when a wound occurred, not months—or years—after. But sometimes, if one worked at it, they could ease the scarring. He pressed his fingertips to his temples. If he could remember that, why couldn't he remember why the hell every memory seemed to be surrounded with violence?

He knew he could take apart his guns and put them back together in seconds because he'd already tried it, the moment she'd gone outside. He'd *needed* to clean his guns.

He knew what ammo he needed for each weapon. He knew he could pull a knife, turn and throw, and hit his intended target with exact accuracy. When he saw someone, he saw targets on them and knew immediately where to strike to kill them if needed. His mind was like a computer, analyzing all the time, choosing kill spots. Did other people live that way?

"Lev?" She stood in the hall looking at him, a worried frown on her face. "Do you need more aspirin? I don't keep anything else in the house."

"No. I'm fine. I was trying to remember something—*anything*—that might tell me I'm a much better man than I think I am."

She sent him a small, crooked smile. It was almost reluctant, as if she didn't really know how to smile. "I think that tells you you're a better man than you think you are." She looked back at the kitchen and then glanced toward the bathroom. "I'm sorry about the mess. It happens sometimes when I have nightmares. My guest bathroom was really flooded."

"Because you dream about fires."

She nodded slowly, her dark eyebrows drawn together. He liked the shape of her eyebrows, the way they emphasized her eyes and those incredibly long lashes.

"Are you afraid you start the fires while you sleep?"

Her gasp was audible. Her eyes widened in alarm. She actually took a step back from him and nearly dropped the mop.

"It isn't that difficult to figure out, Rikki. You're afraid to sleep in the house with me in it. You call to water when you do sleep. You have burns on your feet. And the house on fire in your dream was *this* house. You're scared you're the one causing the fires."

She swallowed hard, but her gaze didn't waver. "It's possible. Maybe even probable. My parents died in a fire. Two foster homes I lived in burned down, and then I lived in a state-run facility until I turned eighteen. I thought it was over until . . . I met someone. A few years ago, my fiancé died in a fire. That's four fires, two that killed people."

He saw past the belligerence to the real terror permeating her entire life. "Rikki. It would be impossible for you to start the fires, awake or asleep. You couldn't do it."

Rikki's frown deepened. "That's *exactly* what Lissa said. *Exactly.* With the same absolute conviction. How could either of you know that when I don't even know it?" She rubbed her palm down her thigh in agitation right along the path of the shimmering raindrop tattoo dripping down her leg, drawing his attention to it even though it was hidden. "I can't take the chance on your life, and you shouldn't want to either."

"It's obvious you're a water element. You're bound to water. You can't start fires. You can only put them out."

"I don't know what you're talking about. I like water, but I'm not bound to it. I just feel safer around it, and when I'm in the sea and the pressure of the water is all around me, I feel different—more normal."

"What in the hell is normal? Not you. Not me. I doubt if there is such a thing."

She regarded him as if he had two heads. "Of course there is normal. There are regular people."

He swung his legs up on the bed and stretched out, linking his hands behind his head. "Come lie down. There's no one close to the house. We're locked up and safe, and you need to get sleep." He patted the bed beside him.

She looked utterly shocked. "We can't sleep in the same bed."

"Why not?"

"Well . . . because."

There was that laughter welling up again. He found himself smiling at the idea of it. "You know, I don't think I've ever actually slept in the same bed with someone either. If I have, I don't remember, and it doesn't feel like I'd trust anyone that much."

"So why in the world would you trust me? Or why would I trust you?"

He kept his eyes locked with hers. He could stare into her eyes for eternity. "What the hell difference does it really make at this point, Rikki? I don't think we can hide from one another, do you? Whatever it is that connected us in that water went bone deep. I'm not getting you out of me anytime soon. So come lie down and just let it all go for the rest of the night."

"I'm not having sex with you."

His smile widened. "Thanks for the compliment. It never occurred to me you would think I'd be capable."

"You have unexpected abilities."

"I won't touch you. The bed's big. I imagine you'd be lost in this thing."

Abruptly she turned back to the kitchen. He heard her rattling around for a few more minutes. More hand washing. The woman loved water. She snapped off the kitchen light and moved a little reluctantly into the bedroom, eyeing him warily.

"I really don't mind sleeping in the swing."

"I mind it. It's raining out there, although that could be your fault. Just lie down and go to sleep. If anyone comes near the house, I'll know."

She stretched out on the bed, keeping several inches between them. It took several minutes before she began to breathe normally. He smiled at the ceiling, there in the darkness, while the scent of her enveloped him.

"Thanks, Rikki. I know this was difficult, letting me in. I don't believe or trust myself, and I sure don't know why the hell you saved my life and helped me, but I'm grateful." His voice was gruffer than he intended. He wasn't used to allowing himself to feel emotion, and just for a moment, there it was, clogging his throat and changing his tone.

She shrugged. "I can't imagine not being able to remember my past, although it might be a good thing. I might not be so afraid to go to sleep."

"I don't want to remember my past."

"You might have a family waiting for you somewhere, Lev. You don't want to leave them wondering. Believe me, until Blythe and the others came along, I'd forgotten there was such a thing as family. You don't want to be without one."

His heart contracted painfully. "I don't have anyone. No one knows me, Rikki. They don't see me, and they're not supposed to. I'm the kind of man who lives in the shadows."

"How can you know that for sure?"

Her voice was soft and got inside of him in spite of his determination not to allow her to come any further. He already felt too dependent on her.

"Because all I know is how to kill."

"You know how to dive. You're very experienced in the water."

"Why do you say that?" He asked curiously. She spoke with conviction.

"The way you acted under water. The water was cold, too cold. You were going into hypothermia. You had no air, no wet suit, and yet you didn't panic, not even when you were injured. It takes a *lot* of experience to behave like that when all the odds are stacked against you."

"But I had you to save me."

She turned on her side and, sticking her elbow on the bed, propped her head in her hand to look at him. "Anyone else would have fought me. I expected you to try to fight me for the air, but you were calm and you breathed with me and allowed me to get us to the surface, decompressing along the way. That isn't just unusual, it's downright rare. Even experienced divers can panic. It took a lot of nerve."

"And then I ripped out your radio. I'll fix it for you."

"I can fix my own radio. I'm not certain you knew what you were doing at the time."

That was the trouble. He'd known exactly what he was doing—had weighed the advantages and disadvantages of killing the woman who had saved his life. What kind of man did that? Not a good one. "I know you don't like people touching you, Rikki, but . . ." His fingers were already on her face, tracing every angle, stroking the softness of her skin, memorizing the details.

She held her breath, but she didn't pull away, as if sensing the deep need inside of him. He didn't understand his connection to her, and he doubted if she did either. Just for this moment, they declared a truce and just accepted that it was there. He had to know her face intimately, as intimately as he intended to know her body, but right now, this was enough. Mapping her face and imprinting it forever on his brain.

She suddenly smiled. He felt it through his fingers before he made out her expression. His body stirred in response. "You don't even know if you can fix my radio."

"No," he agreed, "I don't. But I can take apart a gun and put it back together again in seconds."

"I can see you'll be a big help on the farm."

As soon as the words slipped out, he could tell by the way she stiffened that her expectation of him staying with her had been entirely subconscious. Now that she'd spoken the thought aloud—given the idea life—she retreated back into her world, probably sorry she'd voiced the suggestion.

Satisfaction slid into his gut, a quiet happiness he rarely—if ever—had experienced. Just being in her presence made him feel different, more alive, more sensual, more of a man and less of a killer. Lying beside her should have set off every alarm in his body. He had sex, usually great sex, but it was a tool, and he was never comfortable afterward. He certainly didn't lie on a bed in a semi-vulnerable position and contemplate falling asleep with another living, breathing human being beside him. He knew it was completely alien to every survival instinct he had, yet he wanted her there. The thought of her sleeping outside, at a distance from him, bothered him on a primal level he couldn't explain, not to her and certainly not to himself.

He kept his eyes locked on hers. "I was thinking more like helping out on your boat."

He saw the shock, the instant rejection. She even shook her head. And that adorable frown was back, so that he couldn't help but smooth his fingers over the little lines between her eyes. He laughed softly. "I can see you're completely behind the idea."

"*No one*, and I mean *no one*, goes on my boat."

"I can understand that. *But—*" He put his finger over her pursed lips, imagining her kissing his fingers. The thought was fleeting, but vivid enough to cause heat to flood his body. He didn't seem to have control around her. "As reasonable as that would be, *I've* already been on your boat."

"You ripped out my radio."

"Which I intend to fix," he pointed out. "What's a tender?"

He felt her shock. "A what?" she repeated, but she'd heard him the first time.

He waited in silence, but she had gone stubborn on him. He sighed, and although he was taking a chance, he rubbed her chin in the dark with the pad of his thumb. Once, he stroked a caress across her lips. She was definitely frowning and that made him smile.

"It isn't any great secret, is it? You said your sister Blythe told you that you shouldn't dive alone. She said you needed a tender. What is that?"

"Someone that would drive me insane. They take care of the boat and equipment, sort of keep watch while a diver is under water. They need a permit and have to know what they're doing. I trained a couple but kicked them off after a couple of dives. They're annoying. They don't roll my hoses the right way. And there is a right way. You do it wrong and they're all tangled."

Now that she'd come out with her opinion on the subject, he could see she was extremely hostile about the idea. She hadn't let on to Blythe, but she had no intention of diving with someone watching over her. He had a vague idea that he might change that. "Blythe thinks it's necessary."

"You were eavesdropping on my conversation with Blythe."

"Of course. Would you expect less?"

She opened her mouth and then abruptly closed it. "I

don't want anyone on my boat and that includes you. You'd touch my things."

"I'll learn not to."

Her frown deepened and she narrowed her eyes at him. "You will not. You'll do whatever you want to do. You're one of *those* men."

"If I don't know what kind of a man I am, how could you know?"

"Because so far, you've been on my boat, in my house, touched my things, slept in my bed, and you're probably going to want food. You're demanding."

Laughter spilled over, startling him. A real laugh. Out loud. He sounded rusty, but it didn't matter. He was shocked at the sound, at the feeling, at the freedom he felt with her to laugh. "I suppose you're right about that."

She stared into his gaze, her eyes so black, there in the night with the moon hidden behind the clouds, that she appeared mysterious and elusive, like the storm passing overhead.

"You're damned beautiful," he said, before he could stop himself. "I've never met a woman like you."

A slow smile curved her mouth. He realized, like him, she didn't smile often. "How would you know? You can't remember who you've met and who you haven't. But in any case, thanks. No one ever says things like that to me."

A shadow crossed her face and he remembered the fiancé, the man who had died in a fire. "Tell me about him. His name. What he did. How you met him." *How he died and why you're so afraid you started the fires.*

She blinked, looked startled. "I heard that. What you were thinking. You are telepathic. And you've made me weird, just like you. Okay . . . maybe I was already a little weird, but now I'm way worse than I already was. Am

I going to hear what everyone's thinking? Can you hear my thoughts?"

"You aren't projecting them to me. And that was an accident. I didn't mean to have you hear that, but I honestly am interested."

Rikki laid her head back on her pillow and stared up at the ceiling, her mouth set in stubborn lines. The sound of the rain hitting the roof and windows seemed to drain the tension from her. He could tell she was listening to it, and while she listened, her fingers began to react, tapping against her leg. She didn't seem to notice, caught in the spell of the rain falling.

Lev remained silent, realizing this was a part of Rikki's nature. Certain things—especially anything to do with water, he supposed—took her outside herself, and she focused completely on whatever captured her attention, tuning out everything else around her, tuning out him. His first thought was to bring her attention back to him, but before he could speak, her hand went up and she began to weave patterns in the air, just as he had done when directing healing energy, although her designs were more like those of a conductor with a large orchestra.

At once he detected a difference in the pattern of the rain. The beat changed and then the resonance, the sound, depending on where each drop landed and how fast or hard. He found himself holding his breath. Her control and power were extraordinary, and she didn't seem to notice she was directing the rain. His brain computed her patterns, recognized and spit out the data for him. She was drawing the layout of her farm in the air and directing the heaviest parts of the storm where she wanted it.

The rain over the grapevines was soft and gentle like

the sounds of flutes and clarinets. The rain in the trees and along the creek banks where the ferns grew was much more dramatic. It pounded down to saturate the area and feed the voracious redwoods, the other evergreens and the flora growing in the forest throughout the farm. The garden was treated with a melody of patterns spread out over the various vegetables and herbs, in a symphony of violins and other instruments.

Rikki was so deep into her concentration and focus—obviously completely forgetting him, her surroundings and everything else—that he began to pick up images from her mind. Entire sections of the garden were dedicated to pharmaceutical plants, to plants for making various dyes, to all sorts of flowers, to vegetables of all kinds, and there was another section for herbs. There was an olive grove and an orchard with apples. It was amazing how clear the images in her head were—with exact coordinates, like a map. Just as the map in his head was laid out in grids, so was hers.

He closed his eyes and let the music of the rain soothe him. He could feel her breath, hear the soft variations in her breathing when she changed each chord, when she played one area differently than another. He began to sort the various sounds and rhythms. It was an orchestra of drops, a miracle performance. He would bet his last dollar—and he was fairly certain he had a great deal of money—that the farm was doing extremely well thanks to Rikki's ability to call the water and change how hard or soft it fell.

He turned his head again to watch her face. She was so caught up in the musical aspects of her orchestration, the actual sounds of the drops, he doubted if she was fully aware of what she was doing—if at all. And he doubted, even if anyone else observed her, that they would recognize what she was doing, the enormity or significance of it. Who would ever suspect she was manipulating the rain?

He turned the idea over and over in his mind. She "called" water to her. She couldn't manufacture the water—it had to be available—but she could control it. Rikki was so lost in the wonder of playing that she didn't notice when he got up and went to the window, shoving it open so he could see the silver sheets of rain falling from the sky. The sight was breathtaking. He turned back to look at her. *She* was breathtaking—extraordinary. She was such a rare phenomenon that he could barely believe he'd discovered her.

A gust of wind drove the rain into the house and dotted his chest, shoulder and arm. He knew he'd felt rain a thousand times, yet it felt like the first time. The wonder Rikki experienced when she touched water spilled over to him through their strange connection. The raindrops were sensual against his skin, velvet tongues lapping at him. The liquid was cool, his body hot. He could feel each individual drop.

More than the sensation *on* his skin was the way the liquid felt as if it seeped deeper. There was first a tingling along nerve endings, and then a rush, like a dam opening inside of him. He went very still and allowed the phenomenon to engulf him, to spread like a tidal wave inside of him. He felt renewed, happy, clean and balanced.

Lev turned back to the bed, leaving the window open. He loved the sound of the rain and knew he'd always associate the sound with Rikki. Her face showed signs of exhaustion. She'd worked hard beneath the water, hauled him out of the sea, given him CPR and been up most of the night. Even playing as she was, manipulating water took tremendous energy. He knew she hadn't eaten anything since she'd brought him to the farm. It was no wonder she was so thin.

He stretched out again, shaping his body around hers, careful not to touch her or disturb her, but he sent a "push" to get her to sleep. He used a very delicate, gentle touch, one designed to allow her to drift off slowly, unknowing. While he waited for his suggestion to work, he contemplated the tragedies in her life.

If someone had deliberately set those fires—and it was too much of a coincidence to think it wasn't intentional— was her ability to control water the reason? Had someone realized Rikki was an element with tremendous power, even when she was just a child? She hadn't said how old she was when the first fire had occurred, but she'd been in two foster homes and then was in a state-run facility. Someone had killed her fiancé using fire, the opposite of water. Who wanted her dead? He was convinced someone did. And if so, why the long gaps between the attacks, and why fire?

Her hands dropped to her side and her lashes fluttered. He smiled down at her. "You've come back to me."

She looked around her. "You're still here."

Her voice was drowsy, her eyes slumberous. She'd definitely crawled inside of him and wrapped herself tightly around whatever was left of his soul. He wanted to look at her all night—the rest of his life, for that matter. He found peace in her.

"Yeah. I'm here. I don't think I'm going anywhere soon." If ever.

He *should* go. Whatever he was, he was violent and

deadly, and definitely trouble for her, but . . . He looked around the room. She had a bed, a dresser and a night-stand. The bare minimum. It was that way in every room.

"How long have you lived here?"

She thought about it. "We closed the deal on the farm just before Lexi's nineteenth birthday and she just turned twenty-three, so just about five years. The orchards were already in, and part of the main vegetable gardens. The houses were on the property, but they were all in bad shape. We remodeled ourselves and extended the garden. Last year we put in two greenhouses, a fairly large one for vegetables and one much smaller for flowers. The farm has really done well and produced for us."

It was the most forthcoming she'd been about her life, and he heard the pride in her voice. She loved the farm.

"Who did the work on the houses?"

"We did. All of us. We started with Lexi's house. She needed to feel safe. It was important that she had a home, a place that was hers. Judith, she's our artist, is amazing with a hammer. Between Judith, Lissa and Airiana, we were able to do just about everything ourselves. And Judith helped each of us decorate."

He looked around Rikki's house. His first thought was that not much decorating had taken place, but then he realized he was wrong. Judith, whoever she was, knew Rikki's need for simplicity. The walls were done in cool water tones, producing a soothing atmosphere for her. And her bathroom had been a work of art. The few pictures in the house were watercolors, depicting rain over grass or rain in the trees. Judith "saw" Rikki and designed the interior to suit her needs. He had no doubt she would see right through him and made up his mind to avoid her.

"How did you all meet?"

Rikki's fingers continued to tap a beat along her thigh. He could hear the rain respond through the open window, drumming at the roof, following the beat of her fingers.

"We met through grief counseling. It was sort of my last-ditch effort to save myself. I was fairly certain I was a sociopath or something, at least in my sleep. I didn't really want to keep living. But then I heard Lexi's story, and Judith's, as well as the others', and they didn't make me feel so alone. They believed in me when I couldn't believe in myself."

He was silent, digesting what she told him. "Rikki. Is that why you took me in? I'm not like you, honey. You didn't start those fires. I've killed men. I see the images in my head. I don't know why, but I'm not the nice man you've got in your head."

"I don't think you're a nice man," she protested.

Her vehemence made him smile all over again. "Good. I don't want you to be disappointed when we find out who I am."

"You really don't know?"

"Don't feel sorry for me, Rikki," he cautioned. "I'm glad I don't know. Spending time with you has been cleansing. I feel free. I know that probably sounds crazy, but I don't want to look at who I was, not with the things I'm seeing. How could I have ten names? I don't know what's real and what's made up. But I do know that every memory contains violence. Staying right here with you, lying here listening to the rain with you, I feel at peace. I shouldn't but I do, and I'm going to enjoy it while I have the chance. Who knows? Tomorrow a cop or someone wanting me dead might show up at your door."

"They won't, you know," she offered, turning her body slightly toward his.

She should have turned away from him. If she had any sense, his honesty should have shaken her, but Rikki didn't react like most people. Her eyes were steady on his.

"If anyone is looking for you, Lev, they'll think you died in the ocean. Everyone was gone yesterday morning. The harbor was deserted when I went out. Only Ralph was there when I came back. Ralph noticed you, but he never saw your face."

At the mention of Ralph noticing him, Lev's mind kicked into overdrive, rapidly calculating the benefits of finding Ralph and disposing of him before he could reveal Rikki hadn't been alone. It was an automatic reaction more than a conscious one, and that told him a lot about himself. Killing was a way of life. Killing was an option for removing obstacles in his path. What kind of man thought that way? Rikki had thought of herself as a sociopath because she didn't know whether or not she started fires, but she played in the rain, made water dance and composed symphonies with it. He contemplated killing.

To avoid her eyes, he covered his own with his arm. She saw into him and the last thing he wanted was for her to see him as he really was.

"What's wrong?"

He shook his head. "Go to sleep, Rikki. I'll know if someone tries to come near the house."

Her fingers brushed his mouth. He felt the jolt of her touch like a lightning bolt slamming through his body. There was no gentle stirring of his body. His hard-on was immediate and painful, an aching need that encompassed body and mind. He let himself enjoy the sensation. He'd thought he was incapable of a natural erection, one not planned out, one where he hadn't set up the seduction and controlled every aspect of the scene. Rikki made him feel alive. Real. A human being.

"First tell me what's wrong."

"Damn it, can't you just go to sleep? I don't want to tell you."

"I don't want you in my bed or my house. I don't want you near my boat. That didn't stop it from happening."

"What do you want me to say? That the moment you told me Ralph saw me, I thought about killing him?" He pulled his arm away so his gaze could lock with hers—so he could see her reaction, the revulsion, the horror. He waited for her to order him to go.

Her eyes softened, and God help him, she was looking at him with compassion. "Lev, you believe someone is trying to kill you. You didn't rush off to actually do anything to Ralph." She smiled at him, her eyes as soft and as liquid as ever. "I thought about killing you numerous times, but I didn't. The jury's still out on whether I will or not."

There was a slight teasing edge to her tone. Her voice and the pad of her finger rubbing back and forth over his lips in an effort to erase his frown didn't do much for his peace of mind or his heavy erection. She put a lump in his throat the size of a golf ball, and he felt like he might be choking. He couldn't find a way to believe in himself, yet she did—this strange woman who had pulled him out of the sea.

"Do me a favor, honey," he said softly. "Go to sleep and let me watch over you with the rain. You've done so much for me, let me do this for you."

She studied his face for a long time before she nodded and turned on her side, facing away from him. When she'd removed her finger, he found he could breathe again, but his body didn't relax until long after her breathing became even. He waited even longer, until he was positive she was in a deep enough sleep, before he wrapped his arm around her waist and laid his head near her shoulder so he could breathe her in along with the scent of the rain.

6

Rikki took her responsibilities seriously and Lev was a huge responsibility. He wasn't like owning a cat or a goldfish. She actually had to take care of him. She spent a great deal of her time muttering to herself over the next week and a half. He was unable to get up for more than fifteen minutes at a time. His headaches were horrendous and he'd discovered more aches from his battering against the rocks.

She resumed her normal routine, circling the house morning and night looking for signs of an intruder. She used every can of broth and soup Blythe had bought for her to feed the man. The first few days he ate little and slept most of the time. She worried that she needed to take him to a hospital, but each time she brought the subject up, he was adamantly against it, assuring her he would be fine.

There was one day of beautiful weather, and she thought about going to work but instead spent the day glaring at him. He seemed oblivious. Two days of high surf made it easier to bear, but by the twelfth day she couldn't stop pacing. She felt restless and out of sorts. She decided she had to leave him long enough to sit on the bluffs for a while and just breathe. At least Lev didn't want to talk. He often woke up with a gun in his hand and his eyes cold as ice as he tracked around the room. She was careful never to startle him.

He didn't seem to mind her helping him to the bathroom, and she gave him a massage twice a day. He rarely talked even then and she could tell noise hurt. She didn't mind silence, because noises often hurt her head as well. She knew she would have to find a way to get him clothes—that meant going into a store—and she wasn't ready for that kind of commitment yet. She just wanted to get him on his feet and out of her house.

She hadn't slept very well after that first night. Mostly she stayed in the hammock swing off the kitchen, or, if it was too cold, on her couch. She often paced, worried that Lev wouldn't wake up and then afraid that he would. She was so used to being alone that she was very aware of his breathing, the way he took up her air and her space. She kept the blinds down in her house, and each of her sisters called twice but they didn't ask questions.

The huge news was that a yacht had sunk off the coast in a freak accident. The yacht was owned by a Greek businessman, a billionaire, and everyone on board was lost. Naturally Rikki's sisters didn't want her going out into the ocean until it was pronounced safe, which made her want to laugh. How could going out to sea ever be considered safe?

She knew they assumed she wasn't working because of the yacht sinking. She didn't consider it lying that she didn't give them facts they didn't ask about. But she couldn't breathe anymore, and she had to get out of the house and go where she could see the ocean and just absorb it. That meant leaving Lev alone and unprotected. Her main worry was always fire.

She sat on the edge of the bed and pushed back his hair. The shadow on his jaw had grown into the beginnings of a real beard. "I have to leave for a little while." She knew he was awake. She'd never go near him while he was asleep, but his eyes were closed.

He didn't open them, but he caught her wrist, his fingers a shackle, preventing movement. It amazed her how he could do that, know exactly where her arm was when he had his eyes closed. And she always watched his face, not even blinking. He never so much as peeked, yet he never missed.

"Don't."

"I have to go, just for a little while. I've checked outside and no one's around. I think it's safe. I'll lock the door when I go out."

She could tell it was a struggle for him to open his eyes enough to look at her. The impact of that blue stare gave her a jolt in the vicinity of her stomach.

"You'll come back?"

"I live here." She was ashamed instantly. He seemed to need reassurance. Why was that so difficult for her? "Soon. Don't shoot anyone while I'm gone."

"Take one of my guns."

She could see the worry in his eyes and that caused some sort of meltdown in her heart. Physical reactions scared her, especially physical reactions to men. Daniel had been an excellent diver who helped perfect her diving skills. They'd spent so much time together it seemed a natural progression to get engaged. But she hadn't spent time with him off the boat. They'd talked about a future, diving together, but the one time he'd come to her small rented houseboat to spend the night, a fire had taken him.

"What are you thinking about?"

She searched his face, his eyes, not certain what she was looking for exactly. She didn't want him to die, not in a fire and not on her account.

"Rikki, I need to know."

"Why?"

"You looked sad. Upset. Did I put that look there?"

She couldn't help herself. With her free hand, she smoothed the frown from his face. "No. I am just worried about leaving you."

His fingers moved over her wrist and slid down to the palm of her hand to trace circles there. "I'm a survivor, Rikki. I'll be here. The house will be here as well. Go do what you have to, but come back to me. I won't sleep until you're back with me."

The drowning sensation was acute this time, and she jumped up, pulling away from him. As his fingers slid from her skin, her stomach did a slow somersault. She backed away from him. No one had ever made her feel the way Lev did, such a gut-wrenching *physical* reaction. She could barely breathe sometimes and that's why she had to leave her own house. He was forcing her out with . . . with . . . *this*.

She glared at him. Scowled. Her blackest, scariest, get-away-from-me-now scowl. He should have been intimidated. That practiced look worked every time. He smiled at her. *Smiled*. Not just with amusement, but with a drippy, dippy, you're-so-cute sort of look. She backed completely across the room to the door.

"You forgot the gun."

"*I* don't shoot people," she reminded him with a little sniff, and stalked out. She heard him laugh, but she didn't turn around.

The sound of his laughter was too intriguing. It set off little explosions in the vicinity of her womb. She really needed to get out of there and go sit by the sea, breathe in the fresh air and listen to the gulls. She could almost believe he was a sorcerer who had cast some sort of spell over her. Privately, she would admit to herself that she *liked* touching him. She never touched anyone. And she sure didn't want anyone touching her. But the feel of Lev's hands on her skin, the way he stroked his fingers over her, was mesmerizing. The reaction of her body was frightening, yet at the same time exhilarating.

She found herself almost reluctant to drive away from the property and leave him. She got out and walked around in the trees above her house, quartering the area carefully, searching for evidence of a visitor. She should have gotten a dog after all. She'd considered it, but she'd have to take care of it and it might get seasick because she'd never leave it home alone. She sighed. She was leaving Lev alone.

"But he has guns, Rikki," she reminded herself aloud. "A dog wouldn't have a gun."

Muttering curses under her breath, she marched back to her truck and drove straight to the highway. *This*—this *indecision*—was the very reason she didn't get involved with anyone. Her life was far simpler just living alone. Furious, she made up her mind to throw him out the moment—the *very* moment—he was able to leave.

A siren caught her attention, and she glanced behind her and swore out loud. Damn the man. He'd made her speed on top of everything else. And now she was going to have to talk to a cop. She shuddered as she pulled over and sat, teeth clenched, with her license and registration and insurance out and waiting.

She recognized Jonas Harrington as he walked up to the truck. Her heart pounded and she tasted something metallic in her mouth. She silently handed him the three documents.

"Rikki. You all right?"

She'd seen him around the village hundreds of times in the last five years. Everyone knew him. She knew he was married to Hannah Drake. Her mouth was so dry she wasn't certain she could speak. She nodded, hoping that would be enough, gripping the steering wheel so hard her knuckles turned white.

"You were speeding, unusual for you. Everything all right? All your sisters fine?"

She swallowed and nodded.

He handed her back everything. "With our village being overrun with so many reporters, scientists and investigators, we have to be a little careful. Watch your speed."

Reporters? Scientists? Investigators? Her sisters had chatted on about the yacht that had sunk being owned by a Greek shipping magnate, but she'd only paid attention to the part about the owner having a bodyguard. She was certain Lev was the bodyguard. It would explain his presence in the sea, as well as his weapons. She stared straight ahead, keeping her death grip on the steering wheel. She was thankful Harrington wasn't giving her a ticket but sent a silent prayer that he'd go away.

"I haven't had a chance to talk with Judith but maybe you'd pass along a package to her. She's been working on a special kaleidoscope for Hannah. It's a surprise." He leaned his arms on the door and peered in at her, his eyes hidden by his dark glasses, but his expression friendly.

She swallowed and nodded again, staring straight ahead.

He laughed softly. "You talk too much, you know that?"

She turned her head then and looked at him, frowning. Maybe she should try her drop-dead scowl. But really, he was being friendly and nice. She just had to breathe. She took a deep breath and gave it a try. "I'll take it."

He smiled at her effort. The wind came up and blew at his shirt. He glanced toward where the Drake house sat up on the bluff above the ocean. "Hannah's up on the captain's walk. All of her sisters are on their honeymoon so she's visiting with her parents today. I haven't had a spare minute to get the package to Judith. It's in my car. Can you wait a second?"

Rikki felt it would be wiser not to point out that if he hadn't stopped her, he might have had the time to drop off the mysterious package to Judith himself. Since she didn't want him to change his mind about giving her a speeding ticket and she didn't mind talking to Judith, she kept her mouth firmly closed.

Jonas returned with a very small packet. He grinned at her. "These are all those little things women keep for memories. Judith had this great idea for a kaleidoscope. I wanted something extraordinary for Hannah to focus on when she's giving birth."

Rikki nodded. She had to say something. Being socially awkward didn't mean she was completely inept, and after all, she was representing Judith, not herself. Staring straight ahead, she tried a small smile, hoping he couldn't tell it was forced. "Everything Judith does is extraordinary. She'll make it special."

He looked pleased as he patted her door with his hand and then waved to her. Rikki's hand shook as she turned the key. She was fortunate that it was Jonas who had stopped and recognized her. And she had to ask Judith about the reporters and what Jonas had been talking about. Really, she should read the paper more and at least turn on the news. She saved the newspapers for a week, just in case she wanted to read them. But they were always so depressing.

She turned off the highway to enter the village. As a rule, tourists came from all over to see the small, artsy town set on the edge of the sea. Today, it was packed. Overrun. Her pulse went into a pounding beat she felt inside her head. Ordinarily she would have driven straight to the headlands to sit overlooking the ocean, but she'd promised Jonas she'd deliver his package. She probably hadn't been speeding. He'd most likely taken one look at the mass of people and turned tail and run, waiting for an unsuspecting innocent to do his dirty work for him.

She blew out a disgusted puff of air as she found the only available parking place in town—a good distance from her sister's shop. Even the grocery store lot was filled. Rikki looked down the street and every single parking space was filled. People jammed the wooden sidewalks. And trying to go into the local coffee shop was impossible. There was a crowd ten deep. She'd been thinking about a nice cup of coffee. Damn Jonas Harrington. He was probably somewhere smirking right now.

She sat in her truck for a few minutes, working up the courage to fight her way through the crowded sidewalks to her sister's shop. Far out, she could see the blue of the ocean, and her entire being yearned to be out there where the waves swelled and crested, rolling in beautiful, powerful displays. She understood the sea and the rules there, the life and death survival. But here . . . She looked around her. Here, she was definitely the proverbial fish out of water.

Well, she had something to do. Resolutely, Rikki shoved open the door of her truck and stepped into the street. Out at sea, on the deck of the *Sea Gypsy*, she could keep her legs under her, riding the swells with perfect balance, but here, on land, the uneven terrain always made her feel clumsy and awkward. Maybe it was all the people. She could barely breathe. There was no way to drown out the noise. She had coping mechanisms that she'd developed over the years. Counting her steps sometimes helped, but she'd never seen Sea Haven so packed.

She kept to the street, walking close to the bumpers of the parked cars to avoid the masses on the sidewalk. Her temperature soared and she had to wipe beads of sweat from her face. She kept breathing, her sunglasses firmly in place, wishing she were on her boat where she could see whatever was coming at her.

She had to push through people to get inside Judith's shop and it was difficult to avoid touching anyone. Twice she was jostled and nearly fell to the sidewalk. Once a tall man's elbow struck her in the head, knocking her sunglasses askew. He quickly caught her elbow to steady her, apologizing profusely. She nodded and scurried into the shop, banging the door closed behind her, hoping to keep everyone else out so she could breathe. She stopped, her entire body shuddering. The store was packed.

Judith looked up and saw her. Judith. Her lifeline. Tall, slim, hair flowing like a cascading waterfall of black silk—a heritage from her Japanese mother—Judith came immediately to Rikki, working her way through the crowded aisle, her expression one of concern. Rikki would never have come into her shop with people around, not if it wasn't important. Rikki felt relief, knowing Judith understood.

"What's up, baby? Anything wrong?" She looked back toward the counter and raised her voice. "Airiana, I'll be a minute."

Airiana, another one of Rikki's sisters, looked up with a small frown of annoyance until she saw Rikki. There was instant concern. "Of course. I can handle it. Hi, hon. Everything okay?"

Rikki lifted a hand to reassure her, but immediately turned and shoved open the door, practically falling onto the sidewalk. She needed to be outside where she could gasp for breath. There were still too many people, so she pushed her way through them to the street. She drew in several deep breaths, holding her head down to clear her dizzy brain.

Judith put a comforting hand on her back. "I'm sorry, Rikki. I had no idea you were going to come into town or I would have stopped you. This place has been crazy ever since the yacht went down. Unfortunately, a couple of bodies have been found, so the frenzy started all over again."

"You all talked about a yacht sinking." Rikki straightened and kept her gaze glued on the distant sea. "But I wasn't really listening past the fact that it went down. What happened?"

"It was some freak accident that has all the scientists in the world out there. Apparently methane gas from the continental shelf was released in a huge bubble, and it was the yacht's bad luck to be there at the precise time the bubble hit the surface. Shades of the Bermuda triangle. The gas changed the density of the water and the ship just dropped down. The owner was a businessman, well-known, in fact rather famous. He, his bodyguard and the entire crew were lost at sea. There are reporters and tele-vision crews from all over the world here. Along with that, every curious person in the world has arrived as well. Good for business, but difficult all the same."

"I couldn't get out there diving even if the day was perfect," Rikki grumbled. "There are ships everywhere."

"What are you doing in town?"

"I needed to see the ocean," she admitted. "I got stopped by that moron sheriff, Jonas Harrington, and he asked me to give you a package."

Judith's mouth tightened. "Was he mean to you?"

"No, actually, he was very nice. He didn't even give me a ticket, but he asked me to deliver this package to you and he knew what it was like in town."

Judith smiled. "That's true, but he doesn't know you, Rikki. He probably assumed you'd be coming into the shop anyway."

Rikki shrugged, sending Judith her first small grin. "Yeah, I'm pretty sure you're right, but it gave me a good reason to be mad."

Judith laughed. "Do you need anything from the store?" She glanced down the street to the coffee shop. "Coffee maybe?"

Rikki frowned. "Soup. Broth. Blythe bought me a bunch of cans and I've used them up. I don't know what's good. So anything. And Inez's coffee is fine if you can manage to brave the mob to get me a cup. If not, don't worry about it. Your store was overrun and poor Airiana looked a little overwhelmed."

"You wouldn't believe it, Rikki, but the reporters are so desperate for information, they're filming everything in town and doing interviews. I'm hoping it's good for business. Three different crews have filmed my shop." She indicated a film crew across the street. "Those people are everywhere with their cameras."

Judith was striking with her tall, slim body and waterfall of hair, as well as her sparkling personality. She saw people in colors and tended to shine the moment she walked into the room. Rikki could understand why a reporter might want to talk with her on camera. She would draw the eye of the audience with her animation and personality.

"That's insane," Rikki murmured in agreement anyway. "What can any of you tell them about a freak accident? A few years back I read about the theory of methane leaks causing ships to go down in the Bermuda Triangle, but seriously, who would ever believe it would happen, especially here? I'm out there all the time." Rikki pointed out, glaring at the news crew, silently wishing they'd all go home so she could have her tidy little world back.

"They say it really did happen and that yacht definitely sank."

"How long is all this going to go on?" She meant before she could have her ocean back.

Judith smiled at her sulky face. "I don't know, babe, but just think about all the business we're getting."

"Think about all the business I'm losing," Rikki muttered, and then was instantly ashamed. In a rare gesture of affection, she flung her arms around Judith. The hug was brief but fierce. "I hope they film the inside of your shop and see what a genius you are. I could never have enough of your kaleidoscopes or paintings."

Judith looked out toward the sea and for a horrified moment, Rikki thought there were tears in her sister's eyes, but when she looked back, she was beaming. "You just made my day, little sister. Wait here and I'll get the soup for you. It will only take a minute."

"Airiana is going to kill both of us if it takes more than that," Rikki pointed out, but made no move to let Judith out of the task. "While you're there, can you pick up more toothpaste and a good toothbrush?"

Judith burst out laughing. "I'm on it."

They had a supply room for the farm and it was kept well stocked with everyday items, but when Rikki had checked it, no toothbrushes or toothpaste had been on the shelves. She found a razor and shaving cream. The cream smelled like lavender, but if Lev wanted to shave, he could just make do. Besides, it might lessen his ultramale impact on her.

She tapped the toe of her shoe on the street, counting, all the while keeping her gaze glued to the sea. The whitecaps were foaming and curling, the spray shooting into the air when it hit the cliffs. She found herself smiling, feeling each ebb and flow begin to set her right inside. She wrapped her arms around herself and hugged tightly, needing the pressure to help hold together until Judith returned.

Judith came hurrying out, her straight white teeth flashing, her dark eyes bright. Rikki took a moment just to enjoy the sight of her, the happiness flowing from her. Rikki saw Judith as a burst of color across a monotonous background. She sparkled, and in another world, she would have been a fairy of some kind, waving her wand and leaving happiness in her wake.

"What?" Judith asked as she handed the bag of groceries to Rikki.

"You just look especially beautiful today," Rikki said, idly fiddling with the turtleneck collar, drawing it up around her mouth.

Judith's expression changed. She reached out and touched Rikki's face, pushing down the sweater. "Is everything all right, Rikki? I can close the shop and go home if you need me."

Rikki looked at the masses of people. Today would be a potentially killer day for sales. Judith had rocked the kaleidoscope world, winning all kinds of international awards, and her name was synonymous with quality. She had made her money in art restoration, but her first love was making kaleidoscopes for individuals. She studied the person— Rikki knew she could read their aura—and she made the perfect scope for each customer. Rikki had one that she only had to pick up in order to gain more control; even the feel of it in her hands was enough. When she turned it to look into the swirling sea, she immediately felt serene and calm.

"I'm fine. I'm going out to the headlands and sit for a while. You know me, I just have to be out on the ocean sometimes, and it's been too long."

"Come for dinner tonight. I'll serve salad with a peanut butter dressing."

Rikki burst out laughing. "I think I'll skip it. And you should be happy that I am."

Judith laughed with her. "All right. Go sit by your precious ocean and I'll go see what I can sell today."

"Well, one of us has to be the breadwinner, because it sure isn't going to be me for a while," Rikki groused as she slammed the door of her truck closed and waved to her sister.

She watched Judith go back into her shop before she started her truck. Judith was a true sister of the heart, not born of blood but certainly chosen and very loved. The five women had taught Rikki trust. It was fragile, but she'd learned to count on others when she needed them—at least here on land.

Rikki sat for a long time on the edge of the bluff, knees drawn up, just breathing in the scent of the sea. Almost immediately relief flooded her body, practically a euphoric rush. The waves mesmerized her, transporting her away from a world where she didn't fit, where she was out of sync with everyone else. There was no rhythm for her on land. No order. She rocked gently, picking up the beat of the waves, letting the song of the sea whisper to her, drowning out the noises of the world around her.

She let herself drift off, envisioning the seafloor, the smooth rocks, the forests of kelp, the coral and the crevices. She found herself laughing as she remembered the time she had had an encounter with an octopus just south of Casper where a big rock about fifty feet off the headlands stuck up out of the water. She was relatively new to the area and she anchored her boat there. The floor was some thirty feet down, but she found sea urchins on the rocks at around fifteen feet and began raking them fast into her net, elated at the easy find.

Without warning an octopus was suddenly in her line of vision, bobbing in the water. Normally the ones she encountered were relatively small, but this one was larger than she was. Its tentacles were down, but it was watching her. Thinking it prudent to give the octopus a little space, she moved in a counterclockwise motion around the rock and began working again. The octopus swam clockwise and met her on the other side. Her heart jumped when she saw the creature coming toward her, getting bigger and bigger as it came near.

Again she changed direction. The moment she began picking, the octopus followed about a foot behind her, just bobbing, tentacles down. At that point, Rikki decided the octopus wanted the sea urchins more than she did, either that or it was protecting his den. Whatever—the creature made a rather loud statement she wasn't ignoring.

Laughing at the memory, she rose, her arms outstretched, embracing the sea. Happiness wrapped her in mist and the wind whipped her hair into a wild frenzy. She inhaled and closed her eyes, needing to feel—to absorb the water into her skin, into her blood. She could feel the tides running through her, filling her need for freedom, to be able to be wild and to show every emotion, deep and strong. The force of her passions often shook her. She rarely showed feeling, but the emotions were there, hidden beneath her carefully constructed false calm. Just like the sea, she was turbulent and wild, angry and loving. She felt every sensation, but it was only here, with water around her, that she dared let herself feel so strongly, so passionately.

She opened her eyes to take one last look at the sea before she went back to the farm. The swells were enormous, the sea crashing against the bluffs.

"Oh shit," she whispered, dropping her arms and staring at the turbulent, choppy water. "Did I do that?" There were boats out in the very rough sea.

Swearing under her breath, she raised her arms again to encompass the coastline and did her best to calm her mind, to still the fears she had about allowing Lev in her house and the guilt over not telling her sisters about him. Breathing slowly, in and out, she brought forth the image of a calm sea, of clear skies, of the gulls flying overhead and water lapping gently at the rocks below the cliffs.

She felt the wind tugging at her clothes and ruffling her hair. The mist swirled around her, the spray dotted her skin. Her body, thirsty for the moisture, instantly absorbed the droplets. In her veins the pounding rhythm slowly began to calm and her heart slowed to a gentle beat. Water swirled for a moment just under the bluff, rising like a cyclone in a thin column, leaping up toward her, as if reaching to kiss or embrace her, and then it spun itself out, collapsing back into the calm sea.

She slowly allowed her arms to drop as she looked out over the gently rocking water. Jubilation. Pride. Satisfaction. A dawning hope. Emotions flooded her and her brain began working a million miles an hour trying to assimilate what had just happened. She hadn't accidently turned on a few faucets. She hadn't skipped water out on open sea. She had actually manipulated a huge body of water. *She had a gift beyond price.* Lev had been so matter-of-fact about her ability, so certain she could do it, but this—controlling a large body of water had never occurred to her.

Rikki wasn't certain she believed her own eyes. Turning away from the water, she made her way back to her truck, all the while wanting to practice. She needed a place to go where no one could observe her, and no one could get hurt. The farm had a pond that was used for irrigation. She could sit beside the mass of water to her heart's content and see if she really could do this amazing thing.

She did have the presence of mind to drive slowly so she didn't get stopped again. With her usual single-minded purpose, she drove straight out to the pond and jumped out, nearly running to the pond. The water lay flat, seemingly unresponsive to her, but as she made her way down the slope, she imagined she could see ripples forming, moving toward her, as if she were a magnet.

Rikki sank down on the very edge of the bank. The lip was narrow and she knew it was a precarious perch at best, but she was eager to test her ability. On the drive, she'd begun to doubt, thinking it was much more likely a coincidence, but she'd *felt* the water that time, felt it move through her, inside her, just as she did when she was under the water. She'd felt like she was a part of the sea, connected to it in a way she never had been with anything else. The discovery was both terrifying and elating.

She threw out her arms and closed her eyes, deliberately absorbing the feel of the water. Immediately she could feel the normal centering in her brain that she always felt when she was near water, but beyond that, she could tell there was a difference. The sea was powerful and moody. The pond was serene and lazy, a gentle, steady presence, more peaceful than one that battered and pounded as the ocean did. This body of water didn't tap into her emotions as the sea did. There was no release of anger, of fear, of the golden happiness this farm and her sisters represented, or of the wild sexual energy she was desperate to repress ever since pulling Lev from the sea.

She absorbed the calm, took it in and then tried her dance, singing softly and using her palms to "feel" the water. When she opened her eyes, small columns leapt and played under her direction, just as on the open sea. The small spouts whirled and leapt, racing one another across the surface. Delighted, she stood up, raising the energy, and saw the instant response—the columns grew taller, whirled faster, and more broke off into multiple geysers.

Joy burst through her. This—this gift—was hers. She

couldn't walk down a crowded street or go into a store with fluorescent lights, but she could join with water, make it whisper or roar, be a part of it. She reached out over the small strip of land she was standing on toward the columns of dancing water, her fingertips tingling as she manipulated the many waterspouts across the pond.

She stepped forward and felt the narrow edge crumbling. Desperately she tried to throw her weight backward. Her heart hammered, her palm burned, the pain rushed up her arm. The columns collapsed, sending water spraying into the air as the earth continued to erode beneath her. She flung out her hand to catch an exposed root. Without warning she felt a jolt, like a hand lifting her and flinging her back onto solid ground. The force was so strong she landed hard enough to knock the wind out of her. She lay there, trying to find air, her lungs burning and her mind racing. She should have fallen into the pond.

Rikki rolled over and stared up at the sky, all the while cradling her left arm and pressing her palm against her wildly beating heart. What had saved her from a cold dunk? It would have been difficult to climb out, but she had no doubt she could have. It would have been messy and cold and very embarrassing, but still . . . She looked at the narrow ledge where she'd been. It had collapsed completely in a mini avalanche.

Rikki? Rikki, answer me. I need to know you're all right.

Lev's voice filled her mind. She realized immediately he had done something to help her *from a distance*. Swallowing hard, she rubbed her hand over her face, trying to think. He had to have tremendous power to do something like that. She lived in Sea Haven and everyone there knew the Drake family. It was rumored that seven daughters were always born to the seventh child and each carried tremendous gifts, but she'd never heard of anyone else having such powers, and the Drakes were—well—the Drakes. Everyone accepted them as fact.

Answer me now.

The voice was a soft growl of command. She couldn't stop the instant response. *I'm fine. Don't worry.*

Rikki clapped her hands over her ears. She had no intention of engaging in telepathic communication with him. If he could get inside her head, he might be able to read her thoughts . . .

You could read mine too.

There was relief in his voice. It flooded her mind and the intimacy of his velvet tone shocked her. Her body reacted, coming alive, every nerve ending alert. Electricity sparked over her skin, and deep in her most feminine core she felt empty and needy.

Get out of my head. Trembling, she managed to get her feet under her.

You scared the hell out of me. And my head hurts like a son of a bitch. You might consider that before you go getting yourself into trouble.

She sensed his anger was shocking to him, that he was horrified at his own fear for her safety. Somehow that was unusual—his concern for another human being. He didn't understand their connection any more than she did, and knowing that made it easier for her.

Well, thanks for saving me from a dunking.

He was silent a moment but she could still feel him there in her mind. It was a bit like being underwater, everything in her stilled and steadied as if he anchored her in the same way the sea did.

If you're finished playing, come back to me.

She could hear the pain in his voice, in his mind. Her heart stuttered in her chest and she pressed her palm tight against it. *Lev, did you try to get up?*

I wasn't going to leave you in danger.

For her. He'd tried to get to her. He could barely stand for more than a couple of minutes, just what it took to get to the bathroom and back and even then he was dizzy. Each day had been a discovery of new bruises from the battering he'd taken, yet he'd tried to get to her.

You're not nearly the bad man you think you are.

Come home and find out. He growled it at her, meant it to be a threat.

She found herself smiling as she walked back to her truck. Maybe there was something to this telepathic nonsense after all. When he spoke out loud, she basically wanted to hit him over the head, but when he talked to her in her mind, she could sense his feelings. She didn't pick up nuances of voices or read facial expressions like other people, but she didn't have to when he projected his voice into her mind. He was there inside her and she knew the feeling behind the words.

I'm coming. I hope you're back in bed. I'm getting a little tired of picking you up off the floor.

If you'd quit mopping it so much, it wouldn't be so slippery.

The amusement creeping into his voice made her happy. She knew laughter was even more foreign to him than it was to her, yet for some reason she couldn't quite fathom, he found her funny. Most people thought her odd, but her strangeness not only didn't bother him but he seemed to enjoy her company.

You give me massages.

She swung into the truck and slammed the door, frowning. *I knew it! I knew the moment I let you into my head you'd be trying to go where you don't belong. My thoughts are not for you to go eavesdropping on.*

You were thinking about me. Satisfaction purred in his voice.

Well, think about me becoming very angry with you.

I'd rather think about you giving me a massage.

She choked on laughter. *Doesn't this way of talking make your head hurt?* She had the beginnings of a headache.

I already have a headache. I can't tell what's making it worse or what isn't. All I know for certain is, I want you back here safe in this house with me.

She tried to block the rush she got from his words and the way he said them. It was impossible not to feel the heat spreading or the way her body responded to him, reaching out the way it did when she was near water.

I'm on my way.

7

"**Lev**, you need to listen to me." Rikki glared at his back as he paced around her kitchen. "This is important information. A yacht sank off our coast the day I pulled you out of the water." She watched carefully, but there was no reaction from him. "It's a huge deal. They've got investigators and scientists swarming all over. Everyone is presumed dead."

When he continued prowling around opening all the cupboards, she sighed with exasperation. "Don't you understand what this means? You had to have been on that yacht. It was just a short distance from where I was when it went down."

It had been three days since she'd gone to the village, and this was the first time Lev had been up for more than fifteen minutes. He'd actually showered, and although he'd had to lie down for a half hour, he was back up again and hungry, wanting an actual breakfast, not broth or peanut butter sandwiches. She'd run out of the soups Judith had bought for her, and she was feeling a little desperate, hoping to distract him from eating. And she hadn't been out to sea in more than two weeks. It seemed like months and the effects of her last little visit to the bluff days ago had already worn off, leaving her agitated and distressed.

Lev banged another cupboard closed and she glared at him, irritated.

"Stop that. What in the world are you looking for?"

"Food."

"There's tons of food. Quit slamming the doors. You need to shut them quietly." Or better yet, not touch them. "You're leaving fingerprints all over them and I'll have to spend hours polishing them." She touched her throat. She'd been wearing turtleneck sweaters for freaking weeks to cover up the fingerprints he'd left on her throat. She didn't mind tight heavy sweaters, but high necks bothered her because she tended to fall back into an old habit she had of hiding in them. She'd fought hard to stop that, but wearing one for fifteen days made her want to disappear into the warm material. She was desperate—*desperate*—for the sea.

His gaze shifted to her face, then drifted down to her neck. She suddenly wished she hadn't drawn his attention. His face darkened, and shadows crept into the blue of his eyes.

"How bad is it? Let me look."

He stepped close, looming over the top of her so that she hastily backed up to create more space. When he was in bed, he seemed vulnerable and needed care. She actually could lie on the bed and fall asleep beside him as long as she got up before he woke, although she sometimes suspected he knew the moment she opened her eyes and just didn't say anything to her. She wasn't certain how to feel

about that either, because it meant he sensed how uncomfortable she was with him when he was awake.

Rikki shoved at her unruly hair in agitation. She had
no idea what to do with him. But he had to sit down and
quit walking over her floor. He was barefoot at least. She
might have to hide his shoes if he demanded to put them
on and walk across her clean floor. It was that or kick him
out—which she was certain was the better idea.

"Keep your hands off my neck. In fact, keep your hands
off of everything. You're making a mess."

He hadn't stopped coming at her, not even when she
gave him her blackest scowl. She held up a hand to ward
him off. "People say I don't know boundaries. You have
none at all. Don't touch me. And don't touch my things."

He ignored her hand and pushed at her sweater, exposing her throat. His fingers brushed strokes over the marks.
They had long since faded to little green smudges, but she
didn't want anyone—not even him—to see the evidence.
She had never liked being closed off, and his body trapped
hers between freedom and the table. She held her breath,
afraid she might explode into violence, but somehow the
stroke of his fingers took away the sense of being ensnared.
Instead, sensation poured through her body, like a wave of
heat, brushing over her skin, sinking deeper, until she felt
his touch in her bones.

"I didn't mean to do this. I actually don't remember
grabbing you around the throat."

She pulled away from him and jerked the neckline of
her sweater up, stepping to one side to give herself room
to breathe. "Do you remember the knife?"

He kept his gaze locked with hers. "You should have
dumped me back into the ocean."

"Darn right, I should have," she agreed. "Now that that's settled, sit down. I'll fix you a sandwich."

He looked pained. "I don't eat peanut butter."

That genuinely shocked her. "Who doesn't eat peanut butter? It's the perfect food."

He shuddered. "Even to make up for all the things I've done wrong, I don't think I can do it."

"For a man who carries around as many weapons as you do, you're a bit of a baby."

"It isn't being a baby not to eat peanut butter. I don't think babies eat the stuff."

"That's un-American."

"I'm not certain I am American," he pointed out.

She had to agree with him there. "Fine. You can put peanut butter on waffles. Blythe bought some of those frozen thingies that you put in the toaster. I'm not sure how old they are. Do frozen foods last like four years or more?"

He groaned and dropped into the nearest kitchen chair, pushing his head into his hands. "Death by peanut butter. I never thought I'd go that way."

Rikki found herself laughing. Nothing made her laugh, not out loud, not hurt-her-tummy laughing, not like this. He looked so dejected—a big, tough man done in by peanut butter.

He looked up at her and smiled, and the laughter faded. Her stomach somersaulted and her heart contracted. Suddenly it was hard to breathe again.

"I don't know how to cook," she blurted out.

He looked at the dishes and pots and pans.

"I just wash them to keep them clean, but I've never used them, not once in the four years I've had them. There's broccoli in the vegetable bin. I can't cook it but you can eat it raw," she offered.

"You fed me soup."

She tapped her foot and counted to twenty before she faced him again. Color crept into her face. "I heated it up in the can on this little gas outdoor thing I have. All the soups are ready made so it was easy."

There was a small silence while he studied her expression. "How about I cook for us? If you're going to let me stay here while I recover, that's the least I can do."

Was she going to let him continue to stay in her home while he recovered? Rikki chewed nervously on her lower lip. He would say he wouldn't touch her things, but he would. And she'd have to be very vigilant. Just because the house hadn't caught fire during the last two weeks, didn't mean it couldn't happen—the risk was far greater with someone else in the house.

He sent her a small smile. "You're thinking of kicking me out."

She shrugged. "I'm always thinking about kicking you out." She spread her arms out, encompassing her home. "I'm used to living alone, and it's safer."

"Not really. Not if someone's really trying to burn you out. I'd be damn handy to have around."

He leaned toward her, his blue eyes so intense she lost herself there, in that wild blue sea. "Let me stay with you, Rikki. I have nowhere else to go. I don't have a clue who I really am. If I was on that yacht, everyone thinks I'm dead."

So he had been listening. He'd chosen not to answer—as she often did.

"Maybe this is my chance," he persisted. "My one chance at a new life. I can be someone else, someone different."

"If you don't know who you are . . ."

"I've killed men. Every instinct I have is all about survival."

"That doesn't mean you weren't protecting people, Lev. I saved the newspapers." She got the newspapers but never read them, not until she'd gone into town and seen the influx of reporters. The mess was still going strong. "The man who owned the boat was a billionaire and everyone on board was lost, including his bodyguard. You could have been his bodyguard. Don't bodyguards have to shoot people occasionally?"

Lev shook his head. "You're incredible, you know that? *Don't bodyguards have to shoot people occasionally?* Who thinks like that? Let me stay with you, Rikki."

She wasn't going to kick him out. She'd found him in the sea and she was bound to him. She'd taken him on board her boat and that made her responsible for him. Besides . . . She pressed her fingers to her temples. She'd gone to sleep with him beside her. She'd never even done that with Daniel. She couldn't just abandon him, not when Blythe and the others had given her a chance, not when he'd given her a gift so precious as to know that once—*once*—in her life, she'd been normal enough to sleep beside another human being, which was the *only* reason she'd continued to sleep on the bed. Not because she wanted to be with him.

"I don't know what I'll do with you. And you can't touch my things."

"I'll do the cooking," he volunteered immediately.

She didn't eat anything but peanut butter—not unless Blythe made her go to her house for dinner. Then she forced herself to do it so she didn't hurt Blythe's feelings. His slight grin made her heart turn over. Sheesh, she hated the effect he had on her.

"Do you want to go shopping now? Before breakfast? Inez's market is open."

Instantly his expression went blank. For a moment he looked a little scary, his blue eyes diamond hard. "It would probably be best if no one sees me for a while. We don't want any questions."

She didn't like questions either and she sure wasn't going to answer any of them. She glanced at the clock. It was still very early. She might get there while the store was empty. "Make a list then." It took seconds to go to the drawer where notepads and pens were neatly stacked. She handed him both.

He immediately began scribbling. Twice he opened her fridge, frowned at the milk and broccoli, and wrote more. The cupboards contained jars of both smooth and chunky peanut butter. "I can see you're into variety."

She put on her darkest scowl. "Blythe can lecture me about my eating habits; you can't."

He put down the pen. "I suppose that's fair. I'm not going to be a burden to you financially. Things are coming back to me and I must have money somewhere. Sooner or later I'll have access to it and I'll pay you back. And I can work for you. You need a tender."

Her scowl deepened. "You stay the hell off my boat."

His grin widened. She supposed he had reason to look a little cocky. He had the perfect place to hide out. She was so antisocial no one but her family came to visit her, and most of the time she went to their houses. His contact with outsiders would be minimal.

We'll see about that.

Her gaze jumped to his and the breath left her body in a foolish rush. That intimate voice stroked every nerve ending. Her mouth went dry. They'd never discussed their strange conversation or her near fall in the pond. She found ignoring subjects she didn't want to discuss was usually the best way to go, but he didn't seem to realize he wasn't allowed in her head.

She narrowed her eyes at him. "Give me your list, and I'll go into town and get the supplies." She wasn't arguing with him over the boat—or telepathy. She was the captain. Out at sea, no one questioned her authority.

His fingers brushed hers when he transferred the paper to her. She felt a jolt through her entire system. Everything seemed so out of focus. She didn't like anyone touching her, yet when this man did, she didn't feel thousands of pinpricks as she normally did. The pressure of her wet suit helped to combat the way her body felt as if it were flying apart. She had a weighted lap blanket she used for the same purpose, but she had neither item to help her now. She just stood there looking at him a little helplessly, trying to figure out how to think or feel in such an unfamiliar situation.

"It will be all right," he murmured softly, and his fingers stroked over her face, tracing her bones.

She sucked in her breath, shocked that she could stand there, trembling, feeling nervous flutters instead of pinpricks and pain. She shook her head, trying to throw off the spell he seemed to weave around her.

"Only my sisters ever come here, and they won't with my truck gone. Just keep the doors locked and the shades pulled down. I doubt you'll be disturbed." She turned back to him. "*Don't* kill anyone while I'm gone. They might be important to me."

Rikki started out the door, but Lev caught her arm.

"You won't say anything about me?"

She scowled. "I dragged your ass out of the sea, cleaned

you up and gave you a place to stay. Who the hell am I going to tell?"

He shrugged. "It just matters."

"You're dead. Stay that way until I get back." She shoved her dark glasses onto her nose and marched out, indignant that he thought she was too stupid to keep quiet.

Muttering to herself, she started toward her truck, but she couldn't quite force herself from her normal routine. She cast a surreptitious glance toward the window, but even if he was watching, did it matter? This was her home—her life—she wasn't going to change because she'd hauled some man out of the sea. And he was just as strange in his own way as she was. He was definitely secretive, everything he owned seemed to be a weapon, and his first reaction was usually violence. Yeah, she was *not* going to apologize for who she was.

She circled the house, checking each window, making certain her silk threads were intact. If anyone tried to lift the windows, they wouldn't notice the small thread fluttering to the ground. She examined the flower beds she'd planted beneath the windows. The dirt was soft and damp and would reveal any prints. She checked her hoses, rolled perfectly around the hose reels on each side of the house. She was very fussy about the hoses. They had to be able to be pulled off fast with no kinks in case of an emergency.

When she walked around to the front of her house, Lev stood there watching her. She sent him a dark frown. "What?"

"You don't have to worry with me here."

She tilted her chin. Usually she didn't bother with explanations, and she wasn't going to tell him. Let him find out she had a routine—a ritual—she couldn't go anywhere without performing first. She had a lot of those. He could leave if her ways bothered him. She climbed into the truck and slammed the door without answering him. She did look back in the rearview mirror and felt sad for him. He looked very alone.

She drove along the winding tree-lined road that lead to the coastal highway, and she felt immediate relief. She hadn't spent this much time with another human being since she had been a teenager, and it was stressful. She tried not to stare—looking through him or into him instead—or to get caught up in the small observations that she tended to fixate on. It was darned stressful just to be with people.

Once she'd turned onto Highway 1, she could see the ocean. The sea soothed her, no matter what mood it was in. The expanse of water always helped her to stay centered enough to deal with going into a public place. It was early enough that few people would be out, but Inez's store was a local hangout. People tended to gather there and exchange news—and Inez knew just about everything there was to know about everyone.

Rikki parked the truck at the far end of the lot and got out slowly, taking a careful look around. Thankfully, the reporters and investigators—whatever they were—hadn't gotten up as early as she had. She had the village nearly to herself. The morning air was crisp and a wind blew in from the sea, carrying the feel of salty mist. She could hear the water breaking against the cliffs as she walked across the lot to the sidewalk where she took another long look around. Her blood moved with the same rush in her veins as the waves, and she stood at the top of the hill, just in front of the store, looking down the street to the powerful display the ocean was putting on.

Sea Haven's main street ran right along the actual coast,

separated from the water only by the bluffs. She could be in the town because from just about anywhere she shopped, she could see and hear the ocean. Right now whitecaps danced over the surface and spray blasted up the rocks. The sight was breathtaking.

There was no one out but old Bill. His blanket wrapped around him, he huddled in the small area between the grocery store and the kaleidoscope shop Rikki's sister Judith owned. She lifted a hand toward him. Like her, he was different. He muttered to himself and made a living from the cans people left for him, and he often rode around on his prized possession, the old bike that was propped against the wall of the store—it was his only method of transportation other than his feet. His clothes were old and dirty, and the soles of his boots worn. She made a mental note to remind Blythe that they were going to find him a comfortable pair of boots for the winter.

As she pushed open the door, there was an all-too-familiar tightening in her stomach. At once the walls closed in and she felt like she was choking. Ordinarily she could grab jars of peanut butter and get out, but the list required actual walking up and down the aisles. When she stepped inside, the fluorescent lights seemed to flicker like a strobe. Flashes went off behind her eyes. Her stomach lurched, and even with the dark glasses, she threw her arm across her eyes to protect them and backed out of the store, shaken.

Rikki bit her lip hard and looked toward the sea, trying to breathe in the salt air. It had definitely been too long. She actually felt a little dizzy and it was hard to catch her breath. The store wasn't crowded or noisy, two things she avoided at all costs, so she just had to get past the lights and force herself to go up and down the aisles. Everyone did it. The peanut butter was stocked on the outer shelf and she could just grab it and go, but . . .

She squared her shoulders. People did this every single day. She was a grown woman, the captain of her own boat— there was nothing she couldn't do. She pushed open the door a second time and walked in. Inez Nelson, a fragile-looking woman with graying hair and a slender body stood at the counter, looking up with a friendly smile.

"Rikki. You're always up early," she greeted. "How are you? How are your sisters?"

Rikki nodded to her, ignoring the questions. She moistened her lips, concentrating on putting one foot in front of the other. She could do this, walk into the space between the aisles. Her feet didn't move. She just stood there, frozen, with the lights fluttering, pushing sharp little darts into her brain. Her stomach lurched, and she turned and went back outside where she could breathe.

"Damn it." She was used to being different, but when it interfered with her ability to do everyday chores, it made her angry. She was used to the lights in stores actually hurting her, where she could tell others didn't have the same problems. Noises were the worst, and textures, especially in her mouth, were brutal on her. The taste of silver or plastic just couldn't be tolerated. Certain fabrics hurt her skin. She knew others weren't like her, but for the most part, she'd learned to cope. But this shopping thing was a nightmare. The hum of the lights reverberated through her head until she wanted to scream.

What was she going to do? Ask Blythe? One of the others? They'd want to know why she wanted food she'd never eat. She chewed on her thumbnail and glared at the store. A person could do anything for a short period of time. She had to be able to go into a grocery store, and if she didn't hurry, more people would come and then it would be impossible.

Squaring her shoulders, she went back inside, and this time she managed to make it to the actual entrance to the aisle before she stopped, dizzy and sick. She couldn't enter that small space where the lights pushed needles into her brain that exploded like firebombs behind her eyes. She shook her head, near tears. Anger welled up like a tidal wave, black and ugly—it was a force she often had to fight when she became frustrated.

"Rikki."

Inez's voice was brisk, matter-of-fact, never that pity sound she detested. Rikki turned around to face her, knowing she had to leave the store again and fighting her blurred vision.

"Give me your list. I'll get your things and you can stand over by the window." Inez held out her hand.

Was it defeat? Or victory? Rikki didn't know, but she had no choice. She handed the list to Inez, grateful she seemed to understand the problem.

"You weren't at the wedding," Inez said, all chatty.

Rikki grit her teeth. Did one answer a statement? She made a sound in the back of her throat, the only acknowledgment she could think to make. The timbre of Inez's voice took a background to the hum of the fluorescent lights. The lights were like a strobe now, continually flickering. The needles stabbing through her skull became ice picks.

"The girls looked lovely," Inez added. "Everyone had such a good time. We missed you though. Elle made a stunning bride. And Jackson was so handsome."

She sounded proud of Jackson, almost as if he were her

son. What did Rikki know of Inez, anyway? Other than she knew everything about everyone, so Rikki made certain to avoid her whenever possible. Jackson was a deputy, and as far as Rikki was concerned, that put him right up there with the officials who had relegated her to the state home and accused her of starting fires and killing the people she loved.

"Frank and I danced the night away."

Frank, Frank Warner, was Inez's fiancé, who owned one of the local galleries. He'd been incarcerated for something. Sometimes he was in the store sitting behind the counter; he was quiet and had little to say. Rikki identified with him more than she did most people. She knew others probably judged him, just as they did her odd behavior.

Inez was still talking, the sound of her voice grating on raw nerves, but the woman was doing her a favor so Rikki wasn't going to let the pain in her head make her do something stupid, like get violent. It had happened in the past, more than once. Lexi called them "Rikki's freak-outs," but it was embarrassing not to have control. She did deep breathing, hoping she didn't pass out.

"Thank God you weren't out on the ocean that day, Rikki," Inez was saying, pushing a cart with great efficiency. "A huge rogue wave came out of nowhere and would have hit the beach, but the Drakes did their thing and it was gone. But your sisters must have already told you that."

Now the ice picks were daggers, stabbing through her brain. Rikki put her hands over her ears to drown out all sound and concentrated on her breathing. Inez was working fast. Rikki could see that the woman was aware something was wrong. She was trying to help, obviously talking to distract her, but between the humming of the lights, her voice and the flickering, the pain in Rikki's head had increased.

"You can take anything for a short period of time," she murmured to herself, uncaring that people thought her strange for talking to herself. If it helped her get through this without losing her mind, she'd talk to herself.

"Here you are, hon," Inez said, her voice that same brisk tone. "I'll just run them through fast."

Rikki pressed her fingers to her temples. "Put twenty dollars on Bill's tab and after I leave, will you take him coffee and something nutritious for breakfast?"

"Sure," Inez worked fast. "No peanut butter today?"

"I picked up a large supply a while ago."

"Are you having company? Your sisters over?"

Rikki drew cash from her wallet and put it on the counter, ignoring the query. Inez was still talking but Rikki couldn't make out the words. A thousand needles pricked her body, and she felt as if she was made of lead and could barely move. She couldn't have produced a sound even if she'd tried. She could feel each individual muscle, hear the blood flowing in her veins and pounding in her head. She hated those sensations, the overload that made no sense. It had taken years before she realized everyone else didn't have the same responses to stimuli in the environment around them. Her body felt as though it might break apart on her if she stayed one more moment.

She picked up the bags and hurried out, cursing under her breath. The man better eat these things slowly because she wasn't *ever* putting herself through that again. Feeling sick and disoriented, she hurried to her truck and drove the few blocks to the headlands where she could park and get out and walk around on the bluffs overlooking the pounding sea. She got two feet from the truck and was sick, her stomach protesting the vicious stabbing in her skull.

Rikki stumbled down the narrow path through the heather to reach the edge where she could stand with the ocean stretching out in front of her like a cool blanket of gray blue. Whitecaps broke along the rocks and spray hissed up the sides of the cliffs. Gulls screamed and far out she saw a whale breech.

The wild chaos in her mind and body began to settle enough that her hands stopped trembling. She needed to be out on the water where she belonged. She didn't belong on land, in public, anyplace where there were other people. She didn't realize she was crying until her vision was completely blurred. She yanked off her dark glasses and rubbed angrily at her tears.

Lev had to go. He couldn't ruin her life. She couldn't deal with someone in her house. She knew what she was like. There was no pretending she'd be all right. She had nearly lost it right there in Inez's store. He just had to go. That was all there was to it.

She drove home faster than she normally did, not allowing any other thought to get the upper hand in her mind. She just had to finish this before it cost her too dearly. She parked the truck and, catching up the groceries, rushed up her back porch to the kitchen door. Lev must have heard her coming because he was there before her, unlocking the door so she didn't have to use the key.

Rikki pushed past him, dumped the grocery bags on the table and whirled to face him. "You have to go. You do. Right now. You just can't stay here and that's all there is to it," she blurted out.

Lev frowned and stepped close to her. Before she could elude him, he removed her glasses and looked at her eyes.

"You've been crying. Rikki, tell me what happened to upset you. Talk to me."

She shook her head, stepping back, and to her horror fresh tears spilled over. "No talking. I'm done talking. You can't be here, that's all."

He went to the door, closed and locked it before turning back to her, his expression unreadable. "*Lyubimaya*, you're going to have to talk. I'm not leaving without finding out what happened to you."

She was trying not to sob, her emotions were out of control. She detested being out of control and it was his fault. Why couldn't he see that? "You'll touch my dishes and use the pans to cook with. I'll have to go to the store again and I can't. I just can't."

"You don't have to do anything, Rikki. Not for me. And if you don't want me to use these dishes or the pots and pans, I can buy some others. Come on, *lyubimaya*, what really happened?"

There was no way to make him understand because *she* didn't understand. She'd always thought her strangeness was due to her childhood, but others had suffered all kinds of trauma and they weren't like her. They didn't feel as if their entire body was going to come apart. Everyday noises didn't make their minds so chaotic that they couldn't think straight. They didn't need order the way she needed it— just to breathe.

His voice—gentle, almost caring, velvet soft—was her undoing. She turned and ran for the bedroom, slamming the door behind her and flinging herself on the bed. She reached under it to find her weighted blanket. Made of soft material, it had inner pockets of small pellets to provide the needed twelve to fifteen pounds for her body weight. She pulled it over her and jammed her hand in her mouth to try to stifle the weeping. She hadn't cried in months, and now, with someone nearby, she had to go and lose it.

After discovering that the pressure from her wet suit made her body feel less like it was flying apart, she'd recognized the calming effect of her vest and sought to find something that would help her off the water. She'd read a great deal about the blankets and knew the weight was supposed to help release serotonin by putting pressure on the sensory nerves in her muscles, joints and tendons, for a calming effect. Whatever. She didn't care how it worked, only that it did. And right now, she was feeling foolish and embarrassed and very tired. She wanted to curl up under the blanket and go to sleep. She heard him moving around the kitchen. It didn't sound like he was leaving. Maybe if she drifted off, he'd be gone when she woke.

The door to the bedroom pushed open and she closed her eyes with a soft groan of despair, wanting to just disappear.

"Rikki, I made coffee. Sit up and drink some. It will help. The groceries have been put away. I just want you to explain to me what happened."

She felt his weight on the edge of the bed. She blew out her breath in exasperation and abruptly sat up, dragging her blanket around her for comfort. "Do we really have to do this?"

"You don't owe me any explanations, but I'd like one."

She took the coffee and frowned at the dark liquid, not wanting to look at him. "I just need things a certain way."

"I can understand that, but it wouldn't make you cry."

"Why the hell do you care?" She resorted to belligerence. It usually pushed people away from her so she didn't have to try to deal with emotions she had difficulty keeping under control.

"You saved my life. You saw what kind of man I am and you still gave me a place to stay. I'll admit I don't remember a lot about my past, but it doesn't feel to me as if I know kindness. You showed me kindness."

"I'm not right, Lev." She clenched her teeth, hating to say it out loud. She didn't mind the way she was, as long as she stayed away from people. She liked her life. She was captain of her own boat. She made a good living. Why should she care that she couldn't go into a grocery store? She wouldn't if he wasn't there. She hated feeling inadequate.

"Neither am I. I'm not asking you to change. Tell me what you need to feel comfortable."

"It isn't reasonable for you."

"Rikki, look at me." Lev waited until she reluctantly lifted her tear-drenched gaze to his face. He wanted—even needed—to kiss her better, but she had huddled inside that peculiar blanket as if it were a fortress. "Don't you think I should decide what's reasonable for me? You took me in, not the other way around. I had to lie down the entire time you were gone, and if I didn't come in here and sit down, I would have fallen. I've got nowhere to go. At least give me a chance to put things right with you."

"I don't know how to explain it to you. I live alone. I have a certain order to things and I need it that way." She took a sip of coffee to steady herself. Her hands were trembling and her body reacted the way it always did when she was stressed, flooding with adrenaline and an anger that just seemed to take her over. Happy or angry or sad. There was rarely an in between for her, and anger was a way to keep people away from her. "I don't talk to people."

Amusement crept into his eyes. "Baby, I don't talk to people either. We aren't people. Here, in this house, there's only us. What we do, how we act, doesn't matter to anyone else. If you need order, teach me your order and I'll follow it. You steady me, Rikki. I don't know why, but I feel more balanced with you around."

She nearly spewed her coffee over him. Was he completely crazy? How in the world could she possibly keep someone else balanced? "You really did hit your head hard, didn't you?"

He smiled and touched his head. "Maybe it knocked some sense into me. I'd appreciate you letting me stay here for a while, Rikki. Let me try not to disrupt your routine. I can learn to eat peanut butter."

The look on his face was that of a man going valiantly to his doom. In spite of everything, laughter bubbled up. "I don't know what to do with you. It would be silly to buy new dishes and you can't eat peanut butter if you don't like it."

"Why don't you eat anything else?"

She frowned again, studying his face. "Textures bother me. It was just easier to find something I liked that was high enough in calories to sustain my work underwater."

"So you can eat other foods."

"I used to, before I lived by myself."

"Think of it as a great adventure. You can try new things and tell me what you like and don't like. Once we have a list, we'll stick to it. And I'll keep the dishes clean."

She took a breath to try to still the pounding of her heart. Blythe was always telling her that she needed to stretch her limits, to keep expanding—not just in her thirst for knowledge, but in her social abilities. Living with someone would certainly come under that heading, wouldn't it?

"I can't lie to my family."

"I haven't asked you to lie. If they ask questions, then answer them."

"Swear to me you won't hurt them."

"Honey, it makes no sense that you'd believe me."

"Do it anyway."

She stared into his eyes, seeking the truth. He didn't look away from her and she saw what she'd seen before in him—vulnerability. He looked tough as nails, a big, muscular man well versed in survival, but like Rikki, he wasn't at ease in the world of family and friends. He was an outsider—just as she was. In spite of all the problems having him there caused, she identified with him.

"We can try it, Lev, but living with me isn't going to be all that much fun."

He reached out and pushed strands of her hair from her face. "As long as I don't make you cry, I think we'll be all right."

"I want you to know it could be dangerous. Four homes have burned down around me. I escaped, but others didn't. People I loved. People who lived with me. You're taking a chance."

"You told me."

"I want you to believe me. The fires were arson."

He nodded. "I heard you. I'm not worried. I think you'll be a lot safer with me here."

"I'm not so worried about me, Lev. I don't want any more deaths on my hands."

He closed his eyes briefly and then looked into hers. "Neither do I, *lyubiamaya*, but you aren't responsible. No matter what others led you to believe, you didn't start those fires. A water element could never do such a thing."

"You said that before. What does that mean?" Because she was fairly certain he knew what her special gift was. He'd been there, in her mind, when she'd directed the pond to respond.

"Some people are born with gifts, Rikki. You're one of them. You're bound to water. It answers your call. You play with it, dance with it, call it with song. You're at home in the sea for a reason."

"I'm at home in the sea because I'm a sea urchin diver. I love what I do and it gives me independence. I can't work with other people."

"More likely you're a sea urchin diver because the water called to you. You're gifted with a rare trait. I imagine that your family—your sisters—are gifted as well."

"We chose one another. We aren't of the same blood."

"Elements are usually drawn to one another," he said. "More than likely each of them or at least some of them are bound to an element."

"Are you?" She tilted her chin at him and drew her left hand under the blanket to hold her palm close against her heart. She dared him to lie to her.

"Not in the same way, but yes, I have a few gifts of my own."

"I knew it!" She scowled at him. "I'm not telepathic but I heard your voice. You connected us in some way."

He shook his head. "You did. Under the water. When you saved me."

She opened her mouth and closed it again. She had no idea about elements, gifts or anything else—but she was going to do research. And maybe one of her sisters knew what he was talking about. He was in her home, and in spite of every instinct demanding she throw him out—she couldn't. It wasn't sane or reasonable, yet she couldn't.

Lev smiled at her and drew the pad of his thumb over her lips. "It isn't going to be so bad, Rikki. You'll hardly notice I'm here."

She made a derisive noise in the back of her throat. He was enormous and very male. How could she not notice him? His shoulders took up more space than her furniture. "I'm going to stay in here while you cook breakfast." She didn't want to see her precious dishes or pots and pans get dirty.

"I'll cook everything separately so you can try it."

She wrinkled her nose. "Looking forward to it."

He laughed and ruffled her hair as he got up before taking her coffee cup. She watched him leave and snuggled beneath the blanket, hoping it would help her stay calm.

8

LEV took the pans out carefully, staring out the window while he considered the best course of action. The longer he was in Rikki's company the more he found himself wanting to be with her. She intrigued him. While he was certain others would find her ways off-putting, he found them endearing. Obviously her sensory system was not functioning properly. For a man who had always believed he felt no instinct other than survival, he found he had a protective side. She seemed to bring it out in him.

He was a loner. So was she. Neither felt comfortable in the company of others. Neither liked to be touched, yet he found he liked her hands on him and she didn't seem quite as opposed to his touch either. Never had he trusted anyone enough to actually go to sleep with them, yet he had with her—and so had she. He believed in fate and the sea had brought them together for a reason.

His memory of his past was coming back one small piece at a time, although, truthfully, he didn't remember anything about a yacht or what he might have been do-ing on it. The good thing was that maybe it didn't matter. He was dead to the outside world. Rikki was the only one who really knew of his existence. He could build a whole new life. Start over again. Be someone else.

First, before anything, he had to buy time with her. That was imperative. His gaze swept the terrain outside the kitchen window. The cover was good as long as no one was on the drive leading to her house, or trying to sneak up on them through the trees. He'd told her the truth when he admitted to having a few gifts of his own. While he cooked a few slices of bacon, he studied the grounds out the kitchen window.

Rikki had obviously set up her house with an eye to-ward protecting it from fire. The trees were a distance away. The flowers and bushes surrounding the house itself were plants that held water and would burn slowly. She didn't think in terms of guns. Did he think those fires were aimed at her? Of course they were. The investigators had a scapegoat in a young teenage girl who obviously was a social misfit in their eyes.

Rikki had been a target not once, but four times. No one had bothered her in the last four years and that meant one thing to Lev—whoever was trying to kill her didn't know where she was. But they'd be searching for her, and when they found her . . . they'd find Lev. She wouldn't be unprotected. He settled on pancakes for breakfast, think-ing the texture of eggs might bother her more than the pancakes.

He heard her coming and turned to watch her walk into the room. She flowed, like water, but he could see she was uncomfortable.

"I was reading the newspaper article again," she greeted.

"The bodyguard was identified as Sid Kozlov. Does that sound at all familiar to you?"

He wanted to smile when she studiously avoided looking at the bacon and pancakes. Instead, she went straight to the door and opened it and then began pacing around the table as if her nervous energy was so overwhelming she couldn't stand still. Damn, he found her adorable. How could anyone not see her struggle to overcome whatever sensory problems she had? He couldn't help but admire her for the life she'd created for herself.

"Yes." He had promised himself that he would tell her the truth as much as he could. "It's one of about ten names I recognize."

She sent him her small frown and rubbed the bridge of her nose as she continued to circle the table. "Are you telling me you have ten names?"

He nodded. "That I can remember." He gave a casual shrug. "Who knows how many more I have."

"So Lev is one of those ten names?"

"Yes." His voice was curt, short and clipped.

She hadn't taken her gaze off of him, but she still couldn't tell if she was annoying him. She didn't pick up social cues as easily as other people. "I don't like it when people interrogate me, so anytime you think I'm doing that, it's okay not to answer me."

"Is that what you do when you don't like a question? You simply don't answer?"

She shrugged.

"So if I ask you a direct question, will you answer me?" Because he had all sorts of questions he wanted to ask her. Especially about the men in her life. There was no evidence that she was dating, and he'd looked. He could only stay up twenty minutes at a time, but those twenty minutes had been used wisely. He knew quite a lot about his elusive little sea urchin diver. And he was already building a new identity for himself.

A slow smile curved that soft, unbelievable mouth. He found himself captured. Spellbound. And he thought her frown adorable, but now he was holding his breath, waiting for that full effect. Her dark eyes, so black they reminded him of shining obsidian, sparkled like gems. Her small white teeth flashed at him all too briefly, and his body went into instant predator mode. He felt the jolt slam deeply and painfully into his groin. He was hard and full instantly. Out of control.

Control was his life. Discipline was everything to him. He stood in the kitchen, unable to move or breathe properly with his pancakes burning and his heart pounding. He had come alive, his body, his soul, there in the water. No, there in her eyes. Those dark, dark eyes.

"Um, Lev."

He stared into her eyes knowing his reaction to her wasn't ever going to go away. He could dismiss it if it was physical attraction, but throughout his entire life, he had controlled physical attraction.

She pushed past him, crowding close. Ordinarily he would never allow anyone into his personal space, but his space seemed to be her space. He felt the spatula taken from his hand, but he didn't move, caught in the shock and wonder of that perfect moment. He was real. He was human. He *felt*. He looked down at the top of her head. She had given him something he never thought he would ever have.

"Lev, sit down."

He felt her hand on his arm and she led him to a chair. He sank into it slowly. She wet a cloth and gently dabbed his forehead. He hardly felt her wiping the sweat from him. He inhaled her, that fragrance that was woman and yet uniquely hers.

"You overdid it. You can't be up this long. I'll figure out how to do this and bring you breakfast. Can you make it back to the bed?"

He loved the sound of her voice. She talked just a little differently, with little inflection. Her tone was low, almost husky. Sometimes when he concentrated on the notes and not the words, it sounded like music to him.

She crouched in front of him, worry in her eyes. "Lev, should I call a doctor?"

He framed her face in his hands and let himself fall into her eyes. He wanted to live there. She reached up and touched his face. He realized it was wet. What the hell? Feeling was shocking. Wonderful. Terrible. He leaned down and took possession of that perfect mouth. Warm. Soft. Incredibly generous.

He felt her startle, go still, and he moved one hand to her thick, wild hair, burying his fingers deep in silk to hold her to him, to anchor himself right there. Her lips trembled beneath his, and he slid his tongue along that soft seam and demanded entrance. For several heartbeats he thought she might not comply, but he was patient, his mouth coaxing. She opened her mouth to him and he took possession without hesitating, sweeping inside to claim what was his.

Sex was a practiced art to him. Each move calculated. His brain always worked while he performed, his body seducing his prey with ease, noting each response of his target. But in one moment, everything had changed. She swept him into a tidal wave of pure sensation, and he willingly let go and let her take him with her. Electricity charged through his bloodstream, snapping and crackling, sparks going off everywhere.

The rush was hot, spreading through his body like a fire. She was a water element and he expected cool, but there was nothing cool about the heat encompassing every part of him. More than that, there was the feeling. He didn't know another way to describe it. To him, it would always be "the feeling." His heart nearly exploded in his chest. His belly tightened and his brain dissolved. He found a miracle in her soft mouth and he never wanted to leave that secret haven.

He tasted passion. He tasted emotion. He tasted a world he'd never imagined, one he could never enter. It was right there in front of him, suddenly open to him. Unexpected. Exciting. Scary. He knew he could never walk away, not when he'd lose this dream before it had ever had a chance to blossom. He reached for it, raced to it, embraced his only chance with everything in him.

Lev lost himself there, kissing her over and over, exchanging breath, drowning, knowing he was drowning and uncaring. She'd saved him before and she was saving him now. He would never be the same and he didn't want to be. Her hands found his chest and fluttered there. She felt slight, fragile, warm and soft, and so feminine, yet he knew a core of steel ran through her.

He lifted his head, breathing deep, drawing air into his burning lungs as he rested his forehead against hers. How did a man tell a woman she moved him? Changed him? Took wrong and made it right? How did he tell her she was a miracle? He didn't. He just held her to him, with the strength in his fingers. His body was trembling, allowing feeling to sweep inside and take hold.

"Lev, it will be all right," she whispered, comforting him.

She thought something was wrong—not that being with her was the most right thing in the world. An incredible gift he wasn't passing up. He couldn't lift his head yet, the emotion was too strong, too overwhelming. So he just pressed his forehead against hers and kept his thoughts contained so she wouldn't accidently connect with him and decide to run. He was going to have to be careful, very careful. His woman—and there was satisfaction in thinking in those terms—was skittish at best.

She represented hope. Belief. Trust. And he had lost those things before he'd ever had a chance to know them.

"Come on, I'll help you back to bed." She slipped her arm around him.

He shook his head and straightened, knowing she wouldn't talk about kissing him. She simply ignored the things she didn't want to talk about, but he could see arousal in her eyes, hear it in her breathing. He knew the signs and she'd been just as affected physically as he had been, but her emotions . . . She hid them well and she wasn't meeting his eyes.

"Look at me."

She drew back, flinching, dropping her arms. "Don't say that to me."

She tried to get up, but he caught her arms and held her. He could see she was annoyed by his strength, but she stilled under the shackles of his fingers and turned her dark eyes on him, and they were filled with fury.

"Thank you," he said quietly. "Sometimes I need to look into your eyes."

She clenched her teeth and he could tell she was still seething.

"Why can't I ask you to look at me?"

He felt the wave of fierce anger well up and rush through her. The black in her eyes sparkled.

"What do you think I heard growing up a million times? I was in foster homes and a state-run facility. I don't look at people. I can't tell you why, but I just don't. I can't tell you how many times I got my face slapped for not doing something I couldn't do or didn't understand how to do it. I trained myself to look at a person's nose, so I appeared to be looking into their eyes and then, apparently, I was inappropriately staring." She jerked back away from him and stood up. "This is my house. I can look anywhere I damn well want."

He stood up too, his speed catching her off guard. He tugged her off balance so she fell against him, her eyes spitting fire. He killed coldly, professionally; it was always a job to him and nothing more, simply exterminating where there was a need. But that soft hiss of her memory—*I got my face slapped*—built an instant rage so deep, so extraordinary, he was shaken at the depth of his ability to feel.

"You don't understand, *lyubimaya,* I *love* the way you look at me. I need it the way others need to breathe."

Her stare was so intense. She'd managed with her direct stare to break through the wall his trainers had erected in his brain. She'd penetrated deep with her intensity, finding him beneath the layers and layers of armor. He never thought he'd ever be capable of feeling such intimacy with anyone and knew he wouldn't with anyone else.

He growled the declaration at her, allowing fierce desire to show in his eyes as he bent his head toward her. She didn't move away, going still in that way she had, as if she were making up her mind whether to fight or flee, but she stood under his hands, her face upturned, her gorgeous eyes watching intently as he lowered his head slowly to hers. He felt the small tremor run through her body just before his mouth claimed hers.

She opened her mouth to his and at once he was swept into her secret world of sensation. She kissed the way she dove, with complete and utter focus, with absolute passion—she gave herself to him and took everything he offered. The world vanished. Every disturbing memory in his mind vanished, leaving only Rikki with her sweet fantasy mouth and her soft body. He disappeared into her, the amazing heat and fire her cool body could produce. Tidal waves of sensation broke over him until he felt shaken by his growing need of her.

He lifted his head, brushing the top of her silky hair with several kisses. "I didn't mean to trigger bad memories, Rikki. God knows I have enough of those for both of us."

Her gaze drifted over his face and he had to really resist the need to read her thoughts. A small, brief smile curved her mouth and she shrugged her shoulders. "I don't think you're any better of a cook than I am. You've burned breakfast."

He whipped around to look at the stove. She'd removed the pans, saving what was left of the scorched pancakes and bacon. It took a few minutes to orient himself again, to put the food on the plates and set them in the middle of the table. She sank back into a chair, obviously uneasy.

Rikki cleared her throat. "I've never actually used these dishes before. My sisters gave them to me when we finished building the house." She touched the edge of one of the plates almost reverently.

Realization slammed home. No one had ever given her presents before. These plates represented family and love to her. He touched the same plate, just as reverently. "Then this is a special occasion. Our first time eating from beautiful dishes together. I'll never forget this memory, not even if I take another bump on the head."

He poured a small glass of orange juice for both of them and put one pancake on her plate and a stack on his. He lifted his glass, waiting until her fingers slowly—almost reluctantly—curled around her glass.

"Here's to many more firsts and many more great memories."

Rikki clinked her glass against his and took a cautious sip of the juice, watching him the entire time. Her expression changed as she tasted it. "This isn't anything like I remember."

"Good or bad different?" He encouraged, studying her face.

He loved to look at her. There was no guile there. She didn't look at him, but into the glass, as if studying each tiny drop as though fascinated beyond belief. She swirled her glass and her eyes widened as she watched the juice moving before she took another sip.

He found the way her lips touched the glass just as fascinating as she found the orange juice. He had an unreasonable urge to reach out and stroke back her sweater so he could see her throat move as she swallowed.

"Good different," she said and turned her head to smile at him.

Her smile hit him like a punch. His belly tightened into hard knots. He indicated her pancake. "Since you helped, if it isn't any good, I'm blaming it on you."

Her smile widened, and her eyes lit up, sparkling at him. "I see how you are." She studied the pancake without touching it, looking at it from all angles.

He couldn't take his eyes from her, even as hungry as he was. Food wasn't nearly what he needed anymore. He needed her. He was broken. Shattered. He was wide open, and somehow, she had done it with her penetrating gaze. She'd stripped him of his past and the monster he'd become, and she'd given him life and a purpose beyond use as a weapon. She'd managed to slip past his guard and open him up, and now, when he was at his most vulnerable and should have been terrified and fighting for his survival, he felt at his safest—here—with her.

It was as if he'd melted into her space somehow and become part of *this*. He looked around at the neat kitchen, the cherry cupboards obviously crafted by a master woodworker. She'd done this—carved out a safe haven for herself in a world that didn't understand different. There, under the water where solace waited, he'd found himself trapped in her eyes. She'd never once looked at his past as if it mattered. And to her, whatever he'd done before that moment didn't exist.

She reached across the table, cut his pancakes and lifted a bite to his mouth. He opened automatically, thinking it the most intimate thing he'd ever done in his life. His gaze didn't leave hers as he chewed and swallowed. A slow smile welled up. Happiness. So this was what it felt like. He'd never known kindness or caring. He'd never known love. Maybe love was a woman feeding him pancakes. Maybe it was someone sitting across from him sipping orange juice just to please him.

"It seems I'm a good cook after all."

She grinned at him and a curious fluttering in the vicinity of his belly startled him. He took the fork from her, his fingers brushing hers. The contact gave him intense satisfaction. For the first time in his existence, he knew he was drowning and he wasn't thinking about survival. His head, his heart, hell, everything he was, rushed to take the plunge. What, after all, did he have to lose?

"You think it's safe to risk it?"

Her soft words startled him and for a moment, he misunderstood, certain she was reading his thoughts. Her eyes held amusement and a bit of a mischievous glint. Her face might not be expressive, but he could read it all, there in her eyes.

"I think you should," he agreed and settled back in his chair to watch her take her first bite of pancakes. Who would have thought something so simple could bring such pleasure? He'd made each pancake quite thin in the hopes the texture would bother her less.

She put a thin spread of peanut butter over one. Her knife made lazy little swirls that weren't quite as lazy as he first thought. Each circular wave was exact, creating a pattern. The top of the pancake began to look like the surface of the ocean. Her entire attention was on the peanut butter as she drew waves swelling, cresting and rolling over. Each stroke was deliberate and seemed to absorb her completely. He found himself nearly as mesmerized as she was.

"That's a beautiful drawing, Rikki." He kept his voice low. "Do you paint?"

She startled, raised her lashes and blinked several times before she focused on him. "What?" She frowned, processing his question. "Why would you think I paint?"

He indicated the top of her pancake. "That's a beautiful picture of the sea and it's in peanut butter. If you can do that with a knife, you must be good with a brush."

Her frown deepened and she turned the dish around and around, studying the decorated top from all angles. "I never noticed. It isn't art."

"It was very precise," he commented and forked another bite of pancake.

"I suppose it is. I count." She looked at him, obviously expecting him to find her revelation disturbing. "In my head, I count."

She actually muttered to herself, half aloud, mostly under her breath, but he didn't point that out to her. He liked the little talks she seemed to have with herself, especially when she was annoyed with him.

"It's the ocean." He ate more. His body needed fuel, and he downed a piece of bacon.

"It is, isn't it?" She smiled at the design. "I can't draw. This, apparently, is a secret skill." Her eyes changed and a little frown came back. "When I lived in foster homes or at the state home, whenever they forced me to eat something, I weighed the punishment for not eating it and if I didn't want to pay the price, I counted to focus my attention on what I was thinking and not on how the food felt in my mouth."

A stabbing pain pierced his chest in the vicinity of his heart. He reached across the table to still her hand as she raised her fork. "You don't have to eat the pancake, Rikki."

She shrugged. "I know that." She looked around her

home with satisfaction. "Not here and not on my boat, but Blythe says I should always try to expand my comfort zone. It's hard to do when I'm alone. I just fall into a routine. When I'm with one of my sisters, eating at their houses or going somewhere with them, it's easier to make myself try new things."

There was just a hint—a note—of Blythe's voice in her tone. He knew it was unintentional, that she'd taken on a bit of the woman who she so admired.

He sent her a smile as she put the pancake in her mouth and watched her face. It was silly, really, but he actually felt privileged that she included him with her sisters, trying something new for him. "How is it you've never eaten pancakes before?"

She chewed thoughtfully, made a face and delicately spit the pancake into a napkin. "I probably did when I was a child," she admitted. "I got stubborn as I got older. I didn't like anyone telling me what to do and after a while I just refused to do anything. I got so I liked making people uncomfortable before they trashed me. I figured it was going to happen anyway, so why not? Especially the police. I dealt with them quite a lot when I was younger."

"Didn't anyone recognize that maybe you needed help?"

She blinked. Drew swirls in her peanut butter. Her gaze locked with his. "No one ever asks me questions like that."

"I'm interested."

She sighed. "Lev, everyone believed I murdered people by setting houses on fire. I was strange and that just added to their conviction that I was the guilty one. Maybe I even acted guilty. It occurred to me that I was setting the fires in my sleep."

Lev watched her push away the plate and cross to the

breadbox. She looked over her shoulder at him as she extracted a piece of bread. "Why in the world would someone eat those things when they could put peanut butter on bread?"

He waited until she sank back into her chair, drawing her knees up, feet tucked up where no one could see while she spread peanut butter on the slice of bread. He wasn't going to get drawn into another discussion on the merits of peanut butter, not when she was giving him pieces of her childhood.

"You were thirteen when the first fire broke out?" He prompted. "Do you remember much about that night?"

She jumped up and paced across the floor with a quick, restless movement. She poured herself a cup of coffee before she turned and regarded him from what she must have considered a safe distance. There were shadows in her eyes and her mouth trembled. "I remember everything about that night." She took a small sip of coffee and turned to stare out the window. "My mother told me I could read in bed. I couldn't sleep much and she or my dad stayed up with me as a rule, but if they'd gotten a book I wanted that day, they'd often let me read. I loved reading." She turned around, leaning back against the sink. "They'd given me the complete works of Sherlock Holmes the week before and I was anxious to start it. I'd wanted it for so long, and when we'd gone to the bookstore to get it, there was a terrible wreck on the freeway. A huge pileup. Both my parents were injured and taken to the hospital. I'd been so scared, afraid I'd lose them. I didn't read a word. I sort of made this pact with God, you know—let my parents live and I'll be so good. The kind of thing kids do."

He watched her drink her coffee to steady herself. Her hands trembled slightly. He doubted if anyone else would have noticed that small sign. He wanted to put his arms around her and hold her but he knew she wouldn't allow it. She was holding herself together by a thread and one touch would shatter her.

She sent him a small humorless smile over the coffee mug. "I was already so strange, you know. I couldn't do things like other children. I was clumsy and never quite got their social cues so school was extremely difficult. My parents were my safety zone so you can imagine how frightened I was. My dad was able to leave that night, but my mom couldn't. So my idea was that I wouldn't read my book until she was home."

"Was Sherlock Holmes worth the wait?" He kept his gaze locked on her, observing—*absorbing*—her reaction. He knew he'd been trained for interrogation, for gathering information, and he automatically had fallen into the examination mode. In the back of his head he recognized—as he usually did—that this information was important and he needed to file it carefully for future reference.

She turned abruptly and dumped the rest of the coffee in the sink, set the cup on the counter and simply walked out the back door. He caught the glint of tears in her eyes as she turned her head. Lev sat there quietly finishing his breakfast while his mind turned over what she'd said, continuing to dig through the facts to get to the reasons anyone would target her for death in such a particularly ugly manner.

He sat back and contemplated what to do. His head wasn't completely better, despite all the energy he'd spent trying to heal himself. The force of the waves had been tremendous, slamming his body into the rocks. Even with his special gifts, he hadn't been able to combat the power of the ocean. He was dizzy most of the time and his head still pounded with alarming vigor, threatening to explode if he moved around too much.

All of a sudden, he felt a sense of urgency, and for a man who lived in the shadows with no real name and only one purpose, it wasn't a good idea to ignore his feelings. He had recovered enough memories to know he didn't want the man he'd been to come back from the dead. As far as Lev was concerned, Sid Kozlov was going to stay in the sea, his body lost for all time. He had already identified himself to Rikki as Lev so he'd already come up with a variation of that name, making it more American. It was time to put the finishing touches on his new identity, one he could use here with her, because he was staying and that meant he had to use his head and force his memories to cooperate.

He needed an untraceable computer to finish the process, and he needed to get into the small town close by. He'd left himself a few packages scattered around for emergency exits if the need was there—a major requirement in his profession. He just had to remember where his safety stashes were. He carried the dishes to the sink and meticulously washed them while he tried to force his memory to cooperate.

He knew how to make up a new identity that would pass inspection by any official—he'd been doing it for years. He was certain he had plenty of money and he'd hidden more weapons and ammunition, but he couldn't quite remember where everything was. That small, important fact continued to elude him. So, identity first. He had to get strong enough to go outside her home and study the surrounding terrain and set up warning systems. And he had to get on her boat. Her boat was far more vulnerable than her house. He'd been aware of the harbor, a small open community with a park right there where people could easily come and go. Her boat was tied up to the dock and anyone could rig it to blow, or rig her air compressor so she died of carbon monoxide poisoning while she was beneath the water.

He looked around the kitchen to make certain everything was in place before he went out onto the porch. Rikki was curled up in a chair, her bare feet tucked under her, her dark glasses pushed onto her nose, covering her eyes. He sank into the chair beside her and took possession of her left hand, tracing circles with the pad of his thumb.

"I didn't mean to upset you, Rikki."

"You didn't." She sighed and indicated the trees with her chin. "I love that grove of redwoods right there. That many redwood trees indicate water—a lot of water. I love that I might be living with water running just under me."

"I can see why that would appeal to you." The peace of her farm appealed to him. Trees surrounded the house, tall and majestic, as if guarding her property. She kept everything neat and orderly. There was no lawn, but she had terraces of plants, bright, colorful flowers and shrubs in every shade of green. The rockwork on the terraces was beautiful and obviously done with care by someone who handpicked each stone.

"Tell me about that night. Did you hear a noise? Did you see anyone? Were your parents acting different? Worried maybe?"

She was silent a long time. He waited patiently, giving her space, letting her work out whether she trusted him enough to give him something that personal. The wind rustled the tree leaves overhead and birds flitted from branch to branch. A squirrel chattered and another answered. He noted it all rather absently as he watched in the distance for the telltale dust rising that would indicate a car on the road leading to her house.

Rikki was utterly still, no squirming, no sound, she simply stared out into space, her face averted, her eyes hidden behind her dark glasses. She hadn't pulled her hand away, and Lev pressed his thumb into the center of her palm and closed his eyes, feeling his way. Immediately he "saw" numbers in his head. She was counting to herself, and she was on seventy-eight.

She took off her dark glasses, turned her head to look him straight in the eyes. The jolt was like a powerful punch straight in his gut. Hard. Encompassing. She did something to his insides, where he was tough as nails, strong and impenetrable. She slipped past his guard and managed to penetrate deep. His reaction to her bordered on primal.

"You think my entire family was a target and whoever killed my parents missed me and is still hunting me."

He wanted to pull her into his arms and hold her close, but her entire demeanor screamed "hands off," so he continued to stroke caresses over her open palm, satisfied that she hadn't pulled completely away from him. "If it was a contract hit, they wouldn't stop, not until they were dead, and even then, the contract could be given to another hit man."

"Are you a hit man?"

A day earlier he wouldn't have been so certain. "No." He kept his gaze on hers. "I don't know exactly what I did, and I've certainly killed, but I'm not certain why. My memory is coming back in pieces, but it's definitely returning." And he wasn't all that happy about it.

She moistened her lips, shoved her dark glasses back on her nose and turned to look out over her trees again. "If someone is trying to kill me for whatever reason, why the gaps between fires? And why fire? Wouldn't that be an unusual choice for a hit man?"

"Yes, very unusual. My memory is coming back slowly, so maybe I'll eventually remember someone who uses that method. It isn't in any way familiar, but that doesn't mean it couldn't happen. Were your parents different? Upset? Was there anything unusual that you can remember in the days or weeks before that night?" He pressed her because he was certain he was on the right track.

"You have the instincts of a bodyguard," she pointed out.

He didn't allow his smile to surface. She had no idea what instincts he had, and he wasn't going to enlighten her and risk getting kicked out—but they sure as hell weren't that of a bodyguard. He remained silent, waiting.

She chewed on her lower lip for a few moments. "My mother was my stability. Without her I was lost and all I really remember is being alone with my father. He tried to understand me, but he was disappointed that I was so different. Don't get me wrong. He loved me and he tried to do all the things Mom did, but he was stiff and annoyed most of the time. He tried to hide it, and when Mom was in the hospital, we both were so miserable that anything else would have been impossible to notice."

"The car accident when she was hurt. Could that have been deliberate?"

She shook her head. "It was one of those pileup things,

where everyone is sliding into everyone else. A couple of the cars caught on fire and the rescuers pulled everyone out fast and made us stand as far away as we could get, even those injured. There was such chaos that if someone wanted us dead, they could have killed us right there and no one would have noticed. Several people died in that accident. It was horrible."

"What happened to your mother?"

"Her leg was smashed. She was in the hospital for a week and I remember my father crying, afraid she was going to lose her leg. He was there the first night, with broken ribs and a concussion as well, but then they allowed him to come home with me."

Lev frowned as he brought the tips of her fingers to his mouth and rather absently scraped his teeth back and forth over the sensitive pads as he tried to make the pieces of the puzzle fit together. He had a feeling—more than a feeling; he was certain she was a target, and that meant if there was a contract, she was in very real danger.

"That night, how did you escape?"

"I was reading and the house was very quiet. I was listening to classical music while I read and I had earphones on, but I knew my parents had gone to bed. I checked a couple of times because I liked the sound of them moving through the house turning off lights and getting ready for bed. It always comforted me." She spoke very matter-of-factly and there was no expression on her face.

Lev held his thumb against the center of her palm and let his mind expand to encompass hers. She replayed the sound of her parents moving through the house to herself often. He brought her hand back to his mouth and pressed a kiss there.

She jumped and swiveled around to face him, her eyes wide and startled behind the sunglasses, but she didn't pull away. "I read for a long time after they went to bed and suddenly I was coughing. I noticed it was difficult to see the words on the pages and blinked. Inside me, there was this strange calling, and I yanked off my headphones and looked around. The room was smoky and I could hear a roaring sound. I dropped to the floor and crawled to the door. I wanted to get to my parents. I tried, but every room was on fire. We had a carpet in the hallway and it melted into my skin while I crawled. I remember the sounds and the heat vividly."

"Do you remember calling water to you?"

She nodded. "The pipes in the house burst, at least that's what the firemen told me later. I hadn't realized I'd done it, of course, not until much later, and I still wasn't entirely certain it wasn't all a huge coincidence." She pushed her free hand through her hair in agitation. "My mother couldn't walk. It appeared that my father tried to carry her out and a piece of the ceiling fell on them. The fire burned hot and fast. There was an accelerant poured inside the walls as well as outside."

"Why not in your room?"

"At the time, the investigators said my light was on and probably whoever did it didn't want to risk getting interrupted. Later, of course, they figured it was to allow me an escape, although they couldn't figure out why I didn't go through the window."

He turned his head toward the road, his internal radar sounding off loud. "You're about to have company."

"Probably one of my sisters."

"I'll go inside and wait."

"Don't shoot anyone."

He grinned at her, leaned down and brushed a kiss across the top of her silky head. She felt alone to him. He knew exactly what that was like and he didn't want it for her. "I'll be close if you need me."

She looked up at him, but she didn't reply.

9

RIKKI watched the door close behind Lev and her heart began beating normally once again. She hadn't realized that she'd been barely breathing. Lev had pressed a kiss into the center of her palm and for one moment she'd felt it—*physically* felt it—deep inside her most feminine core. Her womb had reacted with a clasping gasp of shock, and the bundle of nerve endings felt raw and sensitive. She had been unable to think clearly after that brief touch of his mouth on her. She felt raw and needy and so empty inside.

Sex with Daniel had been, at best, rote. She didn't believe she could really enjoy it because she didn't like close contact, but he was good to her and she cared for him. It made sense that they could dive together and make a good living. Daniel was content to have quick sex as long as she was available to him, and because he was the first and only person she'd felt affection—even love—for, she wanted the relationship. They made sense.

Lev made no sense. None. And it was terrifying to feel

the sensations he produced in her, yet she craved his touch now. Craved the way he made her feel both in her head and in her body. His kisses were extraordinary, reaching inside of her and melting her until her entire body flowed against him like water.

Blythe's car distracted her from her thoughts. Her stomach tightened. What in the world was she going to say? Guilt was sharp and edgy, a knife cutting her open. She didn't lie to Blythe—not ever. Not even when she wanted to. She knew Blythe would never approve of Lev, and she wouldn't understand about not taking him straight to the authorities. Blythe believed in the law; she'd never seen what false accusations could do to a person.

Rikki sat up straighter and pushed at her glasses to make certain they were firmly in place. She would *not* betray Blythe by lying. But Lev . . .

Blythe got out of her sporty little Spider and walked up to Rikki slowly. "Are you all right?" She took off her glasses to study Rikki's face.

Rikki was certain guilt was stamped there. Color rose in spite of her determination not to allow it. She shrugged. "Yes." That, at least, wasn't a lie.

Blythe dropped into the chair Lev had vacated, and for a moment Rikki was afraid the warmth of the seat would give him away. She would have noticed and she was certain Lev would have as well, but Blythe was too busy inspecting her. "You don't look sick."

Rikki shook her head.

"You missed a diving day this week. On Thursday, the weather was perfect, the sea was calm and you didn't go. You always go."

"Too many boats out there." Again she felt relief, she was still telling the absolute truth. She hadn't wanted to share her sea with so many and it was dangerous. A boat could get too close and cut her hose.

"Honey. Talk to me. You've had the soup for two months and suddenly you're buying more. And Inez said you were in this morning and needed groceries. She asked if you were putting on a dinner party. I know you better than that. What's going on?"

There it was, the direct question she'd been dreading. She sat in silence, her mind working fast, discarding ideas as soon as they popped into her brain.

It's all right, Rikki, I'll handle it. Lev's voice slid into her mind and she turned, knowing exactly what he was doing.

He pushed open the screen door and stepped out. He looked tough and dangerous, his jeans riding low on his hips and his shirt stretched taut across his broad chest. It was impossible to miss the defined muscles rippling beneath the material. He looked gorgeous to Rikki.

Blythe stood up and backed up a couple of steps, her eyes wide with shock. Lev smiled at her and offered his hand.

"I'm Levi Hammond," he announced. *Make certain you use Levi instead of Lev,* he cautioned Rikki.

Blythe reluctantly shook his hand, all the while looking at Rikki. She couldn't have failed to notice his bare feet or the intimate way he brushed his hand through Rikki's hair before toeing a chair close to her and straddling it.

"Blythe Daniels," Blythe muttered, and raised her eyebrow expectantly toward Rikki as she took her seat, a determined, almost alarmed, look on her face.

"I'm hoping for the tender job on Rikki's boat," Lev announced.

Rikki choked. She glared at him.

I'm telling the truth.

He sounded so innocent. She kept her face averted from Blythe. Damn the man. She could already see what was going to happen. He was going to use Blythe to manipulate her into letting him aboard her boat.

Her mouth tightened. "I told you, I don't need a tender." The moment the words left her mouth she knew she'd made a major mistake. If she'd just kept her mouth closed, Blythe would be concentrating on Lev's dangerous look, not on whether she needed someone watching over her out at sea. And that was exactly how Blythe saw it. She knew nothing about urchin diving, but she wanted someone on board checking on Rikki's safety. And Lev looked like the kind of man who could handle things.

"Of course you need a tender," Blythe objected, falling neatly into Lev's trap. "I've told you so for a long time. It's just much safer with someone up top looking out for you."

Behind the dark glasses Rikki rolled her eyes. Although she'd offered on the day of the wedding to go to sea with her, prior to that, Blythe had refused to even go out in the boat after the first time when she'd been so sick. The water had been calm the day Rikki had taken her out, but Blythe had been terrified. She was certain a great white was going to come up under the boat and take a big chunk out of it, or a giant squid would rise up and wrap its tentacles around the boat, dragging it beneath the sea. Now that the word was out that a methane gas bubble was suspected in the sinking of the yacht, Blythe had one more thing to worry about.

"I don't want to have to go rescuing some amateur," she muttered.

"I know how to dive," Lev asserted.

"Tenders stay in the boat."

"Which I have every intention of doing." He managed to look pious.

"Where did you meet?" Blythe asked, looking from one to the other.

"Out at sea," Lev said. "And we were sort of thrown together in the harbor. She was diving alone and I'm out of work. I know my way around a boat, so I was hoping it might work out for both of us."

He spoke in an easy, casual tone. Believable. Even Rikki believed him. How had he gone from scary, gun-toting killer man to cuddly puppy in five seconds? He was sprawled out, his face in the shadows of the porch, which somehow softened his edged features. He looked open and honest, although still tough and strong, which would appeal to Blythe. She would want someone tending the boat who appeared to be able to pull a whale out of the ocean. She didn't understand sea urchin diving and what the very real risks were.

Rikki took off her glasses and pinned him with her darkest stare.

Blythe nudged her. "Stop trying to intimidate him."

"If he was on my boat, he'd be intimidated," Rikki muttered.

"Are you Rikki's neighbor?" Lev asked, all chatty.

Rikki clenched her teeth together as she pushed her glasses back on her nose. She should have known he could pull out the charm. He was a chameleon, and she was begin-ning to get a sense of how lethal he could be. Blythe wasn't a woman who could be snowed easily, and while she couldn't say Lev was lying, he certainly was misleading, acting like a docile goldfish when he was a really a shark.

Suddenly his head went up alertly. "Someone's coming."

Rikki turned to look at the road, but she didn't see any dust to indicate anyone was traveling on it. She waited a few heartbeats, and sure enough, a small cloud of debris shot into the air. Lev stood up—not exactly stood up, more like flowed to his feet, a graceful, fluid motion, more like a dancer than a big man.

"Would you like coffee, Blythe? Cream? Sugar?"

Blythe looked shocked. Rikki never let anyone in the house. It had taken her months to get Rikki to allow her to go into the kitchen, and there was Levi making himself at home.

Rikki glared at him again. *I know exactly what you're doing.* And she did. His little show of gallantry earned him two things. Blythe would see he was at home in Rikki's house, and it would get him inside where he was not only out of sight but he could shoot someone he considered a threat.

I knew you were a smart girl when you wanted to throw me back into the sea. He was laughing at her even as he took Blythe's order for both cream and sugar in her coffee. *Let the inquisition begin.*

She sat up straighter. She hadn't considered that. The moment he went into the kitchen, she was going to be interrogated like there was no tomorrow. Squirming, she realized there was no way out. She simply handed him her coffee cup in surrender. "No sugar or cream."

He gave her a cocky smile. "I knew that."

Of course he did. He was observant. She sent him another dagger-cutting stare, but he just grinned as he closed the screen after him.

"Oh my gosh." Blythe caught her hand and leaned into her. "He is so hot. Where did you find him?"

"I pulled him out of the sea and decided to keep him."
Rikki's answer was strictly honest.

Blythe burst out laughing. "I'd keep him too. So he
really wants to work with you?"

Rikki scowled at her, her most fierce scowl, usually re-
served for anyone *but* Blythe. "*For* me, not with me. Let's
just keep that totally straight. I'm captain. And he's a lowly
tender." Her palm throbbed, a dull ache that swiftly turned
into an itch somewhere else. She pressed her hand against
her leg tightly, trying to dull the sensation.

*I accept the position of lowly tender. I'm good with
that title.*

"He looks like a man who would be helpful on a boat,
Rikki," Blythe said.

Rikki growled aloud. "I'm a solitary diver, Blythe."
The car was in sight now and Rikki recognized it as be-
longing to Judith. Both Judith and Airiana were inside.
Rikki groaned and covered her face.

"What is this, Blythe?"

"An intervention."

"You have got to be kidding me! Because I bought groceries?"

"You haven't bought anything but peanut butter and
bread in four years."

Rikki was indignant. "I buy coffee and broccoli and
sugar for you."

"We were going to talk about nutrition. You can't just
eat peanut butter all the time, and since you showed an
interest in food, we thought this was a good time to talk
to you."

Rikki glared at her. "*Levi* showed an interest in food."
See, I remembered.

That's my woman.

"I guessed that after I saw him, but you shopped for soup a couple of days ago, which means he's been here for a while."

Rikki tightened her mouth and refused to speak. *Brace yourself. I think they're planning to show up en masse. And when they get going, they're relentless. Last time they came, they insisted I start eating broccoli. It was really annoying.* She wasn't touching the "my woman" comment for anything.

He laughed softly in her mind, sharing his amusement over her obvious disgust of anything green and her cowardice. *As I want actual food, I'm going to be on their side,* he warned.

She growled deep in her throat, warning him of dire consequences. *You do and I'll retaliate. Every time you shower the water is suddenly going to go ice-cold.*

Judith and Airiana walked up the paved walkway, Airiana looking up at the sky and Judith clearly drawn to the colorful flowers. Rikki found herself relaxing a little as she always did when her sisters showed up. She loved just watching them. In their own ways, they were as different as she was. And they accepted her. It didn't matter to them that she didn't like them going into the house. They might not understand, but if it was important to her, it was important to them. She loved feeling their acceptance.

Maybe that was what appealed to her about Lev. Her peculiarities didn't seem to bother him at all. She smiled at the newest arrivals and indicated chairs. "As long as we're not talking about food, groceries or anything green, I'm glad to see you."

Judith burst out laughing and bent to brush a kiss on top of Rikki's head. She was nearly as tall as Blythe. With her long legs, slender figure and exotic looks, she could have been a model.

Rikki tried to glare. "You ratted me out."

Judith looked unrepentant. "I had no choice. Blythe subjected me to her . . ." She whirled her hands around, her long fashionable nails glinting dark red in the sunlight. "That *look* she gives us when she will get her way. In any case, it was Airiana who blurted out that you'd gone grocery shopping."

Blythe laughed. "You all remember my evil eye when you're thinking of withholding information. Actually Inez called me, worried, so I already knew."

Airiana, a small, fragile-looking woman of twenty-five with natural platinum hair and huge blue eyes, flashed a small grin at Rikki. "I was feeling so guilty."

"I'm sure you were," Rikki said drolly.

Airiana started to sink into the chair Lev had vacated. Blythe caught her arm, shaking her head. "That chair's taken." She leaned forward with a conspiratorial air. "By a man," she added, lowering her voice. "A very hot man. He's in Rikki's house."

Judith and Airiana gasped in unison.

"You let someone into your house? A man?" Judith said, clearly shocked. "I'm going to go see." She started toward the screen.

"No!" Panic welled up. Judith couldn't go into the house with Lev. Not two people. Not together. It was bad enough that Lev was in there, but not someone Rikki loved, not Judith. Rikki shook her head adamantly, barely able to breathe. "You have to stay out here where I know you're safe." She blurted out the order, her heart hammering so loud she could hear a roar in her head.

Judith immediately held up her hands and halted in mid step. "I won't, honey."

Calm down, lyubimaya, just breathe. There is no fire. There is no one close other than your sisters. I would know if an enemy was near. I won't let anything happen to you.

I'm not worried about me! She was emphatic. *I don't want anything happening to my sisters.* She hesitated. *Or you. What's taking so long with the coffee?*

Rikki found that she could breathe easier, that her strange connection to Lev steadied her.

I'm just holding back for a minute or two to let the others arrive. They're coming up the drive. Their energy feels happy and affectionate, but I prefer to be certain.

Rikki glanced up the drive. Sure enough, there was a small but telling cloud of dust. How did he do that? "If we keep meeting like this, we're going to need more chairs." She got up, vacating hers so her other two sisters would have a place to sit. She perched on the railing, leaning her back against a post, leaving Lev to bring out a chair or sit in the hammock swing.

Lexi Thompson jumped out from the passenger side of Lissa Piner's bright red convertible. Lexi waved madly, her wild mass of auburn hair flying around as she leapt up and down. She looked like a little pixie with her large green eyes and her pale oval face. Rikki adored her. Lexi, at twenty-three, was the youngest of all of them. She'd had the worst life any of them could imagine, yet she remained an upbeat, positive person, one Rikki looked up to. She'd manage to make peace with herself after meeting Lexi.

"I'm here for the defense, Rikki," Lexi called. "I've totally got your back."

Rikki had to laugh. Of course she could count on the

little rebel. "Way to go. Sit next to Blythe and every time she mentions vegetables, kick her."

"Lexi's the one growing the vegetables," Lissa reminded and stepped out of her convertible.

Rikki couldn't help but admire her. Bright red hair, deep blue eyes, she had curves and a small waist. Rikki was skinny and she didn't have a waist like that. Lissa was the resident martial arts practitioner and her body was a tribute to her abilities. She also was a carpenter and welder. She excelled at blowing glass and showed many of her glass and metal pieces in Judith's store.

"I do eat your broccoli, Lexi," Rikki said as piously as she could manage.

"And I love you for it," Lexi blew her a kiss.

Blythe waited until both women were seated before she dropped the bombshell. "Rikki's got a man."

Five heads turned to stare at her. Rikki lifted an eyebrow and pushed her glasses firmly on her nose, trying to look nonchalant.

"In the house," Judith hissed. "She won't let me in to see him."

"He's not on display," Rikki defended.

"I want to see," Lexi insisted.

Lissa looked at Blythe. "You met him?" There was suspicion in her voice. "Who is this man and how did he get into Rikki's life? Rikki doesn't just pick up men."

Rikki sent Lissa her most ferocious frown. "I certainly am capable of picking up men."

I wouldn't be saying that where I can hear you.

You have nothing whatsoever to do with it.

Maybe not yet, but I will.

A thousand butterflies took wing in her stomach. She wasn't touching that statement. He sounded far too confident and his killer kisses might have given him reason to believe he might have a say in her life, but it wasn't true. No one, *no one*, told her what to do.

She could hear her sisters talking around her, but their voices had faded into the background. Her mind was filled with Lev. His laughter was low and amused and all too male. He cut off abruptly, pulling out of her head. For a moment she was dizzy and nauseated. She breathed deep to allow the feeling to pass when it suddenly occurred to her that it was Lev who was sick and dizzy. He wasn't hiding in the house—well, maybe he was because he was inclined to be paranoid, but he hadn't been able to stand more than fifteen or twenty minutes at a time. He'd been up and even cooked breakfast. He must have been resting and trying to hide it from her.

She brushed her hand over her face, hardly able to breathe. She wasn't the kind of woman to take care of sick people. She just wasn't. He needed to have a doctor, or Lexi, look at him. She started to move, when the sudden hush of chatter warned her and she turned to see him standing in the doorway. Her heart jolted at the sight of him. Tall. Masculine. The two-weeks' growth of beard hiding his stubborn jaw. His eyes were deep blue, just like the sea. It was difficult, looking at the obvious muscle, to think of him as being sick or dizzy. He looked too strong, too invincible.

Judith made a single sound, drawing her attention. Judith had gone pale and she turned her head to look at Airiana. The two women exchanged a look of fear. Lexi, Blythe and Lissa flashed bright smiles. Rikki's stomach tightened into knots.

"I shouldn't have had you getting coffee, Levi." She

jumped up and took the cups to her sisters. "Levi hit his head pretty hard the other day and he needs care."

"You aren't responsible for him," Judith said.

Rikki was startled by the belligerence in her voice. As a rule, Judith was open and caring. Just the bandage on Lev's head should have produced her usual empathy.

"Actually, I am," Rikki countered. It was true. She was captain. She'd pulled him out of the sea. Her code made her responsible. "Everyone, this is Levi Hammond. Levi, my sisters. You know Blythe already. This is Judith, Lissa, Airiana and Lexi."

"So you brought him home with you because you feel responsible," Airiana clarified, ignoring the introduction.

Rikki scowled at Judith and Airiana. "Why are you being rude? He's a guest in my home. I may not have social skills, but in your homes, I'm always polite to your guests." Okay, that wasn't strictly the truth. She usually backed out and left the moment she saw company, or she simply didn't speak. But she kept her dark glasses on and that could be considered polite. Her throat felt funny, a strange tickle.

Lev put his hand on her shoulder. "It's natural for them to worry about you, Rikki." Even as he said it, his head whipped around, looking toward the trees.

"His aura," Judith broke off, gasping, one hand going to her throat. She began to cough.

Airiana leapt to her side. "What is it?"

Judith shook her head and held up her hand as she tried to breathe. Lexi rushed over to her. Rikki went still. She pulled her glasses off and her gaze locked with Lev's. She knew she was giving him the death stare, but if he was responsible, she was *never* going to forgive him. She couldn't tell by his stony expression or his eyes. He was completely inscrutable.

Judith coughed again and Rikki hurried to get water, her mind racing. Lev was telepathic. He'd admitted to other gifts as well. His strongest drive was self-defense. Would he see Judith as a threat to him? She should never have brought him anywhere near her family. It bothered her that she had even conceived the idea that he could be a threat to Judith, but she couldn't get the nagging doubt from her mind.

She handed Judith the water. Lev hadn't reassured her. And she had observed him enough to know he had some healing abilities, but he wasn't rushing to assist Judith. He stayed quiet, out of the way, standing over near the railing where she'd been sitting. He was looking out toward the sea or maybe up to the road, but he wasn't looking at Judith.

Judith managed to get water down, and she slumped in her chair, gasping for breath. Lexi put calming hands on her and Judith drew in more air. "I have an allergy to something, I think."

"Has this happened before?"

The suspicion in Lev's voice startled Rikki. He was still looking out toward the road. A chill went down her spine. What did he sense out there? She couldn't stop herself. She stepped in front of her sisters, all huddled around Judith, and she faced the road as well, trying to make herself larger, even going so far as to spread her arms out.

"What is it?" Lissa whispered, coming up behind her.

"I don't know. Something. Can you feel anything?" Rikki murmured back in a low tone.

Lissa was a warrior woman. If something was wrong, she might be able to feel it.

"Go in the house," Lev snapped. "Now. All of you."

Horror was a metallic taste in her mouth. All of them together in her house? She shook her head. Lev didn't argue, he simply caught her arm and thrust her inside. "You fucking stay there, you hear me? The rest of you get inside and stay away from the windows. You keep Rikki inside and out of sight."

She felt the push in her mind, knew he was using some sort of strong compulsion along with his command. He didn't need it. His demeanor and voice alone would have stopped her sisters from going outside against his wishes. He dragged her through the kitchen into the living room.

Rikki couldn't breathe. The temperature in the house was extraordinarily hot. She broke out in a sweat, she was dizzy and weak. Her panic was full-blown and she couldn't talk, couldn't get the words out. Lev strode past her into the bedroom and began strapping on weapons. She could see him from where she was, but her sisters were oblivious, all peering out the windows. Airiana started to protest, but Lissa stopped her.

"He's right," she agreed. "I feel something out there."

"Call Jonas," Blythe said, all practical.

"Stay the hell away from the windows," Lev snapped, as he stood in the doorway of the bedroom. "Keep Rikki in here." He crossed to her side and bent down, his face close to hers, his hands on her upper arms as he pulled her against him. "I know you're worried about fire, *lyubimaya*, but no one is going to get past me to get to you. Just breathe this away and I'll be back soon." He brushed a gentle kiss across her upturned mouth and abruptly strode away, leaving her in shock.

Blythe, Judith, Airiana and Lexi stared at her with

open mouths, obviously not believing what they'd just witnessed.

Lissa followed Lev through the bedroom to the back window. "I can help."

"He'll be long gone. He's watching the house. He's up on the high ridge to the north. I caught the flash of his binoculars. Could be nothing, but then again, I don't want a pervert lurking around either."

"Rikki can't have us all in the house," Lissa advised, hanging on to the windowsill. It was impossible to see the northern tree line from where they were—which meant whoever was watching couldn't see Lev as he went out.

"I know. You can get her through it. Better a panic attack than a bullet."

Lissa went to catch his arm, but as fast as she was, he was out of reach, his eyes were flat and cold. "Just watch over her until I get back."

Rikki tried to make her feet move, to follow him. She didn't want him going out alone, not with a concussion. He was sick and dizzy, but he was functioning. That made her feel worse, guilty even. He managed. There was nothing wrong with her at all, but she was so upset over her sisters gathered under her roof that she couldn't move.

Lissa put a hand on the nape of her neck and pushed her head down. "Breathe, honey. We're by the door. If the house catches fire, we'll all get out safely. No big deal."

"Lissa's right," Blythe's tone was brisk. "Judith, have you had this happen before?"

"No. Never. But I do have allergies," Judith answered. She took another swallow of water. "That man is very, very dangerous."

"He's out there trying to protect us," Lissa reminded.

Airiana shook her head and stepped close to Rikki as

if to protect her. "Judith is right. We both can see auras and his is very strange. He carries many colors, but the colors are layered and surrounded by a deep red and then covered completely in black. The man lives with death and shadows. Whatever is inside him is eclipsed by his violent nature. I've never seen a man so dangerous."

Judith nodded. "The only two people who even come close to date have been Elle Drake's husband, Jackson, and even more dark is Joley's husband, Ilya Prakenskii. This man, this Levi Hammond, honestly, Rikki, he scares me."

Rikki forced air through her lungs, anger welling up in spite of her belief that they were right about Lev. She didn't like that they were saying aloud what she was thinking. He was violent. She couldn't argue with that, but that wasn't all there was to him—and they had given her a chance. Lord only knew if she was worthy of it. They were all convinced she didn't start fires, but who, besides her, had four homes burn down, two with people she loved in them?

Lissa put a gentle hand on Rikki's shoulder. "He went out the window like a pro. He's fast and silent, and I'm betting very efficient, but he was definitely in protection mode. He'd be handy out in her boat, or any other place for that matter."

Rikki shot her a grateful look. "If we're going to stay in this room, all together, I have to open the front door." There were beads of sweat dotting her forehead and her chest felt on fire, as if she was already desperate for air. She swore she could smell smoke.

"I'll get the door," Lissa assured. "You sit down before you fall down. Maybe Blythe can get you water."

Rikki shook her head. "Everyone should stay together."

She looked around. "Do you smell smoke? My eyes are burning."

Judith passed the glass of water to Lissa. "There's no smoke, Rikki. Take a drink. You'll feel much better."

Rikki inhaled deeply, trying to draw in air, terrified that she was reliving a nightmare that would never go away. Her feet and calves burned, a fierce, bone-wrenching pain. The scars had seemed a little less tight, but now they hurt as if newly formed. Usually they ached when she walked, the tight skin resisting stretching. Underwater she didn't have the problem—she even forgot about the scars until she was back on land.

Her house had been purposely designed so that she could look from the kitchen door, straight through her house all the way through the bedroom door that led to the back of the house. There were doors in almost every room leading to the outside, a safety net should there be a fire. She had wanted sprinklers, but with her penchant for nightmares and calling out for water, her house would have been destroyed in the first few months of occupation. She chose the chair she'd placed in her living room where she could see every door. The kitchen had only the screen door closed, so she had a good view of the outside.

"Lissa, open the front door and the back bedroom door, please," Blythe said. When Rikki started to protest, Blythe put a gentle hand on her. "She'll be in sight the entire time and she's very safe around fire. Your screen doors are dark so no one can see in but we can see out. You'll feel so much safer with the doors open. We'll all watch for anyone close to the house."

"I'll call Jonas," Airiana announced, reaching for the phone.

Rikki shook her head. "No. Not yet. I don't want to talk

to him. I'm too stressed and I don't know if I could handle it. Let Levi see what's out there. Maybe it's my imagination." She huddled in the chair, drawing her feet up off the floor, rubbing at her burning scars.

Lissa opened the back bedroom door and stopped to get Rikki's weighted blanket. "Take this, honey."

Rikki didn't see how cowering under her blanket was going to stop her from feeling guilty. She should be outside, helping Lev.

"He shouldn't be out there alone. He's hurt, Lissa. He really hit his head. He's had a terrible concussion. That's why I let him in the house. Someone had to take care of him."

The women exchanged relieved glances and Rikki realized that made sense to them, that she would bring him home to take care of him.

"You should have told us," Blythe said gently. "We could have helped you."

"I didn't want anyone else in the house," she muttered. That would make sense to them as well. They knew she was extremely leery of having anyone inside her house.

She looked around her at the faces looking back at her with so much open affection. "You thought he was using me, didn't you?"

There was an awkward silence. "He's gorgeous," Blythe said. "Any woman would take one look at him and fall at his feet."

"You mean like Judith and Airiana did?" The scent of smoke was fading as her mind cleared, slowly releasing her from the grip of a full-blown panic attack. She turned her gaze back to the outdoors. She wouldn't—*couldn't*—be comfortable with the people she loved gathered under one roof, so she would have to pull herself together in order to keep them safe. "Or just me? I'm not desperate for a man, you know. I'm quite happy here without one."

"Rikki, no one is saying you're desperate for a man," Judith objected, her voice every bit as gentle as Blythe's. "There are predators in this world, and they look for certain traits in women so they can use them."

"Certain traits?" Rikki sat up straighter, the scent of smoke dissipating altogether as her temper kicked in. "Just what are you saying?" She glared at them all. "No man is going to want to be with me because I'm so different? You think I don't already know that?"

"That's not what I said," Judith replied. "Nor do I think it's true."

"Yes, you do," Rikki said. "I think it, so why shouldn't you? I don't care. That's the important thing here. I honestly don't. I'm happy. I have a life. I don't like other people around touching my things. He used my dishes this morning. He doesn't eat peanut butter. Sheesh. He wants on my boat."

Blythe folded her arms and sat back in her chair. "Let's think about this."

"Let's not," Rikki said. "As soon as he's feeling better, he's gone. No one has to worry about whether or not I'm going to be so desperate for a man's attention that I let him use me." She glanced up at Judith. "Or abuse me, if that's what you're implying."

Judith shrugged. "You can get as angry as you want with me, Rikki, but if you think I'm going to back off from protecting my sister from a predator, you can just get over it. That man is no lamb. He's got teeth, and he's dangerous. It's not some small shadow surrounding him. He lives with violence."

Judith always managed to disarm her with affection.

And Rikki couldn't very well deny that Lev was a violent man. He'd put a knife to her throat and he was a walking weapon. But they'd given her a chance, and she saw something in him that apparently Judith and Airiana couldn't see. She saw *past* those shadows to something altogether different. But how could she explain what she didn't understand?

"I know what he's like, Judith. You have to trust me this time. He's much more than the protection he's wrapped himself in." Rikki looked up at the one person she knew she'd have to convince. Judith always amazed her with her insight into people. She was calm, where Rikki was stormy. She chose her words carefully, while Rikki often blurted out a response, if she bothered at all. "I'm asking as a personal favor to me that you give him a chance, Judith."

Judith sank down in front of Rikki and took both of her hands. "Tell me why you feel so strongly about him, honey. Make me understand."

Rikki shook her head. "I'm not like you. I'm not good with words. But I know him. I know him better than he knows himself. I see him. I can't tell you how, but I do. He needs us. All of us. We have to help him. He's lost—just like I was."

The women exchanged wary looks.

Judith sighed. "You were never violent, Rikki."

"You don't know that. You don't. You took it on faith that I didn't start those fires, but even I don't know for certain. It makes sense. Everyone else believes I did. And don't think Jonas Harrington hasn't had his suspicions about me. He watches me. I've seen him. You gave me a chance when there was no reason to and I'm asking you to do the same for him."

"And if you're wrong?" Blythe said.

"I'll keep him away from the rest of you. I'll be the only one in danger."

Judith shook her head. "Absolutely not acceptable. I'm sorry, baby, but if you take the risk, we all do."

Rikki looked around her. Each of the others nodded solemnly. There was no dissenting vote. It was up to her. How strongly did she feel about Lev? She barely knew the man. She rubbed the pad of her thumb over the center of her palm.

"Why are you doing that?" Airiana asked.

Rikki frowned. "What?"

"You're rubbing your palm. You've never done that before."

Airiana was frightening in her observation of detail. Rikki shrugged and turned her palm over, pressing it against her jeans. "No reason. I'm just confused about all this. I want to give Levi a chance."

Blythe glanced at the others and then nodded. "We're with you then."

10

LEV opened the window in the bedroom, grateful it slid up silently. Whoever was watching Rikki—and how the hell had they found her?—had some kind of psychic power. He'd felt the shift in energy. It hadn't been particularly powerful, but he noticed the two women who he had determined were the most sensitive to psychic forces had been the only ones really affected. Rikki had been with him all week, holed up in her house, so if this was about her, there had to have been a trail leading to her. And if it was about him . . . Well, no one was going to hurt her or the others because of his dubious past.

He did a rolling somersault, coming up on one knee, allowing a couple of seconds to orient himself in the surrounding terrain. The few minutes he'd managed to stay up he'd spent studying the house and the immediate acreage around it. He'd committed the map of the farm to memory so he was fairly certain he could find his way around, but it was imperative he scout Rikki's five acres as soon as possible. He needed to know every shrub and tree, every hollow. Where the tall grass was that might conceal someone. Everything. *Especially if he was going to make his home here.*

That brought him up short. What was he thinking? Living here? With Rikki? Men like him didn't have homes. They didn't have loved ones. Those things were liabilities to his kind. He'd been trained to move, to shed his identity fast and assume another one just as quickly. That was life. Trying to be someone was a certain road to death.

He moved as fast as his pounding head would allow him. Each jolt sent a dagger through his skull. His stomach lurched. He knew his head injury had been worse than he'd first imagined, but it was healing. He was speeding the process along as best he could, and now he needed to be at full operating capacity. He made his way up the terraced flower beds and began working his way over toward the northern side of her property up toward the tree line.

Sid Kozlov was dead. Did that mean Lev Prakenskii was as well? An image of Rikki's little frown filled his head. A few times, when he couldn't sleep and he just lay there beside her, aching, wishing, he fantasized that she was his. That the world he was in was real. Maybe this was his one chance. It was a miracle he'd survived the sinking of the yacht. Another miracle, that although he'd been slammed into the rocks by a powerful wave, he'd lived through it. And Rikki. *She* was the real miracle, with her quirky ways and her eyes that could see beyond his armor and straight to something he'd thought long gone.

Damn. He wanted her. He wanted this life. He wanted it to be real. Were there second chances? It was possible he'd have to walk away, but before he did, Rikki Sitmore was going to be safe. She would know that she didn't start fires in her sleep. She would know she hadn't killed her parents or fiancé, nor had she burned down the homes of her foster parents.

As he made his way through the trees, he tried to figure out what it was about her that appealed to him so much. Passion. She was passionate about everything she did. Everything she was. Who she was. He was fairly certain she had some form of autism, yet she had carved out a life for herself in spite of all the odds and she made it her own. She was the sea she loved so much, moody, joyful, playful, and at times stormy and wild. He was icecold, a passionless floe out in the arctic seas, alone and struggling for survival.

He had faced death every day of his life and never once had he flinched. He'd seen things that no man should ever have to see. He'd made decisions no man should ever have to make. Some might call him courageous, yet compared to Rikki, he saw himself as a coward. She took hold of life and lived it, in spite of her limitations. She forced herself out of her comfort zone for those she loved, while he stayed in his, behind his wall of armor, behind his survival instincts and his vast training.

He wanted life—with her. With Rikki. He wanted to lie awake at night and feel her next to him. He wanted to hear her breathing while she slept. He wanted to know that she couldn't tolerate anyone else in her bed—only him. He wanted to see her frown and the flash of her eyes, hear her breathing change right before he kissed her. They had a connection he didn't understand, but it didn't matter even though everything else in his life had to make sense. She didn't. She just was. And that was enough and that was everything.

He glanced up at the sky, watching until he spotted a hawk in the outer branches of a fir tree. He closed his eyes and summoned the predator, pushing it to take flight. Its talons dug into the branch for just a moment of resistance before the hawk spread its wings and glided into the air. The hawk began the search with a tight pattern, widening each circle as it took in a larger and larger radius.

Images poured into Lev's brain, but none of them were of what he was searching for. He released the hawk with a small nod of thanks, knowing even before he came up on the spot where he knew the intruder had been that the man was already gone. He still moved carefully, wanting to preserve evidence. The watcher had been much lighter than Lev. The storm had left the soil damp and there were impressions everywhere. Crushed grass and sunken boot prints, but not too deep, indicating a lighter build. The man was tall, though, because the needles had been knocked off several branches of the tree he'd been standing under at about an inch or so below Lev's height.

He liked fire. As Lev examined the ground, he had no doubts in his mind that this was the man who had stalked Rikki since she was thirteen, starting the fires that had destroyed her loved ones. Tiny bits of grass were burned in small clumps, as if, while idle, the man had started tiny fires to amuse himself. How long had he been up there? There were four cigarette butts and seven places where the grass was burned. Fortunately the entire area was soaked so there was little chance that the fire would have gotten out of hand, but Lev could see the potential for disaster. Fire generally burned uphill, but that didn't mean the stalker wasn't contemplating a massive strike.

Lev studied the house from this position. Rikki was in the habit of sitting on her kitchen porch each morning and having her coffee. There was a clear line of sight to the porch. The stalker could have been here observing her often, but Lev doubted it. There was no evidence that visits to this particular spot had occurred at any other time.

He tracked the boot prints through the trees back to the road. The man had scouted along the ridge, but he hadn't gone off the narrow deer trail. Lev didn't have the feeling the stalker was experienced in the woods. He'd avoided deeper woods and didn't try to go through heavier brush. He was no professional hit man. This wasn't about a contract. But how could it be personal when the trouble had started when Rikki was only thirteen?

Lev cast around for more signs, but as far as he could tell, whoever was watching her had only come this one time and had stood in the grove of trees above her house, watching long enough to smoke four cigarettes. Lev hadn't caught the smell of smoke, but the wind had been blowing toward Blythe's home.

"Next time," he whispered aloud. He knew with absolute certainty there would be a next time, but he'd be more prepared.

Rikki had set up security around her immediate home. She'd installed an amazing widespread sprinkler and water system throughout her yard and the farm. But she had no surveillance on the property anywhere. He would have to change that. He found where the stalker had parked the truck—not a car—and took note that the back tire was worn. He should have sent the hawk toward the road first.

"Next time," he repeated, and searched for more signs, trying to get a good picture of the man responsible for several murders.

He liked fire. There was no doubt in Lev's mind the stalker had been playing with it while he waited—almost

absently playing with it. Fire intrigued him. Maybe the
man even needed the crackling bright flames like some
addiction—or maybe in the same way Rikki needed water. Elements attracted one another. Could she have run
across another element as a child and this was a bizarre
war she didn't even know she was in?

He turned the idea over in his mind. He had to find a
way to get her to talk to him about the events leading up to
the fire, the days and weeks before the fire. The event was
so traumatizing he doubted if she remembered much before that. And right now, he wanted to lie down for a good
ten hours and try to keep his head from falling off. Unfortunately, he had a lot of work to do before he could rest.

With a small sigh, he made his way back to her home—
the home he wanted for himself. He found his gut tightening, hard knots developing, which was a little shocking. He
wasn't exactly a tense man, but then he'd never had anything this big at stake. He wanted to see her eyes when he
walked through the door. Rikki could hide a lot of things
behind her still face, but she couldn't hide anything she felt
behind those dark, liquid eyes.

Tension didn't suit him. He was a man who cared little about the pleasures in life. He had been programmed
nearly from birth to do a job—exterminate the enemy.
There had been no other way of life for him. His emotions
should have been gone—had been. He killed coldly and
efficiently, just as his handlers had taught him. There was
no room for emotion. Emotion meant mistakes and mistakes meant death. His life was in the hands of Rikki Sitmore and she didn't even realize it. Because if this didn't
work out and he made a mistake, they would send everyone after him and they'd never stop until he was dead. But
who the hell were "they"?

He glided onto the kitchen porch in silence before turning back to take a slow sweep of the surrounding trees. Closing his eyes, he reached out, sending his call to the birds foraging or making their homes in the trees. *Hear me. Watch. Call to me when we are disturbed.* He waited another moment until he felt the positive response. The network of spies and sentries would grow. Once he could show them what to look for, a single vehicle he wanted watched or, better yet, the actual man, he would have an unbeatable alarm system.

He stood in the doorway, his shoulders filling the entrance to Rikki's house—*home*. He inhaled, drawing the scent of it into his lungs. She was sitting in a chair with a clear view of the screened door, and he noted vaguely, somewhere in the back of his mind, how clever the design of the house had been, but he was utterly still inside, waiting for her to look up. Waiting to see his fate in her eyes.

He wasn't a praying man—men like him hoped there was no God to judge them, but he couldn't help the silent appeal stealing into his mind. *Let her choose me.* He'd chosen her with her quirky ways and her adorable frown. And God help him, he wanted to see that right now because it would mean she was serious. He wanted her to be serious about him.

She looked up, her eyes locking with his and his heart stopped. Everything in him went still. Settled. Anchored there in her dark gaze. She was worried. She was relieved. She was happy to see him. There was no smile, no outward sign, but all he needed was in the depths of her eyes. He stepped inside and closed only the screen door. Too many people together in the house made her crazy, and maybe that would never change. He didn't care if it ever did, as long as she could close the doors with him inside and she had that look in her eyes.

Lev smiled as he walked the short distance to her, through the kitchen and straight down the hall into the living room. He ignored her sisters, taking both her hands in his and pulling her close until he could wrap his arms around her and hold her tight against his chest. He needed the closeness more than she did right then. He wasn't used to his emotions being so close to the surface.

He registered Judith and Airiana exchanging a surprised and rather pleased expression, just as he noted the position of everyone in the room, the escape routes and the potential weapons. Observation was his way of life and that would never change, even though he was determined that Sid Kozlov and Lev Prakenskii were dead and buried for all time. He was never going to be anyone but what those nameless faces in his past had made him.

"I was worried," she murmured and reached up to trace his honed features.

"You shouldn't have been," he answered. *You can always reach out and I'll answer.*

Color swept into her face and she glanced back at the circle of interested faces. "Well, I was worried," she told her sisters a little belligerently.

Blythe nodded. "We can see that."

"I take it no one was out there," Lissa said. She didn't sound as if she believed that.

"Someone had been," Lev said. He needed to sit down before he fell down.

As if reading his mind, and maybe she was, Rikki took his arm and led him to the recliner, gently pushing him into it.

"I won't give you a lecture about wearing shoes in the house," she said. "This time."

"Sorry, *lyubimaya*." He leaned his head back because he couldn't help it. It felt good to be off his feet. He hadn't realized just how dizzy he was. "I'll remember."

"Tell me," Lissa insisted.

"He's a fire lover," Lev confirmed. "And he was watching Rikki. He smokes Camels. There were several cigarette butts there. I didn't touch them. While he was watching, he started seven small fires, just playing, but the potential could be disastrous. Fortunately, everything is soaked from the storm."

Rikki sucked in her breath, the color draining from her face. "Do you think he plans to start a forest fire?"

Lev studied her sisters' faces even as he took her hand, his thumb sliding over the center of her palm, tracing small circles there. "I don't know what he plans to do. If he wants to destroy everyone Rikki cares about, then none of your homes is safe."

Lissa lifted her chin. "He'll have to fight all of us."

Rikki shook her head. "No. No way. If he's found me, then I'm getting out of here. I'm not taking chances with any of your lives. Who is he? Why is he doing this to me?"

"And if he didn't know where you were, which he couldn't have or he would have been starting fires before this, then how did he find you?" Lev asked.

"You aren't leaving," Blythe said. "We're in this together."

The other women nodded and Lev liked them all the more for their united stand.

Judith snapped her fingers. "The news. Rikki, you were on the news the other night. I meant to tell you about it."

Lev scowled, his fingers tightening around Rikki's hand. He tugged until she was up against the chair. "What the hell were you doing on television?"

She shook her head, looking confused. "I have no idea what she's talking about. How could I get on the news, Judith?"

"When you came to the village and I went into Inez's store to get the soup for you," Judith reminded her. "Remember the place was crawling with news reporters. You were standing outside by your truck and then there was another shot of you sitting on the bluff with the sea behind you, right out on the headlands."

"I didn't notice anyone filming me."

"They were across the street filming everything. The man who owned the yacht was big news all over the world. And it was such a unique event, a methane gas bubble sinking a ship," Lexi added. "Very strange and sort of spooky. That's why so many scientists are here."

"They've thinned out a lot," Lissa pointed out.

"That's how he found Rikki," Lev said.

"I'm calling Jonas, Rikki," Blythe announced. "I know you're uncomfortable with anyone official, but he needs to know that someone's stalking you."

Rikki shook her head. "He'll think it's me, just like they all do, Blythe. None of them believed me. He'll read all the reports and he'll start watching me."

"Let him," Lissa said. "At least he'll be keeping an eye on things."

Rikki remained silent, but Lev could feel the thoughts racing through her head. She was close to tears, yet it didn't show on her face. She was going to leave them all, try to draw the danger away from them. All of them—even him.

"You're not leaving," Lev said quietly. "I know what you're thinking, Rikki, and no arsonist is going to take your life away again. I know you're saving my life. Maybe I'm supposed to be here to save yours." He said it aloud deliberately so she'd know he was serious. He stated it quietly yet firmly in front of her family, uncaring what they thought. "Do you trust me enough to stay and see this through?"

"And risk them?" Rikki gestured at her sisters. "They mean everything to me."

"Even if you're gone, there's no guarantee that he won't strike at you through them," Lev pointed out gently. "You've been inside my head, you know me. You know what I am. You know I can do this."

She shook her head. "No. I don't want you to go after him. You wanted this chance to be something—someone— different, and I'm not taking that away from you."

"A man has the right to protect his home, Rikki," Lev said. "And his woman." He wrapped his arm around her waist and pulled her to the arm of his chair. "That's what men do."

Airiana inhaled sharply and looked at Judith.

Blythe stood up. "Let's everyone just slow down. What is it, Judith?"

"His aura changes when he's close to Rikki," Airiana whispered. "Judith, did you see that? He's totally different when he's near her."

"I don't know what that means."

Rikki trembled, but she didn't move away from him. He knew in her mind that she was standing with him to protect him, not to commit to him, but her sisters saw it differently and he was damn well going to take her position in the same way they did.

"I tried to tell you earlier," Judith said. "Airiana and I

see auras, colors surrounding people. Every color you have around you, Rikki, is about water and compassion. You're incapable of starting a fire that would kill someone. Lissa has the colors of fire, bright and passionate, but she tempers those things with her protective instincts."

Lev held up his hand to stop her. "She's trying to say that my colors say something else, Rikki." The knots were back, but he kept all emotion from his face.

"You surround yourself with darkness, with violence and death," Judith said without flinching. "Yet when you're with Rikki, other colors pierce that shroud of darkness, almost as if when you're close to her, your true self emerges."

He forced a nonchalant shrug. "If one believes in that sort of thing." He didn't see auras, but he knew they existed. He'd known from the moment Judith and Airiana had approached the house that they were strong psychics. He didn't doubt for a moment that they saw death and violence surrounding him, but it was disturbing to know they caught glimpses *inside*, to the man he hid from the world—hid from himself.

He slowly let go of Rikki and forced himself out of the chair. His head nearly exploded. He needed a quiet place to try to keep healing the concussion, even if only for a few minutes. "If you ladies will excuse me for a time, I need to lie down."

It was true, but he was still retreating. Her sisters didn't trust him—but they wanted to for Rikki's sake. He'd made his claim in front of them, and while Rikki wasn't paying attention, they were, and they were a protective bunch.

Blythe followed him right into the bedroom and he turned a cool stare on her. She didn't flinch. In fact, there was steel in her dark chocolate eyes. "You'd better not hurt her."

He sank down onto the bed, mostly to keep from falling. He was more nauseated and dizzy than worried about appearances. "Is she autistic?"

Blythe shrugged. "I believe so. She certainly has acute sensory dysfunction, and if she is autistic, which we all believe, she's very high functioning. As far as we know, she's never been diagnosed, but she doesn't talk much about her past."

She put her hands on her hips and pinned him with what he could only interpret as a stern "mother" stare. It was very effective. The woman, as elegant and sweet as she appeared, could look intimidating.

"I don't want her taken advantage of."

He laid his aching head back on the pillow. "Do you really think that's possible? Rikki is very intelligent, and more than that, she's tough."

"She's also very fragile. I'm just saying, mean what you say or leave us alone."

"She's not starting those fires, Blythe. She's got someone out to destroy her for whatever twisted reasons he thinks he has. And he's found her. Go up to that ridge and examine it. He was there. I'm not leaving her to face him alone. You don't have to like me—none of you do—but I'm staying."

"Are you a man of your word?"

He thought that over. Was he? He didn't know if Lev Prakenskii was or if Sid Kozlov had been, but Levi Hammond would be. "Yes."

"And you'd never hurt her?"

"Not intentionally." He closed his eyes and allowed himself to sink further into his own consciousness. "Nor will I let anyone else."

"That's good enough for me."

He knew it wasn't. The moment she left, she would be going to someone she knew to have him investigated, and that didn't leave him much time to become Levi Hammond. Fortunately, he'd already done a lot of work on his new identity using Rikki's laptop, and if there was one thing he was exceptional at, it was creating identities. He was a ghost in a computer. There was no database he couldn't find a way to hack. And his online identity—the Phantom—was well known to hackers around the world. They owed him favors and would repay instantaneously when asked.

Levi Hammond already had a complete history, including a few parking tickets, a sea urchin diver's license in Alaska and up and down the coast of California. He had a tender's license, a social security number, a driver's license, a college education and extensive travel on his passport. He also had a gun permit. He'd learned diving in Japan.

His one problem was with the sea urchin divers here on the coast. It was a small group and most of them knew one another—or at least of one another. If he was lucky, no one would ask them about Levi Hammond until he had a chance to meet them and impress memories of him upon them, another talent that served him well. Whoever Blythe asked to check up on him would no doubt be a cop, and they'd look up his criminal history.

"Be careful," he said as Blythe turned to leave. "All of you. Remember, this man killed Rikki's parents and her fiancé. He's just as likely to go after one of you."

Blythe nodded. "We'll be alert. We were prepared for this to happen. We all figured that if he struck at her four times, the chance that he'd do it again would be very high. All of us have security systems, smoke detectors and sprinkler systems." She looked up at the ceiling. "Rikki's got plenty of smoke alarms, but we couldn't install a sprinkler system in her house."

"She had a nightmare the other day," he conceded. "I saw what happened."

Blythe raised an eyebrow. "And that didn't scare you off?"

"I don't get scared off easily," he said. "Rikki has gifts, incredible gifts. If most people want to look at the surface and never see what's inside of her, that's their loss. I'm happy to keep her to myself."

"If you're with Rikki," Blythe warned, "then you're with us."

He smiled and closed his eyes again. "I got that, Blythe, and I'm fine with that."

He heard her leave the room and listened to the low murmur of voices as they talked more with Rikki. He didn't want to leave her alone with her sisters. They had indicated they were willing to give him a chance, but he knew they didn't like it. None of them—well, maybe Lissa would prove to be his ally. She understood his nature more than the others, but even she would want to protect Rikki from a man like him.

He respected them, even understood their need to watch out for Rikki, but he wasn't going to let them influence her away from him. He didn't deserve her, he knew that, but this was his one chance. He'd never met a woman who could make him lose control, who could make his body hard and his heart soft. Something had happened there beneath the sea, and if he chose to view it as a personal miracle, a second chance, then no one had the right to take it away from him—not even her sisters.

He heard the soft footfall of Rikki's bare feet as she

padded into the room. "Lev? Do you need something for your headache?"

He wanted to open his eyes and drink her in, but he waited. "Are they gone?" He knew they were—she was calling him Lev again. He shouldn't allow it, but he liked the way the name rolled off her tongue so intimately. He craved the sound of Rikki's voice. That soft monotone soothed him.

She sat on the edge of the bed and the coolness of her hand slid over his forehead. "Yes, they've gone home. You shouldn't have rushed off like that without help. You haven't even been up for more than a few minutes at a time."

He opened his eyes then, needing to see the proof of her concern, the soft look in her eyes, the slight frown to her mouth. He didn't really remember much about his mother, and he'd certainly never had anyone fuss over him. He doubted if he would have tolerated or liked it from anyone else but Rikki. From her—he needed that anxiety and care.

"We've got to go into a town, Rikki. I need to go to an Internet café, someplace where I can use a computer," Lev announced. His head hurt like a son of a bitch and all he wanted to do was lie down, but he'd set the ball rolling before he had everything up and running. He had to finish putting his identity in place, and fast. Her sisters weren't going to just let him into Rikki's life without knowing who he was. That meant a post office box and sending for necessary documents. He had to concoct a plausible story for losing everything as well. He needed an exit plan too—for both of them. Just in case his past came knocking.

"You can use my laptop." She gave him her little look,

the one that said she knew what he'd been up to. "You've been using it regularly already."

He caught her hand and pressed her fingers against his lips. "I don't want anything traced back to you. Better we use a public computer." Afterward, he'd upload a slow-moving virus that would corrupt the hard drive over several days until eventually it would have to be replaced. If his hacking raised red flags anywhere, the computer would be long gone, discarded by the café, and no one would ever remember who had used it.

She studied his face. "Did you remember something?"

He'd promised himself he wouldn't lie to her. "None of it's good, Rikki. I'd like to be able to tell you I'm a good man, but I don't think I am."

Her gaze never wavered. "As long as you don't lie to me, we'll be all right, Lev. I'd rather hear the truth, no matter what it is."

"And if you can't take it?"

"I'll tell you."

He searched her face. The woman was courageous, he had to hand her that. She meant what she said. "I want to go the nearest big town."

She laughed. "We don't have big towns here, Lev. Fort Bragg is about eight miles or so from here. That's as big as we get. And no, we're not a military base."

"Let's go then." He'd been to Fort Bragg. He recognized the name. That meant he'd already set up an exit and an emergency plan for Sid Kozlov.

"Are you certain you're up to this?"

"If I don't get it done, your sisters will have the cops here throwing me out."

Rikki didn't argue with him. "You'll need clothes as well."

"And diving gear."

"Not a chance. No way. You're not coming on my boat."

He couldn't help giving her a smug look. "Even Blythe thinks it's a good idea."

"Yeah, well, Blythe isn't the captain."

He caught the nape of her neck and drew her head down toward his, eyes open wide and staring into hers. He felt like he'd waited hours, weeks, a lifetime, to feel his mouth on hers again. He gave her the opportunity to pull away from him. He didn't want to push her too hard. He knew he had to give her time to accept him into her life. And touching was hard for her. He had noticed the way she held herself when her sisters had hugged her or took her hands. She never pulled away, but she never relaxed either.

She didn't relax now either, but she didn't resist. Her eyes went that beautiful liquid black, and they were so inviting. Then her lashes fluttered and his mouth was on hers, her lips soft and warm and accepting. He didn't have to coax her this time. She opened for him and he found his sanctuary. The world just slid away until there was only Rikki and the man she saw, the man inside that dark armor of violence and death.

She tasted like freedom. Like life. Like a fucking miracle. Her mouth moved on his and then she gave herself to him. He felt the tension in her fade—that complete stillness she had was gone. She relaxed into him, a soft warmth that made him more of a man and less of a killing machine. She brought out every good thing left in him, traits he had never known he had. She found the man he should have been. It was as if she knew his every battle, his every demon, as if she could accept the broken pieces that were all that was left of him. She knew he was a shadow, nothing more, but she was putting him back together, piece by piece, with her complete acceptance.

He felt safe with her. He'd never been safe with another human being, not since he'd been taken as a child from his home. He'd never been able to trust. He could never give that last small piece—all that was left of his humanity— into someone else's keeping. And now there was Rikki. She let him be whatever he had to be to survive. She didn't ask anything of him. There was no hidden motive. No agenda. Just acceptance. She was different—imperfect, or so she thought—and she knew what it was like to fight to carve out a space for herself. She was willing for him to do that.

He realized he had shifted her and had one hand bunched in her hair while he devoured her mouth. He wanted to feel her skin beneath his fingertips. His body ached to touch her, to feel her warmth and softness without the thin layer of clothes between them, but he forced himself to be satisfied with her delicious mouth. With the solace she offered so freely. Her body blanketed his and she couldn't fail to notice that he was heavily aroused, but she didn't seem to be afraid. She seemed as lost in his kisses as he was in hers.

"We have to stop," he murmured. He wasn't a saint by any stretch of the imagination and in another few minutes he'd lose all good sense.

She pulled back instantly, sitting beside him, her eyes on his face. Her mouth was swollen from his kisses, her hair wild, and her eyes were drenched in desire. He almost dragged her back into his arms, but she was too still, like an untamed animal making up its mind whether to stay or go. He wasn't giving her any reason to go.

"I love kissing you," he whispered, and touched her mouth. "I could kiss you forever." She poured herself into her kiss, giving him everything she was. It was easy to want to give back.

She was silent for a long time, just looking at him. Her smile was slow in coming, but it was heart-stopping. "Funny thing, I kind of like kissing you."

There was a tiny note of teasing in her voice, but mostly there was surprise, more than surprise—shock even, as if she couldn't quite believe it herself.

"I'll take whatever you've got for a headache and let's get going."

Rikki didn't move. She continued to sit on the edge of the bed, her enormous black eyes staring straight into his. For a long moment she was very still, and then she lifted her hand and began tracing his face with the pads of her fingers as if memorizing the bone structure. His heart accelerated, began a pounding that matched the beat in his groin. He loved the way she brought his body to life—the hard, fast need that slammed into him like a well-timed punch. Every nerve ending leapt to life and his blood ignited like rocket fuel, when normally there was ice water in his veins.

"Lev, I'll see this through with you."

His gut tightened. She read him so much better than he thought possible. Or maybe she was as much in his head as he was in hers—and that could be dangerous for both of them. He had things in his head people would kill for.

He couldn't stop himself from touching her, stroking caresses over her arm as she mapped his face. "And if the things I've done are worse than what this stalker has done to you? What then, Rikki?"

Her eyes never wavered. "Then you make up your mind that you're a different person and start again."

"Just like that? You could accept me even knowing I've hurt others?" His throat nearly closed on him, cutting off his air. "Maybe someone like you?"

"I know what it's like to battle every day of my life just for acceptance, just to survive," she said softly. "You're safe here, Lev. You can be who you really are."

"What if I don't know who that is?"

She smiled, her expression so tender he felt nearly paralyzed. "Then you have plenty of time and a safe place to find out." Abruptly she dropped her hand from his face. "I'll find the aspirin."

He caught her hand and held her captive. When she turned back toward him, he felt the jolt through his entire body from the impact of her eyes. She saw him. That was her gift. She saw inside of him and the rest of it didn't matter. She was wholly focused on him, an intense connection that he knew he'd never have with another human being.

"What is it?" Again her voice was incredibly gentle.

"I need to kiss you again." Because he was drowning. He'd lost his footing and he'd sunk hard and fast. He desperately needed an anchor. She was turning him inside out and he wasn't doing a thing to stop it.

Rikki didn't ask questions nor did she hesitate. She slid her hands up his chest and lowered her head toward his. He saw her eyes go liquid and fire with passion, all that cool water flashed so hot that he imagined steam rising around them. He closed his own eyes and just let her sweep him away, take him to paradise.

He hadn't imagined a world of feeling, of passion. He

hadn't known he could feel this way, so hot and achy and on the verge of loss of control. Arousal spread like a tidal wave, up his thighs, tightening his gut and chest. His lungs burned for air. And his cock was heavy and full, an urgent demand. All the while his heart pounded and his breath came in ragged gasps. The feeling was wonderful.

11

"WAIT, stop here," Lev said, and stuck his head out of the truck to look back at the storage facility they'd just passed.

He knew he'd been in the Internet café Rikki took him to at least one other time—*before* the yacht sank. He knew which computer he'd used and he chose it a second time. Rikki hadn't come in with him. She'd tried, but in the end she waited in her truck. He'd spent a great deal of time in the café, but when he returned, she showed no signs of impatience. She had a cup of coffee and was listening to music, and she smiled as soon as he got into the truck.

He was grateful that she'd thought to get him coffee as well. Moving around hadn't helped with the headache, and he was determined to get as much accomplished as fast as possible since they were out in public. He didn't want to attract attention, but he needed clothes and he knew he'd left a couple of suitcases somewhere—ready for a quick exit. He needed to orient himself again and find where he had left them. He had her drive around for a while, while he sipped the coffee and tried to remember.

"I recognize this place," he affirmed. "I've been here before."

Rikki pulled a U-turn and stopped the truck just outside the high chain link fence. "Why would this place be familiar?"

"I always leave a suitcase with money, passport, ID and clothes for a quick emergency exit in several places." He carefully assessed the area. He could see the security camera was broken. He remembered throwing a rock with accuracy to make certain no pictures of him were captured on film. The camera hadn't been fixed.

"Several places?" she echoed. "Why several?"

"I believe in being prepared," he explained absently, his attention on the storage facility. "Which is why we're going to add security to your house. You need to take better precautions."

"Did you rent a space under the name Sid Kozlov?"

He shook his head. "Too dangerous. If I was on the run, I could be traced through that name. I always use a clean identity." So even his handlers couldn't trace him. One never knew when a hit might be ordered to clean up a mess. He trusted no one, least of all the people who had robbed him of his parents, family and childhood to train him to be a top operative. He was a tool, nothing more, and when his usefulness was at an end, they wouldn't hesitate to kill him.

Rikki touched his arm to bring his attention back to her. The moment their eyes met, he experienced a strange pain in the vicinity of his heart, like a vise gripping him hard. That expression, so close to tenderness, nearly shredded his heart. "How terrible to have to live like that. I've been afraid and angry and guilty for too many years of my life, and I've found peace here, Lev. I hope that you do as well."

She *was* peace. That's what she didn't fully understand. Looking into her eyes, touching her skin, kissing her mouth . . . Hell, just watching the expressions come and go in her eyes gave him an immeasurable gift. *I could look at you forever.*

He swallowed what he'd been about to say, because nothing would be right. There was no way to express what he felt without sounding like a complete lunatic.

She smiled at him. "You don't sound like a lunatic, you sound sweet."

He grinned like an idiot. He should have known they were connected, but the flood of warmth was worth sounding like such a fool. "There's nothing sweet about me," he warned.

Her smile widened. "Really? Because I'm thinking the color red suits you very well."

He touched his face. Color had crept beneath the permanent tan of his skin. "That's a first." He leaned over and kissed her, brushing his lips lightly across hers just for the thrill. "Stay here. I'll be back in a few minutes."

"I feel like the gangster's moll in the movies." She leaned out the window and watched him walk around the truck. "Are there weapons in there?"

"Of course."

She laughed and shook her head.

Lev's head jolted the moment he put his feet on the ground and began walking, but her soft laughter changed everything. Nothing mattered. Not pain. Not what was in that storage unit. Only Rikki and the way she just let him find his way. He had his identity in place and he'd sent away for his "lost" items. He even managed a police report in San Francisco where poor Levi Hammond had been mugged. His mother was Russian, his father American. He was born in Chicago. He liked his new past. It was all very normal.

He let his mind rest while he went on autopilot. His body found its way to the third row, where several smaller units were housed in a long line, all looking exactly the same. It didn't matter, his feet took him to the eighteenth mini garage. Using the hem of his shirt, he punched in his code. He kept the code the same, as one nobody would know but him. Nevertheless, he entered the storage unit with extreme caution, going on full alert the moment the door unlocked.

Before entering the enclosed room, he went very still, reaching with his senses, ensuring there was no one lying in wait. Next he inspected the door itself for hidden traps before cautiously stepping inside. The suitcase was exactly positioned where he left it, but he didn't approach it. He studied the floor for signs of disturbance first. There was a light sprinkling of dust over the concrete surrounding the single shelf where the suitcase rested. He could see no prints and the spiderwebs were intact. Still, he was careful as he made his approach, studying the case from every angle before he touched it.

He was tempted to open it and inspect the contents, but he didn't want to chance being discovered, better to walk away while no one was around. He walked back to the truck and slid in. "Let's get out of here."

Rikki obediently started the engine and drove onto the highway, a small frown on her face. "You think someone is going to come after you, don't you?"

"Yes." His reply was deliberately abrupt, clipped, a signal to back off.

"But if you were Sid Kozlov, won't everyone think you died? The odds of you surviving were minuscule. They have to believe you're dead. They only recovered a few bodies, it's a big ocean. Eventually others may wash onto shore, but that isn't guaranteed and the more time that passes, the less likely it is."

He kept his eyes on the rearview mirror. "They won't accept that I'm dead, Rikki. They'll come looking." She glanced at him, but he didn't look at her—he was too busy watching the road around them. "Do you want to go to the boat?" he asked.

"Yes, but we're not going to," she said firmly. "I'm taking you home and you're going to rest. You've been up too much today. And who is 'they'? Have you figured that out?"

He shrugged, not arguing with her. He wanted her to at least be on the water, even for a short time in the harbor, but he was hanging on by a thread. "I'll tell you when we're in bed. In the dark."

"I'm fine with that."

Rikki drove in silence, wanting Lev to rest. She found herself enormously pleased that he'd wanted to go to the boat. That told her he was aware that she had difficulties if she was away from the water too long. A storm was supposed to hit around midnight, and she intended to sit in her swing on the porch and enjoy every second of it. Lev was looking gray beneath his skin. She doubted if anyone else would have noticed the changes in him, but she was aware of every breath he took, and he was hurting again.

When she would have turned onto the road leading to

the farm, Lev stopped her. "Keep driving. Isn't there a back entrance?"

"I can take the road just past this entrance, but it's much longer and leads through the forest, so it's quite a distance coming in through the back. The back gate is kept padlocked."

"I take it that no one travels on that road?"

"Rarely. There's two undeveloped properties off this road and I've never seen anyone come out this far, but then I don't take it that often." She glanced at him. "It's really long."

"Good. Drive in about a mile and then stop on the road and let me examine it."

"For what?"

"It rained, remember? This is a dirt road. I'll recognize the tire tracks of the bastard stalking you."

She turned that over in her mind, afraid to hope. "Lev, are you certain there was someone up on the ridge?"

"I told you I wouldn't lie to you and I won't. He loves fire, Rikki. It would be too big of a coincidence that someone shows up, watching the house and starting small fires just to pass to the time, and he not be the man responsible for the things that have happened to you."

"But it doesn't make any sense. What could I have done at thirteen to make him hate me so much that he was willing to kill people?"

"It doesn't have to make sense to us, *lyubimaya*, it only has to in his mind."

She liked the way he called her that name, the only time he used a Russian accent; otherwise, his American accent was perfect. "How many languages do you speak, Lev?"

He shrugged and continued looking out the window,

examining the ground as she slowed to make it easier. The
road was unkempt, cutting through heavier forest to circle
the farm's acreage. There were two sets of tire marks marring the muddy road, as if two vehicles had traveled there
in front of them. Both led to a gate to another property,
the only evidence of others anywhere on the long winding
road.

"Your neighbor," he asked.

"That property is undeveloped. We actually thought
about trying to buy it, but it's priced a little too high for us
right now."

He sat up straighter. "Stop for a minute." The tracks
indicated that one of the vehicles had driven back out the
way they'd come, but the other had turned the opposite
way and was following the route around the farm. Lev got
out and crouched low to examine the tire tracks. He recognized the tread on one of the vehicles. The same truck
had been parked on the ridge above Rikki's house.

The man had driven in, following a second vehicle,
possibly a real estate agent, and then after the first vehicle
left, he had waited for a while, presumably until whoever
had come with him was gone. While he waited, the man
had smoked the same brand that Rikki's stalker had
smoked. Lev cast around looking for more evidence. He
found what he was looking for just beyond the gate. Small
burn circles in the grass. The stalker had been playing
with fire again. This time, he'd been more creative. The
circles were in a pattern.

Lev walked around the area, studying it from all angles.
He had a continual map in his head and the arrangement of
the circles seemed familiar, as if he'd seen the design before. If he was right, and he would bet his life on it that
he was, the burned areas in the grass were a blueprint of

Rikki's five acres, everything from the trees to the terraced gardens and the house itself. The arsonist had studied the topography of the farm, paying close attention to the five acres belonging to Rikki.

"What is it?" she called.

He straightened slowly. "I believe this man means to come after you again and he's planning an attack."

She didn't flinch. She kept her eyes on his face. "Are the others in danger?"

He shook his head. "I have no way of knowing for certain, but so far, his battle plans seem very concentrated on your immediate property." He climbed back into the truck. "Keep driving. You can see his tracks in the road. I need to see every place he's gone."

Rikki tightened her hands on the steering wheel until her knuckles turned white, the only sign of her agitation, but she drove slow and steady.

"He doesn't know about me," Lev murmured, trying to reassure her.

"He's got to know you're in the house," she argued, "He probably thinks you live with me. You're in as much or more danger than I am."

"I do live with you and he doesn't know a damn thing about me."

Her laughter was unexpected and unraveled a few of the knots in his belly. "I don't know a damn thing about you either, Lev, and you probably don't know much more than I do."

"It's coming back," he told her, his tone grim. His memory was definitely returning, and little of it was good. "And anyone stalking you is in for a nightmare." He wasn't a passive man. He didn't believe in waiting for the enemy

to strike. He struck first and hard, and ended the war before it ever began, but he didn't think it necessary to tell
her that.

He noted a high chain-link fence starting. "And does
this fence actually surround your entire farm?"

"Not the entire three-hundred-plus acres," Rikki said.
"We don't have that kind of money, even with all of us
pooling our resources. The fence surrounds the main part
of the farm where we grow food and herbs. The orchards
aren't fenced either."

She turned onto a dirt road. "We're on our property
now. We keep this road up ourselves. Lexi can handle a
tractor or a backhoe like a pro. She's amazing."

"She's very young. Did she grow up on a farm?"

Rikki stiffened and stared straight ahead, compressing
her lips. It was more than obvious that the sisters didn't talk
about one another. She might tell Lev whatever he wanted
to know about herself, a rare thing for her, but she would
never disclose her chosen sisters' pasts to anyone else—not
even to him. And maybe especially not to him.

Lev didn't press her. She was being unreasonably kind
and generous to him. He'd never met anyone like Rikki
before, and he wasn't about to push her to reveal anything
she was uncomfortable with. He'd been making conversation with her, trying to get more of a feel for the women
she loved.

"It doesn't matter, *lyubimaya*. Keeping your sister's
confidence is far more important than answering."

"It's just that I feel that each of us has a right to decide
who knows us to that extent. I'm telling you things about
myself I've only told them, but I'm giving that to you with
no strings. I'm okay with being different. I'm not hiding it

from you or anyone else. I like my life, Lev. In fact I'm very happy with it. I'm choosing to share with you because I want to."

He touched her face, his fingers trailing over her soft skin, her high cheekbones and stubborn chin. "If you're trying to tell me that you don't need me or any other man in your life, I'm well aware of it. I'm saying I need you."

He should have been hesitant, or even embarrassed or ashamed to admit it to her, but he wasn't. It was now or never. Sink or swim. Live as a human being, or die in the void that had been his life. He wanted out. And Rikki was his savior. He felt it with every fiber of his being.

There was little left of his humanity, just this one small piece that he was handing into her keeping. If she took it, if she chose to allow him to build a new life around her, there was a chance for him. It wasn't what the experts or the storybooks said was a good or healthy relationship, but it was all there was for someone like him. He needed one human being to see him. He could only afford one. Some higher power had chosen Rikki. Fate. Whatever. It didn't matter—all that mattered was that he had been offered a chance and he was determined to grab it with both hands.

Rikki's smile was slow in coming. "Men like you don't need women like me, Lev. Or any woman, for that matter."

"You're exactly what I need." The pad of his thumb stroked over her lips. "You're all that I need. I've told you I won't lie to you and I meant it."

Rikki took her eyes off the road long enough to look at him. He could see she was skeptical and maybe a little confused. She shook her head and turned her attention back to her driving. "We're coming up on the back gate and paved road now. This leads through the orchards to the main part of the acreage Lexi farms. We have olive trees over there. We don't have our own press yet, but we're part of a co-op that owns a press together."

"This operation is enormous."

Her face lit up. "It's pretty awesome. The farm was in ruins when we took over. You should have seen us out there putting up all the fences and building the homes. Lexi mostly took care of the orchards and began planting crops. We have an amazing greenhouse where we grow all year round. The weather here is too cold for most things during the winter months."

As if hearing her, the wind picked up and the sky darkened as clouds blew overhead, rolling and churning, heavy with rain. Rikki glanced up and her hands relaxed on the steering wheel. The road widened and he caught a glimpse of a large house off to his left.

"Whose place is that?"

"That's actually the communal area. We have a gym for working out and a meditation center. Lissa has been working on a training area that's really nice. You might like to use it if you do that sort of thing."

He wanted to smile. Sometimes she was like sunshine with her quirky little ways and the things she said or thought. "He drove through your farm, Rikki. How did no one see him?"

"It's a big place and most of us aren't home during the day, only Lexi, and she could have been anywhere."

They were silent as she drove back to her house and parked the truck. Lev watched her check the ground around the house and each of the windows, taking her time as drops of rain began to fall. She lifted her face to the sky and smiled, holding out her hands as if in welcome. She stood there, focused on the drops, lost in the beauty of individual beads. He found himself caught up in her magic, the childlike awe in her face, her expression one of absolute wonder.

He couldn't help himself, he reached out telepathically, wanting to share the moment with her, *needing* to feel what she was feeling. Awareness burst through him, soothing, calming—he marveled at such perfection, at the actual feel of cool water on warm skin. He was astonished at the myriad of sensations pouring over and into him. The sky glittered with diamond tears, each more perfect than the last, each one multifaceted. For a moment he was caught up in a fascination with nature, just as she was. He'd never noticed raindrops in detail, nor had he ever paid attention to how they felt on his skin.

There was a sensual feel to the pattern of drops, or maybe he was so connected to her that, as usual, when he was close to her, his body came alive. Even that was amazing to him—the fact that he could become full and hard without willing himself to do so. Wrapped in the fresh scent of the rain, he stood beside her and lifted his face to watch the wonder of the drops as they came toward him from the sky. They were crystal prisms bursting over his skin like tongues.

This is incredible.

His mind brushed against hers, an intimacy deeper than anything he'd ever known. His left palm itched and without thinking he lifted his hand and rubbed the center with his stubbly beard. Rikki gasped and swung around to face him, breaking the spell of the raindrops. Her eyes were wide with shock.

He stared into her eyes, those dark pools of mystery that intrigued him so much, and then she turned away from him abruptly to unlock the door and let him in. She stepped way back to allow his entry, but as he strode past her, he brushed his hand over her hair. He loved those shiny sun streaks in all that thick, dark hair. She always looked as if the sun had kissed the top of her head, something he seemed to have the impulse to do quite regularly.

It was a strange thing to look into his past, a black void of duty and discipline, to see the seamiest side of the world, to accept his fate, to know he was trained to kill. Never in those years had he considered any other way of living. In fact, the worse the crimes he witnessed, the more he was determined to rid the world of its corrupt and ugly underbelly. He never once thought himself part of that world. He never considered that he might be doing wrong. He followed his orders and he carried them out without question. It was almost as if he had awakened there in the sea, there in the depths of her eyes, as corny as that sounded to him.

Something had changed inside of him and he'd been reborn. His handlers would come, and if they realized he was still alive, they would never stop until they found him. Sid Kozlov had to remain buried at sea, and the new Levi Hammond had to have a past that could stand up to any scrutiny. He stroked his developing beard thoughtfully. Facial hair and a fisherman's wardrobe would add a layer of protection. If he worked out at sea and remained a recluse as much as possible, laying low for a long time until Hammond was established, he would have a chance at life.

He put the case on the kitchen table in plain sight of Rikki. He wasn't going to hide anything from her. There had to be one person in the world he trusted enough to give his last shred of humanity to. If she couldn't accept him, there would be no one else. Behind him Rikki locked the door and leaned against it, her gaze steady, focused on him and not the case.

Lev studied the lock. It appeared to be intact and with no scratches on it. He crouched low to get eye level. He could hear Rikki breathing, slow and steady, but she didn't move or make any other sound. She simply waited.

He punched in the code and slowly lifted the lid. There was cash, stacks of it, all in American money. Beneath the money were passports and a kit for making additional identities. He put them all aside to reveal two sets of casual clothes. Beneath the clothes were more weapons as well as a small laptop.

"You know how to pack," Rikki observed, her tone strictly neutral.

He glanced at her as he carefully inspected each weapon before gathering them all together and transporting them to the bedroom. Rikki stepped forward and peered into the briefcase, her hands behind her back, that familiar little frown on her face. Lev found himself smiling all over again as he returned and gently but firmly moved her out of his way by lifting her and placing her a foot to one side.

"You might think about food," he said.

"You might think about putting that money in the bank," she countered. "Someone is going to rob you."

He tossed a grin at her over his shoulder. "Who would that be, Rikki? No one knows about the money."

"Me. I'm going to rob you. I happen to have a bedroom filled with weapons. I think I could take you," she added, still staring at the money.

He laughed softly. "I'll spare you the trouble. If you want it, it's yours. I've got at least four more briefcases stashed with the same sum in them and a bank account I've directed money to for years. I'm damn good on a computer, Rikki. When I've come across major corporate conspiracies, I've managed to redirect the cash flow without anyone being able to trace it."

She swallowed hard. "You stole money."

"From criminals." Usually before he exterminated them. "And I received hefty paychecks for certain assignments." Ones he would tell her about if she asked, but he sure wasn't volunteering information. He indicated the money. "Take it if you want it. You certainly have shared with me."

She shook her head and stepped back. "Don't joke about things like that. I'm going into the living room."

It was his turn to frown. He followed her as far as the doorway. She sank down into her favorite chair and began to rock slowly back and forth. He doubted if she was even aware of it. His first instinct was to go to her and kneel down so that he could look into her eyes and see what she was thinking, but with the way she was holding herself, he feared she was already on overload and needed some space.

They hadn't really been apart for very long since she pulled him out of the ocean. He thought he would have difficulties spending so much time with someone when he'd never done it, yet something had happened to him there in the sea. She was struggling to integrate him into her life and it was obvious that change wasn't her forte. He went into the bedroom and found her weighted blanket. She didn't move or look at him while he tucked it around her, but some of the tension went out of her. He stepped back out of the room and left her alone.

He'd never been in a situation where he was unsure of himself. He knew she was drawn to him and their connection was getting stronger, but she was still reluctant at the thought of sharing her peaceful haven with anyone else. He couldn't blame her; giving up hard-won peace for someone like him was a lot to ask.

He stood over the briefcase, staring down into its contents. Too many names. Which one, if any, was really him? He'd been born Lev Prakenskii, but that boy had disappeared long ago. He should never have given his name as Lev, a distinctly foreign name. He'd told Rikki the truth—they would send someone to confirm his death and he'd left a loose end. Someone—Ralph—had seen Rikki put him in her truck the day the yacht sank. He could try to "push" the memory, but as a rule, sea urchin divers were mavericks, freethinkers, nonconformists, and that made suggestions difficult. Rikki hadn't responded to his occasional push.

Ralph worked off the platform for a processing company. If he wasn't a diver, Lev had a chance of making it work. Or he could just kill him. He pressed his fingers to his eyes. How could one shed an old life by starting the new one with the death of an innocent? He swore under his breath. The briefcase brought up a lot of memories he'd rather forget. If he was any kind of a man, he'd walk away from her and leave her untouched by the life he led, but he'd had a taste of freedom, a glimpse of a kind of paradise, and he wanted it so much he couldn't find the strength to walk away.

He hid the stacks of money in several places and secreted a passport and ID with each stash. His radar went off as he was putting his jeans in her closet. Someone was approaching the house. He stuck his head into the living room. "Rikki? We're about to have company."

She pressed her hands to her ears and didn't look at

him, continuing to rock gently back and forth. She stared forward at the large kaleidoscope built into the wall. It was moving, a rolling ocean, waves tumbling and churning. It was one of the coolest things he'd ever seen and he'd have to ask her how it worked. She was totally focused on it and evidently needed to be. He shrugged, checked his gun and headed outside.

Night was falling, and he preferred to be in the shadows where he could see what was coming at him. Most likely it was one of her sisters. He didn't feel a threat at all, but as always, he remained cautious, stepping back into the darkness, just off the porch. The position offered him a good view of the surroundings as well as the road. He studied the ridge. There was no one up there at the moment, but he expected they would have company soon. The nervous small fires told Lev that Rikki's stalker wasn't a patient man.

He recognized Blythe, Rikki's oldest sister. He knew instinctively that Blythe wielded a lot of power in Rikki's life. There had not only been love in Rikki's eyes, but also a deep respect. Her gaze shifted often to the nose of the other sisters, but not Blythe. She looked Blythe in the eye, which to him meant that she believed Blythe could accept her as she was.

He shoved his gun into his waistband at the small of his back and stepped out of the shadows before she pulled into the circular drive. He bent as if checking a hose and straightened slowly, watching as she got out of the car. She flashed him a quick smile. "I brought food. We decided that until you were up and around, we'd take turns cooking for you. Otherwise, you'd be living on peanut butter."

"That's very generous of you but not necessary. I can cook . . ."

"Believe me, Levi, it's necessary," Blythe interrupted. "Rikki can't take a lot of change at once. She needs plenty of time to process and get used to the idea. Her kitchen is sacred to her. It took me months to get her to let me inside to get my own coffee, and after I leave, I'm betting she wipes all the imaginary fingerprints off her cabinets and sink."

"You'd be right about that. I've seen her do it." He glanced toward the house. "She's upset right now. She's sitting in her favorite chair staring at her kaleidoscope. She's rocking."

Blythe nodded. "It calms her. We put in wood floors so she doesn't have to use a vacuum cleaner. The noise hurts her and she can't cope with it at all. Fluorescent lights do the same thing, although she says in a different way. And never wear corduroy, it hurts her skin. She's extremely intelligent, never think she isn't, but when she doesn't want to talk to you, she won't and nothing you say or do will change her mind. Rikki's her own person and she has a good life here. It's been difficult for her."

"I hear your warning."

"Are you hearing what I'm saying about Rikki? Before you turn her world upside down, you make very sure you're prepared for what her world has to be. You have a choice. She doesn't. Certain things have to be in place for her to cope."

"Such as?" Lev prompted.

"Cooking. She's not going to be able to handle grocery shopping or cooking. Not ever. She isn't going to miraculously get better and do it for you when you're having a bad day."

"She made me soup," he pointed out.

"She heated up the can outside, not in the kitchen."

"Then she found a way, didn't she?" Lev countered with a small shrug. "Maybe I don't have as much of a choice as you think I do. Rikki matters to me. I can't tell you why or even how it happened, but I've never felt for any woman what I feel for her. I'm not playing her, Blythe."

He didn't ever explain himself, but he felt Blythe deserved something. She obviously loved Rikki and wanted to protect her.

Blythe leaned one hip against the car. "I wouldn't plan any parties. She doesn't like more than one person in her house. And the reason she goes on dangerous dives is because she thinks she doesn't contribute as much as the rest of us, even though she does all the planting with Lexi. She couldn't take the sound of the carpentry work. I wouldn't ever take her near a construction site."

"So sounds can trigger a problem," he mused.

Blythe shrugged. "Among other things." She kept her eyes on him. "It's never going to change, Lev."

He sent her a smile, more a showing of teeth than actual humor. "You're saying she's autistic, but then I already suspected that, didn't I?"

Again Blythe shrugged, watching him the entire time, clearly expecting him to run or explain why he wasn't running.

There was no explaining his mysterious connection to Rikki or how she made him feel—totally accepted without strings, a freedom he'd never experienced. Or how the things Blythe was telling him tugged at his heart. He didn't feel emotion, that was supposed to be long gone from his life. His trainers would be horrified at the way his heart melted over Rikki. He imagined her as a young girl in a world she didn't understand, stalked by a killer and without anyone to turn to, yet somehow, against all odds, she had carved out a life for herself. He looked at Blythe. With this woman. Blythe had stood for Rikki. She'd believed in her. The fierce protection she and the others felt for Rikki was genuine.

"Is it better to leave her alone when she's overloaded?"

"We do," Blythe conceded. "She calms herself down. If you notice, she keeps things around her that comfort her. She has a blanket that helps, but the ocean is her best resource. When she's away from it too long, she runs into more problems."

She leaned into the car and retrieved the food, two big containers that smelled like heaven. He hadn't realized how hungry he'd become. He was going to be hacking into Rikki's files and reading everything he could about her. If she was autistic, she was too high functioning not to have had some help as a child. He needed to read everything he could about her and get a much larger picture of the things that had shaped her life.

"Thanks for the dinner." Lev watched Blythe get back into her car. She still didn't trust him, and he didn't blame her. He was going to take Rikki and make her his. Blythe knew his intentions and she didn't trust his motives.

He took one more slow, careful look around and locked the kitchen door behind him. He ate while he worked, his fingers flying over the keyboard so that he barely tasted the food when he'd been so hungry. Rikki's juvenile files were more easily accessible because the cases involving the deaths of her parents and fiancé were still open. Her parents had sought medical help for their daughter around the age of two and a half. She was given both auditory and occupational therapy, which continued until she was thirteen, thanks to a very progressive doctor and a parent willing to try newer approaches. She had a speech therapist for a short time while she was in the state-run facility, but she had violent outbreaks to the point that most instructors refused to work with her. She was labeled as unmanageable and even dangerous to herself and others.

Lev scowled at the screen, shocked at the anger and adrenaline coursing through his veins. He hadn't realized emotion could shake him the way looking at her past had. Rikki didn't make any noise, but he sensed her presence and looked up to find her standing in the doorway, watching him. He closed her laptop and pushed it away from him, looking right back at her.

"I'm sorry, Lev. I don't know what to say, except thanks for the blanket."

"Don't apologize to me, Rikki. Not for being who you are. Never do that, certainly not to me and not to anyone else either. You do whatever you have to do, Rikki. This is your home."

She didn't smile, but simply watched him, holding herself still as if she were waiting for something. "I see my sisters decided to feed you."

He flashed her a grin. "I think they took pity on me. I was looking a bit thin."

Her gaze drifted over his body. "I don't think that was it. You look pretty filled out in all the right places to me."

His eyes met hers and his heart leapt. There was a speculative look in her eyes, one that told him that his kisses had paid off and she was definitely noticing he was a man. "Come in, sit down at the table. You need to eat something."

She glanced at the dirty dishes on the table and shook her head, backing out of the room. "I think I'll go outside and sit for a while. The rain is starting to really come down, and I like to sit on the porch and watch it."

He wasn't certain he wanted her outside without him, but there was no way to stop her. She enjoyed sitting in her hammock swing and listening to the rain at night. "I'll be out in a few minutes. Do you want coffee?"

She shook her head. "Not this late. I have a hard time sleeping as it is."

Lev watched her go out through the front door. She hadn't even walked through the kitchen with the dirty dishes on the table. And she wouldn't eat. He had to find a way to get her comfortable with the idea of eating together. He thought about solutions as he did the dishes and cleared the table. He made her a peanut butter sandwich, chopped up a few pieces of raw broccoli and added a spoonful of peanut butter to the plate. Adding a glass of water, he took the plate out to her, sending up a silent prayer that she'd accept her meal on her precious dish and not get even more upset with him.

12

RIKKI swung one foot back and forth as she swayed gently in the swing, staring out into the gathering darkness. She had no idea what to do with Lev. She'd made up her mind he could stay, but she didn't know how to share her life. She needed a certain environment to live in peace, and yet if she was allowing Lev into her world, it wasn't fair to expect him to conform to her needs. She sighed. She was definitely intrigued by the man, and she felt for him. He was lost and trying to find his way, just as she had been. She couldn't do less for him than Blythe and the others had done for her.

She sighed again. Maybe she'd started out helping him because she felt he needed it, but now she wasn't as certain of her own motivation. She was becoming fascinated by him, almost obsessed—and she could really fixate on something if she was interested in a subject. So far, the subject had never been another human being, but her weird connection to Lev seemed to be growing. She thought about him way too much.

"That's your third sigh."

A million butterflies took flight in the pit of her stomach. She brought up her hand and shook her fingers, blowing on them as if putting out a fire. Realizing what she'd done, she dropped her hand quickly. It had taken years of concentrated effort to stop that childhood pattern of shaking her hands and blowing on her fingers repeatedly. The act was mesmerizing and allowed her mind to focus on the repetitious pattern rather than deal with what was new and uncomfortable. She glanced at Lev's face. Yeah. He'd noticed.

"I wasn't counting," she replied.

"You worry too much." He held out the plate with the sandwich. "I brought you something to eat."

Her stomach lurched. Her sandwich was on one of the plates her sisters had given her. This was the second time he'd used them and she couldn't do it again. She folded her hands in her lap. "I don't ever use those plates."

"Why?"

There was curiosity in his voice, but not anything else she could detect. She frowned, trying to think of what to tell him. She didn't use the dishes because she loved them and she was afraid something might happen to them. It sounded stupid when she thought about admitting the reason aloud. Her sisters had given her the dishes to use and yet, for four years, she'd just looked at them. Keeping the dishes in mint condition seemed very logical until she tried to say it out loud. Even Blythe had objected to her not using the dishes.

She looked up at Lev's face. There was no expression on his face, just a gentle understanding in his eyes. That look set off another round of flying butterflies. She wanted to reach out and trace every line on his face. "I know it sounds silly, even to me it does, but no one ever gave me anything, not after my parents died, and I didn't want to risk chipping or breaking a single dish."

He smiled. Her heart jumped. His smile wasn't amused or teasing or even mocking—it was almost tender. "That makes perfect sense to me. I'll put this on a paper plate for now, and we'll buy dishes we don't care about breaking or chipping. You could put this set in a display case. They'd look beautiful." He looked down at the rim of the plate with the shells and starfish surrounding it, all in white, but obviously handcrafted. "Actually, the entire set is a work of art. It would be a shame to see them ruined."

The knots in her belly unraveled and she could breathe again. She hadn't even realized she was holding her breath. She blinked at the sudden burning in her eyes and turned to stare out at the rain coming down. It was soft still but beginning to fall harder. The storm front was coming in off the ocean and bringing a lot of water—which was needed. Her body felt more together and less likely to fly apart with the rain coming down.

"I'm going to see what else I can use."

"I'll take the sandwich," she offered slyly. She couldn't help it if she couldn't eat the broccoli out here on the porch. Usually she just broke off a piece and dipped it into the peanut butter jar. She scooped the sandwich from the plate and took a bite, savoring the taste of her favorite food.

He grinned as if he were reading her mind, which maybe he was, but Blythe wasn't there to lecture her so it was all good. She ate her sandwich happily. Lev disappeared into the kitchen with the plate and she was left alone with the night. The clouds had dropped the veil of darkness early. She swung her foot in time with the beat of the rain and closed her eyes to absorb the sound.

Her heart found the rhythm, then her pulse followed. She tuned her hearing to focus on each drop. The rain was beginning to fall more heavily, and she found herself hearing the music it always made in her head, drowning out every other noise. She was fascinated by the various tones as the drops hit objects—the rooftop, the trees, cement, asphalt, the dirt. Everything made a slightly different sound.

Share it with me.

She became of aware of Lev, close, so close his body heat warmed her, but she didn't open her eyes. His voice in her head was commanding, velvet over steel, a brush of heat that spread like a drug through her veins. The center of her left palm pulsed as if he'd brushed his fingers there, physically stroking her, but she knew he hadn't. She found herself opening her mind without really knowing how she was doing it, but deliberately sharing her world was a unique experience for her—she *wanted* to share it with him.

The moment she allowed him fully into her head, it was as if somehow they merged, skin into skin. She felt him inside. Everything feminine in her responded to the masculinity in him. Electrical currents ripped through the heat in her veins and pooled low and hot. She caught images in his mind, erotic and shocking, both tempting and a little frightening. Her breath caught in her throat and she took a deep breath, drawing him in further.

I want to experience everything that you experience.

She let out her breath. He would know how her body reacted to his. He already knew. Color slid up her neck and into her face. It was normal to be physically attracted to a man—especially one as hot as Lev—but like this? Every single cell in her body was on alert. She was hot, right there in the midst of the rainstorm.

Are you feeling the same? She couldn't ask aloud, but she had to know.

His breath was ragged against the back of her neck. *Even stronger.*

Her heart jumped at his honesty. He wasn't ashamed or embarrassed to feel such an overwhelming sexual attraction.

Is it you? Or me?

I think we have extraordinary chemistry. I have never encountered this need before, so strong that it's a hunger that grows rather than allows control.

There was satisfaction in knowing that she wasn't alone and that he was honest with her about the way his body responded to hers.

Not just my body, lyubimaya, he corrected. *Cool us down with the rain.*

The sheer poetry of his suggestion appealed to her soul. She lifted her hands and began a symphony that for the first time she performed for someone other than herself. Bright diamonds fell from the sky, sparkling and perfect. The sound seemed precise at first, but in response to the commands of her fingers, she began to hear individual notes—the drumming of the rain, harder along the forest edge.

Lev had seen her do this before, but he'd never truly experienced what she did when she disappeared inside her head. Rikki was a water element, but he knew even had she not been, this was her world, this other place where sound wasn't harsh and lights didn't burn.

He inhaled sharply as he was drawn into another dimension, an alternate reality, more vivid, more alive, than the world he lived in. The landscape was painted with sound. Soft at first, like a string quartet, the rain was nearly weeping with joy.

She changed the rate of fall to bring in the various sounds of drums, the pounding rhythm, the midrange snare, the kick of the bass, all flowing together into a symphony of color and magic. She created a complicated, intricate pattern, or maybe it was there all along and he had never been tuned to it before.

He could hear individual notes and, like in a Bach fugue, counterpoints to the building thematic melody. While the music seemed soft, it was also strong and commanding, a force to be reckoned with, nature building on itself. Each individual voice was different, as if a variety of instruments played various tunes, yet somehow they all melded together to create a masterpiece.

Just like the movements in a symphony, the rain sent vibrations through his body, painting the world in a physical map of mountains, valleys and high peaks dropping into deep ravines. The physical structures were all created by sound itself, and the colors were intense and vivid— substance created by sound, by feeling. He realized the emotions in her, so closed off to the rest of the world, were right beneath the surface, a swirling cauldron of heat and fire and cool rain. The vivid colors and sounds expressed what she felt—the amazing intensity of her emotions.

For the first time in his life, Lev shut out the world around him. He was lost in the wonder and beauty of the rain coming down. He was utterly fascinated, experiencing a joyful euphoria, a sharing with Rikki that was inti-

mate beyond imagination. This world, this creation, was
as real as the two of them—he'd just never had an opening
into another dimension before.

The rain swelled and ebbed, pouring over the slopes
and valleys, each section answering with a loud or soft
rush of music, as if there were melodic voices in the rain
calling and answering one another with greater and greater
force. The drops whirled and danced as they came down
over the house, creating small twisters of crystal prisms.

He was lost, caught up in the beauty and sound. Everything sparkled against the night, a million stars rained
down on them. The drops began to touch and then sink
into his skin, absorbed by him until he felt like part of the
deluge, floating in space between sky and earth. This was
her world, just as the sea was. The cool water surrounding
her, carrying her, holding her close to comfort her in a
world she could never understand.

She wanted to live in this world or in the deep sea. He
felt her reach for it, let it take her spinning further away
from reality, and he went with her, free-falling into vivid
color and beautiful sound. The music flowed around him
with the rain. Streaks of glittering color were weeping violins, and then a calypso beat separated the drops once
more.

Abruptly it was gone and he stood there blinking, as if
waking up from a dream, looking around, trying to orient
himself back to a world that was not quite so bright and
vivid. Where was the music? The vivid color? The world
seemed dull in comparison. He put his arms around her
and held her while she came back from her journey into
another dimension. He had no other way to describe what
he'd experienced, but he knew that rapt expression of

focused attention that often came over Rikki meant she was there, in that world that was in her head.

She turned her head, letting it fall on his shoulder, accepting the security of his arms. "You're cold, *lyubimaya*, let's get you inside and ready for bed."

He didn't want her to stay out on the porch alone. He was afraid of losing her to that other world. It would always be there, just as the sea would be, calling to her in a soft, tempting whisper. He kissed the top of her head. It was entirely possible he didn't know one thing about love, but he knew himself inside and out, every strength, every weakness, and he knew absolutely his life was entangled with hers for all time.

He didn't like being away from her. He found himself listening for the sound of her voice, watching for her little frown, waiting for her direct stare so he could fall into the dark depths of her eyes. Free-falling. That's what he'd been doing since the moment he met her. And he wanted this life. He intended to grab it with both hands. Right or wrong, he was falling in love with her, and every moment spent in her company intensified the feeling. He couldn't imagine going back to being without her.

He scooped her up into his arms, not waiting for her breathless protest, and carried her back into the house, kicking the door closed behind them.

"I have to lock it," she said.

"You get ready for bed and I'll shut down the house." He wanted to take a quick look around and set a few extra guards in place.

Rikki stood just outside the bathroom door, shocked at the way she felt when he left her, taking most of the warmth in the room with him. She shivered, aware something had changed between them. Sharing her world with him, allowing him into her head, had only made the connection between them deeper. She was happy on her own, yet, slowly, Lev was inserting himself deeper and deeper into her life—into her emotions.

She didn't let people in because she couldn't risk her fragile happiness. Without Blythe and the others, she'd be dead. She wouldn't have been able to continue her solitary existence, wondering every moment if she was truly a monster capable of burning people alive. Lev was winding his way into her heart. She was getting used to his presence in her home, but more than that, she was getting used to his touch.

She'd never liked being touched, even by the people she loved. She tolerated it because she knew they needed it, but she'd never wanted to feel skin against her skin—until Lev. She rubbed the center of her left hand in slow circles, finding it soothing, almost as if she were stroking Lev's skin. She found him warm, allowing her to almost melt into him, instead of feeling his touch as a prickling that was uncomfortable or at times even painful.

She pushed open the bathroom door and staggered in. She hadn't felt so clumsy on land for a long, long time, but the direction of her thinking had thrown her. She was never going to be able to fall asleep without him if she let him into her life any further. She would never feel happy again if—no—*when* he left. No one could live with her eccentricities. She was fine now in her own skin, but she was fully aware she was not the "standard" model.

She scrubbed her face, looking into her own eyes. She saw him there. Lev. How had he gotten inside of her? For the first time in a long while she was terrified. Not of her kitchen being messed up or that someone else shared her house, but that she was coming to need him. She was meticulous about brushing her teeth, a torture for her as the sensation repelled her, but she also had a thing about teeth and wanted them as immaculate as possible. Each time she brushed her teeth, she remembered her mother brushing and counting, helping her to focus on the numbers and not the sensation. She still counted and that helped to pull her mind away from the terror of falling for Lev—*Levi*—Hammond.

That wasn't even his real name, not that it mattered to her, but he was shedding his old skin and donning a new one. He could be in her life for a short time and shed her just as fast. Heart pounding, she brushed her hair the one hundred strokes she did every night, counting each one carefully before placing the brush in the exact spot she always put it in.

She stepped out of her clothes, her skin sensitive, her breasts aching. Breathing deep to push down the building need, she dragged on a tank and the matching boy shorts, a concession to her femininity. She did like beautiful underwear. She sat on top of the covers, her weighted blanket in reach. She allowed Lev to sleep beneath the covers, acutely aware that he rarely slept with clothes on. She'd become accustomed to giving him a massage at night, telling herself it would help him relax and sleep, but it was really becoming an excuse to trace every muscle in his body until she knew him fairly intimately.

Not tonight. She resolutely pulled out a book and opened it, focusing the light on her bedside table onto the pages. She didn't look up when Lev came in, but she couldn't help but see him—his energy filled the entire room. In spite of her resolutions, her body stirred to life. He moved like a creature of the jungle. Fluid and strong, he was every inch a man, every inch a predator. He could shed his name but he couldn't change what was beneath the skin, and it showed in the way he walked.

His muscles rippled with strength. His thighs were strong columns and his hips narrow. His shoulders were broad, his chest deep, and he was well-endowed, a fact she couldn't avoid either. His symmetry appealed to her. She knew the flow of his muscles beneath his skin. She knew the heat he could generate. The silk of his hair, already growing out and a little shaggy, the long lashes and piercing sea blue eyes all combined to set her pulse racing and her blood stirring.

He slipped beneath the covers after turning off the overhead light so that there was only her lamp shining on the pages of her book. Rikki remained very still, head pressed against the headrest of the bed while Lev shifted position beneath the covers, turning onto his side and laying his head squarely in her lap. For a moment she couldn't breathe. She tried to pretend that she could read but it was impossible, and she knew he knew it.

"Turn off the light, Rikki," he said softly.

She hesitated a moment, still afraid to move, but there was no point in trying to read when his arm settled around her thighs and his head nuzzled into a better position, his breath warm on her bare thighs. The blankets were between their bodies, but the way he held her was the most intimate thing she'd ever felt in her life. She reached out and touched the lamp, plunging the room into darkness. She could hear her own heart pounding in her ears.

Even the sound of the rain didn't bring her peace. She counted silently, not wanting to move, but afraid she might have to from sheer terror at such closeness. Lev was breathing evenly, but she wasn't altogether certain he was any more relaxed than she was. She waited in the darkness, but he made no sound and no movement. She realized he was holding himself even more still than she was, awaiting—even expecting—her rejection.

She let her breath out and dropped her hand onto his head, stroking gently over his thick hair. "Are you all right, Lev?" she asked, her voice soft and more tender than she wanted it to be.

His arm tightened around her thighs. "Sometimes, my childhood is just too close."

They'd spoken of it earlier, when she'd asked him questions he didn't want to answer. "I didn't mean to bring up bad memories," she apologized.

"I've never told another human being about my life."

She knew the feeling of being exposed and vulnerable, turned inside out. She'd had that happen in grief counseling with the women she regarded as her sisters. The outcome of exposing oneself could be, and often was, disastrous. For Lev, she had the feeling it could end in violence or death.

"I'm not asking that of you, Lev," she said. "You don't have to pay that kind of price to be with me. I don't need it."

"Yes, you do. You have to know what I am."

Her heart contracted and then began to pound at an alarming rate. He was giving himself to her. She wasn't ready. She didn't know if she could make a commitment. She was happy with her life, at peace with herself. She liked her life. He would change that dramatically.

"Lev." She wanted to stop him. He didn't have to strip himself naked for her to feel safe with him, and that's what he was most afraid of. "Your past doesn't frighten me."

His fingers began slow, seductive circles on her thigh, right over the tattooed raindrops, tracing each one, committing them to memory. "It should, Rikki. Men like me—we're not supposed to lie in bed with a woman or have a place we call home. We eliminate threats, and anyone knowing us is a threat."

"You've had plenty of chances to kill me, if that's what you're implying, Lev. I'm still alive, so I don't think your threat is very real." She continued stroking his hair, silently trying to send him a message that she accepted him without explanation. Whatever demons were riding him so hard didn't need to be exposed or acknowledged, not unless he needed to tell her.

He sighed. "My entire life has been about survival and survival instincts. I'm not certain you have any. You should never just bring a stranger into your home, Rikki. Especially a man who has so much to hide."

She found herself smiling. He was desperately trying to talk her into throwing him out, yet at the same time, his fingers were moving in those arousing circles and the way his arm was wrapped around her thighs was distinctly possessive. Maybe it was all in her imagination, but she wasn't moving, mostly because he was more afraid of their connection than she was. She'd come to bed so afraid of giving him too much of herself, yet here he was, feeling exactly the same. And maybe that was love. Being so vulnerable and allowing someone else in so far they could hurt you, but they could also give you everything.

"I told you, Lev, I know all about you that I need to know."

He lifted his head slightly, just enough to bite her leg in frustration, the smallest of nips. It felt more erotic than a reprimand. She laughed. "If you want me to throw you out, Lev, it isn't going to happen."

He rolled over enough to look up at her face. "You have to do it, *lyubimaya*, because evidently I'm not man enough to do it myself."

She would have laughed at the drama of his words, but there was too much pain on his face, when he rarely, if ever, displayed emotion. She smoothed the lines there as if she could wipe away the past for him—pursing her lips as if to kiss it away.

"You shared something beautiful with me tonight, Rikki. I want that sharing. I even need it. But I've got nothing so beautiful to give you in return. I've been thinking a lot about that, about what I'd bring to you—and I don't have much of anything useful to give you."

"That's for me to decide," she challenged. "If you need to talk about your childhood, you're safe with me. If you need to break into a million pieces, I'm right here, Lev. I'll find them all, I'm good at details, and I'll put you back together. You're safe here."

The rain beat down and as usual she had the window open wide, needing the soothing sounds and scents. If a few stray drops hit her face or body, she was fine with it. She always made certain there was nothing too important near the open window during a storm. She sat in silence just listening. Usually the rain called to her and carried her away, but now she was too focused on Lev. His ragged breathing. The seduction of his fingers. The need in him.

In his own quiet way, Lev was as desperate to be saved as she had been before Blythe and the others reached out to her. Whatever revelation he was thinking of giving her, it was something he protected fiercely. A piece of himself—the last piece. And he was handing it into her keeping. She recognized the enormity of what he was doing. She remained silent, just waiting, unsure of what he was going to say, but knowing it would change her life forever if he said it, because she would never turn her back on him, never walk away, no matter how difficult it was. If he gave her such a gift, made himself that vulnerable, she would treasure and protect him with every breath in her body.

Lev continued to stroke his fingers along the satin length of her thigh. It was a gift to do something so simple, to lie in bed with a woman, touching her skin, inhaling her scent while the rain poured down on the roof. He wanted her more than anything in his life. He wanted *this* woman, this life with her, yet he felt guilty knowing she didn't see the killer in him. That wasn't fair. He was a violent man, a cold one, his emotions were buried deep, allowing him an expertise few could achieve. He'd watched the suffering of others, his need to go to their aid suppressed in order to focus on accomplishing his goal.

He was risking everything, yet he could never live with himself if she didn't go into this knowing what kind of man he was. He wanted one person to know him. To see him. And if she took him as he was, broken, tainted, twisted even, he would never give her up. She had to see into him. It was the only real gift he could give her. He would love her fiercely, protect her with everything in him, but she had to see and accept who and what he really was.

"When I was a boy, we lived in a tiny apartment. It was cold most of the time. Not like this, but really cold. I remember ice on the inside of the door."

Her fingers stilled in his hair, curled and held on as if she realized the story he was telling her was going to be ugly and horrific but told in a matter-of-fact voice, because he could never face it other than looking at it as if from a great distance and from behind a transparent wall, where emotions had no place.

"There were seven of us, all boys. We were very close in age and we slept together in the same bed, except for the baby. It was how we stayed warm, I think. I can barely remember the faces of my parents, but my memories of them are good. They were good to us. My father was a man who had amazing gifts and he passed them on to all of us. Gifts that allowed us to do things most people can't do."

"We have a family in this town that has extraordinary gifts," Rikki conceded. "Remember, I mentioned them to you."

"That doesn't surprise me," he murmured, turning back to nuzzle her thigh. He rested his head on her lap again. "Sea Haven has a powerful energy. I can feel it every time I walk outside. It's stronger the closer to the ocean we get. Power attracts power, just as elements attract elements. I wouldn't be surprised if several people living in or around Sea Haven have some degree of psychic power."

"I suppose you're right. All of us felt the pull of this place, and I've never been happier," Rikki admitted.

"We didn't live anywhere near powerful energy, but my father had undeniable gifts and at the time, there was turmoil in the government, conspiracies and many individuals fighting for their own agendas. My father backed the wrong party and they came one night as a huge force, very frightening."

"I huddled there with my brothers, so scared. The soldiers burst into our apartment." He could feel her thighs tremble beneath his head, but her hand was anchored firmly in his hair, as if holding him to her, and her arm went around his shoulders. She was very empathetic, and although he was viewing his childhood from a distance, she was feeling what he should have been.

"They executed my father first and then my mother. I was separated from my brothers, and each of us was taken and sent to training facilities. With our particular genetics, they believed we could better serve our government if we were indoctrinated at a young age and held no loyalty to one another or to a family. Later, of course, I realized, as I'm sure my other brothers did, that they feared us, just as they feared our father. Unfortunately, we were so young that their indoctrination and isolation techniques worked."

She began stroking small caresses through his hair. "What did they do to you?"

"They kept me from my brothers and put me in a facility where they trained and educated me. I speak multiple languages and had to perfect each accent. I learned weapons, hand-to-hand combat and sexual technique. I had to learn absolute control and discipline. Fun was defeating one's enemy, and everyone there was an enemy. We were trained to work alone. We were trained to endure torture and not break. My forte was the ability to shed one identity for another. I can blend in anywhere, become anyone, and it has served me and my government well. Since they took me from my parents, I don't recall one time when I was not in training. Duty and discipline were my childhood."

There was no pity in his voice or in his mind. He accepted his life, and he accepted that he couldn't change what had happened to him.

"It must have been a frightening childhood."

"It shaped who I am, what I am. I killed for them, Rikki. Hundreds, maybe thousands in my lifetime. I lived in the shadows and hunted for them. I don't know if it was a good thing or a bad thing. It just was. I still have no idea why I was on that yacht, but I have images in my head of events leading to my boarding the yacht. I think the man I was after was involved in human trafficking. There were women . . ." He shrugged. "I had to make difficult decisions that affected other lives."

Lev fell into silence—touching her mind, he showed her images of women being brutally tortured, of violent death, sudden and horrific, of the cold-blooded kills that stained his soul and over time had chipped most of it away. He waited for the full implications of what he'd told and shown her to sink in. Rikki might not believe him. There were many children taken for political reasons and raised to be assets for the government or the secret police, or even to be special assassins. He and his brothers were feared for their gifts, yet they were also seven of the most useful tools his country had. They were also the most dangerous.

"Have you ever seen your brothers?" Rikki asked, her voice soft, almost a caress.

He closed his eyes and savored the touch of her fingers on his scalp. He should have known she would focus on the loss of his family instead of the assassinations. "I've seen three of them. Our paths crossed on jobs." He didn't—couldn't—elaborate. They had all worried that if it was known that they had spoken, one of them would be chosen as an example to all of them and would be eliminated. They wouldn't risk further contact unless it was an emergency.

Rikki was silent for a long time, turning his revelations over and over in her mind. He had never had a chance at life. He was so alone and lost, just as she had been. He was afraid to reach for something better. She knew how difficult it was to let go of the familiar. No matter how bad it was, one knew the rules in their own world.

She stroked his hair and leaned her head back against the headboard, allowing the rain to soothe her when her heart ached for him. "I think you're better off here, Lev. Stay here awhile and just let yourself live. There aren't any strings. I'm not asking anything of you. Just find who you want to be, who you really are underneath it all. Whoever that person is, will be welcome here."

The burning behind his eyes hurt. He just lay there, holding her, afraid if he moved, he'd shatter, just break into a million pieces. He also knew it wouldn't matter to her if he did—she wouldn't view him as less than a man. She would simply accept him.

He took a breath and allowed himself to feel very real love for another human being. He told her the stark truth. The emotion was strong, swamping him, invading every part of his mind, his heart and his body. He shook with it. He let it consume him, filling up every empty space. Several heartbeats went by before he could speak.

"I want to spend my life with you, Rikki, not just a few moments, not a few nights. If you take me on, we'll work together, no matter what comes up, and we'll find a way to make it all work."

Her heart jumped. He felt it, but he didn't look up.

"I don't want to go back to living in the shadows, *lyubimaya*. If we do this, it has to be all the way, because I don't know how to be any other way than what they trained me to be. Here, with you, I'm different. If I leave you, I'm back in a black void. Maybe I belong there," he nuzzled her thigh with his chin, "but I've had a taste of something else. You're magic to me, Rikki. I don't know why, but I know without you, I don't have a chance of living a normal life."

She made a strangled sound in her throat. "Lev. By any stretch of the imagination, I'm not the norm. Maybe you're not seeing me as I am. I can't even let you use my bathroom. You've somehow managed to get into the bed, but I still wince when you're in the kitchen and I can't watch you cook. Is that the kind of life you envisioned for yourself?"

"My life is killing, Rikki. I stalk my target, immerse myself in their life, kill them and disappear without a trace. There's nothing left of me because I'm not real."

"You're real."

He rolled onto his back to look up at her face. "I'm not real to anyone else. I'm a ghost to most people, a weapon the government lets loose on the world when they need it. When they get to the point where I'm too scary for them to handle, a contract will be issued and then it will be a matter of time before someone just like me shows up to eliminate me."

"But you've been loyal and you've carried out whatever task they've asked of you, no matter how abhorrent to you, right?" Rikki protested. "Why would anyone you've served want you dead?"

"I have too much information running around in my head and I'm dangerous. They would presume that eventually, if I'm not working for them, I'll work against them."

She frowned and he couldn't help himself, he reached up and traced her soft lips.

"Then it's a good thing that everyone thinks you're dead, Lev."

He sighed. "That man on the platform that day. You called him Ralph. He saw me."

"Not your face. I said you were visiting. And why would he remember?"

"You honestly don't know, do you?" He was a bit shocked at her naïveté. "He was trying to flirt with you and you didn't give him the time of day."

"That's just silly. He's friendly to all the divers. And you had a concussion and were imagining things."

"It's my job to catch every little nuance, Rikki. It's the difference between life and death. Believe me, the man was flirting. He finds you intriguing. And it's probably the first time he's ever seen you with a man."

Now her frown reached her eyebrows and he had to trace them as well because he just couldn't resist. "He noticed me, all right. And when they come looking—and they will—he'll mention that you were out on the sea that day and I was with you. That will lead some very bad people straight to you." He wasn't certain if he was warning her, asking permission to kill Ralph or needing to see her reaction to knowing Ralph had been interested.

"You might be just a little paranoid, Lev. Why in the world would he talk to perfect strangers about seeing either of us?"

"Because my government will send their best cleaner and he knows how to get information."

She suddenly smiled. "Well, I guess we'd better have a plan for when that happens."

He stared up at her face for a long time, wondering how he'd found her. The water was so cold, so dark, his lungs burned and his ears had nearly imploded, and his body and head had been battered against rocks, tumbling until there was only death waiting. He'd seen death. It hadn't been any better for him than life. And then Rikki. He touched her with reverence.

"You know that I intend to make love to you."

She went very still, just as he'd known she would. "You haven't tried."

He wasn't certain what that meant, whether she was disappointed or just stating the truth. He figured it was probably the latter. She was very accepting of reality. "It has to be right with you, Rikki. You're different. You're real, not a job. You matter. I've never been with a woman who mattered to me."

"I can't imagine you not getting any woman you wanted, Lev."

He smiled, his heart suddenly lighter as he kissed her thigh right on one of those shimmering raindrops. He was very fond of her boy shorts. The ones she was wearing had little pink stripes wrapping around her as if she were a gift to be opened. "Thank you, but I never wanted a woman for myself. There've been women. Too many. Assignments. I used them to get what I wanted. This isn't ever going to be about using you. This is going to be about making love to you."

He stroked his fingers over her satin thigh, over the drops. Were they tears? How could she be so soft when she spent so much time in the water? There was always a faint fragrance just out of his reach, subtle, yet so Rikki.

"I've got to warn you, Lev"—her voice trembled, and for the first time when he looked at her, she looked away from him—"I'm not very good at lovemaking. It's not like I have a lot of experience, and when someone touches me, sometimes it hurts."

He propped himself up on one elbow and slid her down so that she sprawled out beneath him. "Well, we'll have to go slow and see what you like and what you don't like, won't we?"

13

THE butterflies were out in force, taking flight in the pit of Rikki's stomach. She stared up at Lev's face. So dominant. So beautifully masculine. Why him? Why did Lev send every single nerve ending in her body into high alert? Why did she wait for the brush of his fingers on her skin when she could barely tolerate other people's touch? The center of her left palm pulsed and she closed her fingers over the tingling warmth.

His eyes were amazing. A deep-sea blue she was immediately lost in. If she had a thought of self-preservation, it was gone the moment she looked into his eyes. There was desire smoldering there, a scorching intensity that burned right through her. His eyes couldn't lie, he actually wanted her that much and how could she ever resist?

Rikki touched his face tentatively. His hand was on her bare stomach, his fingers spread wide to take in as much territory as possible. She was acutely aware of the skin-to-skin contact; he seemed to burn a brand right through the surface and deep into her body. She'd never felt like this with anyone. His touch was as real and as vivid as the world of the sea, or the rain.

She became aware of the music in the rain changing—not through her, but through him, as if he conducted now. Dreamy, sensual, an exotic, erotic beat that kept time with the movements of his fingers. Each stroke sent little tremors through her body. She was mesmerized by him, by the sight and feel of him, by the way he looked at her—as if she were the only woman in the world. It was there in his head, that conviction that there could be no other for him. It was a fairly heady aphrodisiac when she'd spent so much of her time alone—when no one had ever really seen who she was and wanted her anyway.

Everything he said, she felt the truth of. The connection between them was so strong, she doubted if he could lie effectively to her. For some unknown reason, and she was grateful for that reason, Lev had settled on her as the one. She'd never really been anyone's *one*.

Daniel had loved her in his way. She was a good companion to him, a diver who understood their world. She demanded little from him. He cared for her and he liked sex with her, but he'd never thought to take his time to try to please her. She had such a difficult time with touch that Daniel had believed in getting things over with as fast as possible, not in trying to find a solution.

Had she used Daniel? She frowned, turning the question over and over in her mind. They'd been a convenience for one another, but she'd felt affection for him—loved him. She hadn't had the same level of physical attraction for him that she had for Lev, but he'd been a good man and she'd loved him for the way he treated her—never as an outcast. As his equal. As a partner. She'd never had that before and there would always be a special place in her heart for him.

Lev lowered his head and brushed kisses up her leg, tasting each raindrop. "Keep your thoughts with *this* man, *lyubimaya moya*." He brushed a kiss across her tummy.

"You sound just a little jealous," she observed.

His warm mouth continued to move over her stomach and his teeth gave a little nip of reprimand. The sting jolted through her body, straight to her center, sending a flood of heat spreading through her body. His tongue swirled over her skin, a velvet rasp of pleasure.

Rikki could barely breathe, her lungs burning while her heart hammered out of control. She took a deep breath and her breasts brushed against his bare chest. Instantly her nipples peaked, and her breasts felt swollen and achy, so sensitive that when he looked up at her, tiny sparks of electricity ran from her nipples straight to her womb. She touched her tongue to her lips, trembling with the unfamiliar sensations.

How could he make her body come alive this way? One look. One touch. She reached up to touch his heavily muscled chest. The pads of her fingers absorbed the texture and feel of him, that exquisite heat flowing from him to her. Her eyes searched his, seeking reassurance. She was so nervous. Before, having sex had been a bodily function; now it was a necessity—she knew instinctively that once she experienced it, she would always crave it.

Lev could see how nervous she was, there was a touch of fear in those mysterious eyes, yet there was hunger too—and trust. He dropped his head to swirl his tongue around her belly button. "We won't do anything you're not comfortable with, Rikki, and if anything hurts or doesn't feel good, you tell me."

Her fist bunched in his hair. "This thing with you, it's growing fast. Too fast. If we do this and you change your mind, I don't know, Lev. I've got a good life. I am happy just the way it is. I don't want to be left behind a mess."

Wanting you. Craving you. Needing you.

He caught her thoughts. She was frightened. His courageous Rikki, frightened of making love with him. She'd given her body to Daniel because that was what couples did when they committed to each another. He had no doubt that she would have remained loyal to the man, but she was committing more than her body to Lev, and that was terrifying to a woman who needed absolute balance in her life.

"It's okay," he whispered against her soft skin. "You're safe with me."

He meant it. She was so innocent. So bright. She had a core of steel running through her, yet she was fragile and vulnerable—too much so. Those who loved her recognized that. He didn't remember innocence or brightness or vulnerability, but she somehow gave it all back to him. He'd read her file and knew she was capable of violence, knew others had misread her inability to cope with the sounds and the environment around her. She'd needed help, and no one had given it to her until Blythe and the others had stepped in. He would always—*always*—protect and watch over them for that alone. Because this woman . . .

He kissed his way up her narrow rib cage to the underside of her breasts, pushing the thin tank top up as he went so that it bunched just over her nipples. He felt the tremor that ran through her and his heart responded with a strange melting sensation. His body was thick and full, more so than it had ever been. He felt an urgent demand for relief, but he knew it was his soul making love to her. His soul needed her brightness and innocence. He knew he was as bound to her as she was to water.

The center of his left palm pulsed and ached, sending a chain reaction through his body so that his erection grew fuller. He was grateful he wore no clothes, because already the blanket was bothering his skin. He threw it off, lifting her to pull it out from under her, so he could shove it away from him, so there were only the cool sheets and the rain outside.

His thigh slid over hers, pinning her down while his hand slid up her arm to her shoulder, just memorizing the feel of her. He closed his eyes to savor her softness. His hand continued up to her neck, her face, and stilled, bunching in her thick, wild hair. He captured her breathy sigh as his lips took hers. He had had sex, yet this was the first time he'd ever made love and he wanted to experience every sensation.

He wanted her until his lungs burned for air and his chest felt tight. He was afraid his heart might explode, and if not his heart, then definitely his cock. Her kisses were like a drug that sent fire rushing through his veins. He would never get enough of that soft, perfect mouth. He kissed her over and over until she was melting into him, her soft gasps turning to soft little pleas.

Only then did he kiss his way to her neck, that vulnerable neck that he'd fantasized about more than once. Her skin had that scent of fresh rain he'd come to associate with her and he fed on it, using tongue and teeth, nipping and teasing, indulging himself while she moved against him restlessly, her breasts heaving against his chest.

Need was a monster that raged at him, clawing and tearing at his belly and groin, while love kept his touch gentle. Did other men feel like this? He'd never believed in love until Rikki. She wiped out every bad place he'd ever been—every bad thing he'd ever done. She took all the broken pieces and fit them together somehow. She thought herself damaged, but really, he was the one lost.

He kissed his way to the top of her tank, one hand resting possessively on her stomach. He felt the muscles bunch there, and she tensed as he lowered his mouth to her nipple right through the thin material. Her hips jerked and she shuddered, wrapping her arms around his head.

"Lev." Her voice was broken, a mixture of pleasure, fear and hunger.

He suckled for a moment, and then pulled back, nipping with his teeth, feeling the answering response in the tremors running through her body. "I never dreamed I'd have a woman like you, Rikki. Never. I never even imagined I could want or have a woman of my own, much less that it would feel like this."

He whispered the words to her. She'd given him a gift beyond measure and all he had to give in return was his loyalty, his love and his words. He couldn't even give her his real name, not without endangering her and his brothers. They would have to live with Hammond, not Prakenskii, and if there was a God, Lev hoped He understood. Lev drew her tank over her head and tossed it aside, lowering his head immediately to the temptation of her breast. Pleasure shuddered through him as she arched into him, pressing her breast deeper into the heat of his mouth. He began to suck on her sensitive nipple, gently using the edge of his teeth as her hips bucked against him.

Very gently he drew her little boy shorts down the length of her legs. She cooperated, lifting her hips, nearly sobbing, kicking them aside, and her body grew hotter beneath his wandering hand and the expertise of his mouth. She was unbelievably soft, her body silky smooth, and each time she cried out his name, he sank deeper under her spell.

His tongue teased her nipple, a velvet rasp that had her crying out and clutching at his hair with both hands. He opened his eyes to look into hers. Those huge eyes were black as the deepest sea, where he'd been so lost. He was still lost, but he was safe with her. She looked a little dazed, as if he might be drugging her with his touch. He bent his head, still watching her, and licked at her nipple like an ice cream cone. Her entire body shuddered and her hips rose to press tightly against him.

His hand slid up and down her thigh in small brush-strokes, caressing that silky skin all around her hip all the way up to the underside of her buttocks. Her eyes went wide and her breath caught in her throat. He took her nipple between his teeth and bit very gently, all the while staring into the black, fathomless depths of her eyes.

He loved watching her reaction. She was giving herself to him, putting herself in his hands and giving him an untutored response worth all the money in the world. His hand slipped around to the moist heat between her legs, covering the silky triangle of her mound with his palm. Color crept up her body, flushing her breasts, her neck and into her face. Her breathing turned ragged and broken.

Lev!

There it was again, his name whispered inside his head. A moan of need, a heady sound that made his cock throb and jerk with demand.

I've got you, luybimaya moya, *you're safe with me.* He answered with the intimacy of telepathy. He needed to be in her head with the same desperate need his body felt for hers.

She swallowed hard and nodded, her gaze never leaving his. He slid his finger into her slick, welcoming heat. Her hips bucked and her lashes trembled, her lips parting in a startled gasp. She went still, her eyes swallowing her face.

"I'm not hurting you." He made it a statement. She looked frightened, but her body responded with a flood of liquid honey.

She frowned and he couldn't help himself, he leaned down to kiss her again, robbing her of what breath she had left. His finger began to circle her sensitive bud, gently, getting her used to the sensation. She cried out into his mouth, a strangled gasp of pleasure. He smiled as he lifted his head to look once again into her eyes.

"Tell me."

"More. I want more."

He nipped her chin with his teeth. *I intend to enjoy myself as I get to know every inch of you. I've been waiting to see if you taste as good as I think you do.* He was burning up, need clawing at him with greedy hunger. His cock lay pressed against her thigh, raging at him with a fierce, almost brutal desire.

Her hands loosened in his hair and moved to his shoulders, a test maybe, to see if he liked her touch. He *craved* her hands—and mouth—on him and he let her see it with the images in his head, with the pleasure in his eyes.

More. That single word was all he could articulate, even in his head. His control was slipping fast, the intensity of his need shredding his discipline. He wanted it gone, wanted *this*, a ferocious love that would consume the two of them, that would burn hot and long and melt them together.

Rikki traced the muscles in his back, touching scars here and there, lingering for a moment to puzzle out what caused each of them. His face was a mask of sensuality, his eyes were intensely blue and filled with a dark lust that thrilled her.

She moved against him, a slow sensuous ripple, her body sliding enticingly against his. Surprise flared in his eyes, and he dropped his head, licking along her breasts and down her ribs, exploring with teeth and tongue and lips. Her seeking fingers stroked near the hard length of his heavy erection as it lay against her thigh. She felt the breath slam out of his body, felt the tremor that ran through him.

Every single place his teeth nipped or his tongue rasped sent hot licks of arousal sizzling through her skin to her most feminine core. Her temperature soared and she couldn't stop tossing back and forth on the bed or writhing under his assault. It felt so good it bordered on pain, but in a good way. It was shocking and exciting.

His hands spread her thighs and he bent his head, his teeth sinking into her inner thigh. She cried out, a soft plea for more as heat poured into her body.

His hot breath pulsed over the junction of her legs, nearly driving her wild with need. "I lay next to you night after night thinking about this, dreaming about it." The dark love in his blue gaze shocked her almost as much as what he was doing.

His hands lifted her hips as he lowered his head and he drank. Rikki heard herself scream—the pleasure swamped her, rocking her into a fevered insanity. Her fingers clutched his shoulders, desperate to anchor herself with something solid. Her head tossed back and forth on the pillow, and she was helpless to stop it as wave after wave of sensation rushed over her. Greedy for her taste, he licked and sucked, making no apologies, taking his time, using his tongue to penetrate first shallow and then deep. Tears burned behind her eyes and there was little air in her lungs, but she didn't want him to stop.

Fear clawed at her as she recognized that he was consuming her with his lust, binding them in such a way that neither would ever be free. It didn't matter. Fear didn't matter, only the spiral winding tighter and tighter deep inside her, threatening her very sanity, mattered. She heard another sob, knew it was her, and she pressed herself hard against him as his tongue stabbed deep, driving her to the very brink, but not tipping her over the edge.

Lev! It was the third time she had cried out his name, and this time she was pleading.

The spiral continued outward, bunching her stomach muscles, tightening her thighs, wrapping her in feverish arousal until she was tossing under him, terrified of losing herself, terrified he might stop and she'd never know where he was taking her.

Patience, lubov moya, *we have all night and I want to savor you.*

She closed her eyes as he licked and sucked and drove her higher and higher, taking her to the very edge of sanity before easing her back each time.

I want you ready for me.

I am ready for you. In another minute she was going to start begging and she didn't even care. Her fingers found his hair and tugged, trying to bring him up and over the top of her. *Inside me, now.*

His laughter was low and amused, a purr of male satisfaction. *You're a demanding little thing, aren't you?*

"You have no idea," she murmured aloud.

She couldn't stop her writhing, her head tossing or her hips bucking. His fingers moved in her and she cried out again—her body was on the brink of a great discovery but unable to reach it. She heard her own moan, shocking her, the sound pleading and desperate. His thumb stroked and caressed her most sensitive bud and she arched against him, shuddering with pleasure.

"Please," she whispered, her voice strained. "Please, Lev."

Lev lifted his head to look at her, at her dazed expression. Her eyes were glazed, shocked, filled with anticipation and trepidation. There was no way to hang on to his fragile control. One look at her face and he was lost.

He knelt between her legs and dragged her slight body to him, spreading her legs around him as he lifted her hips and pressed the throbbing head of his heavy erection against her entrance. Every nerve ending he had seemed to be pressing into that fiery heat. She was tight, a velvet, scorching-hot sheath that, as he entered, inch by slow inch, barely allowed his invasion. He gasped, fire streaking into his belly and down his thighs.

He was an expert in sex, but he was not prepared for the assault on his own senses. It had never happened before. He was too disciplined to lose himself in a woman's body. His life was all about survival, not pleasure, and certainly not about loving a woman. And, God help him, he was loving her with every breath in his body.

He felt fire pouring over his skin as he penetrated deep into her body, joining them together. He was thick and she was tight and the feeling was exquisite. He heard her breath hiss out in a long, ragged rush, and her muscles clenched tight around him. The small movement nearly cost him his last thread of control.

"Don't move, *laskovaya moya*," he cautioned, holding still, waiting for her body to adjust so he could bury himself deeper. "You can't move yet."

She was beyond listening, head tossing on the pillow, body writhing in spite of his hands controlling her hips. She was pushing herself onto him, so that he felt as if he were moving through petals as they opened for him. She was so tight, and her muscles continually clenched around him with every small movement of her body, sending streaks of fire racing to the center of his groin.

He couldn't help himself. Rearing back, he plunged into her over and over, dragging his thick cock across her most sensitive bundle of nerves. He wasn't certain he could survive the pleasure rushing through him. He drove deep, bumping the scalding heat of her cervix. He groaned as she tightened around the length of his heavy erection, squeezing and stroking with velvet-soft muscles. She might not have a tremendous amount of experience, but she was naturally sensual and every movement of her body sent him careening closer and closer to the edge. For a man who believed discipline was everything, it was shocking to be so out of control.

She chanted his name repeatedly, and for him it was pure music, like the rain was for her. Her moans and small little strangled sounds filled him with a fierce protectiveness, a pure male satisfaction that added to his joy. He reveled in his ability to heighten her pleasure with the way he moved. Her head tossed on the pillow, her face was flushed and her eyes dazed. She moaned, a long, low sound that resonated through his cock.

He shifted position, pulling her closer, throwing her legs up and over his arms, wanting better leverage as he set up a fast, hard rhythm, all the time watching her face for signs of discomfort. He couldn't help his own groan as he sheathed himself in her over and over—the heated friction was unbelievable. Her feminine channel was fiery hot, surrounding him like living silk, gripping and clasping, dragging over him so tightly the sizzling fire within him burned hotter and hotter. His balls tightened, the exquisite pleasure was nearly painful. He felt the coiling power wind tighter and tighter, and he knew he was close to his release.

"*Ya tebya lyublyu.*" He took a breath. "Look at me, *lubov moya*, I need to see your eyes." He wanted to soar with her, drown in her, merge so tightly, mind and body, that their connection could never be broken.

Rikki felt the pressure building and building, that same tightness she felt in the ocean when a huge wave was coming. She reached for it, embracing the feeling, equating the sensation with her beloved sea. It started in her toes, a tremendous series of waves rolling over and through her, swelling stronger and stronger until the force was like a riptide rushing through her, building in strength. But it didn't stop. It never stopped.

She could feel him, the length and girth of him, stretching her, driving deep. Her own body was slick and wet, and the erotic tension stretched until she was afraid she'd drown in it. She couldn't quite catch her breath and she couldn't find relief from that ever-building pressure. It was too powerful. Too out of control for someone like her, the waves increasing in strength, threatening to engulf her. Fear slithered into her mind, riding the surge of passion, so that every raw nerve ending felt each acute sensation separately and then together, swamping her.

She heard Lev's voice, far off, in her head, calling her in his own language, his voice an anchor. Desperate, she turned her head to look at him, their gazes colliding. It was like free-falling into the sea, all that marvelous blue. There wasn't enough air to breathe, just like under water, but the beauty of his rugged face, his strength, his enduring calm was like the ever-constant ocean, and she managed to hold on to her sanity by clinging to him.

Stay with me. She pleaded with him. *Stay with me.*

You're safe, lubov moya, *always safe with me,* he assured. *Just let go.*

She kept her gaze locked with his and let herself sink into the bliss. Her body clamped down on his like a vise, and the pressure increased until she feared she would implode. She could feel him growing larger, pulsing with heat and fire, heard his hoarse groan and then the ultimate wave started, a tsunami out of control.

Eyes on his, she surrendered completely, giving herself up to him, letting him sweep her away with him so that there was only the sound of the rain and the rhythmic sound of their bodies coming together. The rogue wave tore through her body, up her legs and through her core, into her stomach and breasts, engulfing her brain, wave after wave of such pleasure she wasn't certain she was entirely sane. Her bones melted, her body turned to liquid and she was floating in the subspace of the sea.

He never looked away—never blinked—holding her to him through his own violent release. His breathing was ragged, his face strained, but his expression was tender as the waves in her body settled into ripples of sweet pleasure.

"For the first time in my life, Rikki, I feel like I'm home."

She lay beneath him, her heart pounding erratically, a little dazed by the actual stunning splendor of an orgasm. So that was what the big fuss was about. She'd wondered why everyone talked about sex and seemed so desperate for it.

Her legs were still over his arms and he gently allowed them to drop to the mattress. She couldn't move, her energy entirely consumed by the swamping waves, and just that small movement had sent another set of ripples racing through her body.

"Are you all right?"

She nodded and reached up to trace her finger over his lips. She was surprised she had the strength to even lift her arm. He eased out of her. "No." The protest burst from her, and she caught his shoulders, holding him to her.

"I'm right here, Rikki, I'm not going anywhere."

Her breath caught in her throat. He wasn't going anywhere and this was her home. She couldn't go anywhere. What was she supposed to do? Should she offer him something to eat or drink? Should she get up and shower? She was going to be sore; maybe a bath. Or should she get out of the house altogether? She could sit in her swing, if she could find the energy to get up.

Shivering, she dropped her hand and clutched at the sheet, frowning. She was going to blow this. It had been so perfect. Absolutely perfect, and she had no clue how people handled the aftermath of making love. She recognized the difference. He'd poured himself into her, body and soul, given her a priceless gift, and she was liable to inadvertently throw it back in his face from lack of experience or knowledge.

Her mind raced round and round, filling with fear. She was going to ruin everything. She was in new territory and it was frightening. Her brain wanted to retreat to familiar places. The rain, maybe, just allow herself to be absorbed by it, but she didn't want to do that to Lev. It was difficult, trying to fight the inclination with her head all over the place and no ability to rein it in.

Lev frowned down at Rikki, suddenly concerned. He laid his hand over her heart to discover it pounding so hard he was afraid she'd have a heart attack.

"What's wrong, Rikki?" he asked, his voice gentle, almost tender.

She shivered and reached beneath the bed for her weighted blanket, her gaze eluding his.

"*Lubov moya*, you're moaning. Are you in pain?"

Her fingers fumbled on the blanket, and he reached over her and found it for her, tucking it around her with care.

"I'm sorry," she managed.

"Don't be sorry, Rikki, talk to me. Let me know what's happening." He didn't wait for her to speak, but pressed his left palm against her left palm and thrust into her mind.

Use your words, Rikki. A woman's voice advised.

Her mother, and it was a memory that often comforted her. She rocked her body a little, as the memory of her mother holding her tight, putting pressure on her chest when she felt her body was flying apart, surfaced.

"I don't know what I'm supposed to do."

She sounded so forlorn, his heart twisted, but he waited in silence. She opened her eyes to look at him. The moment her gaze connected with his, he heard her thoughts. *That face, rugged and strong and so beautiful. His eyes. As blue as the beloved sea. His expression tender.* He felt relieved that she took comfort in his presence and wasn't wishing him gone.

He wrapped his arm around her waist and moved her body with his easy strength, tucking her close to him. "There aren't any rules, here, Rikki."

Her eyes flared wider and a little gasp escaped. "No. No, there have to be rules. There're always rules. What do I do? I don't know."

"What did you do before with Daniel?" He didn't want to bring the man's memory into her mind, not after what they shared, but he needed to find a way to comfort her.

"I left. I got up and left, fast, and went back to my house." She looked around her. "But this is my house and you live here too, and I don't know what to do."

She sounded so confused and vulnerable that his heart ached for her. "Remember what we promised each other?" he asked. He smoothed tendrils of hair from around her face. "We make our own rules. I say we hold one another and talk until we're both either too tired to stay awake, or we're recovered enough to make love again."

She looked genuinely shocked but also more than a little interested. *"Again?"*

"Doesn't the idea appeal to you?" He slid his hand under the blanket and cupped her breast, his thumb sliding over her nipple, teasing it into a hardened peak.

She gave him a dark scowl. "Of course the idea appeals to me, but I never read the rules on sex. Is there a certain number of times a day or a week?"

He smiled at her and bent to take possession of her mouth. He kissed her long and deep and with enough mastery to keep her tongue dancing with his. He loved how she gave herself up to him. There was no hesitation when he touched her. He nibbled on her lips and took a nip out of her chin before he answered. "Two individuals sharing their life together have sex when they choose. It can be slow and gentle or wild and crazy. But it should be an expression of love. And trust me on this, Rikki. I love you. When I'm touching you, I'm loving you."

He kissed his way down her throat to the side of her neck. Her pulse fluttered like that of a bird's wing and then began to pound with alarm beneath his lips. He stroked her hair gently, fear sliding into his mind at the thought of what she meant to him. He knew he had committed himself fully to her, to a new life, but he was still just catching glimpses into her world, into her mind.

She was fragile and vulnerable in ways others weren't, yet amazingly courageous and strong. He knew he never wanted to be without her. And he didn't want to stumble, to upset her without knowing what he was doing.

"So we can just stay in bed?" Her gaze searched his.

"That's right, *laskovaya moya*, we'll stay in bed together. Do you mind if I indulge myself?"

She gave him that adorable little frown of concentration again. "I don't know what that means."

"I want to explore what's mine. I like touching you."

"I didn't think I'd like it," she conceded, "but I do."

"Do you like touching me?"

A small little grin teased the corners of her mouth. "I give you a massage almost every night."

"You've touched me everywhere but my cock, Rikki. Are you afraid to touch me there?"

Her tongue touched her lower lip. "Maybe. A little. I don't want to hurt you. I could do it wrong, you know."

"I'm yours, Rikki. My body is yours. I want to feel you touching me. I want your hands and your mouth on me. You'd be giving me the same pleasure I gave you."

She pushed herself up on one elbow, the blanket slipping down over her breast. "You mean if I touch you . . ."

"Or suckle me," he interrupted.

"I can make you feel out of control with pleasure?"

He nodded solemnly. The idea of her fantasy mouth on him was already making him feel a little out of control and his body was already stirring to life at the thought of it. "How did you not know this?" Her fiancé couldn't have taken any time with her.

She shrugged. "I was never interested in sex. I don't learn about things that don't matter to me. But I'm interested now." She turned toward him.

Lev was still lying on top of the crumpled sheets. The other blankets had long ago fallen to the floor. She let her weighted blanket do the same, kneeling up over him, studying his body. She knew every inch intimately, since she'd given him massages every single night, but she'd never explored his manhood. He was long and heavy and thick, and she had been drawn to the sight of him naked and full many times. He never tried to hide an erection from her, and she'd grown used to the sight of him hard and thick.

Rikki stroked an experimental caress over the broad, flared head of his cock and Lev's body jerked. He gasped. She smiled. He tried to lie still for her. Her hands cupped the weight of his balls. She was very gentle, rolling them, getting used to the feel and texture of them. He could barely breathe, waiting for what came next. Rikki was very focused on what she was doing, just as she often was when she was fascinated by something. Lev liked that his body fascinated her.

At first, she was Rikki, completely enthralled and caught up in her exploration so that, for a time, she was wholly focused on feel and the mechanics of her experimentation. He set his teeth and tried to just let her be in control. She had a natural sensuality that shook him, and when she began using her mouth and tongue, his breath left his body in an explosive rush.

All of his training didn't seem to work around her. It didn't matter that she had no experience; she made up for that in her enjoyment, in the way she savored taste and texture, in the way she lost herself in making him pulse and jerk under her ministrations. He finally gave in with a groan and guided her head with his hands, his eyes wide open, watching her. Without a doubt he found her the sexiest woman he'd ever met. It didn't take long before he could tell he wasn't going to last.

Very gently he stopped her, needing to feel hot silk and tight, scorching heat. "Straddle me," he ordered.

Rikki obeyed him, and breathing deep, Lev pushed upward as she came down over the top of him. He felt her sheath unfurl, an exquisite fire surrounding him. He thrust and she shivered, giving him that soft, sexy moan he loved so much. *Need.* It was alive. Breathing in him, clawing at him, ripping at his heart and mind. He needed this beautiful, giving woman. She was so damned sexy, so giving and generous.

He lifted his hips even as he reached up and covered her breasts with his hands, claiming her. Claiming her body. Wanting to feel her heart beating into his palm.

"Ride me, *lubov moya*," he whispered and tugged at her nipples, feeling the answering rush of heat bathing his cock.

Her hair was disheveled and wild, the way he liked it, the sun-kissed streaks darker from her dampness. There was a sheen on her flushed skin, and her eyes were bright and glazed. He loved that he could do that to her, bring that change—the vivid color, the harsh, ragged breathing and the soft, musical moans.

He kept changing his rhythm, just to hear her gasp, to hear those astonished little whimpers as he impaled her. His hands were on her hips, driving her down to sit on him deeper and deeper each time. He felt the hot clasp of her body as her silky muscles surrounded him, gripping like a vise. She shuddered and the first strong wave moved over her, taking her. He increased his thrusts, driving up into her, holding her to him, wanting to explode with her. Scorching hot ecstasy washed over him, left him mindless for a few sweet moments.

Rikki took his past, took every bad thing and simply obliterated it. He floated in that sea of emptiness. Somewhere, sometime, when his mind began to work again, he realized it wasn't emptiness—it was love and he had it. And he was keeping it.

He reached up and caught her head with both hands, bringing her down to him so he could kiss her long and deep. Very gently he helped her off of him and coaxed her to lie beside him. She was exhausted, and this was the part where she felt awkward and uncertain. He dragged her blanket over her and tucked it around her.

"I'm staying, Rikki. Just so you know." He could tell she was drifting a little beneath the weight of the blanket and the sound of the rain through the open window.

She smiled, her eyes closed. "I want you to stay."

"Rikki," he whispered, holding her close, his mouth to her ear. "When the weather's good, let's go out on the boat together. You can dive, and I'll just rest and enjoy the views."

She stirred, her lashes fluttering. "You can't go on my boat."

He kissed his way from her mouth to her breast, his tongue flicking the tight little bud. She groaned and put a hand on his chest as if in protest, but she turned her body toward his, giving him better access. He suckled for a minute or two, his free hand massaging her buttocks.

"I'll just sit quietly. Not touch anything," he promised.

She made a growling noise, but she didn't look at him and her lashes settled. He lapped at her breast, teasing with his teeth.

"Lev, you can wake me up in an hour." Her voice was so drowsy his cock gave a little attempt to stir to life again.

"I want to watch you work. You look hot in your diving gear."

She sighed. "If you wake me in an hour, I'll let you on my boat. But you can't touch anything while you're on it."

"Not even you?" he prompted.

She smiled without opening her eyes. "I might let you touch me."

He kissed her breast and curved his body around hers before setting his watch. One hour it was.

14

"I can't believe I fell for the oldest trick in the book," Rikki said, glancing sideways at Lev before turning her gaze back to the narrow ribbon of asphalt above the ocean.

Highway 1 was deserted in the early morning hour, and she usually had the coastal road to herself. The sea sparkled invitingly with the sun barely up and joy was already spreading through her. Excitement lent a teasing note to her tone, but as always, she drove with her slow control, mindful of her speed.

Lev glanced pointedly at the speedometer and assumed an innocent air. "I have no idea what you're talking about."

"Sex. You managed to worm your way onto my boat using sex."

He laughed softly. "Any means, *lyubimaya moya*." He was totally unrepentant. "I wasn't about to let you go out to sea without me. Who knows what you might find in the ocean?"

She couldn't help but laugh at the implication. "So you think I'm in the habit of pulling strange men out of the sea and bringing them home?"

"I'm not taking any chances."

She laughed and shook her head as she turned onto the road leading to the harbor. "I love to smell the eucalyptus trees. The scent means I'm close to my boat."

"When we get to the parking lot, hang back, Rikki, and let me check out the boat."

The amusement faded instantly and she stiffened. "The *Sea Gypsy* is mine. I'm captain. If you think something's wrong, it's me that's going to board her first and check it out, not you."

"Protection is my field of expertise. I'm not telling you how to do your job," he said, and his voice went soft and scary.

She glanced at his face. His jaw was set. Not stubborn. Implacable. "I knew you were going to be like this. I *knew* it." She slapped the palm of her hand hard against the steering wheel. "I told you there would be no taking over."

He shrugged broad shoulders in a fluid, casual way that only made him appear bigger and stronger and more dominant. She considered trying to push him out of the truck while she was driving. Maybe he'd topple down the steep hillside and roll right into the river.

"I'm sharing your thoughts," he informed her.

She sent him her blackest scowl. "Then you know I'm not in a mood to be messed with. No one takes over my boat. Not even if they're the best lover in the world. *Especially* not the best lover in the world. He's already thinking he's all that."

Lev found himself laughing. She meant it, that was the

thing that amazed him about her. She wasn't even thinking she was complimenting him. She was too annoyed
with him to be pandering to his ego. She simply thought
he was the best lover in the world, but to her, she was the
captain and he wasn't taking over her boat. Little did
she know, he cared nothing for taking over the boat—just
the captain.

He leaned over and kissed her vulnerable neck. Once
started, it was a little hard to resist kissing her soft skin
over and over. And since he was there, a small nip was in
order so he could use his tongue to ease the sting.

"I'm going to crash if you keep that up. You're sort of
distracting."

He laughed again at her matter-of-fact observation.
"I'm *sort* of distracting? Obviously I need to try harder."

She elbowed him and gave him a look from under long
lashes. "Are you going to be this way the entire day? Because I'm likely to throw you in the ocean."

He flexed his muscles. "I'm willing for you to try.
Might be fun." Even as he teased her, he was already in
survival mode, his gaze sweeping the entire Albion Harbor. There was a single recreational vehicle on the grounds,
although no one was in sight. She drove through the
parking lot to the dock. They were the first ones there, as
they'd hoped.

Before she could exit the vehicle he caught her wrist,
all teasing gone. "He could have been here, Rikki. It's just
as easy to rig a boat to catch fire as it is to burn your house
down. This is where I'd choose to hit you, if I was looking
to kill you. You'll need to check your engine and your air
compressor before you touch anything. And when I tell
you to get off the boat, you move. Captain or not, your life
is more important than anything else."

She sat very still, her expression unreadable. Her lashes veiled her eyes so it was impossible to see into their dark depths, but he felt a small tremor run through her.

"Don't be afraid, Rikki. I'm not going to let anything happen."

Her lashes lifted and the full impact of her black eyes hit him. There was no fear, only a deep anger smoldering there. "I *want* him to come after me. All these years I believed I might have killed my parents and Daniel. He made me and everyone else believe that there was some monster lurking in me that slipped out while I was asleep. Four homes were destroyed, people's lives, everything they owned, and my parents . . ." She shook her head and her eyes flashed a dark promise. "I'm not running from him."

He slid his arm along the back of the seat, his fingers curling around the nape of her neck. "No, but we're going to be smart about it. We'll be prepared and careful. Right?"

She was silent a moment, tense, sitting upright and not relaxing back into him. He waited patiently. It took a few minutes before she allowed herself to relax into his massaging fingers. He remained quiet, simply waiting her out—he'd learned patience a long time ago. He wanted Rikki to trust in him and he knew she wouldn't give that up so easily. She'd taken charge of her own life and found a way to live within a world that was alien to her. She didn't trust or like authority, which was the only reason she hadn't turned him over to the police. There was no pushing her. She had to come to her own decisions and he wanted her to choose him every single time.

Rikki sighed softly and leaned her head back, turning to look at him again. "I can take care of myself. You know that, don't you? I've made a good life here, Lev. I like being with you, but I don't want you to think you need to take care of me. I may be different, but I can think for myself."

He tried not to wince at the word *like*. He wanted her to love being with him. He couldn't imagine not waking up to her soft body beside his, or her face with the incredible eyes and sexy, generous mouth. He recognized that perhaps he needed her a little more than she needed him, but he wasn't trying to own her. Just protect her. And there was a difference.

"Have I made you feel that way?"

She bit her lip, her frown back. "Not really. I just think it's important that you know I can take care of myself and make my own decisions."

"I respect you, Rikki. If I've made you think differently, in any way, then I apologize. I have a certain expertise that I hope you'll choose to make use of, that's all. You're so used to doing everything on your own that you might forget that I can help you." He was going to track down and kill the bastard, but now didn't seem the right time to say so.

She nodded. "Just so we're clear. And I don't like using you. You're starting a new life. The last thing you need to do is deal with some crazy person who decided to kill me for something I did when I was thirteen." She pushed open her door and slid out.

Lev did the same, moving around the bed of the truck to help with the equipment. "Do you remember anyone being terribly upset with you?"

She burst out laughing. "I hate to tell you this, Lev, but just about everyone was upset with me. I didn't look at them. I refused to talk half the time. I just wanted all the noise to go away. If it was too bad, I had violent tantrums. My parents were the only ones who liked me. I have no idea if I slighted someone or hurt their feelings. I spent most of the time just trying to survive without losing my mind."

He followed her along the dock until they came to the *Sea Gypsy*. He was grateful she didn't just jump aboard. She studied the boat first, carefully looking it over before stepping aboard.

"I don't think anyone's been on her. Generally, I can tell if someone's been snooping around her. I'll check the engine and air compressor though, just to be safe. I've taken the engine apart myself and I'll know if anyone's touched it."

He believed her. She had already assumed an air of supreme confidence and authority, as if the moment her feet touched the deck she was a different person—and maybe she was. He'd first seen her beneath the water, her eyes fierce and determined, holding his life in those dark depths, and she had been just as fierce on board her boat.

"Get to it, then. I'd like to get out of here before anyone else shows up. The fewer people who see me up close, the better." He rubbed his hand over the beard on his face. He'd never grown out a beard and it felt strange to him, but it changed his appearance.

"You should have stayed home like I told you."

"And be a kept man? I don't think so. I have my pride."

She paused as she went through her routine check of her equipment to give a derisive snort. "You have more money than I'll have in my entire lifetime. You just wanted to come aboard my boat." She narrowed her eyes. "And if you're considering a mutiny out at sea, I won't hesitate to throw you overboard."

"I was considering sex at sea. Lots of sex. I think the fresh air is giving me ideas."

She laughed and shook her head, stepping past him to peer at the air compressor. "We're working here, not playing."

He loved watching her, especially there with the early morning sun shining down on her. The day was cold but clear, with little wind, and the water appeared to be sparkling wherever the sun hit it. She was lost to him again, taken by the water, but this time, it was all right. He could take her in, watch her unhindered, see the smooth, efficient way she moved on board, listen to the way she hummed—he doubted if she even noticed she was humming. Yeah, she was deep in her zone, and he had become part of her boat.

He smiled, realizing she'd accepted him aboard whether she knew it or not. She would be acutely aware of him, feeling as if he was out of place, in her space, if she hadn't. As it was, she moved from her air compressor to the engine, and he watched her routine, memorizing it carefully, adding it like a diagram to the maps and blueprints stored in his brain. He kept out of her way, and turned his attention from her, to their safety.

She obviously knew what she was doing regarding her engine and air compressor, and she carefully went over both, leaving him to double-check that they had no stalker. He reached with his mind, expanding easily, sending his call to the birds up and down the river, in the harbor and on the sea stacks rising out of the water. In answer, they took to the air in a large migration. There were so many that Rikki actually broke her concentration to look as the air filled with various species. It was quite a sight, so many circling above the cliffs and harbor, over the highway and even along the sandy beach.

The birds called to one another and filled Lev's head

with information on the location of any lone man in the surrounding vicinity. One appeared to be a fisherman and the other was sitting on the bluff overlooking the beach. Lev singled out the cormorant that had shoved the shadowy figure into his head, fought for control and took it, soaring high with the bird, directing it to circle above the bluff so he could see the man for himself. Old clothes, a white beard and an empty bottle of whiskey gave the distinct impression that the watcher had spent the night on the bluff. Beside him was a ragged blanket and curled up on it, a dog. He released the bird and waited, breathing deep to orient himself.

He felt her eyes on him and looked up to stare straight into those dark depths. She had the lines in her hands and a strange expression on her face.

"We're heading out of the harbor, you might want to pay attention."

"Give me another minute."

She knew he had something to do with the birds. She probably felt the subtle buildup of power without realizing what it was. She stayed very still, her body swaying with the boat unconsciously, as if she were already out to sea and riding the waves. He loved that stillness in her, the lack of questions, the acceptance. She watched him without blinking. It took a little longer to send his mind soaring, finding and choosing the bird that had seen the fisherman.

Once again, the man seemed genuine enough, sitting in a small boat just at the edge of the bluffs. But *seemed* wasn't good enough. He set his watchers to spy on the man and to come tell him if the man should move from his spot and head out after them. He smiled at her. She hadn't moved, apparently mesmerized by him. "Are you going to get us out of here?" He gestured toward the parking lot where another truck had pulled in.

She turned abruptly without a word and stepped up to the helm. She looked as if she were part of the boat, one hand on the helm, her hair blowing in the breeze as they slowly made their way up the calm waters of the river to sweep under the Albion bridge into the ocean. He knew he should have been admiring all that wood and metal spanning the mouth of the river—and it was a beautiful sight in the early morning hours—but all he could see was Rikki.

She was transformed. He'd thought her beautiful there on the bed, soft skin offered up to him like a sacrifice, but here she was part of the sea, wild and free and very confident. As much as he loved Rikki for her inexperience and willingness to please him, he was intrigued by this side of her—so certain, from her fluid quick movements to her body language, to the rapt look on her face as she stared out over the water.

All he could think about was moving up behind her and taking her right there, while she took them out over the water. Next time, he'd have her wear a long skirt without any underwear so he could just lift up the hem and bury himself deep. They could move with the rise and fall of the boat, a gentle rhythm, or if they hit a little swell, hard and . . .

She turned her head and looked at him over her shoulder, speculation in her eyes. "I'm not certain you're up to the task." Laughter spilled over before she turned back to look at the sea.

His heart clenched violently in his chest, his emotion for her so strong it was nearly painful. It was nice to know he wasn't part of the scenery and that she'd chosen to stay connected to his mind. He needed the intimacy, even if she didn't. She was bright and shiny, as if a light was inside of her, showing him the way out of shadows.

"I think that's a challenge," he managed to reply, but more than the physical cravings for her, was the knowledge of certainty in his decision. He was risking everything, throwing away everything he'd been, who he essentially was, and she was worth it.

Again she sent him a look from over her shoulder before turning back to look straight ahead at the water as they rushed toward their destination. "That's not exactly the truth, Lev."

She really was becoming adept at telepathy; he'd have to be more careful about guarding his thoughts. He knew she was there, but she was becoming familiar, a part of him already, as if they'd somehow absorbed each other.

"Yes, it is. You're well worth the risk."

She sent him a small grin, her eyes velvet soft. "Silly. Of course I am. Not that part. Who you are is the same. This has always been who you really are, you just never let yourself feel anything. You were a child when they took and trained you. You're a good man, Lev, whether you believe it or not. I'm inside your head and I see who you are. You've always been good."

He watched the shoreline as they followed it, occasionally looking up at the sky to the birds, even as he turned her words over and over in his mind. He didn't know the truth anymore, and really, did it matter? He'd been given a second chance and he was grabbing it with both fists.

They stayed silent, enjoying the morning sun beaming down on the water. From the vantage point of a boat, the view was very different than from on shore. He saw holes worn through large rock masses, the sea stacks where every type of bird made their home or rested and nested. Birds plunged into the sea to fish, and seals occasionally poked their heads up or rested on their backs, watching the *Sea Gypsy* curiously.

Something big moved alongside of them, cutting easily through the water, and he saw Rikki smile and glance down. A geyser of water erupted beside the boat, raining drops on them. She laughed out loud. "He just gave us an invitation to play."

His eyebrow shot up. "Invitation to play? With that?" He looked at the massive, streamlined body moving fluidly through the water. The gray whale had to be a good forty-five feet long and weighed approximately thirty to forty tons. The fluke rose out of the water. It was ten to twelve feet and deeply notched in the center.

The whale disappeared beneath the water again. He spotted more shadows in the water. Rikki slowed the boat and then allowed it to idle while she bent down toward the water, dipping her cupped hand in it and shooting the liquid in a long arc over the surface. As she did, she began to sing softly, so that the water droplets hovered in the air, forming a long chain.

Lev held his breath, aware he was about to witness something probably no one other than Rikki had ever seen. He felt energy building beneath them. The boat rocked. He reached out to touch her, laying his hand gently on the nape of her neck, wanting the physical connection even as he thrust his mind into hers.

The intimate connection, so deep, so strong, shook him—the sensation every bit as pleasurable as making love to her. Her warmth surrounded him, feminine and soft, with no hard edges. Merging wasn't quite the same thing as reading her thoughts. Being inside of her, sharing her mind, brought a hard ache and a need that just kept growing stronger. For a moment his breath burned in his lungs and his heart pounded. Erotic images played through their shared mind and he allowed the waves of pleasure to wash over him.

All the while, he kept his gaze fixed on that chain of water held about a foot above the surface of the sea. Without warning, flukes shot up out of the water, slapping at the chain. Laughing, Rikki danced it out of reach. He could feel the way she anticipated the whale's movements by the strength of the energy pouring up from below them. She didn't cheat, keeping the chain the same distance from the surface. Lev spotted several whales spy-hopping their narrow, tapered heads up out of the water, looking to him as if they were smiling. Gray and white blotches covered their darker skin along with white barnacles. The whales were huge, graceful creatures, migrating down the Pacific coast from arctic waters to the Baja lagoons where their mating and breeding grounds were.

He watched as several in the pod played the game, trying to be the first to slap the chain of water with their flukes. He could hear Rikki's delighted laugh, but more, he felt the exact same pleasure, merged as he was with her. The connection to the sea was so deep in her veins that he could swear her blood was ebbing and flowing with the rhythm of the waves. Joy burst through him, a foreign concept so alien, at first he had no idea what the indescribable feeling was. She gave him that—the gift of happiness.

He watched a big male coming in and knew, just as Rikki did, that he was going to hit that chain of water, slapping it hard with his fluke so that water burst into the air, thousands of crystal droplets raining over them.

Satisfied, the pod moved on, disappearing beneath the surface once more.

"That was incredible."

She laughed and allowed him to help her up, moving against his body with a not so subtle signal. "Next time, I *am* wearing that skirt." She kissed his chin and turned back to throttle the boat forward. "If you keep watch, they'll probably come up in anywhere from three to five minutes. They'll blow in intervals of three to fifteen seconds before they raise their flukes and disappear. They'll often stay under longer, but if you pay attention, you'll notice a general pattern."

"You just throw that out there about the skirt and then change the subject to whales?"

Her laughter teased his groin into a hard ache. He swore for a moment he could feel her fingers stroking him into a heavy erection. "We have work to do, my man."

He stepped up behind her, close, so his body was imprinted against hers, so she could feel him hard and thick, pressed tight against her. One arm circled her waist, and he rested his chin lightly on her shoulder. *I like being your man.* He couldn't say such hokey words aloud, but the emotion inside of him spilled into her mind.

She reached back with one arm to circle his head, turning hers so she could find his mouth. He kissed her long and deep, tasting love in the sweetness of her mouth. She broke away first, turning back to make certain they were on course. They were heading toward one of her favorite spots, just off Elk. She'd told him it was approximately nine miles away and she'd held off working there so she could get a good harvest.

The ride took about a half hour and she never asked him to move until they were coming up on the place.

"The cemetery is just up there," she said, gesturing with her chin, a frown of concentration on her face. "Sometimes I feel the spirits are looking out for me."

He no longer had her attention and he stepped back to give her room. "Is this dangerous?"

"Well, if you don't know what you're doing," she admitted. "You have to know how to maneuver in here. The floor beneath us is virtually a mountain range. You see there's not much rock showing here. There's a three-hundred-foot drop from the road up there. The rocks are real close to the edge but they extend out suddenly about a thousand feet into the ocean."

While she talked, she maneuvered the boat carefully along a hidden path. "The northern end of the mountain is totally under water."

He peered below them, and his heart leapt. He could see rocks on either side of the boat beneath the surface of the water. A few jutted out, but most seemed to be out of sight. As they moved closer, little islands appeared, nothing more than rocks protruding out of the sea.

"I'll go down about twenty feet, right off those rocks, but I have to come in bow to current, so I can go down the chain, otherwise the flow takes me and the urchins away from the boat. This way I can use the current to my advantage."

Each of the little coves formed shelters in the rocks. The stacks were dotted with seals basking along the low-tide rookies. The seals' spotted silvery gray and dark brown coats gleamed in the early sun as the mammals rested with their large bodies sprawled out on the rocks.

"Look at them all. They really are cute up this close, but bigger than I expected."

She laughed. "They're not so cute if you dive in one of

their channels between the rocks. They don't like it and aren't shy about letting you know. All of a sudden they have teeth and claws, and you just get out of their way. Most of the time, they rocket past you when you're down there and you have to ignore them. Never share your catch or they won't leave you alone—they can get aggressive."

Lev studied the seals. They suddenly looked a *lot* larger than they had a couple of seconds earlier. "How big are they?"

She shrugged casually. "They reach five or six feet in length and can weigh up to three hundred pounds. Give them respect and you'll be fine." She gave him a small frown. "You aren't diving, Lev."

"I know that, but maybe you shouldn't dive here either. Aren't there urchins on the other side of those rocks, away from their territory?"

She nodded. "Actually, the front of the rock wall is covered with them. There's a drop of about one hundred and twenty feet, but you can only harvest that spot in three foot swells and no duration. You have to stay buoyant at around thirty to forty feet, but it's pretty dangerous, you can drop very quickly."

"Great. You're using that word 'dangerous' quite a bit."

She shook her head, smiling in reassurance at him. "Here we're protected from any big swells coming from the northwest. The big rocks there break up the string of swells. Of course, you have to contend with the current here. It's like diving in a river. You don't get the back and forth of the wave motion here."

She was so matter-of-fact, so completely confident, and more, she was eager to dive. He could feel her slipping away from him, her attention on her mistress. The sea was definitely calling to her. He knew she loved the water and diving was imperative to her well-being, but it suddenly seemed too dangerous to allow her to go alone. He'd never really experienced fear for anyone else before and it was damned uncomfortable.

He'd certainly gone diving, numerous times, and was perfectly qualified, but she would balk. He was already getting a huge concession just to be on her boat. He wasn't so impatient that he'd lose everything by pushing her too fast. Rikki didn't like change. He'd brought about a lot of changes in her life and she was fragile. He knew the hold he had on her was every bit as fragile as her state of mind.

"Tell me what a tender does," he said. When she snapped him an impatient look, he tried a smile. "While you're getting your gear."

She indicated for him to sit out of her way while she checked her gear again. She'd done it the night before, had gone over it meticulously in the morning and now checked it a third time. He realized she really did take her safety seriously.

Rikki pinned him with her dark eyes. "Basically anything I say."

"Come on, *lyubimaya moya.*" Deliberately he used his accent, his blue eyes drifting over her as she poured warm water into her diving suit. "Give me a few facts."

She sighed and shimmied out of her jeans, exposing her shapely legs and the raindrop tattoo he loved so much. She was very slender, all that working underwater and only peanut butter to sustain her. She needed high-energy foods and a balanced diet. *Easy,* he reminded himself. *One change at a time, and only those things she needs to keep her healthy and safe.*

Rikki sent him a peculiar look as if she'd caught part of

his thoughts, although they were no longer connected telepathically. Maybe something about the water surrounding
them amplified her talents. He didn't know enough about
water elements, only that they were powerful in their own
right. He had psychic gifts, but hers worked differently.
She was bound to water, and water was bound to her.

"Rikki." He kept his voice even.

"You're working very hard at manipulating me," she
pointed out.

He knew she was sharp. "Just give me the general idea."

"Tenders, as a *general* rule, do everything above water
and the diver does everything below. The most important
thing to remember is to slow down. There's no emergency
unless I tell you. A tender does what's asked of him, *nothing* more. Don't make it up as you go along."

She poured baby shampoo into her hands and lathered
her legs and hips and buttocks. She wasn't wearing much
more than a thong. He tried not to be mesmerized by the
sight of her hands flowing over all that skin.

"If everything above the water is my job, I should be
doing that."

She blinked, as if coming out of a trance, and then she
grinned. "You have a one-track mind. And it's important
for me to keep to my routine. I can't deviate. For one
thing, it throws me off and my mind goes into chaos, but
more than that, it's a safety issue out here."

"Got it, no sex on the boat."

"I didn't say that, only don't interrupt my routine before I dive."

"So what do I do?"

"Absolutely *nothing*." Her smile faded and she stared
directly into his eyes. "You can't touch one thing on this
boat."

"Rikki." His voice was gentle. "That's just silly. Let me help you. I won't touch anything unless you tell me to. You trust me with your body, you can trust me with your things." He could see she was already becoming agitated, thrown off by the change in her routine. "Give me something to do. One thing. Diving is exhausting work. I can do the menial things."

She slipped into the bottom half of her wet suit while she thought it over. "I'll hook the bag to my hose and send it up. When it hits the surface, you can pull the bag in— *slowly*—which will pull me up as well. When the bag gets to the boat, secure the hook to the urchin bag and disconnect the hose. I'll either come aboard to rest and eat, or I'll want another bag. If I ask for a bag give it to me before you haul the uni aboard. Fill the urchin hole with the bags first. Once the urchin hole is full cover the bags on the deck with the silver tarp—silver side up."

"I can do that."

She dragged her T-shirt over her head and folded it as neatly as she had her jeans, uncaring that she was bare-breasted, the morning sun playing over her slender curves with a loving hand. She didn't seem to notice her state of undress, but he couldn't help himself, his gaze drifting possessively, drinking her in. She was *his*. This wild, independent woman was a mixture of vulnerability and courage. There would be few people in her life who appreciated her quick mind and bravery facing the challenges of a world she was born too sensitive to function in properly—yet she managed, carving out a life for herself against impossible odds.

Lev found himself with his mouth dry and his heart pounding. The light spun around her, turning her skin to soft cream and making her enormous eyes appear even blacker and more mysterious and exotic than ever. She had the adorable little frown on her face he'd come to know meant she was concentrating, wrestling with her inability to cope with change in her routine. He liked that he was one of the few people she trusted into her life, and he loved that he was the only one she would allow on her boat or in her bed. She belonged to him exclusively, and there was satisfaction and even pride in that.

"Slowly," he agreed when he could find his voice. "I pull the bag in slowly. Urchins in the hold first and then if they're on deck cover them with the silver tarp, silver side up. Nothing more, nothing less, and take my time."

She rubbed baby shampoo over her upper body, her fingers gliding over her skin, her breasts, her small, tucked-in waist. It was more erotic than anything he'd ever seen.

"It's possible someone will see us here, Fish and Game, and they'll check your license. A tender makes certain other boats stay out of a diver's territory. Keep track of where your diver has gone so other divers don't enter my territory."

Smirking, he glanced at the sky. That part would be easy enough. No one was getting near his diver.

"And stop looking at me like that."

"Like what?"

"Like you're about to eat me."

Now his smirk was all for her. "I could, you know. Every morning for breakfast. Right here on the boat. Doesn't matter. I could be as addicted to your taste as you are to peanut butter."

She sent him a look from under her lashes that made him want to kiss her. He folded his arms and regarded her steadily as she pulled on her tight shirt and then hooked her belt around her waist. Her eyes had gone bedroom sexy. She liked the idea as much as he did.

"You're just a little perverted, you know that, don't you?" she said.

He shrugged, unrepentant. "Fortunately you like me this way."

Her answering smile was slow, but it came. "All right," she conceded, "maybe that's true. I've got to go to work."

"You like this, don't you?"

Rikki nodded. "This is my world, Lev."

She didn't look at him again, engrossed in her routine, meticulously going over every piece of equipment. He watched her prepare for her dive, each separate step, committing it to memory, so that he would be able to anticipate anything she might need if she ever allowed a partnership between them. He noted her hoses were wrapped in a loop, each length of the circle exact. Her rake had a knife welded to it, but she didn't carry any other weapon on her person, a concept completely foreign to his nature.

Once again he could see he was completely forgotten. He imagined most men's egos would take a beating when they realized that she simply put them out of her head as if they no longer existed. She was very focused as she checked her lifeline, the air compressor, her hose and her bailout tank, which she wore on her back. She had her instruments strapped to her wrist and her gear on when she suddenly looked up at him and smiled. For him.

His heart jumped again. He'd never been so affected by anyone in his life. "Have a good time, Rikki."

She turned toward the side of the boat and then hesitated. "You'll be all right?"

He stepped up to her and took her face in his hands,

kissing her long and deep. "Don't worry about me. I have plenty to do."

She frowned at him, kissed him again and slipped from his arms, making her way to the edge of the boat. She went into the water and caught the anchor chain, using it to make her way down to the depth she wanted to go. Otherwise, the flow of the current would have taken her away.

Lev watched her disappear, his heart in his throat. He shoved his hand through his thick hair and peered down into the water where she'd disappeared. He was going to be one of those obnoxious men who refused to leave his wife's side. He wanted to be down there with her, with spears and knives and maybe a torpedo or two, just in case. Who knew he would be like this?

He studied the terrain around them. It was beautiful, the air crisp, the sight unbelievable. The cliffs were high, and the long expanse of rock, pointing like a finger from the land, seemed to run straight back to the highway. He found himself settling. This was what he wanted. This place. This woman. Diving with her in the environment she was most comfortable in.

He had money, enough that neither of them would have to work again, but she would never accept that, and he loved that about her. He was already committed, his mind, his heart, definitely his body. She was his life now.

So how was he going to stop the inevitable questions? Levi Hammond had a past. He had created an entire life for himself, adding an extensive diving hobby. Hammond's parents were no longer alive, but they'd left him money, plenty of it, and that had been the most difficult part of building a fake life. Money could be traced. He'd had to come up with plausible ways his parents could have left him an inheritance that if looked into, would appear solid.

Once he'd covered his financial tracks, he considered he was relatively safe—but for Ralph. Ralph was a problem and today, when they brought the urchins to the dock where the processing plant would pick them up, Lev would have to make the final decision on how he was going to start his new life. Risk everything and let the man live, or find a way for an accident to happen. He didn't like either alternative, and he didn't want to go to Rikki with blood on his hands, not the blood of an innocent man.

15

RIKKI felt the cool relief of the water enfolding her body. It had been too long. Every cell seemed to soak up the moisture, she was so thirsty she seemed to drink with every part of her body. She felt the familiar stillness, the calming in her mind, as if, down here in this world of water, everything was synced and perfect. There was no noise to fill her head and pound and stab. She didn't have to watch everything she said and did, as if at any moment she would somehow be stepping on someone's "normal." She could just be.

Massive schools of codfish, mottled blue and black, swam in a flashing wave. Starfish in bright, fiery oranges and deep purples clung to the rocks, rock and spider crabs dappled the walls, living decorations. And the urchin were plentiful. She looked up and the water shimmered in layers of pearlescent color, vivid blue, gray and near the surface an emerald glow. A few jellyfish floated free, tentacles searching. She continued down, just enjoying the view along the way. Orange sea cucumbers and red abalone adorned several of the rocks. Visibility was good and she made out more starfish, anemones and sponges in a variety of shapes and colors. On the bottom there was a brilliant purple pincushion guarding several lemon nudis.

The contour of the underground range was just like aboveground, peaks and valleys and ravines. She was very familiar with the area, it was one of her favorites places to dive. Her life had changed dramatically in the last few weeks, but the ocean was the same, always constant, always beautiful and always very treacherous if one didn't pay close attention to her.

She had to be careful to focus on work rather than on the beauty of the sea life around her. The colorful anemones and starfish always captured her attention. One could easily get lost in the vivid world and forget the passage of time, always crucial underwater when one needed air to breathe.

She began raking sea urchins into her net, losing herself in the rhythm of her work. Curious fish drifted around her, but nothing disturbed her and she was able to get her net filled quickly. The current seemed stronger than usual, but the series of storms had prevented her from diving for a couple of weeks and the rivers had filled and were dumping into the sea.

By the time she'd filled her first net and hooked it and was working on the second, she was getting tired. *Out of shape.* Or maybe she was exhausted from making love so often. Lev and she had been holed up in their house for days. Each evening one of her sisters brought dinner by, but that was the only time they saw anyone else. They spent each day together doing the silliest things and then making love. Talking and making love. Exploring the house and making love. They'd had sex in every single room a dozen times.

Lev was insidious. He just sort of snaked his way into her world and had already become a part of it. And somehow, he'd managed to wheedle his way onto her boat. She'd lived with that reminder for almost a week. Now he was up there, probably touching her equipment. She raked faster, her arms aching.

She sent the first bag to the surface and hooked the second one, allowing it to float up as well. She followed at a more leisurely pace. Lev had been paying attention when she'd given him instructions because he was slowly pulling in the hose, and her with it. After working alone for so long, it was an odd sensation to have someone else helping. She wasn't positive she liked it. Relying on herself was easier and safer. If she depended on someone else, eventually, in a crisis she might hesitate, and seconds counted under water.

When she'd worked with Daniel, he'd owned the boat. They'd dived together, and they'd done cleanup together. They'd been diving buddies, but Daniel, because the boat was his, had been the captain. He shared the work with her and they never had so much as a squabble. But when she was diving, even with him, she'd totally relied on herself. The few times she'd tried working with a tender, her need for an exact routine had always made it impossible.

Nearing the surface, she caught a glimpse of something exploding out of the rock as if shot from a gun, rocketing toward her through the water. A huge lingcod with a mouthful of wickedly sharp teeth had emerged from a dark crevasse in the rock and charged straight at her. It came right between her legs and she rolled over in an effort to get away. The mottled fish had to be a good fifty inches in length and weigh in at sixty pounds. With eighteen large teeth coming at her, she whipped around to keep a wary eye on it.

The cod continued on past her, evidently intent on a good-sized cabazon swimming back down to the floor where it preferred to hang. The cod grabbed the cabazon, shook him three or four times as if the twenty-pounder was nothing, split him in half and spit him out. For a moment the cod watched with evident satisfaction as the two halves of the cabazon floated away. The cod ignored her and swam back to his rock.

She stuck her head above water, hanging on to the anchor chain so the current couldn't take her away from the boat and watching as Lev carefully pulled up the urchin nets. He followed her orders exactly, placing them in the hold and covering them. She signaled for another net. She had close to a thousand pounds and thought she might be able to pull in another three to five hundred for a good day's work if she was lucky.

The wind had picked up a bit and mist had begun to drift in from out at sea. She didn't want to take any chances with Lev aboard.

"You tired?" he called.

She shrugged. "I'll come in after this next haul."

He nodded and gave her the net. "Be careful, Rikki."

"I always am," she said.

A gull screamed and Lev turned his attention skyward. Rikki shoved her regulator into her mouth and started back down, trailing the net. She turned her head at the first sign of movement and found the cod back, this time, charging straight at her. It was ugly, the huge mouth wide-open, showing teeth. Its bulging eyes fixed on her. Instinctively she thrust the net in front of her to protect herself. The cod rocketed so fast through the water that he burst into the net, nearly striking her anyway. She just managed to shove the net to one side, avoiding the contact, but he was so strong and swimming so fast he nearly jerked her arm out of the socket. Adrenaline rushed through her veins and without thinking she lifted the net out of the water and tossed, throwing the fish out.

She watched it fly through the air in a high arc and begin its descent. Her stomach dropped. No sound came out of her mouth, although she really did try to call out a warning. The sixty pound cod landed almost on top of Lev, furious, fighting, flopping and jumping, snapping with his teeth. Lev whipped out a gun and aimed it at the ferocious fish.

"No! My boat," Rikki shouted.

He did a little dance, trying to get away from the thrashing creature, catching at the gunwale, prepared to leap over the side as the fish snapped at him.

Laughter bubbled up. Lev, the ruthless assassin, was about to abandon the boat because of a fish. He shot her a long look of reprimand and drew a lethal-looking—*big*— knife. Rikki nearly drowned herself laughing as he stabbed down and caught the fish with the blade and heaved it back into the water.

"That was dinner," she called. "I thought you'd be happy."

"You're not going to be laughing so hard when you get back in this boat," he predicted ominously.

Lev watched Rikki prudently disappear beneath the water. The last he saw of her were her laughing eyes. He found himself grinning. So she was throwing fish at him. He shook his head and poured himself a cup of coffee from the thermos he'd brought. He wanted to be down there with her, but he'd be content with getting a foot in the door, so to speak.

He studied the rocky shores. There was a wild beauty to the coast, a primal feeling of untouched wilderness, even though houses and small villages dotted the bluffs. Just beyond the shoreline, dark forests stood tall, great redwoods and groves of eucalyptus and cypress. The clear sky had slowly disappeared under a layer of mist, which was thickening to a pale shade of gray. He watched it come in, fingers of fog drifting lazily, pointing toward the shore.

The seagull cried out again, drawing his attention. The fisherman was on the move. Lev sighed. He'd known his government would send someone to make certain he was dead. He had hoped they wouldn't move quite so fast, but he was a liability to them if he was out from under their control and they had to make certain.

Everything in him settled. Emotion was gone and his survival instincts took over. He'd been waiting, had planned, and he was ready. Now that the cleaner was finally here, he could breathe again. This was *his* world and he was very familiar with it. Life or death. Cat and mouse. He rolled his shoulders and felt the calm that came to him with every assignment. He had a purpose, a mission to carry out, and this time, it was to secure a new life for himself.

There was only one real threat to him and that was Ralph. He knew he would do whatever he had to do to protect Rikki. He had every intention of meeting with Ralph and "pushing" his memory to the back of his head before the fisherman found him—and he would find him. He wouldn't leave a stone unturned before he went home and reported back to his masters.

Lev reached for the bird and this time it was easier connecting. The bird circled above the blue sea and made his way back toward the harbor. Moving high in the fog was a surreal experience, the bird's sight mainly on the sea and the activity below it, looking for an easy meal. The dizzy, disorienting feeling caused by his blurred vision always threw him for a moment as he adjusted to the difference in his sight.

The seagull took him along the shore, past craggy rocks and windswept trees, and then around the bluff to the other side of Albion Harbor. Lev directed the bird to spiral down for a better look. The fisherman had returned his rented boat to the harbor and was making his way along the bluffs, stopping occasionally to talk to a few people. In spite of the clothes and cap, Lev could not miss that fluid, rolling walk.

Petr Ivanov. Lev recognized the way he moved. He'd run across Petr more than once, a robot of a man. They'd been in training together when they were in their teens. Even then, Petr had displayed an inability to connect with anyone. His trainers had capitalized on that, keeping him emotionally disconnected from everyone. He was used to clean up messes. It didn't matter who the mark was, man, woman or child. No matter the age or circumstances. He never questioned, he just did the job.

Of course they would send Petr. Who else? He wouldn't fear finding Lev. He was a machine. He wouldn't kill unnecessarily or with passion. He would hunt until he was satisfied that Lev Prakenskii was dead, and until then, he'd keep digging until he found answers. There was satisfaction in knowing he had been right. He'd expected Ivanov to be the one they sent after him. Knowing his enemy was half the battle.

He turned the seagull toward the harbor, needing to see if the processing company had already sent their truck for picking up the day's catch. The bird flew over the dock and no one was yet on the platform, which meant Petr Ivanov hadn't yet met up with Ralph. Ivanov was in the beginning stages of his investigation, assuming different characters. He'd go to the authorities with an official inquiry, but he would visit local bars and hangouts, looking for anyone who worked along the docks and in fishing boats that might provide clues to any survivors.

Lev disengaged from the bird and sank down in the boat, shaken. Taking possession of another creature's sight was disorienting and weakened him. The use of any psychic gift always took a toll, but that particular one seemed to use up the most energy for him. It seemed to be different for those who were elements like Rikki. She never displayed weakness after using her gift. She seemed to manipulate the energy effortlessly.

He drank coffee and waited, lighter somehow, now that Ivanov was actually here and the waiting was over. This was a world he could get used to, the peace of it, the wildness. He was a man who would always live outside of society, but here, in this unique place, maybe there was room for him—with Rikki.

He sighed again. *Rikki*. The miracle of Rikki. Did he have the right to stay and expose her to danger just because he wanted a life with her? How selfish was that? He wanted to protect her, but the danger from a man like Ivanov was far worse than her stalker. Ivanov was a cold-blooded killer, capable of wiping out her entire family to get to him. So what did a man do? He loved her. He'd never thought to experience love, and maybe that in itself had been all the gift he was supposed to keep. He blinked

up at the sky, as if looking for an answer, but the fog had
rolled in and covered the bright blue with a gray, smoky
mist.

The net surfaced and Lev pulled it in slowly, helping to
assist Rikki to the top. He was a little surprised how relieved he actually was when he saw her head above the
waterline. He trusted in her skills, he'd seen her in action,
yet now he worried about her. He found himself smiling—
worrying was such a domesticated thing to do.

He had to admire the way she used the anchor chain to
pull herself over to the boat, so the strong current didn't
have a chance to push her away. She'd obviously done it
often and came aboard with ease. He hauled in the net and
covered the sea urchins with the silver tarp, careful to
keep from touching the spines. His hands performed all
the right tasks, but he was watching her, observing every
movement.

She was exhausted. He could see that instantly. She
flashed him one quick smile, but it was a greeting, no more.
She stripped, right there on the boat, rinsing off, smearing
a lotion over her skin before she shimmied back into her
jeans. He could tell sex and flirtation hadn't even entered
her mind, but it was an erotic sight, maybe because of her
complete lack of awareness, almost as if he were a voyeur,
catching a glimpse of a sensual woman through a window.

He handed her the water bottle and watched her drink
it down. He *felt* her peace, her serenity. She found something to sustain her, there in the water, in that other world.
He could feel those dark eyes on him, watching him as
intently as he was studying her.

"What is it?" She wiped her mouth with the back of her
arm. "Something's different. What happened while I was
down there?"

He reached out slowly and touched her face. He needed the contact with her. Dread filled him, a weight in his heart, in his mind.

Her eyes darkened even more and she frowned at him as she shook her head. "No, Lev. I don't want you to go. I want you to stay with me. What's out there for you? Tell me that. Do you really want to live in the cold and dark, in the shadows, without a name or family?"

"No. But I want you safe, Rikki."

She burst out laughing. "Are you insane? Look around you, Lev. I don't live safe. I don't need or want safe. I want to *live* life. If you don't want me, that's fine, but if you think you're being all noble and protecting me, then just think again. You're somebody here. You're concrete, real, not insubstantial like a ghost."

His hand curled in her wet hair, fisted there, drawing her slowly toward him until she was standing so close he could smell the ocean on her. "What am I going to do with you?" His hands framed her face. "I feel like you did the first time we made love. I don't know the rules, Rikki. I'm in new territory."

She smiled at him, and he stroked caresses over her soft, curved lips with the pad of his thumb. The knots in his belly unraveled just a little.

"Then we make up our own rules, Lev. Who you are, that's safe with me. Stay, don't slip back into the shadows. Just stay."

"It's that easy?"

Her dark eyes probed his until he swore she could see inside of him. "Yes." She nodded, very solemn, making him shatter inside—and give her everything he was or would ever be.

He didn't want to leave her. He didn't want to go back

to being alone, not knowing right from wrong, having to make life and death decisions, watching torture and horror for a greater goal. He was tired. And he needed Rikki.

"You're sure? Be absolutely certain, Rikki. This could get ugly."

"I'm sure. And I'm hungry. Hand me a sandwich and tell me what happened."

A slow grin spread across his face. He liked that she was so pragmatic in the face of adversity. He found her a sandwich and they sat together while she ate hungrily.

"I spotted a man I know. He cleans up messes, meaning he disposes of problems."

"And you'd be that problem."

He nodded.

She twirled her sandwich in circles with her thumbs and index fingers. The movement was fascinating. She didn't appear to notice she did it.

"You knew he was going to come. He'll ask questions of the people up and down the coast. Fisherman, divers, the people most likely to have seen a survivor."

He nodded. "Hospitals, clinics. He'll be thorough."

"So hole up at the farm."

"Your sisters . . ."

She shrugged. "Won't say anything. Judith and Airiana will read him like a book. There's no reason for him to question any of them."

"You make it sound so easy, Rikki."

"It *is* easy. You stay out of sight, and he'll go away and declare that you're dead."

"What about Ralph?"

She took another bite and chewed thoughtfully. Washing the peanut butter down with water, she ate a couple of cookies before she answered. "He never actually saw your face that day. He'll see Lev Hammond today, an old diving buddy."

He shook his head. "Not Lev. Don't use that name. It's *Levi*. A Russian name as common as Lev is bound to be a trigger. And we were more than diving buddies in the past."

She made a face at him. "*More* than diving buddies? What does that mean *exactly*?"

"It means you were such a little diving hussy, you were sleeping your way up and down the coast and I've had to come chasing after you *again*."

She opened her mouth to object and he kissed her. She tasted like peanut butter. He was beginning to think he might actually come to like the stuff. His hand bunched in the back of her hair, holding her in place and he kissed her again, just because he could.

She blinked up at him, a small smile on her face. "There might be a few perks to being a diving hussy. Up and down the coast, hmmm?"

His fingers tightened in her hair. "You just remember I carry a gun at all times."

"Ah, but now I know what that gun is for—killer fish."

She burst out laughing again, the sound floating around him like the droplets of fog, enveloping him in a misty, melodic embrace. It was a strange sensation, sharing her love of the water and the feel of moisture on his skin. Individual drops felt as if velvet tongues licked over his skin. The sensual stimulation was more than just sexual—it was elemental to life, feeding his energy, building barriers that helped him cope . . .

He bent his head to hers once more. He was so connected to her that he was in her brain, feeling her sensations as if they were his own. He took his time, ravaging her mouth, trying to convey without words what was in his heart. She'd turned his world upside down. She'd given him a safe place to hide until he was fully healed or a place to live. He chose life—with her.

"I like calling you Lev," she whispered, a small frown drawing her brows together. "I like the way the name sounds—very much like the real you, like *my* Lev."

His world righted as he inhaled sharply. She would always be his miracle, and no more so than right at that moment with her little confession. He wanted to give her that much of his past, maybe keep the memories of his family, so long ago lost, with that name, but it was a danger. Had he not had a concussion he would never have identified himself with his true given name.

Her little frown disappeared and she smiled at him. "I'll call you that when we make love. A much more intimate name between the two of us. Something sacred."

His heart twisted. She could bring a man to his knees. "I like that idea."

"We'd better get moving or we won't make it back into the harbor."

She turned away from him, all business, dealing with the hoses and equipment. When he bent to help, she sent him one fierce scowl and he backed off, both hands up in the air in surrender. He couldn't help smiling as he watched her work, noting the way she wrapped hoses in patterns and fussed meticulously over her equipment and wet suit. They made their way back through the thickening fog to the harbor.

He had to admit his heart accelerated a bit as they neared the harbor itself. The swells were beginning to pick up, dashing against the rocks jutting up out of the water. White spray burst into the air and the fog seemed alive, moving now, which meant wind.

"You scared?" She sent him a cheeky grin over her shoulder.

Her cheeks were red, her hair wild, her dark eyes bright. He could see she loved this. Loved the hint of danger, loved the sea rolling beneath her feet.

"You'd like me to admit that to you, wouldn't you?"

Her laughter was music to him. She sounded carefree. Happy. So alive. "Don't worry, you're safe with me, *Levi.*"

He knew he was safe with her. She'd accepted him into her life and she was intensely loyal. He watched her as she maneuvered the entrance to the six hundred feet of river. The swells were increasing and she had to bring the boat in just perfectly to keep from being swamped. Concentration was on her face, complete focus. She had fought her own battles—and won. She'd found her own strength and knew exactly who she was. She might have wished she'd been born someone else at some time in her life, but she'd accepted what life had given her and she'd made the most of it.

Happiness settled over him. Peace. He was finished living in the shadows as an insubstantial ghost. He'd found home and astonishingly, home was a woman. He folded his arms across his chest and kept his gaze on her as they rode out the increasing swells, shot beneath the bridge and into calmer water. She laughed and turned her head again to look at him, to share the experience with him.

Rikki took the boat straight to the dock. She'd called in the morning and knew the processing plant would have the truck waiting when she came in. It looked as if she was the first boat to come back in. The others wouldn't be far behind her, not with the wind picking up so suddenly. They'd never get back into the harbor if the swells increased in strength.

"We just got here," Ralph called to her. "Mike's the only other boat out from Albion today. Danny went with him. The weather's closing in on us again." His speculative gaze wasn't on her but on Lev.

She nodded. "Supposed to be a good day."

Lev looked at her face. She'd retreated, become closed off. She was all business, hooking the nets to the pulley so Ralph could weigh and tag them before dumping them into the totes. He watched carefully until he knew exactly what to do, and casually took over, one hand moving Rikki gently but firmly out of the way.

"Levi Hammond," he said as he guided the sea urchin net over the platform.

"Ralph Carlson."

"Yeah, I remember. I'll be around for a while again. Decided to come back and claim my woman," Lev said. "We've been dive partners on and off for years. Been roughing it in Alaska, but figured if I waited too long, she'd replace me."

Rikki's gaze was cool as it swept over him. "I'm still considering it."

She played her part so perfectly he could have kissed her. He dropped an arm around her shoulders and was content with kissing the top of her head.

"Best damn diver up and down the coast," he said. "Bossy too. She's not letting me touch anything on her boat."

"I'm still mad at you," she sniffed and pushed him away.

Lev laughed and climbed up onto the platform to help Ralph swing the sea urchin nets to the totes while Rikki took her boat back to the dock to tie up.

"Rikki doesn't talk much," Ralph said. "She's been diving in this area for about four years and has never said more than a few words to anyone."

Lev nodded. "That's Rikki." He stepped a little closer to Ralph, using a very careful "push" to test the man. "Been a while since I've been here." He planted a vague memory, nothing more than a shadow, laughing together in a bar.

Ralph immediately filled in the blanks, providing an atmosphere and details, dumping them into the memory to enhance it. "Long time."

"Alaska's wild. Great diving, but cold—and lonely." Lev grinned at him. "After a while all I could think about was getting back to Rikki."

"You're lucky you came when you did. I was thinking I might ask her out."

Lev smiled but his eyes went cool, then frosty. "Yeah, I wouldn't try that, I'm the jealous type."

He pushed a little harder, distancing the memory of Rikki bringing back a passenger, so the timeline was vague. Ralph rubbed at his head.

"Headache?" Lev asked sympathetically.

"Yeah. Came on all of a sudden. And I've got one more coming in."

"I hear him now," Lev said, and stepped off the platform with a lift of his hand.

It was all the damage control he could do for now, and maybe it would be enough. Ivanov would find Rikki. He would talk to all the divers. It was a fairly common practice for agents to charm their way in, using women as shelters when they needed a safe house. Petr Ivanov would definitely question Rikki and ask questions about her.

Rikki was scrubbing her boat and equipment with bleach in preparation for the next dive. She glanced up at him. "Thanks for not pulling out your gun and shooting him. I worried a little that you might have gone one too many days and just needed the practice."

"Ha ha." He started to board but she gave him that fierce scowl that told him he wasn't welcome. "And I wouldn't have used a gun. I'd want it to appear natural, like a heart attack."

She paused again and gave him her look. "I'd better not die of a heart attack. I'll come back and haunt you."

"Well, your boat is looking pretty good. And you don't share well with others."

She laughed softly. The second boat came around the bend in the river out of the fog, looking a little ghostly. The two occupants stared at Lev as they passed the *Sea Gypsy*.

Lev crouched on the dock, staying low, bending toward her. Voices carried on the water, so he used the more intimate telepathy. *Tell me their names and something about them.*

Dan Ferguson and Mike Carpenter. That's Mike's boat. Dan has his own, but the engine is down. Mike's married. Dan is looking.

She stepped out off the boat and he took most of the gear from her. They walked together, Rikki slightly ahead. The two divers cut off her escape before she could make for the parking lot, as Lev had been certain they would. Divers knew one another. It was a small world and it stood to reason that they would be protective of their only female diver—especially since she was considered "different."

Rikki stopped directly in front of the shorter of the two men, her little frown on her face. Lev reached past her, offering his hand. It was obvious to him that she respected Mike.

"Mike, long time." He gave a little push, directing the vague shadow into the other man's mind. Immediately he turned to the taller of the two men, needing to give the shadow time to work. He'd already felt the resistance in the diver. "Dan. Good to see you're still at it." The same shadow slid into his head. "Levi Hammond," as if he was reminding them.

Mike scowled and rubbed at his temples, regarding Lev with some confusion. Dan picked up the shadow and enhanced it first. He smiled and shook Lev's hand again. "Been a long time."

"Too long. Nearly lost my woman. She was getting ready to dump me—*again*." Lev's fingers settled possessively around the nape of Rikki's neck. "I'm not the best letter writer."

Rikki made no response. He could feel her body vibrating and there was the gentlest of rocking. He knew she wasn't aware of it, but her distress level was increasing in direct proportion to the number of people crowding close to her.

"You okay, Rikki?" Mike asked, looking at her, not at Lev.

She nodded. "Just tired. The current was strong."

"There's an outsider hanging around asking questions. He's asking about the divers. I don't know what he's after, but be careful, Rikki," Mike warned.

"I'll look after her," Lev said.

Her frown deepened and she took a step away from him. "I don't need looking after. That's what got us into trouble before, remember?"

She'd missed her calling. She needed an Oscar, blending her annoyance with their fictitious previous relationship. He was very aware her step had taken her closer to the two men and it bothered him on some weird primal level. He shouldn't be a jealous man. He shouldn't really have those kinds of emotions. Nevertheless, he considered this might be a perfect time for target practice.

Lev forced a grin. "Yeah. I remember. Little Miss Independent. She spit on my money."

He took her hand and drew her around the two divers back toward the parking lot and the safety of the truck. These men needed time for the shadow memory to work. They would think they knew him but were having trouble placing him. And he didn't dare stay long around Mike, the man was too perceptive by far and he was fighting the planted memory.

She shrugged. "If you'd rolled the hoses properly in the first place, we wouldn't have needed the money to replace them."

Definitely an Oscar. They sounded like they'd been together forever, and the men had to know how fussy she was about her equipment. They were divers. They were probably just as fussy. He laughed. "You're not suckering me back into that old argument. Come on, let's get home."

She went with him, lifting her hand to the divers as she climbed into the driver's seat. "You know they think you're kissing ass just to get back into my good graces."

He smirked as he carefully stowed her gear. "They also know the balance of power will swing right back once I worm my way inside your little heart again."

"You should write fiction. The *Sea Gypsy* is *my* boat. If you want to be captain, you'll have to go buy your own boat. You have enough money."

"I'm content to work under you." He gave her another male smirk as he seated himself on the passenger side, his dark glasses firmly in place.

She rolled her eyes and started the truck. "You're good at role playing, Lev—Levi."

He turned his head. She had a tone. Thoughtful. Speculative. His gut knotted up again.

"Yes. I play roles to survive, Rikki. I slip from one identity to the next."

Without speaking, she drove up the narrow, steep road lined with eucalyptus trees that led to the highway, but her frown was back and this time, it didn't bode well for him. He waited, letting her work it all out in her mind. He knew the direction her mind was going.

She drove all the way back to the farm without saying a word. He respected her silence. At the house, she took care of her equipment first, making certain everything was ready for the next dive, just as she'd done on the boat. He went into the house and left her to it, powering up the laptop so he could be sure that everything for Levi Hammond was in place. His social security, driver's, diving and tender's licenses were all being replaced after the theft dutifully reported to the cops. He even had a copy of the "police" report.

Levi Hammond had a secure history, as did his parents and his grandparents on both sides. Lev was always thorough. He even had set up a history of credit card use, with an excellent credit rating as well. The credit cards were coming along with his birth certificate. He double-checked that no one had tried to access any of his records, including his school records. Obviously, Petr Ivanov hadn't heard of him or become suspicious of anyone in Rikki's life.

On the other hand, he'd put a flag on Rikki's records and someone had been looking into her life. He doubted if it was the local sheriff. The man had had plenty of time to look at her if he was suspicious of her in any way and wouldn't go back for a second look. No, Ivanov had heard of the female sea urchin diver and she would be his first choice to look into.

Someone would remember she hadn't been at the wedding on the day the yacht sank. Ivanov by now would have visited the local sheriff and the hospitals and clinics. Finding nothing, he would have started trying to blend in and get acquainted with the locals to hear all the gossip.

Rikki came in, breaking his concentration, and went past him without a word. He heard the shower start up a few minutes later. He sighed and sat back. The woman was beginning to make him a little crazy. Where had all his training and discipline gone? He erased his history and logged off.

Leaning on the doorframe, he studied her through the glass as she showered. She was wholly focused on the water and obviously wasn't aware of him. *Laskovaya moya, do you believe I'm playing you? Using you?*

She didn't look up. Nor did she stiffen. She left the water running over her shoulders and back as if she ached. *It occurred to me that it was possible until I felt my palm aching.* She rubbed the center of her palm and he felt the touch as if it were physical, stroking and caressing his cock. *I'm in your head and you're in mine. It might work for a short period of time, but you can't hide from me any more than I can hide from you.*

She turned her head and looked back at him through

the glass. Her eyes met his, locked and held. He felt that look stab deep, penetrate straight through his chest to his heart. There was love in her eyes. She didn't bother to hide it. She never voiced the sentiment aloud to him. Maybe she didn't realize he said it to her because he always used his native tongue, but he could see it there in her solemn eyes.

I see you, Lev. I will always see you, no matter what skin you have to wear or how many times you have to shed it and grow a new one. I'll see you when you're in the shadows. The real you is always safe here with me. I'm not going anywhere.

His eyes and throat burned. He couldn't move, couldn't turn away from her, and he knew the raw emotion was there on his face for her to see. He broke open and spilled out in front of her. The man he'd wanted to be, the man who had fallen so hard for a woman he couldn't ever find his feet—or his heart—again, could only look at her and know for certain he was where he was supposed to be.

16

EYES locked on Rikki's, Lev pulled his shirt over his head and tossed it aside. It took a minute to remove his shoes and socks and strip off his pants. She waited, her eyes darkening with passion. He could drown in her eyes, he decided, locking his gaze with hers, stepping close to pull open the glass door.

She inhaled sharply, tilting her head as he came closer. Lev wrapped his fingers around the nape of her neck and drew her to him. The moment he touched her, he felt complete. The water poured over both of them like an exotic waterfall. The entire shower had been constructed to appear as if they were out in the wild, the sea surrounding them, and the water, either rain or a cascading fall, added to the effect. She belonged in that setting, and when her body moved against his, she was relaxed and welcoming.

He loved the scent of her, the womanly fragrance drifting around him like a heady perfume. The trust in her eyes, the need and passion, aroused him as nothing else could. Her hands moved over his chest, her fingers tracing defined muscles. There was possession in her touch for the first time. A claiming of her own.

The breath slammed out of his body when her fingers closed over his engorged cock, trailing sizzling sensation up and down its length and around the thick girth. She knelt there on the cool gray and blue tile, and cupped the weight of his balls in her palms.

"What are you doing?" He could barely get the words out as he felt her breath, already hot, already sweet, bathing the throbbing mushroom head. With shaky hands he changed the cascade of water falling on them to a gentle rain.

"Practicing," she replied in a husky, sensual tone. "I like to be good at whatever I do and I like pleasing you." She licked at the pearly drops and then hummed, savoring them as if he had given her the finest of wines. "You taste good."

"I have to say I'm glad you think so. What would we have done otherwise?"

She gave him a sassy smile. "I would have smeared peanut butter over you and licked it off," she offered. "I still might."

Happiness burst through him. And then she took him in her mouth, allowing his cock to slide down the silken heat of her tongue and his mind just slid away from him. Always before, Rikki had become wholly focused on what she was doing, leaving his body in heaven, but he'd known she was somewhat detached from him, completely mesmerized by what she was doing, by her exploration of his body. Now, her eyes met his and she watched him, wholly focused on him, not just on the mechanics, and just like before, when she'd touched him, he knew there was blood and not ice water running in his veins.

Her mouth, growing hotter by the moment, felt subtly different—her tongue, teasing the underside of the head of his cock in the most sensitive spot and then flicking over the head again, had him groaning. He had no time to assimilate the sizzling streaks of pure heat rushing through his veins. Her teeth scraped gently and his cock jerked. Her lips slid up and down, then over his sac, teased the base and then once more engulfed him.

There was fire in her mouth, pouring over him, and the alternating tight suction and dancing tongue kept him off balance. Pleasure seemed almost overwhelming, and through it all, he was lost in the dark pools of passion in her eyes.

He felt that first tentative stirring in his mind as she connected so gently, so lightly. He knew what she was doing, but he opened to her anyway, allowing her to stroke caresses inside his head, to heighten his pleasure by allowing him to experience hers and, most of all, to follow the images in his head. He gasped as she took him deeper, swallowing, the tight muscles constricting around him.

The water fell around them, clear and fresh, adding to the beauty of the moment. The tiles shimmered as if the sea had come alive. The soft lights played over Rikki's skin, turning soft flesh into a creamy delight of pure satin. The water caressed her body, ran in rivulets over her shoulders and down the valley between her small, perfect breasts.

All the while those dark eyes held him captive. There was love, there was pure enjoyment and a desire for him every bit as intense as what he felt for her. Her mouth never broke contact, although she would slide him to the very edge of her lips and then slow, so slowly, enclose him with tight, fiery heat.

He knew every trick there was to heighten the pleasure of his sexual partner, yet he'd never experienced the true generosity of love. His hands bunched in her hair and he lifted his face to the gentle rain of the shower head, his eyes burning. Warmth flooded his mind, surrounded him, pushing out every horrific image from his past, until there was only Rikki with her sweet mouth and her giving, accepting nature.

His body coiled tighter and tighter, and he tugged at her hair, needing desperately to be inside of her, a part of her. She moved into his arms without hesitation, wrapping her arms around his neck as he lifted her, guiding her legs around his waist. She locked her ankles behind him and he settled her body over his. She sheathed him with that same exquisite slowness she'd used with her mouth. He felt her body open to his, a little reluctantly. The tight petals unfurled as his thick shaft penetrated her deeper and deeper until she was seated on him, constricting and gripping so that he shuddered with the pleasure of her.

He let her find her own rhythm and she began to move, undulating like the waves she loved so much, up and down, yet making tight, small circles and moving her hips as if she were riding with the surf. He loved the growing confidence in her, the way she stretched to arm's length, fingers linked behind his neck, throwing her head back while her hips continued that slow rhythm that was certain to drive him mad. The expression on her face was priceless, pure bliss, sexy—she was a wanton woman lost completely in her chosen lover.

The water ran down her body to where they were joined, pooling and then running in small rivers down their thighs. The droplets sizzled as if electrified. He didn't know if it was the water running hot, or his sensitive skin, or something she did as a water element. It didn't matter how, just that a thousand velvet tongues licked at his skin, and when she moved in that slow, sensuous ride, he felt hot liquid bathing the very head of his cock.

Her feminine sheath, tight and hot, gripped and moved as if alive, surrounding him with living silk, wrapping, milking, strangling and causing heated friction as he slid nearly out and then she was once again seating herself to the hilt. Tension grew, coiling inside him like a hot spring. His toes, his legs, his thick thighs, shuddered with arousal. The boiling magma pooled and heated, the pressure building in his jerking, pulsing cock and his tight, relentless sac.

With a low moan, he gripped her hips and took over. He slammed into her, deep and hard, bottoming out, bumping her sensitive cervix so that she cried out and dug her fingers into his shoulders, preparing for a wild ride. He gave it to her, switching from those slow, rising waves, to a crashing stormy sea, surging into her again and again.

Her music started, those soft little whimpers and moaning pleas he found himself waiting for. Her voice blended with the sound of flesh coming together and the beat of the rain shower. He lost himself in her, allowed her to wash him clean, to drive away people, places and the things he'd done and seen. He was just Lev Prakenskii, consumed by the woman he loved more than anything or anyone on earth. Thunder roared in his head. His heart pounded, and his blood scorched his veins as the magma boiled hotter and began to build in his balls. He felt her first tremor, then the ripple, the quake, sweeping him with her tremendous orgasm, so that he lost all control and emptied himself in her, deep and hard and so satisfactorily.

For a moment his lungs burned and his heart nearly exploded. His legs shook. He eased her against the wall to keep both of them from landing on the floor. Pressing his forehead against hers, he fought for breath.

"*Ya tebya lyublyu*, Rikki," he murmured softly. "I love you. I know you think it's too soon. And I don't want to frighten you, but it's true and I have to tell you. So I'll tell you in my native language and you can't be afraid."

Her dark eyes swallowed him, and then she leaned forward and took possession of his mouth, a sweet, tender kiss, pouring herself into him. "I love you right back," she whispered, pulling back to look down into his face. "Maybe it is too soon. All my sisters would think so. But I've never felt like this. Not ever. Don't think I have to hear pretty words, Lev, I'm not asking for forever . . ."

"I want forever." He tasted the word. "I'd never considered that I'd have a chance at forever. I like the sound of it. I'll take that. Forever with you."

She kissed him again. While the ripples of pleasure ran over their shared body, her fingers slid into his hair and she rode him gently until they were both completely spent. She lowered her legs, reluctant to part with him.

"I love when you're inside me." Her hand stroked his bare chest. She bent forward to capture a drop of water clinging to his hard pebble of a nipple.

He cradled her head to him. "I love being inside of you."

Picking up the shampoo, he washed her silky hair, his fingers gently massaging her scalp. Rinsing, he took his time soaping her body with her shower gel, lingering in every place that made her jump or shiver with need.

"I could spend all day here with you," he told her, sponging the soap from her skin.

She took over. Her hands were familiar now, moving over his body with such tenderness, he ached inside.

"It won't be so fun when the hot water turns cold on us, which it's about to do."

Her hands stroked lovingly over his groin, slippery with soap, washing him thoroughly before she rinsed him off. He grinned at her, gathered her into his arms and kissed her again. She looked so tempting, with those dark eyes and slicked back hair, her lips slightly swollen from his earlier kisses.

"You're right. The water's turning cold." He turned it off and handed her a towel before drying off himself.

A bird called. Another answered.

"Let's just sit on the back porch and watch the sky tonight. A small storm is supposed to make its way over the ocean inland. I love to watch them come in. It's not a big system, but the sky is always so great with churning clouds. They get heavier and darker, and you can just feel the rain in the air."

"Someone's here, *laskovaya moya*," Lev whispered. He put her gently from him and stepped hastily into his jeans. He couldn't help taking the time to look at her, wet and disheveled and looking very much as if she'd been thoroughly made love to. He padded barefoot into the bedroom and checked his weapons.

Rikki followed him to the bedroom door and stood regarding him with amusement, absently toweling herself off. "Only my sisters come visit me," she pointed out. "I think you're safe."

"I prefer to be certain," he replied, flashing a small,

reassuring smile. She might be amused by his safety precautions, but they were ingrained in him and he would
never be completely free of his training.

Survival was part of the reason he had grabbed at her
with both hands, committing fully almost before he even
realized what he was doing. Survival was at the very core
of who he was, and Rikki represented existence for what
had been left of the original Lev Prakenskii. That man had
slowly been consumed by the phantom that slipped through
the world unnoticed, assuming new identities, shedding
his skin and his identity at the drop of a hat. She had no
real concept of his world and the danger that came from
accepting him into her life, but he also knew, even if she
had fully recognized the risks, she would accept them.

"You're distracting me," he pointed out, stepping close
to her, one hand cupping her bare breast, as he leaned
down to capture her mouth with his.

He loved the feel of her skin, baby soft, silky smooth.
The way she shivered at his touch. The way she tasted. Everything. All of her. He kissed his way to her ear, nibbling,
pressing butterfly kisses over her chin and neck and back to
her delicate earlobe. "I could eat you up, Rikki."

Her nipple hardened into his palm and he transferred
his attention to her breast, rolling and tugging and then
bending to draw the silky flesh into his mouth. She cradled
his head to her, holding him, the tremors rocking her, the
small little whimpers enveloping him in her music. He
pressed his forehead against hers and inhaled, taking her
feminine fragrance into his lungs.

"You're so beautiful, Rikki."

"Actually, I'm pretty thin," she said matter-of-factly. "I
don't have a lot of curves."

He couldn't help but smile. She wasn't fishing for compliments, she meant it literally. He'd not only meant her outside, but her inside as well.

"You have enough for me. And we'll work on the thin part. I'm a good cook. You just have to learn to eat something other than peanut butter." He pulled away from her before he was lost again. "You're also a terrible distraction."

He caressed her bare bottom as he slipped past and made his way to the kitchen. The drive teed and went into a circle. Rikki, as well as her family, always used the parking at the back. There was more room and the drive circled right back to the main road. He didn't turn on lights, but waited in the gathering darkness as a car he recognized as Blythe's made its way to park beside Rikki's truck. She sat for a moment, staring at the house, obviously disturbed by something, before she opened her door and got out. As soon as he saw that she was alone and bringing dinner, he went out to help her.

"Blythe, good to see you," he greeted, taking the containers from her. "I really can cook now. I do appreciate all of you keeping me from starving to death, but we're going shopping tomorrow and I'll cook. We'll do a little trial and error, and see if we can find other things Rikki can comfortably eat."

Blythe followed him up the stairs to the porch, but stopped at the door. "You have to go slow with her, Levi."

He nodded. "I'm learning that. It's a good journey though. Come on in."

Blythe shook her head. "I don't know how she manages to accept you in her house, but she gets very distressed when we all come in. She barely held it together when we had to enter the house the other day."

"But not because of her autism," Lev said. "She's afraid

for you. If you don't stop that now, it's going to become part of her routine and she'll lose the ability to have guests in her home. That's too limiting for her. Her home is her safe haven. Her refuge. She has to be comfortable with her family in it. Come in and just act natural."

Blythe moistened her lips nervously, but she stepped into the kitchen, looking at him with speculative eyes. Lev knew his hair was damp and his shirt open. She knew he was more than a man passing through Rikki's life. He also knew she was worried. He couldn't blame her. Her sisters had read him accurately, but he was going to stay. Blythe would have to learn that Rikki was his world and she was safe in his hands. He put the dinner on the table and padded barefoot on through to the living room, Blythe following reluctantly.

"It's Blythe, Rikki. She brought dinner," he called.

"Oh, good. I wanted to see her," Rikki called back. "I was going to tell her what a great hunter you are, almost bringing us back a huge lingcod." Laughing, she emerged from the bedroom, her hair disheveled and still damp, her eyes bright with laughter, hands still buttoning her shirt.

The smile faded from her face the moment she saw her sister standing in her living room. "Oh." She pushed her hand through the wet strands of her hair in agitation. "I thought you'd be waiting outside on the porch for me."

"It's a little cool out there to be comfortable," Lev said smoothly. "I asked her in. I knew you'd want her to stay warm."

Rikki opened her mouth twice to say something and closed it, swallowing hard. Her frown was back, dark brows drawn together. She turned in a circle, looking helpless and vulnerable.

Lev wrapped his arm around her waist and pulled her close to him, dropping his chin on the top of her head. "You aren't worried about your stalker, are you, sweetheart? I've got a good warning system. He can't sneak up on us. Your sister is safe."

Her fingers plucked nervously at his shirt. "Are you certain?"

"Absolutely," he said. "I would never put your sister's life in danger."

"He manages to hurt or kill everyone I care about," she said.

"Not this time, honey." *Laskovaya moya, trust me. I am beginning to know him and his days will be numbered. He will not be allowed to harm you.*

Lev kissed her neck and then waved Blythe to a chair. "Rikki threw a fish at me today. One with gigantic teeth."

He forced a small grin. Rikki was still tense. He was definitely pushing her comfort zone by having Blythe in the house with them. He causally crossed to the door and opened it, leaving the screen in place, but allowing Rikki to see that they had a clear escape should a fire start.

"She threw a fish at you?" Blythe settled into a chair with an encouraging smile. "Did you really, Rikki?"

Rikki dropped into her favorite chair and glanced uneasily at the kitchen door. Lev obligingly went through to the kitchen to open it for her.

"He's always complaining about my peanut butter so I thought I might help him out with dinner."

"The fish was possessed," Lev picked up the story. "It was snapping and flopping and trying to chew my leg off, and she's in the water laughing."

Rikki's laughter was genuine and the tension in him unraveled.

"He looked like he was doing a wild rain dance. And he was going to bail, give up my boat to the fish."

"I was not." Lev couldn't take his eyes from her face. He loved watching her expressions. Maybe he'd never looked at people before. They meant nothing to him. He could never see their pain and suffering. He couldn't let it touch him or he would fail in his mission. The mission mattered, the ultimate goal, not the individual. Laughter was never heard. If you allowed yourself to hear or feel amusement, you would hear and feel pain.

As if she was reading his thoughts, Rikki took his left hand in both of hers. "He definitely was, Blythe. He was going to abandon ship."

The pad of her thumb slid over the center of his palm. He felt her caress, not on his skin but deep in his body, an intimacy that connected them beyond all expectations. *Stay.* She'd whispered that to him. Given him a choice. She didn't want him in the cold—in the shadows. She saw beyond the ghost to the man and somehow gave him substance. She'd given him a home, a refuge. And now she'd given him this—intimacy beyond imagining.

He wanted to take her into his arms all over again, bury his body in hers and merge them together until they were sharing the same skin. He didn't think it was possible to love a woman, to love anyone, the way he loved her. He felt Blythe's gaze on him and he forced himself to look away from Rikki. Instincts honed by years of survival kept him from showing his feelings. Rikki made him vulnerable, and his feelings for her made her the perfect target if anyone wanted to get to him.

Lev cleared his throat. "If I want to hear gossip, where's the best place to go?"

"Inez at the grocery store," Rikki and Blythe said simultaneously. They looked at each other and laughed.

"Everyone talks to her. She knows everyone and sooner or later, everyone spills their guts to her," Rikki added.

"But I don't want to paint her as just a gossip," Blythe clarified. "She's not like that. She's genuinely interested in people's lives and cares about them. She doesn't disclose anything confidential and she protects the people in the village. The Drakes, one of our most prominent families, are very close to her. Joley is a star in the music industry and Hannah was a supermodel. Kate writes novels and they're bestsellers, so often, reporters come into the village, especially for those tatty little gossip rags."

"Blythe is a first cousin to the Drakes," Rikki volunteered. "Her mother's name is Blythe as well. It's a huge family. I swear, there're so many cousins they could take over the town."

Blythe nodded, her gaze fixed on Lev. "We probably could. And recently there was quite a wedding."

"Your family sounds interesting. I didn't have any siblings so I've always wondered what it would be like to have a large family."

"Noisy," Blythe said. "And happy. I have a lot of cousins, but no siblings. My mother managed to have me, but no others. She had six sisters. She was third to the oldest and quite talented in her way. I could never lie to her." She laughed softly. "It wasn't so easy during my teenage years, but all the get-togethers with my cousins were fun. Holidays were the best."

"So you're close to your cousins?"

She nodded. "I see them often. That's why I came here,

to be close to family. I found this great piece of property. Most of the farm was already developed."

"Why didn't your family go in with you on it?" Lev asked.

Her expression closed down. "I didn't ask them. I felt it was very necessary to be on my own." She indicated Rikki with her chin. "I'm glad I did. I never had younger sisters and this farm has allowed me to have a big family of my own."

Rikki smiled. "And I'm very glad you did as well."

Blythe studied Lev's face. She seemed to be staring at his eyes. He knew his facial hair hid a great deal. He had scars on his arms and hands, and he was certain she'd noticed them but she hadn't asked any questions.

"You remind me of Joley's husband just a little bit. Something around the eyes, or maybe it's the way you watch people. You're very still like he is. He's Russian and worked for some sort of government agency. I'm not really certain which. His last name is Prakenskii."

Prakenskii. He didn't even blink. Survival took over. His body remained relaxed and he appeared mildly interested, no more. Had someone taken his pulse, it would have been rock steady.

Do not look at me, Rikki.

Rikki rocked gently in her chair and idly picked up the handheld kaleidoscope Judith had made especially for her. Lev could see it was beautiful, the exterior blues and aquas shimmered as if one was underwater looking up toward the surface to palm trees overlooking the ocean.

Keep looking into your kaleidoscope. She is fishing and we can give nothing away. It would put her life in danger.

Aloud, he spoke to Blythe, not even glancing at Rikki

to see if she understood. He had to trust her to handle this inquiry without hesitation.

Lev looked Blythe straight in the eye and gave a casual shrug. "Must be my Russian mother. Well, half Russian. Her mother married a contractor who had consulted with a huge building project there. She was a translator. Maybe she gave me Russian eyes."

"Were you aware," Blythe asked, "that although the yacht that went down was a Greek vessel, one of those lost aboard was a Russian? I've heard someone's been in Inez's store asking around about survivors, particularly the Russian."

Rikki took a breath and held out the kaleidoscope, as if the conversation was an idle one and didn't concern her in the least. "You have to look at this, Levi."

"Really?" he said to Blythe as he took the proffered scope. "I thought it was confirmed that everyone was dead. I haven't been keeping up with the news."

Blythe nodded. "Judith told me he showed her a picture of the man he was looking for. He was about your height and weight."

Lev smiled at her. "I suppose you're implying that I might be this man?"

"It's plausible. You turned up around the same time."

He put the kaleidoscope to his eye and looked down the tube. The liquid-filled cell captured the image and feel of being both in the water and under the water simultaneously. Judith was clearly remarkable when it came to design. The kaleidoscope was perfect for Rikki—the effect, calm and soothing, gave one the feeling of being at home in the sea. The cell contained a variety of ocean colors—aqua, turquoise, various shades of greens, coral, natural shell colors, pearly finishes, cool silvers and warm golds. Inside he found many objects including fish, shells, sea horses, kelp forms, bubbles, wave shapes and crystals that suggested the sparkle of the sun on the water.

"This is beautiful, Rikki," he said, his voice tender, handing the scope back to her and brushing a kiss on top of her head. "Your Judith is a genius." He turned his attention once more to Blythe, giving her an easy smile as only Levi Hammond could do. "If you're worried that I might be this lost Russian, it's easy enough to check me out. I'm sure you know people."

She kept her eyes on his. "There are quite a few people in law enforcement in the family."

Rikki put down the kaleidoscope and frowned at Blythe. "Are you accusing Levi of something, Blythe? What's wrong with you? I thought we were past that."

Lev could have kissed her. She had the right touch of outrage, her eyes accusing. When he touched her mind, he realized she wasn't playing a part. As far as she was concerned, her family had indicated they accepted Lev, so their loyalty should extend to him.

It doesn't work that way, Rikki. She loves you not only as a sister, but as the child she never had. Whatever she heard made her feel the need to protect you, and we are, in fact, lying to her. It's possible she senses that and it makes her uneasy.

Blythe looked uncomfortable. "The Russian said things that were frightening. He said the man who was on that yacht was an assassin, that he was extremely dangerous and anyone he befriended he was only using. He claimed he would find a woman, make her fall in love with him, use her to hide him, and in the end he would kill her to keep his identity safe."

There it was. The truth and yet a lie. He didn't dare

look at Rikki. What if she believed Blythe? The information was impossible to ignore. Rikki reached over and took his hand, her thumb pressing deep into the center of his palm. She stroked a caress there and filled his mind with warmth, with love.

You forget, Lev, I am in your head at times. Blythe doesn't have that ability. I know your feelings for me are genuine. I'm not always certain they make sense, or that one day you won't wake up and realize that bump on the head interfered with your intelligence, but I'll take that risk.

The relief was immediate, and physical, his legs were a little shaky, his heart clenched tightly in his chest. He knew how much he'd invested in Rikki—*everything*. Without her, he would be back in the cold, but this time on the run.

I'm not going anywhere, Rikki.

"I know this is difficult for you, Blythe. You don't know me. I just showed up with Rikki one day and moved in. Of course you want to protect her. I can only give you my word, which I've never broken, that I will never intentionally hurt or harm Rikki. I want to marry her and live out my life with her." He held up his hand to forestall her protest. "I also realize this relationship happened fast. Rikki and I fit. It isn't just about physical attraction. She's my miracle. I can't explain it better than that. I'm not used to explaining to anyone, but you matter to her. You're her family and she loves you. I want you to accept me into your family as well."

Blythe pressed her trembling lips together as if she might be close to tears. "I want to believe you."

"All I'm asking for is a chance."

Outside the house, there was a flutter of wings and

something heavy brushed against the screen door. An owl screeched. Another echoed it.

Rikki jumped, her fingers clutching at the kaleidoscope. "He's here," she said, her voice low, scared.

Lev dropped a hand on her shoulder. "Stay in the house. I mean it, Rikki. Blythe keep her inside. Watch the doors just in case."

He moved fast, before either of them could protest. He'd deliberately donned a dark-colored shirt and he went out through the bedroom window, already reaching for his spies. One owl circled above the house while another sat in the high branches of a tree just up on the ridge. Both were agitated.

Lev swore under his breath and glanced at the sky. There were clouds, some dark and heavy, which might be a good thing. He started up the ridge and the owl circling screeched a warning. He let his mind expand. He hadn't wanted to take possession and see through the owl's eyes because it weakened him, but he had no choice. The frantic cries of the bird indicated trouble elsewhere. He circled the house, coming in under the cover of a small terraced section of rhododendrons.

The scent of gasoline was strong. A wide swath of brush and grass had been soaked in a large circle surrounding the house. He could just make out a dark shadow moving fast for the ridge. He gave pursuit, drawing his weapon and racing over the uneven ground. The shadow turned and what looked like a gun was attached to a hose that led to a pack on his back.

Flames shot from the gun and spread across the ground until a dozen fires flared up. The man used his hose as a fireman might, and all along the wide circle more fires blazed red and orange. Hungry tongues licked at the fuel and rolled over the ground to connect like the bright dots of the tail of a fiery comet.

Energy sang in the air, a large powerful force, dark with hatred and a determination to destroy. The man had gained the ridge where he could watch his creation take shape. As he directed the flames to flow together to close any possibility of escape, Lev attacked, using the owls, calling them down, talons extended, eyes and ears sharp.

Rikki! Get on the porch. Call the rain down. Do it now and do it fast!

Lev had complete faith in her. If there was water in those heavy clouds, she would bring them pouring over the flames. Sprinting, he skirted around the edge of the circle of fire. As he started up the terrace, a bullet whined next to his ear. The arsonist had a gun of his own.

Attack, Lev ordered the birds.

He dropped flat, counted to five and took off running again. The owls dove at the fire starter, dropping out of the sky like bombers. Birds of prey were predators first, and they went for the face and eyes. The man screamed horribly and threw his arms up to protect his head as he stumbled, running for his truck.

Lev didn't have a clear shot at him, but the arsonist fired three more times, presumably at the owls diving at him. The truck took off, fishtailing down the road.

Follow him, Lev ordered.

The owls circled and took off in a straight line, wings flapping hard, silent predators stalking prey. The clouds burst open and water poured down, drenching the farm, the house, the grounds surrounding the house and the trees and plants. Smoke billowed into the air and the fire hissed in protest. Rikki walked toward the fire, her hands that of a conductor. He could hear her voice in the distance now, a song of love, rising with the ferocity of the rain, pounding the fire with a deluge fit for a waterfall.

The fire was no match for Rikki's concerto, no longer fed by a fire element, no longer pushed by a dark force, it ceased roaring, tried snarling and then succumbed with a few more hisses to the onslaught of the downpour.

He stood admiring her, with her face upturned to the rain, walking unafraid toward her worst enemy. He loved her more in that moment—with the dark clouds rolling and thunder cracking, Rikki stood unflinching as she directed her symphony. She calmly circled the burned grass, unhurried, taking her time to make certain there was no stray ember working its way beneath the layers of pine needles and vegetation to erupt when least expected. She ruthlessly soaked the area, until the water stood in deep puddles. Only then did the torrent ease.

Lev looked past her to Blythe, who stood on the porch, one hand pressed to her heart, her expression awed as she watched Rikki. He felt the same way, shocking admiration and wonder, overpowering respect at her ability to manipulate water. He was used to psychic gifts, but an element— that was true power.

There was no point in trying to track the arsonist. The owls would do a better job and in any case, he would need medical attention for the artwork on his face caused by the slashing talons. His time was definitely running out.

Lev walked back much more slowly to Rikki. She was drenched from the downpour, but she didn't seem to notice or care. She walked the entire circle around her house twice, allowing the rain to distribute much more evenly, so the water had a chance to soak into the ground. The wide swath of blackened ground was now mud, a large moat circling her home.

When she looked as if she might start a third time
around, he dropped his arm around her shoulders. "It's
out, Rikki. Come back to the house."

She looked up at him, her eyes as drenched as her
clothes, a dark pool of relief, of horror. "I didn't start
those fires, Lev—Levi. Someone killed my parents and
Daniel. It wasn't me and now I know for certain."

A small sob, somewhere between joy and sorrow escaped. "All these years of not knowing . . ." She trailed
off, her shoulders shaking.

He simply lifted her, cradling her to his chest, striding
back across the rain-soaked ground to the porch. Blythe
had rushed back into the house and she emerged with a
large, thick towel. He set Rikki on the porch and dried her
off gently.

"Of course it wasn't you. We all told you that."

"I know." She sounded a little shell-shocked. "But not
for certain. There was this little part of me that still was
afraid."

She went into his arms and he held her close. "You're
soaked, Rikki. Go take a warm shower."

"You're wet too."

He kissed her forehead. "We'll spare your sister this
time. You know what happens when we shower together."
He pressed his body close so she could feel how aroused
her performance with the rain had made him.

Rikki tilted her head, a small smile breaking through.
"You can have the towel."

He took it, more to cover up than to get dry. He watched
her as she moved into the house. The fluid, easy step was
gone and she walked a little awkwardly, as if, back on
land, without the water, she was out of her world.

"Did you know she could do that?" Blythe asked. "My cousins can do things, but that was pretty darned incredible."

He rubbed at his dripping hair. "She's pretty darned incredible."

17

RIKKI returned, showered and warm in a soft pair of sweats, and snuggled down into her favorite chair beneath her weighted blanket. Clearly, she still was in a state of shock, although her color looked better.

Blythe pushed a cup of coffee into her hands and picked up her teacup, looking at both of them with cool, steady eyes. "We have to call Jonas," she announced into the silence.

Rikki gasped, nearly spilled her coffee, and put down the cup, shaking her head. "No. No, Blythe. We can't do that. You can't do that. He's the sheriff." She began to twirl her fingers in agitation, rocking back and forth.

Lev put a hand on her shoulder to calm her, but she continued to grow more agitated. He lifted his eyebrow at Blythe, warning her off. Rikki had been through enough. Pushing her any more would only cause her to retreat into herself, in his estimation.

"Exactly," Blythe said, ignoring Lev. She leaned toward

Rikki. "Honey, not everyone with a badge won't listen. I've known Jonas since he was a boy, and he's a good man."

Rikki bit her lip. "I know that he thinks I started those fires, Blythe. I can see it when he looks at me."

"We have proof that you didn't," Blythe said calmly.

"I know he thinks I did," Rikki insisted, "and I don't want him here. I don't trust him."

"None of us has ever discussed your past with anyone," Blythe said. "He has no reason to think that. He has no reason to know anything at all about you."

Rikki turned dark, haunted eyes on her. "Jonas is the kind of man who would investigate anyone who came near his family. And you're family to him whether you like to think so or not. He's looked into my background and all of our other sisters."

Blythe sighed. "That may be true, but it doesn't negate the fact that he won't automatically think you're guilty because investigators speculated that you were. And now we have irrefutable proof that you're not guilty."

Rikki continued to rock, her fingers twirling in her lap. Her eyes went a little wild, her gaze darting around the room as if looking for an escape. She kept shaking her head. "I don't want him here, Blythe. I can't have him here looking at me like he does."

Lev crouched down in front of her, putting his hand over hers. "We don't have to have him here, Rikki."

Blythe glared at him. "Rikki, think about *Jonas*, not the other police officers you've been around. Every time he's been near you, how has he treated you? How has he looked at you? Don't superimpose the past on a man who isn't like that. He doesn't have preconceived notions about anyone. Jonas is his own man and he weighs the facts before he makes up his mind. He believes in giving people chances, and if you're honest with yourself, Rikki, you'll admit I'm right about him."

Lev caught Rikki's chin in his palm. "Look at me, *laskovaya moya*." His voice was tender, his gaze loving. "I'm right here with you. Blythe, Judith and all the others know you didn't start those fires. I know you didn't. Does anyone else really matter? We're you're family. We'll stand by you. I'm not wild about bringing the sheriff into this, and if you really don't want him, I can handle this for us."

"No!" Blythe was adamant. "Think about what you're asking him to do just because you're afraid, Rikki. Levi wants to stay here with you. If violence occurs, he might have to go, and somehow—and I'm not psychic—I think he'll protect you with every means at his disposal. No matter what either of you say, I believe he is the Russian missing from that yacht. And if he doesn't want anyone to know, then there's a pretty good reason."

"Don't do that to her," Lev said sharply.

Rikki swallowed hard and reached for Lev's hand, clinging hard.

"I'm not trying to scare you, honey," Blythe said, ignoring the dark menace in Lev's voice. "I just want you to think rationally. I know it's hard to let Jonas into our circle, but he's a good man. If you trust me, I'm asking you to extend that trust to him. Levi deserves to start a life without anything hanging over his head. Whoever is out to kill you used a gun tonight. Do you really want Levi to have to use one as well?"

"I won't need a gun." Lev's quiet voice spoke volumes.

Blythe shivered, but she looked straight at Lev. "I believe in second chances. We all need them. If this is your chance, then you have to start it right."

Rikki rocked for a few more minutes, making a strangled sound of distress that broke Lev's heart. Blythe sat back and waited and he took his cue from her. Rikki had to find her own way. She'd been doing it for many years, and whatever physical response it took to help her get there, he was willing to let her work through it. She wouldn't want interference. She was independent and that state of mind was hard-won. She deserved whatever time it took for her to work it all out.

Rikki flapped her hands in front of her face and blew on her fingers as if the tips were burned. "You can call him, Blythe. But he knows about the other fires."

"Maybe he does, Rikki," Blythe conceded gently, "but that doesn't mean he's not willing to give you the benefit of the doubt; otherwise, don't you think he would have come to me and warned me?"

Rikki rocked for a few more moments, but her hands settled while she frowned, thinking it over. Lev found himself breathing normally again at the sight of that little frown. Her brain was functioning again, driving out the chaos. Rikki was very fragile, and he would always have to be alert to the fact that their home would need absolute routine and balance. He had been prudent, although for a moment or two, the urge to pick up Blythe and chuck her right out the door had been very strong.

Rikki chewed on her lower lip until Lev was afraid she'd draw blood. "Maybe you're right. He stopped me the other day and he was nice. He could have been mean and he didn't give me a ticket."

"Then let's call him and ask him to go out and take a look at where this man has been watching the house and the damage he's done tonight," Blythe encouraged. "If you want, I can talk to him. I can tell him I was with you when the fire started."

"You know the cop is going to want to talk to Rikki," Lev said. His tone was level, but he meant it as a reprimand. Blythe meant well, but he objected to misleading Rikki. The cop was going to want to talk to all of them if he was any kind of a lawman.

"Perhaps." Blythe shrugged. "But even if he does, Rikki knows him. And she knows me. I'm not about to let Jonas intimidate her, which I'm certain he never would." She leaned over and took Rikki's hands, stilling her fidgeting fingers. "Baby, listen to me. You know Levi better than anyone else. What do you think he would do to protect you?"

"Don't." Lev's tone turned low and deadly. "Don't put her in the position of thinking she has to protect me."

"She does," Blythe said quietly, "from yourself."

Rikki's eyelashes fluttered twice before she looked up into Lev's eyes. He felt the impact of those dark velvet depths in the pit of his stomach. She was definitely back and thinking. Blythe had found the right incentive to force Rikki back from the edge of meltdown.

Laskovaya moya, *you are not to worry about me. I can take care of myself. It's what I do. And this man, this fire starter, will not be an issue soon. I'm tracking him now.*

Lev. She whispered his name in his mind. Intimate. Tender. A reprimand. "Blythe is right. We need to do this the right way. We'll call Jonas and give him a chance."

He sat back on his heels. "You know there is danger in that as well."

"Only if you try messing with his head. He's got his own gifts," Rikki said. "I feel his energy every time I'm near him."

"Good energy or bad?" Blythe prompted.

Lev straightened, turning cold blue eyes on Blythe. "You can stop any time."

"Levi, this is important. That man not only tried to trap us inside the house, he had a gun. If he wasn't so determined to kill her with fire, he could lie in wait for her. What defense does she have against that?"

"Me." His voice was implacable. Certain. Confident. "No one is going to harm her."

"Then use the law. Let me call Jonas."

Unexpectedly, it was Rikki who changed everything. *If you're really going to be Levi Hammond and not Lev, the shadow man, we have to jump with both feet. Let's do it. Let's call him. If it doesn't go well, then we'll explore option two.*

Lev sighed, turned away from the two women and paced across the floor. This house—the farm—was his refuge, a safe haven from outsiders. Every moment away from it increased the danger to him. Every person who saw him was a threat. He hadn't had time to plant enough seeds, that shadowy memory that would grow with each sighting. He had wanted to go into Sea Haven in the early morning hours and see Inez, the woman who would ultimately convince everyone that Levi Hammond had been in and out of Sea Haven and her store for years. He would have the reputation for disappearing, chasing after dreams, but they would all eventually swear they knew him.

A sheriff. One with gifts of his own. He rubbed his beard, that soft hair he now kept neat and trimmed, and that altered his appearance and covered old scars. He would have to choose every word carefully, keep to the shadows, allow the women to do the talking, but it could be done. He'd been in worse, tighter situations.

"Levi?" Rikki prompted.

He nodded, his stomach rolling. He had too much to lose. He'd never had anything to lose before. He had a strong urge to grab Rikki, throw her in the truck and get the hell out. His future, his life, was there in her eyes. It wasn't about the farm, or the house—the perfect hideaway. It was all about a woman.

He locked his gaze with Rikki's, looking her directly in the eyes, trying to tell her the enormity of this one decision—what it could cost them. She took a breath, the darkness of her gaze gleaming with intelligence, with understanding.

"Call him, then," Lev said, and abruptly turned away, striding through the house to the back porch.

He had never relied on another human being for anything, until Rikki had come along. Survival instincts were screaming at him, clawing deep, his training protesting the decision. It went against who and what he was, the core of him, yet if he wanted this life, he would have to concede certain things. He'd have to learn, like others, to live within the law—or as close to that as he could possibly get.

He heard Rikki's bare feet padding out of the house, coming up behind him. She wrapped both arms around his waist and laid her head against his back. Leaned into him. He stared into the night, inhaling the scent of smoke and rain. The scent of Rikki. He put both his hands over hers.

"This is risky, sweetheart. You know that, don't you?"

There was a small silence. Frogs called to one another, happy for the rain. A cicada sang its song. Rikki turned her head enough to press a kiss into the small of his back before resting her cheek against his spine. "We can do this."

He smiled without turning his head. With that simple declaration, she had tied them together, made them one. *When I marry you, I can't use my given name.* There was regret in his voice—in his heart. *I want you to marry the real man, not the one I made up.*

She held him to her without hesitation. There was no shrinking away from him, not with her body or her mind. *I will always have the real man, whatever name he chooses for us to live by. You're real, Lev, not a shadow someone created.*

His smile widened. At last he understood the mysteries. Standing there on the porch with darkness surrounding them, listening to the chorus of the frogs, he knew what was inside all those houses across the world. He'd stood outside of them often, listening to the murmur of voices, the sound of children's laughter, and wondered what they were feeling, why they chose one another, why they would risk everything.

I was born Lev Prakenskii. Not everything about me is a lie, Rikki. I will never let you down. What I feel for you is real. It's all encompassing, and it's lasting. The things your sister said to you in there, they were things taught to me, survival techniques vital to a man cut off from all aid and hiding. I am not doing that with you. I can give you my real name, one we will never be able to use, but I want you to know it.

She simply continued to press her body against his, allowing the night to enfold them. The sudden burst of rain she'd drawn from the clouds had become little more than mist without the pull of her energy. It shrouded the trees in a veil of smoky white, closing them off from the rest of the world. He enjoyed the silence, the sound of the frogs playing in the puddles after the heavy rain.

Lev turned slightly and wrapped his arm around Rikki, bringing her from behind him, to his side, under his shoulder where he could keep her warm in the gathering mist.

Blythe cleared her throat. "I've heated dinner. Come eat, you two."

Lev had been aware of her moving about the kitchen and it was impossible to ignore the smell of food. No matter that his world might come crumbling down in the next few hours, his body needed fuel. He turned his back on the night and, keeping Rikki beside him, went back into the house.

He looked around the spacious kitchen. This was their home. Blythe had set the table with the dishware Rikki loved so much. He calmly picked up all three plates and restored them to the china hutch. "Rikki has a fondness for that set of dishes," he explained as he substituted paper plates. "We're going to find another set that doesn't matter if we chip or break it."

Blythe took in his matter-of-fact words with a small shake of her head. "I see" was all she said.

Lev pulled out Rikki's chair and she seated herself, looking regal in her sweats.

"You're good for her," Blythe said, watching Rikki pick up a fork, instead of protesting that all three of them were sitting down to a meal together in her kitchen.

"She's good for me," Lev corrected, and sank into the chair beside Rikki.

"She's right here, listening to the conversation, and contrary to what appears to be the popular belief tonight, she's got great hearing." Rikki took her fork and began to move the green beans around on her plate.

Lev burst out laughing. "She's also a comedian," he pointed out. "And she thinks we're not going to notice that she isn't actually eating."

"I'm studying these things. They look a little like great

big green caterpillars." She wrinkled her nose as she stared down at the offending vegetables.

Blythe laughed. "Green beans are good for you."

Rikki rolled her eyes. "You're obsessed with all things green, Blythe." She appealed to Lev. "Don't you think they look a little fuzzy?" She pushed the beans around a little more on her plate, made a happy face out of them and then changed it to a frowning face.

Lev felt an unexpected jolt of happiness in the region of his heart. He couldn't help himself, he leaned over and brushed the pad of his thumb across her lips. Her little frown matched the one on her plate. "Try the potato, sweetheart. You'll like that."

She made a face and touched the stuffed potato tentatively with her fork, as if it might explode on her. "It's yellow and white."

"Good colors," he commented. "Not sea colors, but cheese colors. I suppose next time you might consider injecting blue dye into the cheese, Blythe."

Blythe nodded. "I will. I hadn't thought of that."

"Very funny, you two. Now who're the comedians?"

Lev pulled her plate over to him and cut the cheese-stuffed potato into small bites. "There's nothing green in this. Just cheese and potatoes."

Rikki inspected the contents carefully before taking a small portion onto her fork.

"I wouldn't poison you," Blythe assured.

"You might try to poison Levi," Rikki pointed out, "and I might have accidently gotten the potato with arsenic in it."

"You do have a point," Blythe agreed cheerfully.

Lev found himself laughing, comfortable now with

Blythe. They'd come to an understanding. Maybe she could see—or feel—that what he felt for Rikki was genuine. He found himself including Blythe in the very small circle of people he was allowing to enter into his life. She was a good person, with good motives. And he loved how she loved Rikki.

"It would have served you right had I brought home that enormous and very ugly fish for dinner," Lev said.

Rikki put a small bite of the potato in her mouth and chewed, swallowed and flashed a quick, teasing grin at him. "That thing was never going to make it into this kitchen." She took another forkful of potatoes. "These aren't half bad, Blythe."

Blythe pressed a hand to her heart. "Such praise."

"The highest," Rikki admitted, chewing another mouthful. "I think I like this."

"I'll definitely need the recipe," Lev said. "I'm collecting as many as possible. I've gotten her to eat only two of the dishes all of you sent over. Mostly it's peanut butter."

"Hey!" Rikki protested, shooting a quick, almost guilty look at Blythe. "I eat that broccoli every single night."

Lev nodded, affirming it was true. "She dips it raw into peanut butter."

Blythe shuddered. "Whatever works. At least you're eating something healthy."

They finished the meal with Rikki trying to explain the wonders of peanut butter nutrition and how the calorie intake was just what she needed when she was diving. She actually ate the entire potato, one green bean and a small portion of chicken before she pushed the plate away and indulged in a handful of peanut butter cookies.

They threw away the paper plates and restored the kitchen to the pristine order Rikki needed to feel comfortable in her home. They were wiping every smudge from the counters, when Lev's radar went off. An owl hooted twice, calling from the trees. The bird took flight, passing silently by the kitchen window.

I see them. Lev sent the reassurance to his sentinel. "We have company," he said aloud.

Rikki stiffened, her expression stricken. Lev softened the lighting in the living room, ensuring there were plenty of shadows for him to slide into.

The car came around to the front drive, the first time Lev had ever seen anyone doing that, signaling to him that these visitors were first timers. The sheriff was a tall, well-built man. He parked the car close to the front door and immediately went around to aid his passenger. He stood for a moment looking around carefully, studying the wide moat, the blackened grass shriveled beneath the dark layer of oily water.

The sheriff took the arm of the woman as they walked to the door. He moved with fluid grace, his gaze shifting around the property, although he gave the appearance of giving his full attention to the woman. Lev slipped back to allow Blythe and Rikki to greet them first, wanting to assess the pair before they were fully aware of him.

The woman coming through the door was shockingly beautiful and very pregnant. She smiled shyly at Rikki and hugged her cousin. "Blythe. It's been too long since we've had a good visit. You should drop by more often." Her voice was musical. Soft like a warm breeze.

Lev recognized power when it walked into the room. Hannah Drake Harrington had been a supermodel for some years, appearing on magazine covers and walking the runways all over the world, yet for all her composure, she seemed just a little hesitant. He read people easily, one of his own gifts, and she was very uncomfortable, although it didn't show on her face.

The man coming in behind her, one hand on her waist, his face strong, eyes taking in everything, saw Lev immediately and assessed him that quickly.

"Hannah, Jonas, you both know Rikki. This is a good friend of hers, Levi Hammond," Blythe performed the introductions. "Levi, Jonas Harrington is the local sheriff and Hannah, his wife, is my cousin."

Rikki actually backed away, toward Lev, her face stark white. She bumped into him and he laid his hands on her trembling shoulders. It was difficult when he was always conscious of keeping his hands free, but she needed his touch. *I'm here,* lubov moya, *you're safe.* He stroked caresses in her mind even as he reassured her.

Reaching around her, he shook the sheriff's offered hand. Jonas had a strong grip, but didn't try any male games, just gave his hand a firm shake and let him go. But he was taking in the way Lev held Rikki as well as noticing Rikki's obvious agitation.

Hannah smiled gently. "Rikki, how good to see you again. We met a couple of years ago in Judith's store, remember?"

Rikki nodded and waved her toward a chair. "Thanks for coming over." Her voice was strained, pitched very low, but she managed to sound hospitable.

"Jonas told me you'd called and I thought it would give me an opportunity to see you, even though it's a business call," Hannah said.

It was difficult for her. Lev could hear it in her voice. She had come for Rikki, to make this visit easier on her. Had it been her idea or the sheriff's? He thought it had been the sheriff. Without warning, Jonas looked straight at him, his shrewd eyes studying him. There was danger there. Recognition.

Lev had never seen Jonas before, but he seemed to recognize Lev. An impossibility. There were no pictures of him. No trace of the man who had died on the yacht. He knew with absolute certainty that they had never met, yet there was recognition on Jonas's face. He moved away from the sheriff, his hand sliding down Rikki's arm, tugging her over to a chair away from the light, where he could stand behind her, back in the shadows.

"Have we met, Mr. Hammond?" Jonas asked, taking a seat on the couch beside his wife.

The opening of the game had just begun. Lev shrugged casually. "I would think I'd remember, but I've been around on and off for years, so it's possible."

Blythe placed a cup of tea on the table beside her cousin and handed the sheriff his. She settled comfortably into a chair facing them. "Thank you for coming. I've wanted to talk to you about this matter for some time, Jonas, but we had no proof until tonight." She told him about Rikki's parents, the foster homes and finally her fiancé's death.

Hannah looked close to tears. "Rikki, I'm so sorry. How terrible for you. I had no idea."

Her reaction was genuine. Lev kept his eyes on the sheriff. Jonas had to know Rikki's story, yet he hadn't shared it with anyone, not even his trusted wife. And he did trust her. The love between them was tangible. Jonas Harrington played his cards close to his chest.

Jonas leaned toward Rikki. "He came tonight?"

"It wasn't the first time," Lev answered for her. Rikki seemed incapable of speech, a low, strangled sound emerging from her throat. He found her weighted blanket and tucked it around her. She managed a small grateful smile.

"He was up on the ridge watching the house about a week ago. I found where he'd been playing with fire. And then the other day, we came in using the back road and found he'd been studying the layout of the farm. I think he contacted the Realtor selling the property next to this one."

"You didn't think to call me then?" Jonas asked. His tone was mild, but he gave Blythe a look that was definitely a reprimand.

Lev shrugged. "Rikki needed to be able to come to a decision herself."

He kept his face in the shadows as he spoke, and he kept his face slightly averted from Jonas, presenting few defining features. His fingers settled around the nape of Rikki's neck, easing the tension out of her. She was trying, he had to hand her that. He could tell she was following the conversation instead of retreating into her head, but it took a great deal of effort. She kept her hands under the weighted blanket and he knew her fingers were twirling, a compulsion she couldn't stop when agitated.

"And tonight?" Jonas prompted.

Blythe took up the story. "Rikki always keeps the doors of the house open when anyone she loves is with her. As you can see, when we designed the house, we made certain that with the doors open you can see completely through the house to the outside, front and back. Levi realized the arsonist was out there and went out to confront him."

"You didn't call me right away, Blythe?" Again it was a reprimand. Quiet, but the man was very annoyed. "All of you could have been killed."

Blythe, usually composed, looked away, color staining her cheeks.

Rikki stirred beneath her blanket, her dark eyes going nearly black. "She would never go against my wishes.

I was afraid to call you." Her chin tilted. "I haven't had much luck getting cops to believe me."

Jonas nodded. "I can understand that, Rikki. I found a few things in those reports that seemed to be overlooked. I was afraid this man would find you."

"You knew about all of this?" Hannah asked.

He took her hand as he nodded. "Blythe told us about buying the farm with five other women and . . ." He shrugged.

"You investigated them," Hannah concluded.

"Of course." There was no apology.

Lev liked him for that. He would have done the same thing. "What was overlooked?"

Jonas brought Hannah's hand to his mouth and kissed her knuckles before releasing her. "Timing for one thing. Her burns were severe in the first fire. She was hospitalized for weeks and then needed special care because she was so traumatized. She wasn't anywhere near her houseboat when the fire consumed it and killed her fiancé. There were several witnesses who saw her down at the harbor cleaning a boat."

Rikki pressed her hand against her mouth and rocked, speaking behind her trembling fingers. "I was late. It was the first time he'd ever been to my houseboat. I get focused on something and I don't notice time passing." She sounded distant, as if she was far away from them. "I should have been there. He was waiting for me. I didn't realize what time it was until one of the divers asked me where he was. We usually cleaned the boat together, but he wanted to shop for food for dinner." She looked at Jonas with shocked eyes. "I don't cook."

Jonas nodded. "It's all right, Rikki. I read everything carefully and made notes. I looked them over before I came, that's why we didn't get here right away. I think he searches for you and when he finds you, he plans out his fire and then takes action. It took him a while to find you after the first fire. You went from the hospital to a care-taker and then to a foster home. When he found you, he tried to kill you with the same method as before. You were able to alert the family. The couple as well as their son all said you'd saved their lives, but the investigators were suspicious because you were unable to answer their questions satisfactorily. There were a few gaps in your story."

A tremor ran through Rikki. Blythe stirred, but Jonas sent her a sharp look.

"I'm filling in the blanks with my own guesswork. You were traumatized after losing your parents. Being autistic and needing routine, another fire must have sent you spin-ning again. You probably were incapable of answering questions."

"They should have known that," Blythe said in a low, angry tone.

"I agree." Jonas kept his eyes on Rikki, obviously judg-ing her abilities to cope with his narration of her past.

Rikki moistened her lips and swallowed hard. "I'm fine. I just want him caught."

"Again he lost track of you, and I suspect he was grow-ing angry, and that he continued to start fires, although probably not so public ones. I had my brother-in-law check for me and there were several suspicious fires in the city where you grew up. Abandoned warehouses. An empty store. Two dilapidated houses, again empty. Several grass fires. I think he was practicing. Waiting for you and bid-ing his time, keeping himself amused."

It made sense. Lev had had the same thoughts even

without the information. Rikki's stalker would never be truly happy without his mistress—fire. He would need her, and the need would grow like a craving for a drug until he couldn't resist and he would succumb to temptation. The cycle would repeat itself over and over. If he had managed to kill Rikki, he would still never be able to stop, although it was likely he told himself that he would.

"He found you a third time, and again, you somehow managed to save the family and everyone got out alive."

Rikki shook her head and a small sound escaped. She began to slowly rock. "Not everyone."

Jonas frowned. "Everyone got out, Rikki," he assured her.

"Not the dog. Not their dog." She grew more agitated, flapping her hands now, a sure sign she was headed for a breakdown.

Lev crouched down in front of her, uncaring what the others thought. *Look at me* lubov moya, *see only me. You're safe with me. If you want to end this, we will. I'll make them all go.*

Her dark eyes found his, and this time, it was Rikki that might have been drowning. She looked frightened, and when he touched her mind, he realized she feared retreating in front of their company more than anything else. This was her home, her haven, and she'd set things up so she could live as comfortably as possible. He took both her hands very gently in his.

It occurred to him that both Hannah and Jonas spoke in low, gentle voices. They had known coming into the house that Rikki was autistic and needed her environment to be as soothing as possible. Jonas had not told his wife about Rikki's past. Lev was certain Hannah knew Rikki was autistic from her cousin.

"Do you need to take a break, Rikki?" Jonas asked.

Lev could have kissed the man. He showed respect for her. Addressed her, not Blythe or him. She blinked several times, took a deep breath and, still looking into Lev's eyes, shook her head.

"I'm all right." She mumbled the words, but they were audible in the silence of the room.

Lev moved back behind her, his hand gripping hers, his thumb moving along her wrist.

Jonas resumed talking. "You were safe in the group facility because they kept moving you and he could never know for certain where you were. I can't imagine that he didn't try looking and he was probably frustrated. Based on that theory, we looked up the years when you were between sixteen and eighteen, when you were released. There was a cluster of fires, arsons, and this time the homes were occupied."

At her gasp he shook his head. "The families were away at the time he started the fires, but their houses and everything in them were destroyed. He needed something to feed his addiction. It was growing."

"And he blamed Rikki," Lev said. "Why?"

"That's the burning question, isn't it?" Jonas said. He looked at Rikki. "Any ideas?"

She frowned. "I've tried to figure that out." She looked at Lev. "We both have. We've gone over and over this. I was thirteen when he attacked the first time, and honestly, even at school, I had an aide. I couldn't manage the lights and noise very well. I mainstreamed, but it was very difficult. I could get extremely violent when someone crossed me."

"Did you ever start a fire?"

Jonas dropped the question so gently, a skilled surgeon

with a scalpel, slicing through to the very marrow of the matter.

Lev felt Rikki stiffen in outrage. He touched her mind and found blind fury. She jerked her hand and he had the feeling she might fly at the man, taking his question as an accusation. He tightened his fingers around her wrist, shackling her to him, although the others couldn't see.

He is trying to get a rise out of you. Take a breath. He's testing you, using a classic interrogation method. Don't react. Think before you speak and then tell him the truth.

Aloud, without taking his gaze from Rikki's, he addressed Jonas. He kept his tone low, velvet soft, but it was a warning—the only one he intended to give.

"You can't use tactics like that on Rikki. Her world has been a nightmare and she doesn't react as others usually do."

"Jonas," Blythe began.

Rikki turned her head and for the first time looked Jonas in the eye. "I could never start a fire." She shuddered. "I can't have a gas stove, because I can't be around an open flame. As a child, I would become violent and hit my head on the floor. It would be impossible for me."

"And yet, you thought you were responsible." Jonas leaned forward. "In your statement, after your fiancé died, you said maybe you were somehow starting the fires subconsciously. Why would you think that?"

Her teeth began to chatter and Lev couldn't take any more. "We're done here," he said, making it clear that he was ending the interview and that he was in charge. If Jonas persisted, he would be dealing with someone other than Rikki. "Rikki didn't start the fires and she may have been traumatized enough in the past to entertain the idea, but she knows better now. He was here. I saw him. The evidence is outside this house."

Jonas's cool blue gaze slid over him, but he merely nodded.

"This man not only loves fire, he needs it," Lev said, changing the direction of the investigation. "You're going to find him in a job that allows him to be around fire all the time."

Jonas nodded. "I believe you're right. He's hiding in plain sight. Now that he's found her, he isn't going to rest until he finishes what he started."

"He's hurt," Lev said quietly. "His face is torn up a bit. Probably bad enough to need stitches. He'll lay low until he's healed and can cover the scars."

Jonas straightened slowly, his blue eyes going diamond bright. "You tangled with him?"

Lev shook his head. "No, I was too far away and the fire was between us. He shot at me, but I saw a couple of owls drop down, maybe defending a nest, but they came in hunting and his face was raked. I heard him scream."

"So there's a blood trail."

"Yes." Lev could tell the sheriff was thinking that over, watching him closely now, curiosity open on his face, but he didn't demand to know why an owl would fly from a tree and attack Rikki's stalker.

"Let's go see," Jonas pushed himself out of the chair.

18

JONAS stepped off the porch with casual grace. Lev had seen his kind hundreds of times over his years in the shadows. Jonas Harrington was far more than he let on. He was a big man, but he moved with fluid grace. His knuckles and hands had seen combat. He carried his weapon as though it was part of him. He had a holdout strapped to his calf and a knife in his boot. He didn't speak as Lev led him away from the house to the blackened circle surrounding the house.

"He planned it well. He soaked the ground fast, very fast, with an accelerant," Lev began.

As he turned, a fist flew at his face. Jonas was fast and it was a surprise attack, but Lev managed to slam a block hard into his forearm, deflecting the blow to step inside and deliver a hard one-two punch to the sheriff's gut. Hitting the man was like hitting an oak tree. He grunted, but didn't fold, nor did he draw a weapon.

"I'm going to give you the beating of your life, you son

of a bitch." Jonas spat the words at him, a low, controlled, rage smoldering in his tone.

Lev didn't reply. He had no idea why the sheriff would want to give him a beating, but as skilled as the man obviously was in hand-to-hand fighting, his training could not compare to Lev's.

They circled one another, two grim warriors, eyes cold, faces determined. Jonas exploded into action, driving in with a hard front kick, which Lev deflected, but as Jonas stepped into him, the sheriff threw a hard straight punch that grazed Lev's jaw as he pulled his head out of the way. The blow, despite only being a graze, was hard, the force behind it appalling. They moved in and out of each other's space, trading blows and blocks, as well as the occasional kick. Lev kept it light, uncertain what the beef was. He could kill Jonas, fast and efficiently, but he would lose Rikki and his haven.

As they fought, one thing became very clear to Lev—Jonas Harrington had seen combat, but he was no killer. He could fight, but he didn't have the kill instinct. There was no doubt in Lev's mind that he was capable if there was need, but he didn't have the lack of emotion needed to be a killer. Jonas Harrington was fighting because in his mind, Levi had done something to deserve a beating. Lev, on the other hand, had slipped back instinctively into his training. He saw a dozen opportunities to kill the sheriff and planned—and dismissed—each one in his mind. Coolly. Calmly. Without emotion.

"You might want to let me know what this is about," Lev suggested during one of the moments when they'd broken apart.

Jonas wiped his mouth with the back of his hand and

spat out a mouthful of blood. "My sister. Elle Drake, you bastard. You let that son of a bitch rape her."

Lev knew the name Drake, but not an Elle Drake. He remembered names and faces. The blow to his head had erased things for a while, but his memories had come back in pieces. He shook his head. "I'm sorry. I have never met Elle Drake."

Jonas had been moving into the attack and that stopped him. He stood, his cool eyes on Lev, while he dragged air into his burning lungs. "You're a Prakenskii. I'd know those eyes anywhere. You're Ilya's brother, and you were on that yacht. Hannah and Elle wouldn't recognize you because they weren't expecting you, but Ilya told me you were guarding that bastard Stavros."

Lev remained silent. He did have a brother named Ilya—the youngest of them—torn from his mother's arms by men in masks, as she screamed and begged them not to take her baby.

"Elle was working undercover and your boss kidnapped her."

Lev's stomach lurched. He remembered her. He'd tried to get her off the yacht when he realized Stavros's intentions to take her. They hadn't known she was working undercover, but she had psychic power and Stavros was determined to use that for his own gain. Stavros was as dirty as they came with fingers in everything from gun running to human trafficking. He was also buying defense plans. Lev's job had been to work his way into the organization and become a trusted member in order to get the full scope of Stavros's operations and find those supplying him with the women, the guns and the secrets—mostly the secrets.

Lev had been close, but he hadn't gotten the job done. And then the ship had gone down, killing Stavros, leaving Lev without his answers and years of work wasted. And a chance at life, away from making decisions about who lived, who died, who was left alone to meet a fate of torture, of sexual servitude so someone could find answers and shut down an entire network.

Save the individual? Or the masses? He'd never allowed himself to think too long on those questions. He was a tool, nothing more, to be used and discarded. He remained silent, closing his mind to the roar of pain for the unanswered questions, for the nameless faces of individuals he'd left behind. The killing had never bothered him. He'd been molded and trained and programmed for that. But the victims . . . That had been much more difficult to shove behind a locked door in his brain.

He let Jonas have his shot. A hard right to the jaw. Pain exploded through his already damaged head. He shook it off, sidestepped the second blow and held up his hand. He could feel the adrenaline flowing hot and bright, the rush of power moving through his body, and knew his eyes were arctic cold, gleaming with repressed fire. He breathed away the instinct to kill, never taking his watchful gaze from the sheriff's.

"You get one free because I couldn't find a way to save her. But being civilized is new for me. I have instincts and they aren't just going to go away. You come at me again and I'm going to put your ass hard into the ground, and then your ego is going to kick in. Right now you're angry. I accept that. But don't be stupid. If you know my brother, you know what I'm capable of."

He hadn't seen Ilya since they'd ripped him from their

mother's arms. All of the boys had fought to get him back—the guns, the fists, the smell of blood and death in their nostrils. No, he wasn't going to apologize for his life. Not to this man who could never understand. Rikki could accept Lev's sins. He had every confidence in her, but he wasn't asking for forgiveness from anyone else.

"You want to help me find the bastard trying to kill Rikki, or should I do it on my own?"

Jonas slowly straightened, his expression hard. "Do you think this is finished? That I'm just going to let a killer into my town where Elle's going to have to live with seeing you every day?"

"She'll be the first to tell you I was doing my job," Lev said quietly. "You don't have to like it and neither do I. It's evident you've seen combat. Are you telling me no innocents ever suffered because you had to carry out your mission?"

"What the hell are you doing here?"

"Making a choice to live. I'm Levi Hammond and I intend to make my life here."

Jonas shook his head. "I don't believe you."

"You don't have to believe me. Only Rikki has to believe me. On the other hand, I will find this man threatening her and you'll never find the body if you walk away from this. I had a choice whether to involve you, and I chose to let Blythe make the call. Levi Hammond's history doesn't have a single hole in it. In a few days people will start to vaguely remember him. I can have a life here. I'm not willing to give that up because you don't like what I did."

Jonas never took his eyes from Lev's face and Lev could feel the power in the man, the energy swirling around him. Harrington had a few secrets of his own. Lev remained still, allowing the man to make up his mind.

"You're a cold-blooded bastard, Prakenskii. We've got a man in town. He says he's investigating the death of a Russian citizen, but it's damned easy to tell that he's an exterminator. He finds out you're here, he's going to put a bullet in your head."

Lev's smile held no humor. "He'll find it isn't all that easy to manage."

Still he waited. Jonas didn't seem to understand the danger he was in and right now, with this threat, he was skirting very close to the edge of the precipice. The horrible accident was all planned out, step-by-step in Lev's mind. Not now of course, the torn knuckles and bruises would point right to him, but Harrington was in a high-risk job. Easy enough to lure him out to a deserted area, so many of them in the forested lands, and the man would meet with an accident.

Jonas studied his face for a long time. "Your brother makes his home here."

Lev didn't like the flutter of anticipation he couldn't quite suppress. Emotions were difficult to control once let loose. "Is that supposed to be some kind of a threat?" He kept his voice mild. "My brother was trained the same way I was. He'll understand."

"Your brother is married to Joley Drake. He might not be as understanding as you think," Jonas warned.

Lev shrugged. "He can take his best shot."

"He's not the one you're going to have to worry about. Jackson and Elle are on their honeymoon, but Jackson may have a few words to say to you."

Lev spread out his hands, so they encompassed the

farm. "This is it for me. This is where I'm making my stand. They can all take their shot."

"Why here? Move on."

"This is Rikki's home. She has a life here and she's worked hard to get it. I'm not leaving her behind and I'm not taking her away from all of this."

"Do you expect me to believe that you've fallen in love with Rikki Sitmore?"

"I don't particularly give a damn what you believe."

Jonas shook his head and turned away, presenting his back. His stance told Lev the sheriff was on alert in case Lev attacked him. Lev crouched down beside the blackened ground. Most of the water had slowly seeped into the ground, so that only an inch remained in places and most of it had disappeared, leaving behind muddy, blackened grass. It reeked of a mixture of gas and smoke.

Jonas took his time, thoroughly examining the area, taking a series of photographs, collecting the water in several places into small tubes and then taking bits of the burned grass.

"You said you saw him?" Jonas prompted, crouching beside Lev to touch his fingers to the water once again.

"He was tall but fairly slight. His tracks indicate maybe one-sixty or one-seventy. He moved fast though, and he's strong. He had a flamethrower on his back and he must have packed in the gasoline. He's had a lot of practice. By the time I was aware of him, he'd run around the house."

And that meant the owls had gone hunting and hadn't discovered the arsonist until they'd returned. That had been his mistake and it could have cost all of them their lives. He couldn't allow himself to get so lost in Rikki that he put aside his survival instincts.

"How did he get the fire going so fast? The ground had to have been soaked from the previous storms. Even with an accelerant . . ." Jonas broke off, shaking his head.

"You're married to a Drake. I have to presume you know about manipulating energy."

Jonas stood up and paced away from Lev, using his flashlight to pick up the smashed grass where the arsonist had run through on his way back to the ridge. "Keep talking."

"He's an element. He manipulates fire."

Jonas stiffened but he didn't reply, following the tracks up toward the ridge. The slope was slippery and several puddles of water stood full and unexpected. Jonas walked back and forth, taking in the longer strides, and the sudden halt, where the assailant had whirled to fire his weapon. The sheriff spent a great deal of time taking more pictures and locating the spent shell casings, carefully collecting them as well.

"Looks like a dam broke," Jonas commented as he skirted around two of the larger puddles. "Where did all this water come from?"

"We were lucky. It rained."

Jonas glanced at the clouds. "It didn't rain in Sea Haven or at our house, just a few miles from here. The mist is thick, but not enough to create this kind of flooding."

He was fishing. A good tactic, but Lev was comfortable with silence and said nothing.

Jonas sighed. "Do you want to catch this asshole or not? You have to tell me everything."

"What does a hard rain have to do with catching him?" Lev countered. "And I could catch him myself. His tire tracks are all over the place. He works with fire. His face is messed up and requires stitches. He comes from the same city as Rikki. And he's in your town. I'll bet he's not that hard to find."

Jonas crouched again, this time finding the spot where the owls had attacked the arsonist. There were spots of blood in the wet grass, but not as much as Lev thought there would be. The rain had stamped out the fire, but it had also destroyed evidence. Jonas searched the ground, moving first in a tight circle, and then widening it slowly. He found two feathers and several spent cartridges. All of it went into evidence bags and then he added several scrapings of the blood. Again, he took his time, very thoroughly going over the ground.

"What the hell was he shooting at? You? Or the birds?"

"He fired off a few rounds at me, both from here and back there." Lev turned to indicate the spot where the assailant had stood. "Then he was shooting at the owls."

"The ones that attacked him." There was open skepticism in Jonas's voice.

"I don't carry spare owl feathers in my pocket," Lev said.

"Yeah. I'll bet you don't. I'd like to know what you do carry there," Jonas muttered, under his breath, once more crouching low and shining his light over the ground. "He went up that way to the road. There are drops of blood scattered along his trail." He placed the measuring tool and took several pictures of the shoe prints in the mud.

"He prefers that spot over there," Lev pointed out. "He can see Rikki's house and has a great view of her back porch, where she likes to spend most of her time when she has company."

"He's sheltered here," Jonas said, circling the area, shining his light over the ground.

Lev let him find the small blackened area where the

arsonist had idly played while watching Rikki. Jonas spent another few minutes placing markers and photographing everything, concentrating on the pattern the arsonist had created.

"He's sure of himself, isn't he?" Jonas commented.

"Not anymore."

"No," Jonas agreed. He sighed and straightened, turning to face Lev. "Now he's going to be angry. He'll go to ground for a while, until he's healed, but when he comes back, he's going to go for the money play this time."

Lev wondered if the sheriff knew what that would be. The arsonist would be afraid to approach Rikki's house with the owls playing guard. He would go for her boat. Rikki loved her boat and whether or not he got her with that fire, taking her boat would hurt her. And the arsonist definitely wanted to hurt her—to make her suffer.

"How does she escape?" Jonas wondered aloud. "He's got to be furious over that. How many times has she slipped away from him? And who hates a child that much?"

"Another child."

Jonas stopped abruptly and turned on Lev. "What the hell did you just say?"

Lev shrugged. "You asked who hates a child that much? Not an adult. What adult could harbor that kind of concentrated hatred for a thirteen-year-old girl? Especially one who is autistic? This has to be a personal attack. It's directed at Rikki. Not at the foster families or even her fiancé. This is about wiping her from the earth. Cleansing the earth, so to speak."

"Maybe someone who targets autistic children?" Jonas mused. "I'll check the other fires in the past, see if any of the families have children who might be autistic."

Lev nodded in approval. "Good idea. Although . . ." He trailed off.

"Spit it out," Jonas took pictures of the prints leading up to the road and the tread marks of the tires in the mud. "Any idea is worth listening to."

"It feels personal to me. He's seething with hatred for her. Not just any child. Rikki. He wants her dead. Otherwise, why select houses that were empty when he was practicing, when he couldn't find her? Why not just select another autistic child?"

Jonas's frown conceded the point.

An owl cried out, drawing Lev's attention. He glanced overhead and two owls circled above, wings silent as they dropped lower.

"Friends of yours?" Jonas asked.

Lev didn't answer. The owls pushed the image of water and rocking boats into his head and he took off running. Jonas kept pace.

"Tell me," he snarled. "I'm not joking around with you. This is my town. My people."

"He's at the harbor."

"You armed?"

"Yes. And Levi Hammond has a permit to carry a concealed weapon."

Jonas spat out another curse and waved Lev toward his vehicle. "I'm calling for backup. Don't shoot the bastard. I mean it, *Levi*. You'll create a tangled mess just when you don't want one. Let me do the shooting if there has to be any. You sure as hell can't afford to draw attention to yourself with a cleaner in town."

"You going to hesitate?"

Jonas glanced at him briefly, face grim, mouth set, eyes

hard. He turned his head and backed out of the driveway, spinning the wheel with one hand while reaching for his radio with the other. "Which harbor?"

"Albion."

Yeah. Jonas Harrington could and would pull the trigger. Lev could see why Ilya had befriended this man. He was fiercely loyal, not afraid to take command, and he would get the job done, no matter how abhorrent. But he'd feel it. He'd go to bed at night with it. A measure of respect crept in.

"So how many shots am I going to have to take to live here?" It was a concession. The only one he could give. He knew what he'd do to any man who had anything to do with harming Rikki. He might not have been able to understand had he not met her. They were on the highway, lights flashing, sirens blaring. "Maybe we should go in quietly and not tip him off. Just a suggestion."

"Just clearing the way. I'll cut the lights and siren before we turn off the highway."

"I see the heavy traffic," Lev said. There wasn't a car on the road.

Jonas sent him a look. One. Lev repressed the urge to laugh. Jonas was trying very hard not to like him, but the man had a sense of humor. If Lev was going to do this, convince this man that he meant to stay and live in peace, he had to trust his brother's judgment and give Harrington a reason to trust him. It wasn't easy. He was a man who kept secrets close to his chest and certainly didn't share with strangers—American strangers. He took a breath and jumped off the cliff.

"The government secrets I was referring to earlier weren't only being siphoned off by my government, but yours as well. Three countries I knew of. Someone went after one of your big thinkers, a man named Wilder. Damon Wilder. Tried to kidnap him, killed his partner. Word is, Wilder's still working and whatever he's been designing they want."

Out of the corner of his eye he caught Harrington's re-action. To the name? To his knowledge? Jonas didn't look at him, but his body posture had changed subtly and he was definitely listening, paying attention.

"We have the equivalent to your Wilder. A man by the name of Theodotus Solovyov. His bodyguard, a man by the name of Gavriil Prakenskii, was severely wounded, stabbed seven times while preventing a kidnapping. He was able to prevent them from getting Solovyov, but he was permanently injured. He was forced to retire, to take on a new identity in order to stay alive."

There was a short silence.

"So going after Stavros and finding who he was work-ing for . . ."

"Partners with," Lev corrected.

Jonas nodded. "It's personal. Another brother?"

"We don't get retirement like other people. We're part of a shameful past. No one quite knows what to do with us. It's easier to kill us than to wonder if we would ever expose the past and the secrets we carry. They do not trust us, yet in our way, we are all patriots. We love our country. This information I've given you on Theodotus Solovyov is hardly a state secret. It's public and was in the newspaper, as was the attack on Wilder. With a little work, it is easy enough to find."

"Do you know where Gavriil is?"

That information would never be shared. They'd set up an emergency signal when they'd met, passing it from brother to brother. Gavriil had checked in. When he knew he was safe, Lev would check in as well. He remained silent and Jonas didn't push.

"Jackson is one scary son of a bitch," Jonas offered in return. "Kind of like you. He'll have a few things to say. He's damn good with a sniper rifle. I've seen him make shots only one or two others in the world could make. You don't want to be looking over your shoulder waiting for him to come up on you. He's got patience. He'll bide his time. Make it right with him."

Lev breathed an internal sigh of relief. Harrington had accepted him enough to give him a chance.

"He's on his honeymoon and he'll be gone for a while. He plans to take Elle on a long trip to give her more time to recover before she returns home to be part of Sea Haven again. That should give the rest of the family a little time to get used to the idea of you being around."

It was both acceptance and a warning. "I'm not going anywhere. Rikki needs Blythe and her other sisters. She needs her diving and this coast. It all works for her here." He made it a statement. Calm. Matter-of-fact. Without defiance. He wasn't asking for forgiveness or acceptance, only to be left alone. He had Rikki and her world, and he fit there.

Jonas cut the lights and siren about a half mile before he came up on the turn to the harbor where the eucalyptus trees stood in silence, swaying slightly in the wind coming off the ocean. They barreled down the long, winding hill and through the short park to the entrance of the harbor, the spotlight illuminating Rikki's boat and the man with one foot on the dock and one on the *Sea Gypsy*.

He turned and ran back toward them. The spotlight pinned him, revealing the deep wounds covering his furious face. He held a gun in his hands, attached to a flexible pipe leading to the three canisters making up the rig on his back. He sprayed the car with flames, engulfing it immediately in bright-hot heat. For a moment they were in hell, the air sucked from inside, the scorching fire burning over the car and along the ground. Visibility went to zero, only the flames surrounding them, climbing up and over the vehicle.

"Shit!" Jonas slammed on the brakes, jerking the wheel away from the spray of fire. The car spun, dirt and rocks flying high into the air, but at least they were able to breathe.

Bullets tore into the front of the car and cracked the glass of the windshield, a neat hole appearing just to the right of Lev and spiderwebbing outward across the entire glass. Both men ducked and Jonas shoved open his door, diving to the ground away from the flames, rifle in hand. Lev tore off his seatbelt and followed, crawling on his belly across the seat to get to the open door as more bullets tore through the car.

Jonas returned fire, trying to provide Lev with some cover, spraying his bullets through the fire in a straight pattern. Their assailant was on the move, running up the hillside, spreading flames as he went. He set the night on fire, uncaring of the homes or the landscape. Dozens of fires started up and there was no Rikki to call down the rain from the clouds overhead.

Lev landed in the dirt beside Jonas, who was barking orders into a radio, presumably calling the fire department. The trees and ground were damp but not soaked, and the arsonist was using a highly flammable accelerant.

The hillside was lit up a bright orange in the night. The crackling flames leapt and breathed in answer to the man's demands. He couldn't get the *Sea Gypsy*, although he'd tried, spraying out the flames in a wide arc as he'd run for the hills, hitting the dock, burning it black, but not igniting the wet wood. Smoky vapor rose from the dock, the heat mixing with cold and rising like a gray mystical cloak, surrounding the boats and obscuring vision out over the river.

Sea Haven and most of the adjoining towns were too small to have a paid fire or police department. The sheriff patrolled the long coastline and volunteers manned the fire trucks. Jonas didn't wait for backup; he started up the hill, trying to make his way through the fire line to get to the arsonist, but it was impossible. In the end, Lev and he worked as fast and as hard as they could to save the structures and trees as the fire tried to rush up the hill toward the heavier forest.

It seemed hours before they could go back to the farm. More photographs. Statements. The fire department thoroughly putting out the last of the blazes. They had shell casings to bag and every scrap of evidence taken. Both of them were covered with black smoke. The car didn't look much better, but it had survived with only superficial damage. Apparently that was also included in evidence.

By the time they returned, tired, throats hurting and eyes burning, the women were obviously upset. Jonas collected his wife and Blythe looked both men over thoroughly before she left. Lev waited until the cars were far down the drive before he allowed himself to look at Rikki. Her eyes were overbright, as if she might have been crying or might be close to tears.

No one had ever cried for him. He touched her face with gentle fingers, tracing a path from the corner of her eye to her chin.

"You're alive, then," she said, her voice husky. "That's good."

"We missed him, *lubov moya*. He managed to slip away from us. The cops are searching for him, but they aren't going to find him. He started multiple fires and you weren't there to put them out."

"Come take a shower and then you can tell me what happened." She tugged at his hand, dragging him through the house to the bathroom.

He was fairly certain she couldn't talk. She kept her head down, but he could see she was very shaken. He started to give her reassurances, but she just shook her head and pointed toward the bathroom. Glancing in the mirror, he could see why. His face was streaked with grime and he was certain he smelled like smoke.

"I'm throwing your clothes away," she announced once the water was pouring over him.

"I don't have very many clothes," he pointed out. "Maybe we could wash them."

"I'm taking them out to the garbage."

She slammed the door and he took that as the final word. Smiling, he turned his face up to the water. He was beginning to love it as much as she did. He took his time, allowing her the space she needed to cry out her relief in privacy. His heart beat hard, though, at the thought that she'd been worried about him—that she cared enough to cry.

He padded barefoot and naked from the bathroom, toweling off his shaggy hair. Over the last few weeks it had grown out from his military cut, spilling down around his eyes. He would have to get a trim, but he thought the longer hair added something to Levi Hammond's personality.

"Where are you, Rikki?" He knew where she was. In her inevitable hammock swing on the back porch, but he'd wanted to give her the courtesy of a warning.

"Out here," she called back.

He heard the rustle as she slipped out of the chair and came to the door to watch him come toward her. She'd definitely been crying. Tears tangled and clung to her long lashes, leaving them spiky and glittering with liquid diamonds.

"You all right, *laskovaya moya*?" His voice was tender as he wrapped his fingers around the nape of her neck and drew him to her.

Rikki wrapped her arms around Lev and buried her face against his chest. "I was so scared for you. Why did you go without me?"

"I was perfectly safe."

"You weren't safe. Don't lie to me. I could feel you were in trouble. I would have tried to touch your mind with mine, but I was afraid I would distract you and you'd get hurt."

He stroked her hair, loving the way her body melted into his like liquid velvet. She would always remind him of the sea, stormy and gentle, welcoming and mysterious. Like the waves against rock, he could break into a million pieces, scatter into molecules, tiny particles, and fall whole into the warmth of her love.

"Come lie down with me," he invited.

"Lev, I was so afraid for you." She looked up at him and those dark eyes were drenched with tears. "I didn't know I could feel like that."

"Now you know how I feel about you. You terrify me, Rikki, with the risks you take."

He brushed back her hair and bent to coax kisses from

her. Her lips were trembling, and he caught her full lower lip between his teeth and tugged gently. She opened her mouth to his, taking as much as she gave. Her slender arms circled his neck, holding his head to hers, her body pressing into his.

"I don't take risks. I'm a safety diver," she whispered into his mouth. She kissed him with growing hunger, each kiss longer and more demanding.

"Come to bed, Rikki." Lev took her hand and drew her into the house, locking the door and leading her through the rooms to the bedroom, pausing only to turn off the lights.

There was little moonlight shining silver through the window, but enough to spill over her pale body as he tugged her shirt over her head. He kissed his way from the corner of her mouth to her breast, one hand cupping the soft weight in his palm while he fed. He trailed his other hand across her bare tummy, the pads of his fingers massaging gently. There was possession in those long, spread fingers as he teased the underside of her breast, enjoying her reaction, the shiver of excitement, the small tremor that ran through her body, and the small whimper that told him she was already wet for him.

He tugged her jeans down over her slim hips, taking her panties with them as he slid them from her legs. She put a hand on his shoulder to steady herself as she stepped out of them, leaving her completely naked. He walked around her, drinking her in. She didn't move as he circled her, his fingers caressing her waist, then her hip, rubbing her buttocks and the seam where thigh and bottom met. He loved stroking her soft skin, loved the way she simply gave herself so completely to him.

Back in front of her, he skimmed his hand over her

breasts and flicked her sensitive nipples on his way to the
junction between her legs. His hand caressed, fingers sliding deep and then coming shallow to circle, so that her
body flushed and her breathing changed. He felt the heat
of her channel close tightly around his fingers, and her
hips moved in an involuntary response.

He closed his eyes and savored the feel of her silken
heat. For him. A welcoming. Her hands came up to his
chest as she rocked against him and she licked at his flat
nipple. As if on an electrical wire, the sizzle ran from her
tongue to his groin. His heavy erection grew even fuller
and pulsed in anticipation.

Lev bunched her hair in his hand and pulled her head
back, indulging himself, kissing her over and over, devour-
ing the sweet taste of her, reveling in the way she opened to
him and took him in. He swallowed her moan, that soft
sound that hardened him even more. He dreamt of that
sound sometimes, and woke up hard and aching. When he
turned to her, she always, always met him with eagerness.

"On the bed, *laskovaya moya*, before I have no
control."

Her eyes darkened and she lay back, beckoning with
her finger. His hands parted her thighs and just the warmth
of his breath made her cry out. Then he lapped at her, a
cat after cream, using his tongue, driving her up hard and
fast, taking her right to the edge and then pulling back
again. He loved the way her body shuddered, the way her
hips bucked and the way that soft, breathless music played
in her ears. She tasted wild and free, and his need for her
grew each time she writhed and moaned.

He inhaled her scent, the fragrance of his woman, and
rubbed his beard between her thighs, watching the ripples

of arousal move up her legs to her channel and even her belly, where the muscles bunched tightly in reaction.

Lev.

The sobbing plea he'd been waiting for, signaling she was coming undone, that he'd pushed and stretched her limits just a little more. He caught her body and flipped her over, dragging her hips up and back to him, so she was on her hands and knees. He kept one hand on her back, forcing her head down so her hips were in the air.

She gasped as he pressed the throbbing head of his cock into her entrance. She pushed back, trying to impale herself on his thick shaft. He stroked his fingernails gently down her back and over her buttocks. Again there was a ripple effect, her legs shaking, her body trembling. He gripped her hips and slammed home.

Her body took his into her tight, hot haven, wrapping eagerly around him, stroking and caressing as she slowly, almost reluctantly allowed his invasion. There was always that exquisite moment when she was so tight he was uncertain if he could force his way into heaven, but the petals unfolded and allowed him entrance. Scorching hot. Velvet soft. Tight and constricting, gripping him, as he surged deep, withdrew and drove home again.

He set a fast, hard rhythm, her position allowing him even deeper access so that it felt as if he'd welded them together for all time. His blood turned hot, flowing like liquid gold, rising from somewhere deep inside him, spreading like a firestorm of passion through his system. He bent forward to kiss her spine. The movement set off ripples in her body so that she clamped down on him like a vise.

"Not yet, not yet," she chanted. "Not like this."

He took a breath, set his jaw and stilled. "Tell me."

"I want to see your face," she whispered. "I have to see your face."

He clenched his teeth together as he obediently withdrew. She cried out as he left her, turning to sprawl across the bed, her thighs open for him, feet flat on the bed, knees wide. He caught her bottom with one hand, wrapped her hips with his arm and, gaze locked with hers, buried himself deep with one thrust, sinking to the hilt. Lights and colors seemed to burst behind his eyes, even as he watched her face, that miracle of beauty, the gaze, the breath, the flush as he took her higher.

He trailed his free hand over her breasts, down her stomach to the soft mound where they were joined. She arched her back, her hips moving into the rhythm of his, time suspended. There was only the sound. The scent. The sensation. He let go, let himself drown, giving himself up to her soft music and the love in her eyes. Her body clamped down on his, held him as the ripples turned to swelling tides and his hot release washed inside of her. He felt the rush through his body, through hers, through their joined bodies.

He waited, locked inside her, fighting for breath. Waited. She just looked at him with a glazed, sexy, *giving* look that turned him inside out.

"Say it. I have to hear you say it," he ordered, holding her beneath him.

She didn't pretend to misunderstand. She smiled at him, that Rikki smile that could take his breath. "I love you, you goofball."

He stared down at her for a few more seconds, and then rolled over laughing, gathering her close to him. "I've never been called a goofball before. There're just so many firsts with you." He wrapped his arms around her and buried his face in her neck. "Go to sleep."

"Already there," she murmured drowsily. Her hand moved over the top of his and they fell asleep together, bodies tight against one another.

19

LEV scowled as Jonas Harrington swung out of his truck, and Blythe slid out of the passenger side. Rikki, in her hammock swing, stiffened, but she covered it well, taking a sip of coffee and peering at their visitors over the rim of the steaming mug. Just to give her added confidence, Lev moved close behind her, dropping his hand casually on her shoulder.

"I was hoping not to see you for a while," Lev greeted. He rubbed his jaw. "I'm a little stiff and not certain I want to go another round."

Rikki glanced up at him, her dark eyes searching his face. He winked at her.

Jonas followed Blythe up onto the porch. "I think I got the worst of the deal, so don't complain. I wouldn't mind a cup of coffee, since no one's offering."

Rikki flushed. "I'm sorry. I should have . . ."

"Rikki," Jonas interrupted gently. "I was teasing. I grew up with the Drake girls and spent my younger years tormenting them. I have a tendency to do that with those I consider family. You and Blythe are family to me."

"I'm getting the coffee," Blythe said.

"There goes my morning," Lev muttered.

Rikki sent him a reprimand from under her long lashes, just as he knew she would. He bent to whisper in her ear. "Little miss prim and proper."

He felt her laughter in his mind, but she didn't laugh aloud. Beneath his hand, he felt some of the tension slip away. He took a swallow of coffee and waited for Jonas to tell him why he'd shown up again, this time with Blythe. The sheriff wouldn't have brought Blythe unless he thought Rikki would be upset by his visit.

Jonas remained silent until Blythe returned, studying the blackened strip surrounding Rikki's house, while Lev studied him. Definitely, he was worried about Rikki's reaction to his news. His fingers slipped to the nape of Rikki's neck, gently massaging, wanting to keep contact.

"Rikki," Blythe said, as she passed a coffee cup to the sheriff, "Jonas would like to talk to you about an official who wants to ask you some questions." She glanced up at Lev, her expression worried.

Rikki went still. "About the fire?" Her voice was low, strangled. The fingers of one hand turned white as she gripped her coffee mug, while the other dug into her denim-clad thigh.

Jonas shook his head. "No. There's a Russian making inquiries into the death of a man who was on board the yacht that sank off our coast a few weeks ago. Apparently he isn't entirely satisfied that the man drowned."

Rikki didn't react as Lev expected. She actually relaxed a little, took a sip of her coffee and met Jonas's gaze steadily. "What has that got to do with me?"

"You were diving that day. He apparently checked with the processing company and they had sent out a truck to collect your catch."

She frowned, tilting her head to one side. "Sure. I remember. The wave came out of nowhere with no warning and threw me into the water. It was lucky I had my diving gear on."

"He thinks this Russian survived."

Jonas never looked at Lev. Not once. He didn't give away the fact that he knew Levi Hammond was Lev Prakenskii, the "dead" Russian. Lev had to tell Rikki the truth, that Jonas knew, but the night with her had been too perfect to mar it with worry over what Jonas might do. Right now, he seemed to be indicating that he had accepted Levi Hammond into his community. It might be an uneasy truce, but Lev could accept that.

"The water is too cold," Rikki protested. "I doubt anyone could survive for long without a wet suit, especially under the conditions that day."

She didn't exactly lie. No one could have survived without a wet suit, not for long. Lev suppressed the need to shiver, feeling the water close over his head as the yacht dropped into the cold water. No one had had a chance to scream, they simply went down into that cold abyss, the darkness settling around them. He'd fallen, sliding along an almost invisible bubble. The fall had seemed endless. A million faces, the wails of the dead, the cold, cold water.

He'd tried to swim, going deeper, trying to find a way out. The wave took him, tumbling him over and over like a washing machine, slamming him into something until he was so disoriented and sick he didn't know where he was or how to get out of the situation. Her hands had been

surprisingly strong, anchoring him, but it was her eyes
that had saved him.

He'd felt himself drifting toward the wails, the dead
beckoning him closer. She had jerked him around, stared
into his eyes. Her gaze was determined. Reassuring. He
was safe with her. He could fall. He could break. He could
live. He *would* live. She shared her breath, her air, the es-
sence of life, all the while holding him to her with her
eyes. He was no longer alone in the dark, deep cold. She
was there, sharing her soul. There was forgiveness. Re-
demption. There was hope. It was all there in Rikki.

He felt the pressure of her hand, her thumb sliding over
the center of his palm. Blinking, he wrenched himself
out of the deep cold and found himself looking into her
eyes. She smiled at him. Slow. Tender. Love slid over him,
warmed him. He bent his head, unable to stop himself and
brushed a kiss over her upturned mouth. His heart contracted. When he looked up, Jonas was watching him
closely and he immediately swept all expression from his
face.

"Rikki doesn't need to be talking to any official from
Russia. There's no reason for her to go through that."

"He's not going away," Jonas stated. "Not until he's
satisfied."

"Bring him here," Rikki said. "I don't have anything to
tell him, but if it helps him to close his case and maybe
bring resolution to that man's family and friends, then I
don't mind."

"Rikki . . ." Lev warned.

"If you'd like, Rikki," Blythe said, "I can stay with you
while Jonas gets him and brings him back. Levi, I know
you have things to do today, but I'll stay with her."

Jonas made a single sound of annoyance. Lev knew the sheriff had recognized Lev because he'd been expecting the missing Russian to be Ilya's brother. He'd known a Prakenskii was on the yacht and Prakenskiis didn't die so easily. He didn't like the situation with Blythe and Rikki not being honest with him, but he was going to allow Levi Hammond to exist.

Lev shook his head. "If Rikki talks to him, I'm staying."

"Don't be an ass," Jonas snapped, scowling.

Lev stared him down. "I didn't say out in the open."

Jonas held up his hand. "Don't say another word. And Levi Hammond had better have his gun permit up-to-date and able to stand up to scrutiny."

Lev shrugged casually. "Be my guest." There was absolute confidence in his voice. Already, his ID was in place and every document had already arrived in Rikki's post office box. He had enough paper to convince the world that Levi Hammond did in fact exist and had a long and memorable but very varied career.

"Blythe can't stay," Rikki said. When Blythe tried to protest, she shook her head. "No way. The sheriff will be here and that's enough. I need to know that you're safe. I don't want attention called to any of you."

Blythe started to protest, but Jonas put his hand on her arm. "I agree this time, Blythe. Let's just get this done." He leveled his gaze at Lev. "Make yourself scarce. I'll be back in a half hour."

"I'll be sitting right here," Rikki said with a small, secret smile.

Jonas frowned and then nodded. "One other thing. Does the name Gerald Pratt mean anything to you? There were fingerprints on the dock and we got a hit almost immediately. We checked the prints against jobs working

with fire, such as firemen. Gerald Pratt works for the for-
estry department in the Big Sur area. He happens to have
grown up in the same city as you, Rikki. He would have
been about sixteen when you were thirteen."

She frowned, obviously trying to remember. "I swear,
I've never heard the name before. I might have gone to
school with him, but if I did, school was so difficult, I
wouldn't have remembered anyway. I was the weird girl,
always losing her mind. Kids made fun of me a lot, but I
can't remember specific names."

"He didn't go to any of the same schools with you,"
Jonas said. "So far I can't find the connection—or him,
but I'm still digging. I haven't had a lot of time. Pratt was
working this last week, but he's off at the moment and no
one has any idea of where he might have gone. He took
two weeks off."

"Gerald Pratt," Rikki repeated aloud. She shook her
head and looked helplessly at Lev and then Blythe. "I
don't know him."

She sounded so lost. Blythe put her arms around Rikki
and held her, murmuring soft reassurances. "We'll sort
this out, Rikki," she assured.

When she straightened, Rikki shook her head. "How
could I have upset someone so much that they would want
to kill not just me but everyone I care about, yet I can't
remember them?"

Jonas crouched in front of her, looking up into the eyes
that studiously avoided his. "Rikki, sometimes people are
ill. You don't know what sets them off. If they live in another reality, whatever they believe becomes true. Nothing
a thirteen-year-old girl could ever do would be justifica-
tion for this man's actions."

"Are you certain it's him?" Lev asked.

Jonas shook his head. "He's a suspect. We've got the blood and he left his DNA on the cigarette butts, but that doesn't mean he started the fire. It means he was on her property. Also, the accelerant used was Jet A, a higher octane fuel that burns hot and fast. This guy knows what he's doing."

Lev said nothing. If Pratt had his face ripped open by the owls, there would be no question. He'd be coming at Rikki soon. He didn't have that much vacation time left and he needed to finish her off now. Pratt had a taste for killing with fire as his chosen weapon. Now that he knew where Rikki was, he'd be back.

"Don't do anything stupid," Jonas warned Lev and escorted Blythe back to the car.

Rikki was silent, swinging gently, moving her bare foot up and down.

"*Laskovaya moya*, I want to talk about this Russian coming to talk with you. I know you're worried about Pratt, but he is nowhere near as dangerous as this man. He will be conducting an interrogation, not a discussion," Lev said, taking her hand, his thumb stroking little caressing circles over the center of her palm. "You don't have to do this."

She turned the full power of her dark, beautiful eyes on him. His heart contracted. There was courage there. Determination. "Of course I do. If you're going to be rid of them, I have to be the one to do it. He knows I was out on the water that day."

"I don't like it," Lev said.

She shrugged. "You don't have to like it. I'm a grown woman and I've been making my own decisions for a long time. We're in this together, right?" She looked at him.

Challenging him. "Right? Or did you think I wouldn't assert myself because you think I have a disability?"

His eyes glittered fiercely and he swung around, squatting in front of her, one hand spanning her throat, his thumb tipping her chin back. "Where the hell did that come from? We're not fighting about this, Rikki. I'm stating my opinion, that it's dangerous and you should have enough respect for me that you trust that I'd know. I respect your abilities in the water."

She flushed and her gaze slid away from his. "I'm sorry. I have a hard time with arguments. Discussions," she corrected. "Quite often, because I'm different, people think I have a low IQ and can't grasp the situation. They want to make my decisions for me."

"That's not me," he countered, then wiped his hand over his face. "Okay. Maybe it is me, but *not* because I think you aren't smart enough to see a situation. I don't like you in danger. When a man finds the only person of worth to him, that one person who matters more than anything and makes everything he's ever seen or done or gone through worthwhile, believe me, Rikki, the urge to protect her is overwhelming. If that bothers you, then I'm sorry, because it's going to be happening over and over throughout our years together."

She touched his face gently. "I can accept that. Just don't ever treat me like I'm not intelligent."

He caught her hand and kissed the tips of her fingers. "I'm not that stupid, Rikki. So if you're really going to do this, I'm going into the house and remove any evidence that I've been there. Your man, Levi Hammond, comes around when he isn't running up and down the coast diving. He crashes here sometimes. Be vague."

"I'm not letting him into the house."

"You'll have to if this is going to work. He's going to find a way to get into the house. Don't make it easy, but let him in. It's the only way he'll be satisfied. While he's on the porch, I can cover him, but once he's inside, it will be more difficult. Don't go in with him." When she looked at him, he sighed. "For me. Stay out where I can see you."

"You stay away, Lev," she dictated. "Leave this one to me." She sent him a mysterious, mischievous smirk. "I'm actually a good actress. And I have a lot of experience to draw on. That state facility I was in provided all kinds of wonderful practice for me."

He tasted fear in his mouth. "Listen to me, *lubov moya*, hear what I'm saying. This man is the most dangerous man you will ever run across. He kills without feeling. He's like a robot. He cares nothing for anyone. He doesn't work with a purpose to save governments or to try to stop gun running or human trafficking. He cares nothing about drugs. He kills. That is his only purpose in life. Once set on a target, he never stops until he has completed the assignment. That is his one joy, the victory of winning. His win is the kill."

She frowned. "And this man is after you?"

Lev nodded. "It is his job to make certain I am dead. If I kill him and he doesn't return to those who sent him, they will know I'm alive and they'll send another and then another until one day I make a mistake. If this one goes home, he will tell them I'm dead and they'll believe him."

"Then that's what he has to do," Rikki said.

Lev shook his head. "It isn't that easy. He's interrogated hundreds of people. He can sense a lie. He knows body language. He knows the little things that give people away when they're lying."

Rikki smiled at him. "He should come here when I'm alone then."

His gut reacted, protesting. The thought of Rikki alone with the cleaner was absolutely terrifying. "No way. That isn't going to happen. He can bring the sheriff with him. That's the only way he gets close to you. If you make a mistake, he'll come back alone without Harrington and I'll kill him. We'll decide what to do after that."

Rikki sighed. "You know, *Levi*, you have to get over the whole, 'I'll just kill him' thing. That might work for Lev, but not Levi. People don't solve their problems that way."

He clenched his teeth. "This might have to be an exception."

He turned his back on her and went into the house, carefully cleaning up all the dishes and putting them away. Only Rikki's coffee cup remained. There wasn't much food in the house. Blythe had already taken away the remains of their dinner from the previous night. He examined the contents of the refrigerator. Very sparse, it definitely looked as if only one person was living there.

Quickly and efficiently he stripped the bed, remade it with fresh sheets and placed the others in the washing machine. The bathrooms were next. Rikki was very particular about the bathrooms so there wasn't much evidence of him there either. He erased all proof of his existence in her home. It wasn't hard. He had a habit of making certain he touched few things wherever he was living. And he wiped every surface fast. His briefcase was packed and went with him, along with the weapons, when he left the house.

He didn't go to Rikki, he couldn't. If he did, he doubted he would have gone through with the plan. He still was considering just shooting the bastard.

Rikki watched Lev stalk across the yard and disappear into the trees. A bird called. Another answered. He was carrying his briefcase, and she knew he would be up in a tree somewhere, covering the house, but this was her world, and no one, not even some big-shot cleaner everyone was afraid of, was going to come onto her property and take what was hers. She was captain of her boat and she'd pulled Lev out of the ocean. That meant he was hers. She took the law of the sea seriously. She was responsible for him. She'd told him he would be safe with her, and he would be.

She swung her foot back and forth, was slightly mesmerized by the small circles she made, deliberately allowing her mind to concentrate on the way the early morning sun poured like gold into the small puddles of water standing in the yard. The water seemed to gleam, diamond bright. She blinked to bring it into focus, or more precisely, out of focus, so the edges of the pool seemed to spread out like rays.

At once she was lost in the beauty of the symmetry, those perfect crystalline streaks radiating from the center of the pool. The colors grew deep and vivid, and small waves sent ripples skimming over the surface as the breeze gently blew across it. The water dazzled her, so that little colored lights burst behind her eyes and she could see the puddle taking on its own life, growing into a three-dimensional image. A world had come alive in that small puddle.

Living insects played above the water, and shadows swam below, patient and deadly, waiting for one of those fragile-winged gossamer creatures to make a mistake. The buzz of the bugs grew until they were musicians playing in time to the breeze blowing ripples in the puddle, driving the shadows into a frenzy of movement. Crevices and cracks held a myriad of creatures of bright colors wiggling arms and legs and tentacles in the search for food.

"Rikki!" Jonas's voice dragged her back from the edge of her fascinating world.

She looked up a little vaguely, blinking rapidly. Her gaze avoided his and she kept her head down, looking past him, studying the second man out of the corner of her eye. She began to rock ever so gently. The official-looking man beside Jonas was carefully quartering the yard and surrounding grounds. As he walked past her truck, he looked inside and she had the feeling even in that quick glance, he'd noted every item.

Jonas crouched in front of her, his voice very gentle. "Rikki, this is the man I told you about, the one who wants to ask a couple of questions about the yacht sinking. His name is Petr Ivanov. He's with the Russian government and is investigating one of their people who had been aboard the yacht. I've explained that you're autistic and you don't like people around your house. He won't touch anything and we won't be here long. Okay?"

She nodded her head repeatedly, increasing the rocking just a little more. Already her brain was very close to that place, her own world, where she was safe and no one could touch her—not even a master interrogator.

Petr Ivanov studied her face for a long time. Her fingers were continually moving, spinning in strange little circles, and occasionally she'd lift them to her mouth to blow on them. Spin, one, two, three times, and then blow.

"You're a diver?"

She nodded.

"Sea urchin diver? And you were diving the day the yacht sank off the coast here?"

She nodded again. The fingers continued to spin and she blew on them every third time, as if she was blowing out candles. Her gaze fixed on the puddle just past the stairs leading to the porch.

Petr glanced at Jonas. The sheriff shrugged. "She doesn't talk to people much, rarely to strangers, and she has a thing about people entering her house or going on her boat."

"I told you it was necessary," Ivanov said. "This man uses women. He's dangerous. I'll know if he was near her."

"I doubt she'd let a stranger close to her, and I can't imagine she'd let him in her home. She's been here nearly five years and I've entered her house once. Surely the other divers told you about her."

The conversation flowed around her. Rikki was immune to it, the words a vague whisper in the background as the insects and frogs took up the chorus of her song. The ripples in the puddle grew into waves.

"I need to know what you saw out there," Petr said, and snapped his fingers under her nose.

Rikki's rocking increased in strength. Her hands began to flap, fingers spinning and then she'd blow on the tips as if putting out a flame.

"You have to ask her a yes or no question," Jonas said. "And step back away from her."

"Did you see a man in the water that day? Someone alive?"

Rikki shook her head violently. "A wave. Big wave." She let herself slide away, down into the gleaming waters of the puddle where the ripples had come to life.

There was a silence as Ivanov studied her growing agitation. He sighed. "I'm not going to get anything out of her. I have to see the house."

The flapping increased. So did the rocking.

Jonas was extremely gentle. "Can we look around, Rikki? We won't touch anything."

She rocked for a full minute then nodded, her eyes glued to the puddle.

The Russian swore and pushed past her to the door of her kitchen. The moment he touched the door handle, she began to make a strangled sound in the back of her throat, her only protest. Jonas, clearly torn between Rikki and the Russian, followed him inside.

"Don't touch anything," Jonas asserted. "She gave permission for you to look around, that's all. She . . ." his voice faded, leaving her fully in her own mind.

She didn't see them leave. She was too far into her mind. She didn't hear them anymore, only the sound of her own world where she retreated when the noise and pain became too much. The Russian could never find her there, and he couldn't find Lev either. He couldn't follow them into her mind, no matter what training he had. She could keep Lev safe until he came to get her. She didn't like anyone to witness her "breakdowns" but this time, she *allowed* it to happen. It had been her choice and she wasn't ashamed.

Come back to me, laskovaya moya, Lev's voice shimmered in her mind, penetrating the rippling waves. *You kept me safe, but now I need you back with me.*

It was a wrench to return to a place where the colors and detail seemed so dull at first, after the fascinating, mesmerizing underwater realm.

"He won't be back," Lev greeted her, pulling her into his arms. "That was a very brave thing to do, and I won't forget it. Not ever."

She smiled up at him, blinking, a little disoriented.

"He'll never believe that I would let you anywhere near me, my boat, or my house."

"Why did you?" Lev asked, and plucked her out of the hammock, to take her into the house. "Why did you choose me?"

She traced his strong jaw beneath the smooth beard. "Your eyes. I see right into you, and I know you in a way I could never know anyone else."

They made love all afternoon. Jonas called asking after Rikki, obviously worried that they had pushed her too far. He assured her that she had convinced Petr Ivanov that his last hope that Lev was alive had faded. No one had seen a stranger. No one believed anyone could have survived in the cold water and there was no trace of a survivor. Ivanov had left for the San Francisco airport, to fly home.

Lev cooked dinner, a careful preparation of salad, which she nibbled at as if she were a rabbit, picking through it to discard anything she thought looked scary; a baked potato, which she liked; and a small piece of a steak. He had to take every bit of fat off of it, and she pushed it around for a long time before she actually ate any of it, but she did eat it and he felt as if he'd scored a huge victory.

Late at night, they lay on the bed together, lights off, his head in her lap while he brought up a subject he'd wanted to broach for a while. "You know, *laskovaya moya*, I've been thinking. We should plan our wedding. A little civil service right here. With just your sisters. Nothing fancy, just us." Lev watched her face carefully. "I'm good at pushing paperwork through fast."

Her fingers stilled in his hair, her dark eyes going black. For a moment it was silent enough in the room that he could hear her heart pound. He took her arm, sliding his hand down to her wrist where her pulse beat into his palm.

"Did I frighten you, *lubov moya*, because I didn't mean to. We spoke of marriage."

"Speaking isn't the same thing as planning."

"Why should we wait?"

She moistened her lips. "You have to think about that, Lev. Really think about it. There're so many things I can't do. This is my world, right here, but it's very narrow. I don't travel—not at all. This is my home. I plan to live my life here. The farm and my diving. I work outside, sometimes with Lexi, but I rarely have company. I live a solitary life on purpose. I need routine. I have a difficult time accepting changes in my life. I can't go into stores where there's fluorescent lighting—which is just about everywhere."

He smiled up at her. "That's a long list. Let me see. I've traveled my entire life and I'm ready for a home—a permanent one. I like working with my hands and diving suits me just fine. I prefer a solitary life. I'm uncomfortable around a lot of people. I don't mind routine in the house, outside may be more difficult, but we've gotten good at compromise. You let me into your bathroom for showers."

"Only because there are one or two perks."

She did flash a smile at him, but it was strained. He'd definitely frightened her. Lev brought her hand to his mouth and nibbled gently. "Do you think I'll leave you?"

She frowned and he had the mad desire to bring her head down to his and kiss that look right off her face. He caught the nape of her neck and did just that, his mouth moving over hers, kissing her again and again, indulging his need to taste her, getting lost in the beauty of her response.

"*Laskovaya moya*, I'll do the shopping in the stores for us. I'm asking you to believe in me the way I believe in you."

"You've only just gotten a taste of freedom, Lev. You can go anywhere now. Everyone thinks you're dead. You can have any life you want. Any woman." She forced a small smile and her fingers bunched in his hair. "One that can have children."

He went still inside. There it was. The problem as she saw it. "The life I want is right here. The woman I want is right here. As for children, I never considered having any, so if we don't, I won't miss anything I never thought about in the first place."

"If we had a child, I'd be afraid it would turn out like me," she admitted in a low voice.

He kissed her again, aching inside. "A woman of courage? One who makes her own way in the world? One who succeeds no matter the odds?"

"It's difficult growing up abnormal in a world where different is not accepted. A small thing like changing the lighting in the schools might have helped, but it was easier to get rid of me rather than spend the money. Teaching children understanding and tolerance might have helped as well. I don't want my life for my child. Don't think I'm complaining, Lev, because I'm not. I just think the odds are greater that any child I have would have to struggle every day of her life just for acceptance."

"I'm fine with getting all of your attention," he said. "I want to grow old with you, Rikki. I'm asking you to give yourself to me all the way."

Her eyes went soft and tender. "Then yes. Absolutely yes."

Outside, an owl shrieked, then a second. Lev rolled off the bed, leaping to his feet, reaching for his gun and slamming it into the harness he'd laid on the table. He slipped the harness on, jerked a jacket on and took off running.

"Call Jonas. Pratt's here. He's damned close too. I don't know how he slipped past the sentries. And get the hell out of here, go up to the highway and wait."

He didn't wait to see if she'd comply, he was already streaking out the door. A determined killer with a lot of experience could do major damage. The arsonist had to be stopped now. He moved fast, this time following the images the owl projected back to him. Gerald Pratt was in the garden area on the slope leading to Rikki's house.

Swearing, Lev raced across the uneven terrain. Pratt had come in through the back entrance. As with many unbalanced people, he was cunning, and he came in downwind, taking care not to alert the birds. He had laid his fire lines like a general. The ground was wet, but not soaked, and with enough fuel, it would burn hot and fast and run uphill right to Rikki's house.

As Lev sprinted through the trees, he could smell the kerosene, thick and strong, and knew Pratt had been at work for some time. Tree trunks surrounding him had been splashed with the flammable liquid. The arsonist was working his way slowly and very carefully around Rikki's house to trap her inside. Pratt had been so overcome with the need to destroy Rikki that he hadn't waited until they had lowered their guard. He'd come up with another plan of attack and implemented it immediately.

Jet A fuel would provide the needed heat to dry out the

ground between the thick vegetation and Rikki's home. Once Pratt started the fire, he could manipulate the flames, until they burned hot enough to race up the hillside, consuming everything in their path, including Rikki's house. This time, Pratt would cut off all escape by soaking the trees on the ridge above her as well. Had Pratt not been a fire element, Lev wouldn't have been so alarmed. The ground wasn't dry and ready for the least little spark, but Pratt had the ability to control his fire, make it burn hot enough to do the damage he intended. The heat would swirl around behind the flames, creating more oxygen and feeding the fire as it grew in size until everything in its path would be consumed.

Heart pounding, tasting fear in his mouth, Lev cursed himself for not having made certain Rikki was safe. He'd been so focused on removing Pratt from her life, that he hadn't considered she might be trapped waiting for Jonas and the fire department. He glanced at the sky. There were clouds, but not as heavy as the other night. A few appeared gray and dark, but not many.

Lev, where is he?

He let himself breathe. The arsonist wouldn't know they could communicate in silence. He turned his head to glance over his shoulder and stepped into a pool of liquid. The ground was saturated with the fuel. He knew instantly the man had expected company. He was in the profession and had been educated in the way fires worked. He would have studied the topography of the farm and surrounding forest.

Rikki's home was considered urban interface—a home surrounded by tremendous amounts of fuel. She had cleared away hazards close to her house and planted only low-growing and fire-resistant plants within thirty feet of her home. She'd convinced her sisters to do the same

thing. Most of the plants held water, making them perfect
to get through droughts, and to aid in the resistance of
fire. She pruned regularly and removed all the dead vegetation, staying extremely vigilant because of the fires in
her past. Wild strawberry, beardtongue and fuchsias were
closer to the house, while plants like lavender, yarrow,
monkey flower and redbud provided a middle circle with
the sage and concha on the extreme outside. Throughout the entire garden, she had sprinklers and a vast water
supply.

*Don't come through here, Rikki. He's got fuel every-
where. And remember, he's got a flamethrower. The moment he knows we're out of the house and in the forest, he's
going to ignite that accelerant. I want you to get out of
here.*

*Well, that isn't going to happen. I'm drawing all the
moisture I can into this area, both from the sky and below
us. I can't use it until he makes his move. Once that happens, I'll cut off his escape using the pond. He has to figure
he'll get out that way. I'm not letting our farm burn. The
sheriff and the fire department are on their way. I told my
sisters to leave immediately.*

That was his woman. Cool under fire. Determined. She
could face a trained Russian interrogator and use what
others called a weakness as her greatest strength, and then
just as coolly and deliberately go out into the night and
work with him, in spite of the danger, to save the farm. Of
course Pratt had an escape plan. He was going to set the
hills and forest on fire. He had to have given himself a
safe path out.

Staying low, Lev moved in a semicircle, slower now,
reaching for the birds to give him a clear idea of where the
fire starter was working. He moved in silence, knowing if

Pratt heard him coming, he would immediately use his flamethrower and trigger the ignition source. It would definitely burn hot enough to start a fire on the hillside.

Rikki had to be out in the open. She could never gather the clouds together from inside the trees. He didn't know which would be worse, knowing she was in the woods where any moment Pratt could turn the entire forest into roaring flames or out in the open where she might be an easy target for a gun. He couldn't see her as he worked his way through the trees and brush, back around toward the lower valley where the irrigation pond was situated.

On the other side of the valley, some forty yards away, he could see Pratt, working furiously, jetting the fuel from a pack on his back. The arsonist sprayed a generous splash over the bushes leading to the first ring of protection of Rikki's house, the sagebrush. Pratt saturated several areas as he raced around the outer perimeter of her personal yard. Shedding his pack, he thrust it out of the way near the road leading down to the pond and donned his flame-throwing pack.

Lev took aim at the man's temple. Before he could pull the trigger, Pratt stumbled on a large tree limb that lay in his path and sprawled onto the ground, taking him out of Lev's sight. Flame burst orange red, igniting the gases. The world around them exploded. The gas on the trees around Lev ignited, flames leaping into the air until he could see nothing else. Heat seared him. Oxygen was gone, feeding the hungry flames, pouring into the fire so that he was left gasping. He dropped to the ground to try to find a way to breathe.

I'm trapped.

Rikki was ready for just that moment. The sky opened up just over the forest and small slope where Pratt had so carefully prepared his assault. She had concentrated the rain in the exact area where the arsonist had set his fuel. Water slammed into Lev, drenching him, plastering his hair to his head, running in rivulets down his neck. The roar that had surrounded him as the fire sprang to life, so loud just seconds before, turned to the hiss of a snake. There didn't seem to be individual raindrops, but buckets of water pouring over the trees and his head.

The rain fell in two concentrated places that Lev could tell. It was difficult to see through the thick gray veil, but water poured into the irrigation pond, already filled to capacity and now running over its banks, and onto the trees and small valley. The valley was a funnel, catching the water running off the slope and sending it rushing like a river toward the road and pond. Water bubbled from underground, adding to the sudden supply, which was rising fast and furious.

Lev crawled forward on his hands and knees through the trees to the edge of the forest. He couldn't get a good shot at the arsonist and he didn't want to tip him off as to his presence, so he continued to move forward through smoldering brush. Pratt struggled to get to his feet, but was knocked back to the ground by the tumbling limb of a large broken branch. He rolled, seemed to get tangled for a moment and then fought to gain his feet.

Water swirled around his ankles, rising fast, pouring now from the sprinkler systems throughout the farm. Water came off the roof of Rikki's house, running down the gutters to the channels leading to the ditches. The entire area had been designed to preserve water. Every ditch led to the main funnel, which Pratt seemed caught in. He gave a halfhearted spray again with his flamethrower, but he knew it was impossible.

Lev used his elbows to propel himself through the mud and grass to work his way around to get in position to take a shot. Pratt suddenly stiffened, his head whipping around, looking up the slope toward Rikki's house.

She stood at the top of the hill, her face upward, toward the sky, hands graceful as she conducted her wild symphony. The rain responded to her commands and every third beat, her right hand would move upward, palm up. She looked like an ancient priestess worshiping the rain goddess. Lev tried to call out to her, to warn her, but thunder cracked and the wind whipped the sound of his voice away. Pratt tossed aside the flamethrower's trigger and pulled a gun.

Without hesitation, Lev fired several shots, knowing the angle was wrong, but all he cared about was distracting the man away from Rikki. He leapt to his feet and ran toward the arsonist, firing as he did so. Pratt turned to face the immediate threat, spitting bullets at Lev. He was just as blind, trying to see through the pouring rain to the shadowy figure coming at him. Unable to see Lev, he half turned and fired at Rikki. The water swirled around his knees now.

Lev skidded to a halt as he realized he was about to run right into that gathering force of water. He slammed a new clip into his gun and knelt, trying to get a clear shot, firing to draw Pratt's attention back to him.

Pratt was in trouble and knew it. He fired several times at Lev and then abandoned every attempt at killing, trading his need for retribution for survival. The water crept up his thighs, and now the current was strong, tugging and pulling, driving him toward the pond. He was strapped into his heavy pack and couldn't get the buckles loosened with the rain pouring down on him.

He fell again, tumbled over, the pack pulling him down. He was wearing boots and the water had filled them. His heavy jacket and clothing added to his weight. The current swept him straight over the bank into the irrigation pond. He went under, surfaced with a thin, terrified scream and went under again.

Rikki collapsed at the top of the hill and Lev's heart nearly stopped. He clawed his way through the slippery mud to get to her, even as he tried to keep an eye on Pratt. The body came up once, rolled like a heavy log and disappeared again, this time in the center of the pond. Lev reached Rikki. She was lying faceup, her eyes open, staring at the rain as it came down. Without her orchestration, the rain slowed considerably.

"Are you hit?" His hands ran over her body.

"My calf feels like it's on fire."

She was remarkably calm while he felt insanity taking hold. He ripped her jeans with the tip of his knife, frantic to see the damage. The bullet had barely clipped her, taking more denim than skin, and he hung his head, his stomach heaving. He didn't have time to vomit, he heard a noise above them and whirled, gun rising. Jonas appeared, flanked by several others. Lev simply laid the gun on the ground and lifted Rikki into his arms. By the time he reached the porch, the rain had stopped altogether.

Several hours later, a team had recovered the body and collected evidence, and Jonas came to join them on the back porch to take their statement. "Are you all right, Rikki?" Jonas asked gently. "Did a paramedic look at that wound?"

"Yes, Blythe got here a couple of hours ago and insisted. She sent coffee to your crew."

"Bad luck, Pratt falling into the pond like that with his pack on. He didn't have a prayer," Jonas commented.

"I wouldn't call it bad luck. And I want my gun back when you're finished with your investigation."

Rikki remained silent, head down, hands covering her face. Lev and Jonas exchanged a long look above her head.

"They're almost gone, sweetheart," Lev murmured.

She rocked back and forth silently, and he dropped to the porch beside her and wrapped his arm around her shoulders, pulling her into him, sheltering her with his chest and arms.

"Rikki," Jonas said softly. "Gerald Pratt and his family were in the same accident as you and your parents, just before your thirteenth birthday, the huge pileup on the freeway. Do you remember that accident?"

Lev felt her take a deep breath. She nodded, but didn't lift her head.

"The Sitmore car hit the Pratt car from behind, launching the Pratt car into the air. It hit a fuel tanker and ignited from the sparks another vehicle that was sliding along a guard rail, metal to metal, was throwing into the air."

"There was fire everywhere," she murmured, her voice that of a child. "All around us. My mother was hurt. People were screaming. A car hit ours very hard from behind and pushed us into the car in front of us. The noise was terrible."

"The accident wasn't your parents' fault and it certainly wasn't yours. Anyone reading the report could clearly see the problem started with two trucks colliding, causing a chain reaction behind them. Visibility was poor, the roads slick, and disaster struck." Jonas pushed a tired hand through his hair. "He's gone now, Rikki, and he can't hurt anyone you love." When she remained silent, he sighed and started to turn away.

Rikki sat up, squaring her shoulders. "Why did he want me and my family dead?"

Jonas shrugged. "Who knows what happened to his mind. He was in a burning car with his parents, someone pulled him out, but he watched them die in the fire. He became obsessed with fire after that. He took classes, became a volunteer at a young age, continued his schooling and then joined the CDF."

Blythe came out of the house, and dropped her hand on Rikki's shoulder. "I'm going home, honey. Get some sleep."

"Thanks for the coffee," Jonas said. "We all appreciated it."

They watched her drive away, too tired to get up. Rikki leaned her head against Lev's shoulder and looked at Jonas, actually meeting his eyes. "He blamed my family and wanted us to die the same way, didn't he?"

Jonas nodded. "I think so. He wasted his life on trying to get revenge for an accident. It was just bad luck that your car was behind theirs. You two get some sleep, you both look exhausted. And watch that wound, Rikki, you don't want an infection. "

Lev held out his hand to Jonas. "Thanks."

"It's what I do," Jonas said, shaking Lev's hand before turning away.

Lev lifted Rikki into his arms and carried her into their house.

20

RIKKI woke up humming. Lev lay for a moment, listening to the joy in her voice. The night before she'd pored over her tide book and double-checked the weather. She rolled over and looked at him. His breath slammed out of his lungs. He ran his hand over her head, stroking down that thick, wild, silky-soft hair, allowing the wash of love to swamp him.

She smiled. His heart jumped.

"It's going to be a perfect day today. A dive day."

The joy in her voice sang in his veins. She kissed him and jumped out of bed. "We'll need a high-calorie lunch packed. And a big breakfast."

She was already in the bathroom, a flash of bare skin, all curves. He could see the marks of his possession on her and it gave him a strange, primal satisfaction. She wore only the shimmering raindrops falling down her shapely leg and his ring, a plain gold band. They'd been married in a quiet ceremony with only her sisters attending. Blythe and Judith had been their witnesses. It had been cold and windy, but they'd bundled up and had the wedding outdoors where Rikki felt safest. He cared nothing about the where, only that it was done and that Rikki was permanently his.

He lay on the bed, fingers linked behind his head, staring up at the ceiling, remembering the night before their wedding, when he'd finally summoned the courage to tell her what Lev Prakenskii had been doing aboard that yacht and just who Stavros was. He told her he believed Ilya Prakenskii was his brother and that Ilya was married to a Drake. He had confessed that he'd been present when Elle Drake had been kidnapped and brutally abused by Stavros, and that he hadn't freed her in order to carry out his orders. He'd been undercover, working his way into Stavros's confidence, slowly gaining his trust, so he would lead Lev to his partner, and ultimately, the leak in the government.

He'd told her everything he could, there in the dark, wishing for the sound of the rain to soothe both of them. She'd been silent, her breathing even and soft against his shoulder. Once, she'd slipped her hand into his, closing her fingers around his, as though to give him courage. And it had taken courage, every ounce he possessed, to risk losing her by telling her the truth, letting her know what kind of man he'd been, and that if she remained with him, if she married him, she might very well become an outcast in Sea Haven when Elle Drake returned.

Rikki's reaction was total Rikki. She merely wrapped her arms around him and held him. He would never forget her response. She meant what she'd said when she'd first committed to him. He could break apart, spill every dirty secret, and she would pick up the pieces and put him back together. She had kissed his mouth, murmured that she loved him and snuggled close to him, holding him to her as she fell asleep. He had no idea how he'd held it together until he heard her even breathing and then he had cried for the first time that he could remember since he'd been a boy. He just lay there in the dark, holding her, his face buried in her dark hair, so filled with love he was afraid he might really shatter.

She stuck her head around the door, breaking his reflection. "Get a move on. We want to get out there early. And peanut butter is *definitely* on the menu."

Lev scrubbed his hands over his face, shaken at the memory, knowing he always would be. Shaken that someone could really love him that much.

"You're going to get fired before you ever get started in this job," she warned.

He laughed and sat up, hearing the water go on. He hadn't heard joy in her voice in a while. The aftermath of finding out Gerald Pratt had targeted her family to die because of a car accident none of them had had any control over had been upsetting to her. In a way, he supposed, it would have been easier for her to think she'd somehow offended someone with one of her outbursts as a child. At least it would have made more sense to her.

In the days that followed she'd lost too much weight and seemed fragile. A series of storms had prevented her from diving. Even their wedding hadn't removed the shadows from her eyes. He'd stayed close to her, venturing out only to do a little shopping. He continued to plant the vague memory of Levi Hammond in the few people he met even casually, building a solid history for his life.

"*Lev!*" Her imperious voice made him laugh all over again. Who knew some little slip of a woman could boss him around and he'd like it?

"I'm on it," he called back, failing to keep the laughter out of his voice. He'd asked to be the cook and tender, now he was going to have to back it up with the grunt work, preparing a feast for the day while she went over her diving gear for the millionth time.

He worked fast and had breakfast ready and a huge lunch packed by the time she ran into the room. Instead of her blue jeans, she wore a coral colored tank and a long skirt that swirled around her ankles. He turned his back on the sink and inhaled sharply, his gaze drinking her in. She never failed to surprise him. The skirt was full and moved lovingly around her slender legs as she walked, the swirl of muted watercolors falling over her hips to her ankles in a cascade of pure temptation.

"You have anything on under that skirt?" he inquired.

That easily she could get him worked up. He'd gone from total control to absolutely none. He was smiling all over again. It was the simple things, he decided, that made a man happy, like his wife remembering a small detail he'd mentioned to her.

"Probably not," she answered with a lift of her eyebrow. "I'm diving. You can't wear too much when you're diving."

He nearly groaned, but he wasn't going to give her the satisfaction. He handed her the usual diving breakfast, her beloved peanut butter and banana sandwich and a cup of coffee. "You'll need to down two of those."

"I'm driving," she said. "No time."

"The boat," he countered.

"You don't *drive* a boat," she sneered. "I was referring to my truck."

"Oh no, *laskovaya moya,* I've been reading the laws of this wonderful state, and I believe that truck is now half mine. *I'm* driving *our* truck."

Her eyes darkened. Little sparkles heated the cool depths. "Really? I don't think you have a prayer because I've got the keys." Laughing, she dangled them in front of him and, scooping up gear, ran for the truck.

Lev followed at a more leisurely pace, locking the house, double-checking that they had everything, especially water. The moment they finished packing the truck and she turned toward the driver's side, he stepped into her path, trapping her slender body with his much larger one, his arms caging her there on the tailgate. "I have one thing you don't," he murmured against her neck, turning his head and nipping her earlobe.

"What?"

His tongue teased her ear. "Brute strength," he whispered and removed the keys from her hand even as he captured her mouth with his. He didn't let her up until she kissed him back thoroughly, until her arms slid around his neck and she melted into him.

He drove the truck with great satisfaction, smirking at her. "Manly man, here, woman."

She snorted indelicately. "Until you board that boat. Then you're a lowly tender."

"I do believe I have a license to dive with you."

"You have a license, which I don't believe for one minute is real," she said, "and you can go dive on Mike's boat."

He glanced over at her, taking in the tight coral tank lovingly cupping her breasts, and shook his head. "I like the perks on your boat."

She laughed and ate her second peanut butter sandwich. As they turned onto the eucalyptus-lined drive leading to the harbor, she thrust her head out the window and shouted, "Today's a *dive* day. Woo-hoo!" It was impossible to contain her happiness.

He didn't think he'd ever seen her look more beautiful as they cast off and she took her position at the helm, guiding them along the river, sweeping under the bridge, through the harbor and out to sea. She was amazing. The sun kissed her dark hair, the wind put color into her cheeks, and her joy made her eyes bright. He knew he would never want to be anywhere else. She took his breath away, and his love for her was so overwhelming that for a few moments he could only stare at her.

Lev watched her, knowing he would never forget the way she looked there at the helm, hair blowing in the wind, utter confidence on her face. She lifted her face to the sky and laughed, the sound carried away by the wind. Her tank top plastered against her small, firm breasts so that her nipples peaked beneath the thin material, beckoning him. In the wind her long skirt blew around her ankles, swirling, sometimes revealing her bare, shapely legs and then dropping the colorful veil over the enticing sight.

He wanted her. There in the early morning sunlight, with the gulls flying overhead and the water beneath them. How could he not? She was his world. Without a doubt, when she was the captain of her boat, she was at her sexiest. His body reacted of its own volition. He didn't will the blood to flood into his cock, despite his training and experience in sexual arts; this was natural, a reaction to loving his woman. He found joy in that simple pleasure—his body reacting without command.

He stepped up behind her, close, knowing—certain— that she would welcome him. She leaned her head back onto his shoulder and laughed again. The sound was an aphrodisiac, bursting through his veins like champagne bubbles. He wrapped his arms around her waist and pulled her body back against him. His cock was as hard as a rock, thick and long and pulsing with energy. He knew she could feel his need by the way she pushed back tight against him.

One of her arms came back up and around to circle his head, bringing it down to hers as she turned her face enough to kiss him. "I've been giving it some thought," she whispered against his mouth.

"What thought?" One hand found its way under her tank top to caress the underside of her breast.

"That there might be a few perks to having you diving with me after all."

His fingers found her nipple, tugged and rolled, then went back to massaging her supple breast. He felt her stomach muscles bunch beneath his palm where he held her tightly to him. He bit the junction of her neck and shoulder.

"I'm certain I can provide as many perks as you'd like," he murmured, licking from her pulse to the lobe of her ear. "Both above and below water."

She rolled her bottom against him, a clear enticement. "When I was putting your diving suit into the truck, I found that little opening right at the crotch very intriguing and fraught with all sorts of amazing possibilities under water." She turned her head more until their eyes met. "I can hold my breath a really long time."

His cock reacted with a hard jerk. The pressure from such a heavy erection was nearly painful with his jeans on. With one hand he unbuttoned the front of his jeans to get some relief. The cool air hit the scorching heat of his shaft, and he pressed closer to her, using the warmth of her body, burrowing into the delicious separation of her buttocks. He trailed his fingers over her hip and down her leg to her thigh. Very slowly he began to bunch the material in his fist, pulling it up inch by inch.

"I have to admit, *laskovaya moya*, I've noticed you have excellent skills under water."

The wind tugged at the skirt and he continued to inch up the hem so that her bare leg and then the left side of her firm round buttocks and hip came into view, revealing all those shimmering raindrops scattered along her bare skin, the ones he loved to taste.

"*Superior* underwater skills," she corrected. "Skills I'm quite willing to improve on. I don't mind practicing. In fact, I *enjoy* practicing."

He knew she was telling the truth. Each time her lips closed over his cock, it was her idea, and there was something so amazing in her eyes that at times he wondered whether that was half of the pleasure, the way she loved him, the way she enjoyed pleasuring him. She gave him back every bit as much as he gave her.

His hand caressed bare skin. He shaped her bottom, rubbed and massaged. "How good are you at driving this boat?" His voice was pitched low to challenge her.

"Expert." There was no hesitation.

"Really?" He bunched her hair in his hand and pulled her head back to take her mouth. Dark hunger spread like the sun across the water. Deliberately he took his time, exploring her sweetness, taking what he wanted, kissing her deeply over and over.

The boat continued over the water toward their destination without so much as a waver. When he released her mouth, she caught his lip with her teeth and nipped. Her tongue licked along the marks. "You'll have to do better than that," she whispered, a husky invitation.

His hands bunched on either side of the long skirt, slowing bringing the material up so he could caress her bare skin. He didn't mind meeting challenges, but there was something amazing about skimming over the water in the early morning with the sun pouring down on them, and the feel of soft, warm skin against his palms. He believed he might be the luckiest man in the world.

He savored the moment, resting his chin on her shoulder, holding his body tight against hers as he massaged her legs and buttocks, feeling the vibration of the engine and the rise and fall of the waves beneath them. He took his time, sliding his hand between her legs to push against her inner thighs, insisting she widen her stance. She took the direction, her hips moving back against him.

He leaned into her. "You're not supposed to move. You only get to stand there." Deliberately he bit her neck again, found her soft skin too warm and enticing to do anything but linger so he added his mark, all the while he cupped her mound in the palm of his hand.

He felt her breath hitch in her lungs. Damp, welcoming heat met his palm. He took his time, using a slow, gentle hand, fingers circling and rubbing, slipping into her to test those tight silken muscles and tease her sensitive bud, only to slide away when her hips bucked against his hand. He didn't know who had more control—Rikki or him.

Her soft little whimper, *Lev*, went straight to his heart. He went to his knees, staying behind her, leaning in to take a nip at the delicious indentation in her hip, right where the raindrops started, those shimmering, enticing drops he loved to follow up—or down—her leg. He started at the bottom and found each one, swirling his tongue along that familiar path. He followed the intriguing little drops up her thigh to her hip.

"I think you need to add to this tattoo." He murmured as he kissed his way to the front of her thigh. "You need a drop here." He nipped her inner thigh. "And here." He nipped again, higher, near the blazing heat. "And here." His tongue plunged deep and one of her hands fisted in his hair. It was long enough, shaggy enough for her to get a good grip, but he sent her flying anyway.

She cried out, a soft sound the birds diving for fish answered as they plunged deep into the sea. *Please.*

I intend to always please you.

He stood behind her, her skirt billowing in the wind, one arm circled her waist, locking her to him, and he entered her, welding them together with her scorching heat. The vibrations of the engine ran up his legs to their joined bodies. The boat flew over the water, her hand steady on the helm. They were joined together, one skin, hearts pounding the rhythm of the sea and nothing—nothing could have been better.

He was exactly where he wanted to be. Where he was supposed to be. This was his world—Rikki—and he had everything.

Keep reading for an excerpt
from the next Carpathian novel

DARK PERIL
by Christine Feehan

Coming soon from
Piatkus

I was half alive for a thousand years.
I'd given up hope that we'd meet in this time.
Too many the centuries. All disappears
as time and the darkness steal color and rhyme.

DOMINIC TO SOLANGE

CARPATHIAN males without a lifemate didn't dream. They didn't see in color and they certainly didn't feel emotion. Pain, yes, but not emotion. So why had he been reaching for a dream for the past few years? He was an ancient, an experienced warrior. He had no time for fantasy, or for imagination. His world was stark and barren, a necessity for battling an enemy who was inevitably a friend or a family member.

Over the first hundred or so years after losing his emotions, he had held out hope. As centuries passed, the hope of finding his lifemate had faded. He had accepted he would find her in the next life and he was carrying out his resolve to do his last duty to his people. Yet here he was, an ancient of great experience, Dominic of the Dragonseeker line, a lineage as old as time itself, a man of wisdom, a warrior renowned and feared. He lay awake beneath the rich soil, dreaming.

Dreams should have felt insubstantial—and at first his

had been. A woman. Just a vague idea of her looks. So young in comparison to him, but a warrior in her own right. She hadn't been his concept of the woman who would partner him, yet as she grew in substance over the years, he realized how perfect she was for him. He had fought far too long to ever lay down his sword. He knew no other way of life. Duty and sacrifice were bred in his very bones and he needed a woman who could understand him.

Perhaps that was what dreams were. He'd never dreamed until a few years ago. Never. Dreams were emotions, and he'd long ago lost those. Dreams were color, although not his. But they felt like color as the years shaped the woman. She was a mystery, sheer confidence when she fought. She often had fresh bruises and wounds that left scars on her soft skin. He'd taken to examining her carefully each time they met—healing her had become a traditional greeting. He found himself smiling inside, thinking how she was entirely the opposite from confident when it came to viewing herself as a woman.

For a few moments, he contemplated why he should be smiling inside. Smiling was equated with happiness and he had no emotions to feel such things, but his memories of emotions were sharpening as he moved toward the end of his life, instead of dimming as he had expected. Because when he summoned the dream, he felt a sense of comfort, of well-being and happiness.

Over the years she had become clearer to him. A jaguar woman. A fierce warrior with exactly the same values he held on loyalty and family and duty. He would never forget the night, only a week ago, when he saw her eyes in color. For a moment he couldn't breathe, looking at her in wonder, shocked that he could remember colors so vividly that he could attribute an actual color to her cat's eyes.

Her eyes were beautiful, glowing somewhere between gold and amber with faint hints of green that darkened when he managed to elicit a laugh from her. She didn't laugh often or easily and when she did, he felt it was more of a victory than any of the battles he'd won.

As dreams went—and they only occurred when he was awake—they always seemed a bit out of focus. But he looked forward to seeing her. He felt protective toward her, as if his allegiance had already swung toward his dream woman. He wrote to her, songs of love, saying all the things he wished to tell his lifemate. And when she refused to rest, he'd lay her down, her head in his lap, stroking her thick mane of hair and singing to her in his language. He'd never felt more content—or more complete.

He stirred, disturbing the rich soil surrounding him. The moment he moved, the pain took him, thousands of knives ripping from the inside out. The tainted vampire blood he'd deliberately swallowed had been thick with parasites and they moved in him, replicating, seeking to take over his body, to invade every cell, every organ. And as often as he purged some to keep the numbers down, they seemed to work harder to multiply.

Dominic hissed out his breath between his teeth as he forced his rising. It was not yet fully night and he was an ancient Carpathian with many battles and kills to his name. As a rule ancients didn't rise before the sun had set, but he needed the extra time to scout his enemy and get his bearings in this land of walking myths and legends.

Deep within the cave he'd chosen in the Amazon forest, he moved the earth gently, allowing it to settle around him as he awakened, wanting to keep the area as undisturbed as possible. He traveled only at night, as his kind did, listening to the whisper of evil, on the trail of a master vampire, one he was certain had knowledge of the plans to destroy the Carpathian species once and for all. His people knew that the vampires were coming together under the rule of the five. At first the groups had been small and scattered, the attacks easily fended off, but lately the whisper of conspiracy had grown into a roar, and the groups were larger and more widespread than first thought. He was certain the parasites in the tainted blood were the key to identifying all those forging an allegiance to the five masters.

He'd gleaned that much over his days of traveling. He had tested the theory several times, coming across three vampires. Two were relatively new and neither had the parasites and were easy for an experienced hunter to kill. But the third had satisfied his questions. The moment he came into close proximity, the parasites had gone into a frenzy of recognition. He had listened to the vampire bragging for most of the night, telling him of the growing legions centering in the Amazon, where they had allies in the jaguar-men and a human society that had no idea they were in bed with the very ones they sought to destroy. The *masters* were using both humans and jaguar-men to hunt and kill Carpathians. Dominic had killed him, a quick extraction of the heart and, calling down the lightning, incinerated him. Before leaving the area, he had taken great care to remove any trace of his presence.

He knew time was running out, fast. The parasites were hard at work, whispering to him, murmuring evil enticements, unrelenting in their quest for him to join with the masters. He was an ancient without a lifemate, and the darkness was strong in him already. He had accepted that his lifemate would come in the next life, and he had dedicated his life to helping his people. His beloved sister had disappeared hundreds of years earlier—he now knew she was dead and her children safe with the Carpathian people. He could do this one last task and end his barren existence with honor.

He rose from the rich soil, as rejuvenated as one with parasites in his blood could possibly be. The cave, deep beneath the earth, kept the sun from touching his skin, but he felt it anyway, knowing it was just outside the darkness, waiting to scorch him. His skin prickled and burned in anticipation. He strode through the cave with absolute confidence. He moved with the easy self-assurance of a warrior, flowing over the uneven ground in the darkness.

As he began the climb to the surface, he thought of her—his lifemate, the woman in his dreams. She wasn't his true lifemate of course, because if she were he would be seeing colors vividly, not just her eyes. He would see the various shades of green in the rainforest, but everything around him remained gray hued. Was finding solace with her cheating? Was singing to her about his love of his lifemate cheating? He longed for her, needing to conjure her up at times to get through the night when his blood was on fire and he was being eaten alive from the inside out. He thought of her soft skin, a sensation that seemed amazing when he was like an oak tree, hard iron, his skin as tough as leather.

As he neared the entrance of the cave, he could see light spilling into the tunnel and his body cringed, an automatic reaction after centuries of living in the night. He loved the night, no matter where he was or what continent he was on. The moon was a friend, the stars often guiding lights he navigated by. He was in unfamiliar territory, but he knew the De La Cruz brothers patrolled the rain forest, although there were five of them to cover a very large territory and they were spread very thin. He had a feeling the five, who were recruiting the lesser vampires against the Carpathians, had deliberately chosen the De La Cruz territory as their headquarters.

The Malinov brothers and the De La Cruz brothers had grown up together, more than friends, claiming a kinship. They'd been regarded by the Carpathian people as two of the most powerful families, warriors unsurpassed by many. Dominic thought about their personalities, and the camaraderie that had turned into a rivalry. It made sense that the Malinov brothers would choose to set their headquarters right under the nose of the very ones who had plotted theoretical ways to remove the Dubrinsky line as rulers of the Carpathian people and then, in the end, had sworn their allegiance to the prince. The Malinov brothers would become the De La Cruz brothers' most bitter and unrelenting enemies.

Dominic's logical line of reasoning had been confirmed by the vampire he had killed in the Carpathian Mountains, a very talkative lesser vampire who wanted to brag about all he knew. Dominic had made his way, taking no prisoners, so to speak, surprised at how the parasites were such a fantastic warning system. It had never occurred to the Malinov brothers that any Carpathian would dare to ingest the blood and invade their very camp.

Going closer to the entrance, he was hit by the noise first, the sounds of birds and monkeys and the incessant hum of insects in spite of the steady rain. It was hot, and steam actually rose from the floor just outside the cave as the moisture poured down from the skies. Trees hung over the swollen banks of the river, their root systems great gnarled cages, the thick tendrils snaking over the ground to create waves of wooden fins.

Dominic was impervious to rain or heat, he could regulate his own temperature to stay comfortable, but those thirty feet or so from the entrance of his cave to the relative safety under the thick canopy were going to be hell and he wasn't looking forward to it. Traveling in the sun even in another form was painful, and with the sensation of glass shards ripping his insides into shreds, he had enough to contend with.

It was difficult not to reach for the dream. In her company, the pain eased and the whispering in his head ceased. The constant murmurs, the parasites working on his acceptance of the *masters* and their plan, were wearing. The dream gave him solace in spite of knowing his lifemate wasn't real.

He knew he had slowly built up his lifemate in his mind—not her looks but her characteristics, the traits that were important to him. He needed a woman who was loyal beyond all else, a woman who would guard their children fiercely, who would stand with him no matter what came at them, who he would know was at his side and he wouldn't have to worry that she couldn't protect herself or their children.

He needed a woman who, when it was just the two of them, would follow his lead, who would be feminine and fragile and all the things she couldn't be during the times they would have to fight. And he wanted that side of her completely to himself. It was selfish, maybe, but he had never had anything for himself, and his woman was for him alone. He didn't want other men to see her the way he did. He didn't want her to look at other men. She was for him alone, and maybe that was what a dream really was— building the perfect woman in your mind when you knew you'd never have one.

He saw her fighting skills easily. He saw the battle scars. He could respect and admire her when he walked with her, yet he couldn't really see her image for so long. In dreams she came to him, shielded by a heavy veil, their exchanges in images more than words. It had taken a long time for either to reveal other than the warrior. They'd built trust between them slowly—and he liked that in her. She didn't give her allegiance easily, but when she did, she gave it wholly. And it was to him.

Again he found himself smiling inside at such a ridiculous fantasy at his age. It must be a sign of his mind deteriorating. Senility had set in. But how he missed her, when he couldn't bring her to him. She seemed closer there in the heat of the forest, with the rain coming down in silvery sheets. The veil of moisture reminded him of the first time he'd managed to peer through that haze in his dream and see her face so clearly. She'd stolen his breath. She'd looked so frightened, as if she'd deliberately revealed herself—finally taken a chance, but stood trembling, waiting for him to pass judgment on her.

At that moment he'd felt the closest to actual love that he ever had. He tried to compare the feeling with what he'd felt for his sister Rhiannon, in the early days when they'd all been happy and he had still had his emotions. He'd held on to the memory of love all those centuries, yet now, when he needed the feeling to complete his dream, before he went out fighting, the feeling was entirely different.

Feeling. He turned the word over and over in his mind. What did it mean? Memories? Or reality? And why would his memories be so sharp all of a sudden, here in the forest? He smelled the rain, inhaled the scent of it, and there was an edge of pleasure to the sensation. It was frustrating, to almost catch the feeling and yet have it elude him.

It wasn't simply a by-product of ingesting the vampire blood—he'd begun "dreaming" much earlier. And the dreams took place while he was awake.

He was suspicious of all things that didn't make sense. He wasn't a man prone to dreams or fantasies, and this mythical woman was becoming too much a part of his life—of him. She was tricking him into thinking she was a true lifemate, a reality instead of a myth. Yet here in the land where myths and legends came to life, he could almost convince himself she was real. But even if she was, it was far too late. The continual pain clawing at his belly told him his time had run its course and he had to carry out his plan to infiltrate the enemy camp, gain their plans, send them to Zacarias De La Cruz and then kill as many as he could before he went down. He chose to go out fighting for his people.

He shifted, taking the form of the lord of the skies—the harpy eagle. The bird was larger than normal, and the harpies were large birds. His wingspan was a good seven feet, his talons enormous. The form would help to protect him as he went into the sunlight before reaching the relative shelter of the canopy. He hopped on the ground into the sunlight. In spite of the heavy rain, the light burst over him. Smoke rose from the dark feathers, pouring off even the bird's form. He'd suffered burns and his body remained ravaged with the scars, although they'd eased over time, but he would never forget that pain. It was branded into his very bones.

Sucking in his breath sharply, he forced himself to spread his wings and rise toward that hideous burning mass of heat. The rain sizzled over him, spitting and hissing like an angry cat, as the large bird took flight, wings flapping hard to get height and take him into the trees. The light nearly blinded him, and inside the eagle, he shrank away from the rays, no matter how diffused by the rain. It seemed to take forever to cross the thirty feet, although the bird was in the trees almost immediately. It just took a few moments to realize the sun was no longer directly on the feathers. The hissing and spitting gave way once again to the calling of the birds and monkeys, this time in sharp alarm.

Below him, a porcupine dropped the figs he'd been dining on as the shadow of the eagle passed overhead. Two female spider monkeys, drunk on fermented fruit, stared up at him. The Amazon forest passed through eight borders, extending through the countries with its own diverse life forms. A silky anteater, climbing in the branches of a tree, paused to gaze at him with a wary eye. Bright red and blue macaws called warnings as he passed overhead, but he ignored them, expanding his circle ever wider to take in more and more territory.

The eagle moved noiselessly through the forest, as high as the canopy would allow, without emerging above it, covering miles. He needed the shelter of the twisted limbs and heavy foliage to block the light. With the eyes of the harpy eagle he could see something as small as an inch from more than two hundred yards. He could fly up to speeds of fifty miles per hour if he was in open territory, and drop with dizzying speed if needed.

Now, eyesight was the primary reason for having chosen the eagle's form. He spotted hundreds of frogs and lizards dotting the branches and trunks as he swept by. Snakes coiled along twisted limbs, hiding among blossoms drenched in rain. A margay shrank deeper into the foliage of a tall kapok tree, its large eyes fixed on prey. The eagle dipped lower, inspecting the overgrown vegetation. Limestone blocks lay half buried in debris, strewn about as if by a willful hand. A sinkhole shimmered with blue water, testifying to an underground river.

The eagle continued to expand his circle, taking in more and more miles, until he found what he was looking for. The bird settled high in the branches of tall tree on the edge of a man-made clearing. A large building made of steel and bolts had been brought in piece by piece and constructed sometime in the last year. Growth around it had been encouraged, presumably with an eye to hiding it, but there hadn't been enough time for the forest to reclaim lost terrain.

Something had blown a hole through the metal from the outside, and a fire had started. The smell of smoke couldn't mask the stench of rotting flesh rising to make his skin crawl even deep within the form of the bird. *Vampire*. The scent was there, although faded, as if many risings had gone by since the undead had visited this place. Still, the wail of the dead rose from the surrounding ground.

The right side of the building was blackened and the hole gave glimpses of the interior. A very recent battle, perhaps in the last couple of hours, had taken place here. The sharp eyes of the eagle could see the furniture overturned inside, a desk and two cages. A body lay on the floor, unmoving.

Outside, two men—human, he was certain—stood outside the building in combat gear, large guns strapped to their shoulders. One tipped a bottle of water to his mouth and then stepped back into the relative shelter of the doorway, trying to avoid the steady rain. The second stood stoically, the water drenching him, as he said a few words to the first guard, before moving on to circle the building. Both watched vigilantly, and the guard in the doorway favored his left leg, as though he'd been injured.

The eagle watched, motionless, hidden in the thick, twisted branches and umbrella leaves up above the clearing. It wasn't long before a third man appeared, coming out of the forest. Naked, he was thick-chested with stocky legs and heavily-muscled arms. He carried another man over his shoulder. Blood streamed down his shoulder and back, although it was impossible to tell if it was from the unconscious man or him. He staggered just before he reached the door, but the guard didn't move to help him. Instead, he stood to one side, the muzzle of his gun barely raised, but enough to cover the newcomers.

Jaguar-men. Shapeshifters. There was no doubt in Dominic's mind. Someone had attacked this facility and done a considerable amount of damage. Obviously the human guard was leery of the jaguar-men, but he allowed them into the building. The second guard had hung back and covered the two shapeshifters, his finger on the trigger. Clearly it was an uneasy truce between the two species.

Dominic knew the jaguar-men were on the verge of extinction. He had seen the decline a few hundred years earlier and knew it was inevitable. At that time, the Carpathians had tried to warn them of what was coming. Times changed and a species had to evolve in order to survive, but the jaguar-men had refused the advice. They wanted to stay to the old ways, living deep in the forests, finding a mate, impregnating her and moving on. They were wild and bad-tempered, never able to settle.

The few jaguar-men Dominic had spent any time with had tremendous feelings of entitlement and superiority. They viewed all other species as inferior, and their women were little more than a vessel to carry offspring. The royal family had a long history of cruelty and abuse of their women and female children, a practice the other males viewed as example and followed. There were a few rare jaguar-men who had tried to convince the others that they needed to value their women and children, rather than treating them as property, but they were considered traitors and shunned and ridiculed—or worse, killed.

In the end the Carpathians had left the jaguar-men to their own devices, knowing the species was ultimately doomed. Brodrick the Tenth, a rare black jaguar, led the males just as his father and his ancestors before him had done. He was considered a difficult, brutal man responsible for the slaughter of entire villages, half-breeds he deemed unfit to live. It was rumored he had made an alliance with the Malinov brothers as well as the society of humans dedicated to wiping out vampires.

Dominic shook his head at the irony. Humans couldn't distinguish the difference between a Carpathian and a vampire, and their secret society had been infiltrated by the very ones they were trying to destroy. The Malinovs were using both species in their war against the Carpathians. So far, the werewolves hadn't come down on either side, staying strictly neutral, but they existed, as Manolito De La Cruz had found with his lifemate.

Dominic spread his wings and moved closer, tuning his hearing to catch the conversation inside the building.

"The woman is dead, Brodrick. She went over the cliff. We couldn't stop her." There was weariness and distaste in the voice.

A second voice, one filled with pain, added, "We can't afford the loss of any more of our women."

The third voice was lower, a growl of sheer power, stunning in the absolute authority it carried. "What did you say, Brad?" The voice conveyed a distinct threat, as if the very idea of any of his subjects having a thought of their own in some way made them a traitor.

"He needs a doctor, Brodrick," the first voice hastily intervened.

Dominic watched as a large man dressed in loose jeans and an open shirt emerged from the house. His hair was long and shaggy, very thick. Dominic knew instantly he was looking at Brodrick, the ruler of the jaguar-men. His prince had decreed the Carpathians should leave the species to their own fate or else Dominic would have been tempted to kill the man where he stood. Brodrick was directly responsible for the deaths of countless men, women and children. He was consumed with evil, drunk on his own power and the belief that he was superior to all others.

Brodrick looked at the two guards contemptuously. "What the hell are you doing hanging out in the doorway? You're supposed to be doing a job."

The second guard kept his gun pointed in Brodrick's direction even as the two human men moved in opposite circles, the one who'd been sheltering in the doorway, limping badly, confirming Dominic's belief that he'd been wounded. Brodrick scowled up at the rain, allowing it to pour onto his face. He spit in disgust and stalked around to the side of the building where the fire had been. Crouching, he searched the ground. He was thorough about it, leaning down to sniff, using all senses to pick up the trail of his enemy.

Suddenly he sat back on his heels, stiffening. "Kevin, get out here," he called.

The jaguar-man who had carried the wounded one hurried out, barefoot, but in jeans and pulling on a T-shirt that strained across his chest. "What is it?"

"Did you get a good look at whoever broke in and freed Annabelle?"

Kevin shook his head. "He's a hell of a shot. He took out two guards, the bullets so close together, everyone thought only one shot had been fired."

"There aren't any tracks. None. Where the hell was he? And how did he know the precise place to blow the building to free Annabelle? There were no windows."

Kevin glanced in the direction of the guards. "You think someone helped him?"

"What happened out there?" Brodrick gestured toward the forest.

Kevin shrugged. "We went after Annabelle. She ran through the forest toward the river. We thought maybe it was her man, the human she spoke of, coming to try to save her. We didn't need weapons to fight him, so we both shifted. We'd be faster traveling through the forest than Annabelle, even if she shifted."

It had been logical thinking, Dominic conceded from his lofty perch above them, but they'd lost the woman.

Brodrick shook his head. "How did Brad get shot? And where's Tonio?"

Kevin sighed. "We found his body just on the other side of the caves. He'd tangled with another cat. Brad was kneeling beside him, and the next thing I knew he was on the ground and we were pinned down. I had no weapon and I shifted to try to circle around and find the shooter, but I couldn't find any tracks."

Brodrick swore. "It's her. *She* did this. I know it was her. That's why you didn't find any tracks. She took to the trees."

Neither said who *she* was. Dominic wanted to know who the mysterious woman they obviously hated and feared could be. Someone he wouldn't mind meeting. Four of the five De La Cruz brothers had lifemates. Could the elusive woman be one of their lifemates? It was possible, but he doubted it. The De La Cruz brothers would not want their women in battle. They had already been men who had fiercely protective natures, and coming to this part of the world had only increased their dominant tendencies. They had eight countries to patrol, and the Malinov brothers would know how impossible it would be to cover every inch of the rain forest. They would never, under any circumstances, send their women out alone. No, this had to be someone else.

The eagle spread its massive wings and took to the air. The sun was beginning to fade, making him a little more comfortable, but the whisper of the parasites grew louder, tempting, pushing his hunger to a ravenous level, until he could barely think straight. It was only the bird's form that kept Dominic's sanity as he tried to adjust to the rising level of torment. As the night grew closer, the parasites went from sluggish to active, stabbing at his internal organs while the vampire blood burned like acid. He needed to feed, but he was becoming more and more worried that insanity was grabbing hold and he wouldn't find the strength to resist the temptation of a kill while feeding.

Each rising he'd woken voraciously hungry, and each time he fed, the parasites grew louder, pushing for a kill, demanding he feel the rush of power, the rightful rush of power, promising a coolness in his blood, a feeling of euphoria that would remove every pain from his body.

He kept to the shade of the canopy as he expanded his exploration, heading for the site of the battle, hoping the eagle could spot something the men hadn't. He found the cave entrances, very small and made of limestone, but these didn't seem to curve back underground to form the labyrinth of tunnels as the cave system miles away had done. There were only three small chambers and in each, he found Mayan art on the walls. All three caves showed evidence of occupation, however brief, but violent in some way. There were dried spots of blood in all of them.

He took to the sky again, a vague uneasiness in his gut. That bothered him. He had seen horrific sites of battle, torture and death. He was a Carpathian warrior, and his lack of emotion served him well. Without a lifemate to balance the darkness in him, he needed the lack of emotion to stay sane over a thousand years of seeing cruelty and depravity, yet the sight of the blood in that cave, and knowing women had been brought there by the jaguarmen to be used as they wished, sickened him. And that should *never* happen. Intellectually, perhaps. An intellectual reaction was acceptable, and the honor in him would rise up to abhor such behavior. But a physical reaction was completely unacceptable—and impossible. Yet . . .

Unsettled, Dominic expanded his search to include the cliffs above the river. The rain continued, increasing in strength, turning the world a silvery gray. Even with the clouds as cover, he felt the bright heat invading as he burst into the open over the river. A body lay crumpled and lifeless in the river, caught on the rocks, battered and forgotten. Long thick hair lay spread out like seaweed, one arm wedged in the crevice two large boulders made. She was faceup, her dead eyes staring at the sky, the rain pouring over her and running down her face like a flood of tears.

Cursing, Dominic circled and then dropped. He couldn't leave her like that. He just couldn't. It didn't matter how many he'd seen dead. He would not leave her, a broken doll with no honor or respect for the woman she'd been. From what he'd gleaned from the conversation between Brodrick and Kevin, she had a family, a husband who loved her. She—and they—deserved more than her body battered by water, left to swell and decompose and be fodder for the fish and carnivores that would feast on her.

The bird settled on the boulder just above her body and he shifted, covering his skin with a heavy cloak, the hood helping to protect his neck and face as he crouched low and caught her wrist. He was strong and had no trouble pulling her from the water into his arms. Her head lolled back on her neck and he saw bruises marring her skin, even prints around her neck. There were circles, black and blue, around her wrists and ankles. Again he was shaken by his reaction. Sorrow mixed with rage. Sorrow was so heavy in his heart that it slowly blotted out the rage.

He took a breath and let it out. Was he feeling someone else's emotions? Did the parasites amplify emotions around him, adding to the high the vampire received from the terror his victim felt—the adrenaline-laced blood provided? That was a possibility, but he couldn't imagine that a vampire could feel sorrow.

Dominic carried the woman into the forest, every step increasing the heartache. The moment he entered the trees, he scented blood. This had to have been where the second battle had taken place and Brad had been wounded. He found where the third jaguar-man had shed his clothes and had gone on the hunt, hoping to circle around and take the shooter.

There were few tracks to show the jaguar's passing, a small bit of fur and a partial track the rain had filled, but it wasn't long before he found the body of the cat. There

had been a battle here, one between two cats. The dead
cat's prints had been heavier and spread farther apart, indicating he was larger, but the smaller cat had obviously
been a veteran fighter; it had killed with a bite to the skull
after a fierce struggle. The foliage was soaked in blood
and there was more on the ground.

Dominic knew the jaguars would return to burn the
fallen cat, so after carefully studying the ground to commit the victorious jaguar's prints to memory, he carried
the woman into the most lush spot he could find. A grotto
of limestone covered in tangled vines of flowers would
be her only marker, but he opened the earth deep and gave
her a place to rest. As the soil closed over the woman, he
murmured the death prayer in his native language, asking
for peace and for her soul to be welcomed into the next
life as well as asking that the earth receive her body and
welcome her flesh and bones.

He stayed a moment while the rays of the sun sought
him out through the cover of the canopy and rain, burning
through his heavy cloak to raise blisters on his skin. The
parasites reacted, twisting and shrieking in his head, his
insides a mass of cuts so that he spit blood. He pushed some
of them from his body through his pores. He found that if
he didn't relieve the number, the whispers grew louder and
the torment impossible to ignore. He had to incinerate the
writhing mutated leeches before they slipped into the
ground and tried to find a way back to their masters.

He moved the vegetation on the ground to cover all
signs of the grave. The jaguar-men would come back to
remove all traces of their species, but they wouldn't find
her. She would rest far from their reach. It was all he
could give her. With a small sigh, Dominic checked one

last time, making certain his chosen spot looked pristine, and then he shifted once more, taking the shape of the eagle. He needed to find where the victorious jaguar had gone.

It didn't take long for the sharp eyes of the eagle to spot his quarry several miles from the site of the battle. He simply followed the sounds of the forest, the creatures warning one another of a predator close by. The eagle slid noiselessly through the tree branches and settled on the broad limb high above the forest floor. The monkeys howled and shrieked warnings, calling to one another, occasionally throwing twigs down at the large spotted cat weaving its way through the brush toward some unknown destination.

The jaguar was female, her thick golden fur spotted with dark rosettes and, in spite of the rain, blood. She limped, slightly dragging her back leg where the worst of the lacerations seemed to be. Her head was down, but she looked lethal, a flow of spots sliding in and out of the foliage, so at times, even with the eagle's extraordinary eyesight, it was difficult to spot her against the vegetation of the forest floor.

She moved in complete silence, ignoring the monkeys and birds, moving at a steady pace, her muscles flowing beneath the thick fur. So intrigued by her dogged persistence in traveling in spite of her severe injuries, it took several minutes before he realized the hideous whispers in his mind had eased significantly. All the times he had drained off the parasites to give himself some relief, he had never had them cease their continual assault on his brain, yet now they were nearly silent.

Curious, he took to the skies, circling overhead, staying within the canopy to keep out the last rays of the sun. He noted that the farther he was from the jaguar, the louder the whispers became. The parasites ceased activity the closer he got to her, so that the stabbing shards of glass cutting his insides remained still and for a short time he had a respite from the brutal pain.

The jaguar continued to move steadily into deeper forest, away from the river, going into the interior. Night fell and still she traveled. He found that he couldn't leave her, he had no wish to leave her. He began to equate the strange calming of the parasites with her as well as the even stranger emotions. The rage had subsided into an unrelenting sorrow and anguish. His heart was so heavy with a burden he could barely function as he moved overhead.

Below, large limestone blocks appeared, half buried in the soil. The remnants of a great Mayan temple lay cracked and broken, trees and vines nearly obliterating what was left of the once-impressive structure. Scattered over the next few miles were the remains of a long-ago civilization. The Mayans had been farmers, growing their golden corn in the middle of the rain forest, whispering with reverence of the jaguar and building temples to bring sky, earth and the underworld together.

He spotted a sinkhole and beneath it the cool waters of the underground river. The jaguar continued without pause until she came to another Mayan site, although this one had been used more recently. The thick growth of tangled vines and trees put the date nearly twenty years earlier, but clearly there had been more modern houses here. A generator long since rusted was wrapped with thick lianas and shoots of green. The ground wept with the memories of battle and the slaughters that had taken place here. The sorrow was so heavy now, Dominic needed to ease the burden. The harpy eagle flew through the canopy a distance away from the jaguar and remained motionless, just watching, as the jaguar made her way through the ancient battlefield, as if she were connected to the dead who wailed there.

DARK SLAYER

*The dark destiny of a betrayed woman. The terrifying
fate of a cursed man. Now after a century of longing, the
instinct for survival has united them.*

A rumour has persisted in the vampire world of a
dark slayer – a woman – who travels with a wolf pack
and who destroys any vampire who crosses her path.
Mysterious, elusive and seemingly impossible to kill,
she is the one hunter who strikes terror into the hearts
of the undead. She is Ivory Malinov. Long ago betrayed
by her people, abandoned by her family and cast out
by everyone she held dear, she has sustained her sanity
by preparing for one purpose – to destroy her greatest
enemy. Until the night she picks up the scent of a man.
Her lifemate. The curse of all Carpathian women.

He is Razvan. Branded a criminal, detested and feared,
he is a Dragonseeker, borne of one of the greatest
Carpathian lineages, only to be raised as its most
despised – and captive – enemy. Fleeing from his lifetime
of imprisonment, Razvan now seeks the dawn to end his
terrible existence. Instead he has found his deliverance in
the Dark Slayer. In spirit, in flesh and blood, in love and
in war, Ivory and Razvan are made for each other.

978-0-7499-4164-2

DARK CURSE

Born into a world of ice, slave to her evil father, Lara Calladine knew paralysing fear as a child. Only by escaping with her mysterious gifts unbroken did she survive to claim her great Carpathian heritage as a Dragonseeker. She walked her chosen path alone, trusting no one. For beyond the frozen hall of her youth was a world of even greater mystery and danger.

Now, Lara is in search of the source of her nightmares – the cold, dark corners of her childhood. Only one man has the power and the will to help her: dangerous, arrogant Nicolas De La Cruz. Centuries of hunting and killing have taken their toll on him but he still longs to feel sensual love without the hunger for blood. A tenuous trust emerges between Lara and Nicholas, and a passion neither of them has ever experienced but, as much as they long for a future as lifemates, they are also haunted by the unknown dangers of the dark curse.

978-0-7499-0953-6